A September Day and Shadow Thriller

FIGHT OR FLIGHT

Book Four

AMY SHOJAI

Copyright

This is a work of fiction. Names, characters, places, and incidents either are the product of the author's imagination or are used fictitiously, and any resemblance to actual persons living or dead, business establishments, events, or locales is entirely coincidental.

First Print Edition, July 2018
Furry Muse Publishing
Print ISBN **978-1-948366-02-1**
eBook ISBN **978-1-948366-01-4**

FURRY MUSE
PUBLISHING
P.O. Box 1904
Sherman TX 75091
(903)814-4319
amy@shojai.com

PART 1 BORN to LOVE
(*February*)

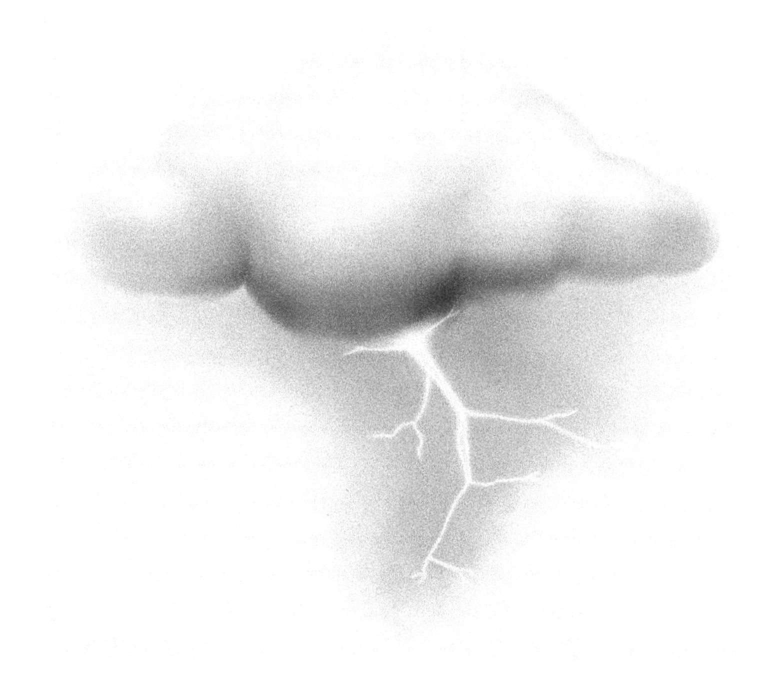

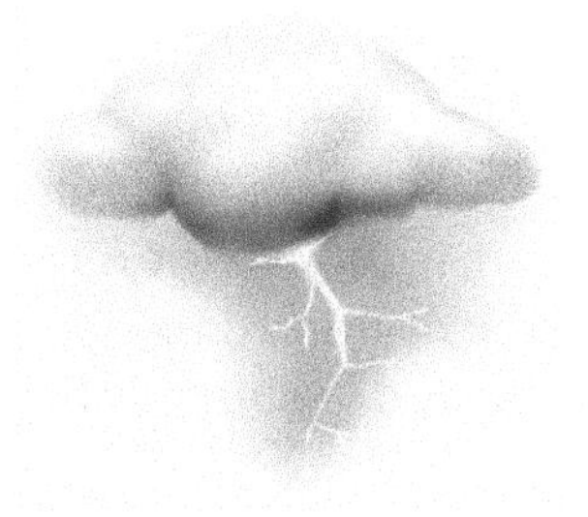

Chapter 1

The flash flood swirled Shadow down, down, and scraped him head over paws against the muddy bottom before thrusting him up in a stomach-wrenching rush. He gasped, and his yelp became a strangled gargle when water smothered his cry. Deafened by the roar, scent blinded and sight dimmed, Shadow struggled to tell down from up, wind from flood. Forelegs churned the water to dingy froth, and he struggled to keep his black shepherd's muzzle above the surface.

The night's frigid air set fire to his flayed cheek. It would be easy to give up and let the tide take him, and erase his pain. But Shadow had to return to his family. To his-boy, Steven. And to September. Especially to September, his person. She needed him. And he needed her.

He gasped, this time without choking, and snatched another two breaths without wasting further air on fruitless wails. Shadow timed gasps to match the roller coaster surge that swept him along before he fetched up hard against a floating tree.

Shadow yelped when the trunk caught his tender middle where the boy-thief had kicked him. He thrashed and managed to scrabble a toehold across one limb. Weakened by his recent battle with the bad-man and now the wicked current, Shadow couldn't pull his 80-plus weight any higher. He clung to the limb while the flood snatched at a good-dog's fur and tried to swallow him whole.

One with the detritus, Shadow caught his breath as he hitched a ride on the log that now took the brunt of the flood's abuse. Neither the sting of his scraped cheek, fire on his neck, nor his throbbing gut could compare to the empty ache inside. He'd left his family behind, without a good-dog to protect them. The bad-man could return to finish what he'd started. September couldn't protect Steven or even herself, not without Shadow by her side.

On the bank ahead, Shadow spied a car. He barked for help. Cars meant people, and people helped good-dogs. But the water's roar swept his cry away. He barked with anguished frustration when the women stared back at him, without any offer to help. Shadow caught a whiff of their scent, which shouted names louder than any human scream—Robin Gillette and Sunny Babcock—before the tree floated him out of sight.

The log he rode caught on something below the water's surface, and spun in slow circles in the current. Shadow managed to lunge enough to pull himself onto the trunk. When the tree's underwater anchor let go, Shadow crouched and braced himself against the thick upright limb. But the log sailed only a short distance before it thumped into a metal dumpster tumbled about by the twisty black cloud. Shadow stiffened, sniffed cautiously, but detected no sign of the hated boy-thief, just stale garbage and animal stink.

Shadow waited another heartbeat, but the log didn't swim any closer to the bank. So he levered himself upright and took slow, shaky steps while his stomach roiled. The tree dipped, and the overhead limb slammed the metal box with clanging blows.

Loss of the limb spun the trunk and spilled Shadow back into the cold water. Energy spent, only the thought of September spurred him to flounder and hook one foreleg across the bobbing tree. His eyes half closed, as he floated helpless in the chill water, and yearned for home that seemed a world away.

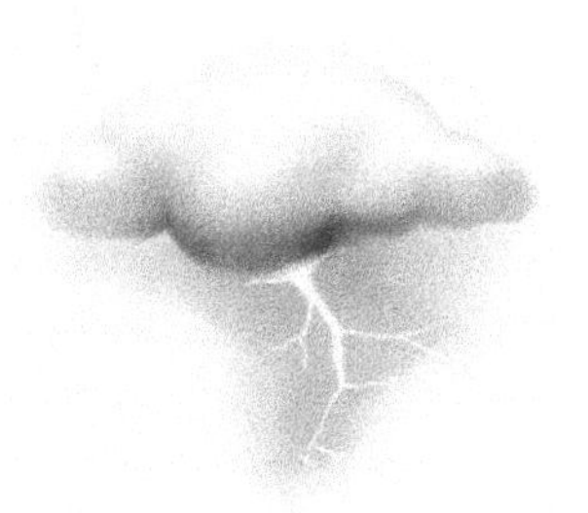

Chapter 2

Lia Corazon squinted at the clouds muddying the North Texas horizon. Wind whipped her goldenrod hair into a tangled froth, pulling it free of the hazel-green kerchief that matched her eyes. Parallel furrows etched her brow, but she couldn't change plans over the weather. It'd be close, but with luck, the storm would hold off long enough to get this meeting behind her.

She stooped to tighten the laces on one shoe, stood, and then trotted in an exaggerated loping gait across the fenced yard. A pack of black puppies galloped after her, their rust colored muzzles yapping with excitement. A couple out-paced her, with the rest satisfied to tag along in her wake.

Her words jollied them along in a high-pitched singsong designed to ramp up excitement. "Puppy-puppy-puppy, that's the way, who's gonna win?"

Once at the far end of the enclosure, Lia leaned against the chain link. The cool metal soothed heated skin through her damp sweatshirt, and she mopped her brow with one pushed up sleeve. February should still be cold, but the weird muggy weather that frizzed Lia's hair also frazzled her nerves. So much depended on today's client. At the thought, her pulse jittered in her throat.

Time to take charge of her own life, though, even if it kept her sideways of the prim-and-proper grandparents who'd raised her. That's why she'd dropped out of college two years ago and "gone to the dogs" (as Grammy called it). Now Lia was smack-dab on the cusp of making her own dream come true. Never mind that Grammy and Grandfather expected her to fail. It all depended on the new client. If all went well, Corazon Boarding Kennels would become a reality.

She needed to calm down. She needed a puppy fix.

"Puppy-puppy-puppy! Come-a-pup!"

With ears flopping and stubby tails held high, excited yaps spilled from nine furry throats as the four-month-old Rottweiler babies raced to meet her. "Puppies, COME." She used the command with intent. She liked to imagine she shared a special level of communication with animals, as had her mother. Once they responded to the chase-and-follow game, she associated the command word with the action.

Lia didn't used the clicker anymore—too easy to lose—and instead preferred a tongue-click to signal THAT (click!) was the desired behavior. She'd already taught the pups a handful of commands in a series of games designed to reward their natural puppy curiosity and urge to play. *It's a tough job, but somebody has to do it.* She grinned.

Thirty-six short furry legs churned, with some of the pups preferring to chase and wrestle each other rather than complete the recall. But over half of the litter, five sleek black and rust beauties, responded to the command and raced to reach Lia.

"Oh you're so smart! What smart brave puppies, good COME."

She clicked her tongue as the biggest girl pup, the one wearing a purple collar, skidded into her ankles. Lia rewarded the puppy-girl with taste of the stinky-yummy liver treat all the pups wanted. She watched the girl-pup chew with relish while the late comers milled and whined about her legs in a furry sea of disappointment about her legs. "You snooze, you lose. Life's not fair, puppies. Gotta be quicker next time."

The first two-dozen times they'd played the game, all the pups got the reward, so they knew the stakes. Now at four months of age, the litter had reached the puppy delinquent stage. They already knew a lot—how to sit, down, come and walk nice on leash—but tested boundaries and often ignored lessons they'd nailed last week. Lia called it their "make me do it" phase, so she increased the stakes of each training session.

For the past four days, the winner of the recall race got the prize. The sharpest pups understood right away, and those that didn't care weren't the best training prospects anyway.

Lia knew from hard experience that life wasn't fair and not everyone got to win the prize. Dog life worked the same way, and for the elite in this litter, the race-game prepared the Rottweiler pups for their future role as police dogs. The technique spurred those puppies with the correct temperament to respond to her command without hesitation, in order to win a reward. Her mentor, Abe Pesqueira, had taught her that trick, one of the best ways to train a reliable recall no matter the age of the dog. God, she missed Abe.

Not all pups were police dog material—hell, maybe one or two would qualify—but all could still be delightful companions or canine partners in other ways. All dogs benefited from training, and a reliable recall saved dog lives. Lia's job prepared them for life with people, no matter what that role might be. After all, Lia was nobody's pick of the litter, either.

As if that thought summoned the call, Lia retrieved her buzzing phone, not surprised at the caller. She debated whether to answer, but knew Grammy wouldn't give up. Not until she got her way.

"I'm in the middle of training, Grammy." Lia pulled a tattered rope toy out of her other pocket and dragged it across the brown grass for the puppies' pleasure. Two of them went after it. Purple Collar girl won the prize by shouldering her brother aside. The pup grabbed hold and tugged, growling with ferocious ardor and Lia grinned as she held on. "And I've got a client on the way."

"In this weather? You realize the county is still under a tornado warning." The gentile southern drawl masked hidden steel as inflexible as Grammy's helmeted coiffure.

Lia rolled her eyes. "Yes, I know. My phone alarm keeps going off." She eyed the clouds again as she walked back toward the kennel, towing the tugging puppy with her. The rest of the litter followed, all hoping to snatch more of the tasty liver reward.

"I don't know why you're so stubborn. We have a storm shelter here. Let us help out." Grammy pronounced, and you were expected to comply.

William "Dub" Corazon and his wife Cornelia lived on a 4000-acre spread that had been in the family for six generations. Corazon Stables bred and trained champion cutting horses.

"I'll be fine, Grammy. I have responsibilities here."

Grandfather had never had much to do with Lia. She'd catch him watching her from a distance, his spicy aftershave vying with the cigar smoke that wreathed his scowling brow. Grammy tried to tame Lia's wild streak with strict curfews, home schooling and stifling supervision. Lia had always believed that was why her mother Kaylia eloped at age fifteen, to escape the smothering Corazon expectations. She knew better than to suggest that out loud, though.

Grammy grew insistent. "For heaven's sake, your Grandfather and I just want you to be safe."

She bit her lip. Grammy and Grandfather wanted to "help" when it suited them. They'd told Lia "no" often enough. *Let it go, Lia.* The client would be here any minute, they'd conclude their business, and Lia would never have to beg crumbs from the Corazon table again.

Lia smiled when Miss Purple Collar switched her focus from the tug toy and attacked Lia's moving feet. *Need to capture that behavior, and put it on command.* "Grammy, you've already said I can't bring the dogs."

"Of course not. They're dogs. And they don't even belong to you." Grammy tittered. "We don't bring our *horses* into the storm cellar, nor the prize bull, and just one of them is worth more than—"

"I know, you've said it before. *Worth more than all of Lia's pipe dreams combined.*" Lia mimicked Grammy's condescending tone while she glanced around, taking in the decrepit building and grounds. "The dogs are my responsibility, and so is this property, even if one of your horses costs more."

Thunder grumbled overhead, echoed in the phone Lia held. "Be reasonable, Lia. Storm's coming. Grandfather and I just want what's best. You've received every advantage, the best education, introductions into the proper social circles. Yet you prefer to mix with . . ." She hesitated, and Lia knew it was for effect. Grammy had never been politically correct.

"I'm an adult. I get to make my own decisions." Lia couldn't hide her exasperation.

"You are a *Corazon*, you have a position in this community. Don't waste your talents on losing propositions. Your Grandfather would happily support your choice of an *appropriate* career." She spouted the same old argument. "Instead, you take every opportunity to embarrass your family. People laugh at us, they laugh at you. Don't throw it all away—"

"Like my mother?" It always came back to that. The all-powerful, all knowing Corazons chose an *appropriate* career. Never mind what Lia might want.

Grammy remained silent. Lia pictured Cornelia's ice blue stare, flared nostrils and creamy complexion that had no need of Botox. She imagined Grammy smoothing her perfect platinum hair with shaking, bejeweled fingers. Mention of Lia's dead mother was the one weapon guaranteed to crack Cornelia's carefully crafted image.

Lia had never known her mother, described as petite with golden hair and skin, a firecracker personality and looks true to her Spanish heritage. *While I must look more like my father, whoever the hell he might be.*

She took a shaky breath. "I'm not *her*, Grammy. I can't ever be Kaylia, no matter how much you and Grandfather push." *Or how hard I try.*

"That's certainly true."

Lia gasped, and then squared her shoulders. They'd become very good at hurting each other. She fingered the flowers on the old baby bracelet for courage. She never took it off, in part because she couldn't resist poking an ant's nest. Lia had found the baby bracelet and an antique braided leather lariat several years ago, hidden away in a box of Kaylia's things Grandfather hadn't managed to destroy.

Grammy had a conniption and refused to discuss their provenance. Lia asked Grandfather about the lariat, made in West Texas, according to a tooled maker's tag. He turned red, blustered and stammered, and threatened to disown her if she ever asked about that *no-account bastard* again.

She hadn't. But she still wondered, and had promised herself to ferret out the truth, someday. Meanwhile, she honored her mother by wearing the bracelet, and worked Kaylia's lariat until she could out-rope anyone. She kept the lariat handy, hanging on her office wall.

"Why make everything so difficult, Lia? I'm sure the dogs and everything else will be just fine. Everything's insured, after all, and can be replaced. Come home."

Just like her to think living creatures were replaceable. "This is my life and my home now! My future. None of it's replaceable." She'd gone to her grandparents for a loan but her dream wasn't appropriate for a Corazon and they'd refused. She couldn't help thinking they wanted her to fail.

"Oh Lia, don't be so melodramatic." Grammy's drawl turned brittle. "Go on then. I'll tell your grandfather you'd rather huddle up with those worthless dogs that don't even belong to you. Just pray that failing business doesn't collapse into rubble around your ears. Go ahead, since that's more important than your family." Grammy disconnected.

Lia touched the bracelet again. It'd be different if her mother had lived. Why had her mother's mysterious Romeo abandoned them? Abandoned *her*. Lia always imagined Kaylia died of a broken heart when he left, but nobody spoke of the details. Lia had been born. Kaylia died. Her father hadn't wanted them.

Except her name on the baby bracelet—her *real one*, not the short version the Corazon's gave her—told a different story. The bracelet's dainty plumeria flowers framed a name spelled out in tiny individual letters:

Apikalia.

She'd looked it up. The flowers and the name were Hawaiian. It had to mean something.

Angry with herself for rising to the old bait, Lia bent down and scooped up Miss Purple Collar. She relished the smell of puppy breath when the baby slurped her face, and Lia kissed the top of her smooth black head. "How about we play a new game? We'll call it, *TRIP*. Sound good, puppy-girl? My little Karma?" This one attracted all kinds of trouble, but Lia liked her attitude and drive.

If Grammy and Grandfather considered her a mutt, a *poi dog* unworthy of the Corazon name, so be it. Dogs loved you no matter what. The Karma-pup didn't care about unknown fathers or dead mothers

Apikalia meant *my father's delight*. Had he chosen her name? Or was it her mother's wishful thinking?

Too many unanswered questions. Lia wanted—no, she *needed* to know where she came from before stepping into her future.

Lia bounced Karma in her arms, and hurried to round up the rest of the litter. Everything depended on what happened today. Failure would mean a continuation of the Corazon's *told-ya-so* hell.

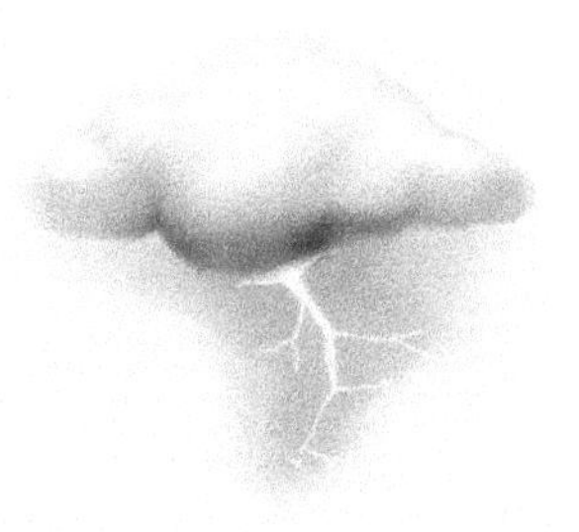

Chapter 3

"What's your name, honey? Talk to me. No, don't sleep; you need to stay with me." A hand slapped first one cheek and then the other.

She roused enough to try and answer the EMT "Thember." Licking her lips, she tried once more. "Sem-ber."

"She said September, September Day." Detective Jeff Combs sounded gruff. "She'll be all right, won't she?" He squeezed her hand underneath the blanket, and then stepped out of the way when the medical team pushed near.

The EMT ignored Combs. "Good, that's right, you're September Day. Do you know where you are?" A light shined in each eye made her squint. They'd already cut off her clothes, and piled a mound of dry warm blankets over the top of her.

September shook her head, brow furrowing with concentration. Her tongue felt thick and her body remained numb. Constant tears drenched her cheeks. How long had she been in the icy floodwater, cradling … who? She'd lost something important, but her mind dodged around the details, maybe protecting her from the memory.

She remembered the tornado, sheltering in the barn with others, fighting someone and then . . .

"Where's my dog? Find Shadow, please oh God find him you've got to—" Crushing reality returned. She struggled to throw off the covers, leap off the gurney and find her dog.

"Calm down, sugar, you're not going anywhere except the hospital." The medic restrained September's weak form. She collapsed back onto the gurney. The flash flood stole Shadow away, and she'd been helpless to save him. Others, too. She shuddered; great sobs wracked her slight figure. Had anyone survived?

Turning her head from side to side, September strained to see a familiar face amid the bustle of the EMTs. She glimpsed Steven's tiny figure swaddled in layers of blankets with just his big-eyed face exposed before an ambulance whisked him away.

Combs returned to September's side, and again shifted the blanket to hold her hand in both of hers. "Can't you warm her up?" He chaffed her hand between his. "What's the holdup?"

"Step back, Detective. I know you're worried, but she's tipping into severe hypothermia. Any vigorous or jarring movements could trigger cardiac arrest. We got to be gentle." The EMT adjusted September's the blankets to cover the top of her head so only her face peeked out. "We're transporting the child first. Tornadoes injured folks all over town, so we're running ambulances in shifts. Weather report says there's more to come. Be grateful she's first in line to get help."

The world shifted and stars spun overhead. September closed her eyes to quell the dizziness.

"Eyes open, September, stay awake. Talk to me." The familiar voice anchored her to the painful NOW when she'd rather slip into oblivion. A hand squeezed her shoulder, and she blinked. Combs gazed at her as he walked beside the gurney. "You're going to be okay." His voice caught as if he doubted the words as much as she did.

"Did your kids get away?" The horrible confrontation came back to September in a rush. Combs's children, along with Steven and several others escaped the barn before the tornado struck.

Combs nodded. "Thanks to you, Willie and Melinda and everyone's safe. Well, except for one boy. We're still looking for him." He paused. "They're taking all the kids to the hospital, just to be sure." His rough hand smoothed her cheek. "You, too."

"Shadow's gone, isn't he?" Her throat ached from grief. "Combs, I have to find him. Please." She sobbed again, and painful shudders racked her body as her shiver reflex returned.

"Right now we have to take care of you. Here, drink this."

He pushed a straw to her lips. She forced herself to sip the warm, sweet liquid designed to warm from the inside. She pushed it away. "Promise me, Combs, you'll help me find him. I know people got hurt, too, but I can't just give up."

The E.M.T interrupted again. "Let's get you warmed up." He squeezed two fluid-filled plastic bags between his hands to activate their warming properties, and applied one compress to September's neck and the other on her chest. "We want to warm up your core first. Heat applied to your arms or legs can move cold blood back to your organs and make your body temp drop further."

September nodded. She'd come close to dying before, and had no wish to further tempt fate. Besides, she couldn't go after Shadow while sick, so she had to get well as soon as possible.

When the ambulance returned, Combs started to climb in, too, but September waved him away. "Go see your kids. I'm in good hands. I'll see you at the hospital and we can make plans to find Shadow."

An oxygen mask covered her face, feeding her warmed air to breathe, and an IV inserted into her arm administered warm saline solution.

The bumpy ambulance ride spared the siren in deference to the multiple tornado warnings that split the air. Her personal struggle might be over, but the weather still had plans for the rest of Heartland and the surrounding countryside.

The look on Shadow's face as the floodwaters whirled him away haunted September. Pain. Fear. Hope. Trust. Such a good-dog. He'd saved her life—again—and she'd let him down.

She choked back sobs the EMT insisted she stifle. Never mind what the doctors said. As soon as the world stopped spinning, she'd go after him. Combs would help. Family did that for each other.

Wait! September's mind cleared. She gasped and her eyes blinked wide open. Pulling the mask from her face, she cried out to the EMT. "Call Combs for me. Call Detective Combs!"

"You have to be still. We're almost to the hospital."

The soothing tone just made her angry, and she struggled to sit up.

"Quiet! I won't have you die on my watch." He put the mask back over her lips, and she caught his hand.

"Call Combs. Please. We can't wait, or more storms will make it impossible." She took another breath, and smiled. "I know how to find Shadow."

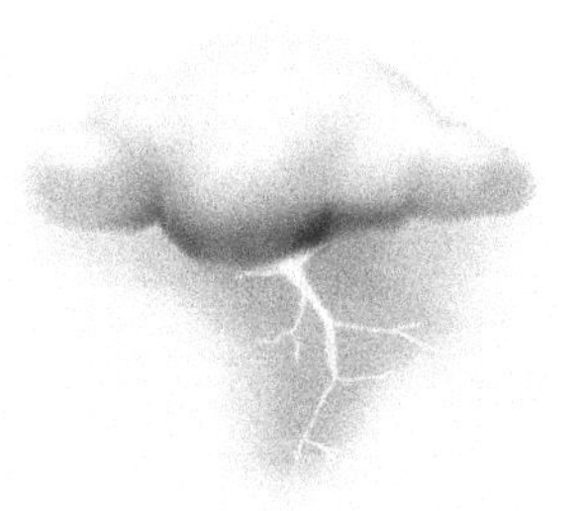

Chapter 4

Karma struggled in Lia's arms. She hated restraint. The girl's hugs didn't hurt, but reminded Karma of her mother's discipline. Even though Lia had the right to tell Karma what to do—she was the leader, after all—the unpleasant sensation made Karma squirm.

Then the girl made soothing mouth-noises and Karma stopped complaining when she recognized her favorite word.

Game!

That changed everything! The idea of a *game* made Karma's tummy flip with excitement. Little whimpers of anticipation bubbled up her throat and her mouth grew wet, knowing yummy treats often came with the girl's playtime sessions.

Her littermates bounced around the girl's feet, and Karma enjoyed her elevated view from Lia's arms. The familiar building they approached meant home and safety, but it shut out the best sniffs and sounds that made life exciting and fun. And Karma yearned for adventure. She wanted to explore beyond the wire walls of her kennel and escape the protective flank of her dam, Dolly. Even at her young age, Karma's confidence outshone that of her mother and siblings combined.

A loud rumbling growl sounded overhead. She strained to look upwards. Did a dog hide above? Dark billowing shapes mounded and surged as far as she could see, perhaps pushed by the whim of the earth's invisible breath that combed the grass of the nearby field.

"Puppy-puppy-puppy, COME!" The girl's sharp command brought the litter surging through the open wired door, back into the kennel where Karma's dam waited, shy as always and curled up tight in a corner. A handful of tossed treats onto the pavement prompted a rush of squeals and happy barks. Even Dolly roused enough to claim a few morsels.

Lia's arms tightened when Karma wanted her share of the treats. "Not you, puppy-girl. We've got a new game to play."

Karma barked and grinned. She knew two of those words. Sometimes she learned words all by herself. She was smart that way. What would happen when both *play* and *game* words came together? Her short black tail stood straight up, and her entire back end wiggled. That happened a lot when she recognized happy words.

The girl unhooked a target stick hanging on the wall before she set Karma back on the grass. The pointer helped Karma know where to look while learning new games.

Cold mud squished under Karma's feet as she bounced across the yard. The wet on her paws reminded her of another urgent need, and Karma trotted off a short distance to squat. She didn't even wait to be told to *take-a-break*. She finished and looked around with a hopeful wag. Sometimes she got paid for peeing. She liked it when that happened.

But not this time. She cocked her head, and focused on Lia for some clue about the game. Karma knew many of the mouth-sounds people used, the important ones like *tug* and *play* and *Karma*, and the sniffing game where she got to ferret out treats hidden around the yard. She also knew the less exciting words like *come* and *sit*. Karma loved hearing her name because it signaled something fun would happen. But she didn't care as much for *sit* or *come*. Beckoning sniffs, sights and sounds distracted and led her astray. But if treats or a game of tug were involved, Karma could be persuaded to do most anything.

She took a moment to sniff the warm wet spot she'd made—self-smell made her feel happy and safe—before racing after Lia's churning feet. The skipping shoes triggered her instinct to chase-chase-chase, to grab and grapple and wrestle.

People covered their feet, muffling the good sniffs that came from between their toes. Karma wondered why Lia avoided the delicious feel of grass and dirt on her foot pads. How did people nibble an itchy paw? Balancing on two instead of four paws must be hard, too. How did people run at all without bare claws to dig into the ground for purchase? Maybe that's why people ran so slow and funny.

The girl stopped, and lifted one of her shoes and wiggled it just as Karma skidded to a stop within nose-touch range.

Karma tipped her head at the swiveling foot, and looked up at the girl's face, seeking a clue. Karma knew the rules of the game. She had to guess what the girl wanted, and when she got it right, Lia would make a CLICK-sound with her mouth and give her a treat. Even better than the treat, guessing right made the girl smile and laugh. And that made Karma's chest swell with a warm happy feeling. She wasn't sure why, but she liked that. A lot.

The girl extended the tip of the long target stick, and Karma focused on its movement. She'd learned to pay attention because it often gave clues about the game. When the tip came to rest on top of the girl's elevated shoe, Karma stretched her neck forward until she nose-poked the foot. Immediately, she heard the CLICK mouth-noise that said she'd guessed right. Karma couldn't help drooling, and smacked her lips after she gulped the treat without chewing.

She looked from the girl's smile, and back to the target stick, wagging her back end so hard she lost her balance. She liked this game. Touch the foot, get a treat. Easy.

Next, Lia girl put her foot on the ground before tapping the shoe with the stick. Without hesitation, Karma bounced forward and nose-poked the shoe again, and stared up with her mouth ready even before the CLICK sounded. She chomped the treat, head swiveling to follow Lia's next move.

When the girl turned her back and trotted away, Karma gave chase. Her four paws overtook the girl, and this time she didn't wait for the target stick to direct her action. Foot movement through the long grass mimicked prey and she pounced, grappling the girl's ankle and mouthing the strings on the foot covers. The CLICK mouth-sound came, just as the girl tumbled forward and rolled onto the ground.

Karma released the girl's foot, and danced away. She'd never seen people fall over. How exciting! She bounced forward again, growling and yapping with excitement. When the girl moved the target stick back to the same shoe, Karma nose-poked the foot, but stood puzzled when no CLICK followed. She poked the shoe again. Nothing. One last nose poke, and then with frustration, Karma grabbed the shoestrings and tugged.

CLICK!

With delight, Karma took the treat. She returned to the shoestrings, grabbed, growled and tugged, even shook her head to subdue the shoe.

CLICK! A whole handful of treats fell from the girl's hand.

She didn't know where to sniff and gulp first. Snuffling through the grass to collect the bonus reward, Karma's brain processed the game as the girl regained her feet, and trotted to the other side of the yard to repeat the lesson. Karma abandoned the few treats left, because the excitement of the new game offered way more fun. Karma dashed after Lia, eyes focused on the girl's moving feet. This time, she needed no prompting, and tackled the shoe, ferocious play growls and happy yelps filling the air. She wriggled with delight when the girl didn't fall at once, instead tugging back and struggling to step forward. What fun, a tug game with chasing.

"*TRIP!* What a good *TRIP*, good girl, Karma. *TRIP!* That's it, *TRIP!*"

Karma continued to grapple the girl's foot, understanding few of the words but registering the percussive final word and the repetition. She wasn't sure just yet, and continued to test and refine what the girl wanted.

She bit harder—it felt good to bite—so she adjusted her grip and tugged, too. When the girl fell forward, rolling onto her side, Karma let go and danced out of the way. But that garnered no CLICK sound. Lia stuck out her foot, shook it and repeated, "*TRIP!*" So Karma launched herself once more at the shoe, biting it, and even clasping and humping against the girl's foot in the ultimate display of dominance.

"Good *TRIP,* what a smart Karma, good-dog. So you like the *TRIP*-game? Good girl, Karma." The girl laughed and pulled out a handful of treats, tossing several for Karma to find in the grass. While Karma collected the yummies, the girl adjusted the padding on her lower legs before standing and starting the game again.

Each time they played, the girl changed something. Not much, just a little bit. Just enough so Karma had to think and figure out what was different. She watched, smelled, and listened to every detail, paying exquisite attention to the girl—what she did, what she said, and especially Lia's facial expression. Every wrinkle of her brow, flare of nostril or quirk of Lia's lips spoke to Karma. The treats didn't matter as much as figuring out what the girl wanted.

More than anything else, Karma wanted to please the girl. So much so, she only struggled a little and didn't growl at all when Lia scooped her up in a hug to end the game.

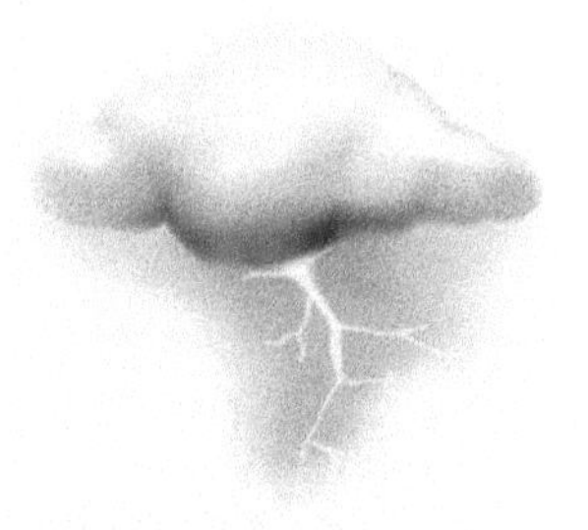

Chapter 5

The muggy atmosphere and dark clouds turned the day claustrophobic, and Lia unzipped her light windbreaker to relieve the feeling of constriction. She'd settled Karma back in the kennel, but hadn't bothered to remove her shin guards and leg pads. The client might want a demo.

She didn't trust the bizarre weather. Her phone alarms kept her updated on the storm's progress and she still couldn't believe the warnings. Most February weather brought ice storms that downed power lines and shattered creaky trees. At that thought, she eyeballed the nearby bois d'arc when the wind made claw-limbs scrabble against the kennel's tin roof. The nails-on-blackboard sound made her teeth ache. Luckily, her two Pit Bull boarders were used to the noise and remained silent. She'd inherited their owner Sunny Babcock from Abe's clientele, but now the woman could afford luxury digs since landing a role on a reality TV show.

The litter accepted the noisy invitation. Once one puppy started, the whole group raised the doggy alarm with each thump, scrap, or blustery breath of wind. She sighed.

The building needed refurbishing she couldn't afford without more paying clients. But unless she spiffed up the facilities, Corazon Kennels couldn't attract the high-end boarders she needed. Chicken-or-egg syndrome.

It all came down to the puppies. If Derek Williams approved of the Rottie litter's progress, his recommendation could put her on the map—and clients like Sunny would come in droves.

Derek's parents ran in the same circles as Grammy and Grandfather, and they all came from old money. His folks bragged on him and indulged his hobby-du-jour while they groomed him to take over the family business.

Lia had hoped her own family connections would bring referrals to her new venture. Instead, Grammy apologized for Lia, and got a pinched look like she'd stepped in something with any mention of the kennel.

Whatever. She'd make a success of this, no matter what. She owed it to Abe to keep his legacy alive.

The black extended cab truck appeared in the distance, bumping far too fast down the narrow road. Lia held her breath, fearing the driver would slide off into the rushing water on both sides. Rain over the past two weeks had overflowed ditches. Weather in neighboring counties left a wake of damage over the past 24 hours, with more in the forecast. At least so far, her kennel roof had passed the leak test. Replacing the roof would cost more than the property was worth.

Lia stood with her hands on her hips as Derek arrived. She stood in the doorway of the main building that doubled as her office and apartment. His truck tossed mud against the office window when he skidded to a stop. He was late. But she couldn't afford to piss him off, and besides, it wasn't as if she had anything better to do.

When Derek dropped off Dolly and her litter of eight-week-old pups after Christmas, Lia hadn't yet closed on what was then called Pesqueira Board & Train. She'd grown close to Abe while working at his kennel, and bought the business after he got an offer to go home and manage the cattle dogs in Waimea, Hawaii. Before he could get back to the Islands, Abe died.

The papers had been signed, but Abe's death left a number of issues unresolved. Lia's inherited clients had reservations for spring break vacation next month. But that income wouldn't arrive for weeks, and the seasonal after-Christmas slump was a killer. Derek's much needed fees would bridge the income gap.

Today, Derek wore jeans with fashionable rips in all the right places, custom running shoes, and a silk tee shirt that outlined his muscles and exposed a full sleeve tattoo of some mythical beast. His outfit cost more than her ramshackle truck. A second man, someone she didn't know, climbed more slowly out the passenger side.

"You have everything set up?" Derek hooked a thumb at the older man. "I got a buyer interested, and some others long distance, so let's get this started. I want out of here before the next wave of storms hit."

She nodded, conjured a tentative smile and offered her hand to shake. Derek ignored the gesture, brushing by to reach the office. Her shoulders tightened, but she followed without a word. Lia held open the door and waited for Derek's guest to precede her into the tiny room.

A large dog roused from his foam bed beside the desk. Lia stooped to stroke Thor's neck. She showed him her palm with an emphatic gesture signaling him to stay and not move from his place.

"That's not a Rottweiler, Derek." The older man hesitated, his double chins quivering with concern. "It looks sick."

Lia smiled. "Thor is a Bouvier. He's not sick, he's just old. He came with the kennel." The old dog had belonged to Abe. How do you tell a dog his special human would never come home? Thor deserved a happy time during his golden years. "I'm Lia, by the way. And you are? . . ."

"Samuel Cooper. Call me Coop." He nodded, tugged his sweater vest down over his ample girth, and wiped the soles of his alligator boots on the doormat before stepping into the room proper. He sniffed the air. His lip curled.

Lia hid a smile. Thor had always been gassy. It seemed to go with Bouviers.

"Mr. Cooper owns a slew of car dealerships in Dallas." Derek looked at Lia. "He needs some furry protection."

Derek planned to sell the puppies to him, untrained? Unprepared?

Derek caught her expression. "You said it'd take years to properly train up a police dog. And I don't have the time. Besides, not all will be a fit for K9 work. What am I supposed to do with the rest?"

True enough. Temperament evaluations at eight weeks changed as puppies matured. Today's test would be a better gage of future potential. With Dolly's sketchy personality, they'd be lucky if any of the nine pups made the grade.

Lia hadn't considered what would happen to those that washed out. Derek owned the dogs and called the shots, even though he hadn't a clue about breeding or training. She'd need more than doggy daycare clients to make a go of the business, so this could be the opportunity she needed. Added to the daily boarding fee for Dolly and her nine pups over the past two months, some basic puppy training could help build her reputation.

Derek pulled the office door shut, glancing around the shabby room, and Lia could almost hear his thoughts. But never mind his opinion. Once Derek settled his account, Lia could pay the overdue insurance premium, with enough left over for office face lifting. She waved both men toward the interior door. "I've got everything set up for the temperament test through there, in the last run on your right." She hurried to open the door. "Derek, I put Dolly up in the first run with the pups across from her in a separate space, so she wouldn't be a distraction." She hadn't expected this second temperament test to be a sales pitch, too. Her shoulders bunched, unsettled by the notion. She'd grown attached to the pups, especially the biggest female, Karma.

"Coop, wait until you see the litter." Derek grinned. "Four months old and already game as hell. Exactly what you want for your, uhm," his eyes cut to Lia and away, "your *purposes*." He clapped the older man on the shoulder, and continued to boast about the attributes of the puppies.

Hiding her disquiet, Lia preceded the two men. She wondered why Derek even bothered. Nobody made money breeding dogs, and he didn't need the income. Couldn't be that he liked dogs. This was the first time he'd visited Dolly and her litter since dropping them off. On top of that, Dolly was at best a marginal example of the heroic Rottweiler breed.

Descended from ancient Roman cattle dogs interbred with Swiss and German mastiffs, the versatile athletic breed excelled at everything from hunting bears and guarding cattle to pulling kiddie carts or sharing a beloved human's pillow. Only the elite with the best temperament and physique were suited for the rigors of protection, military or police work. Poor Dolly didn't come close. It had taken Lia weeks to earn the mother dog's trust, and that told Lia volumes about Dolly's short life. The bitch was just a year old, far too young for a litter. If Dolly was her dog…

But then, Derek hadn't asked for her opinion. And Dolly didn't belong to her. Neither did the puppies. Their sire must have been magnificent, though. Lia could already tell several of the pups had potential. Her fists clenched. If she handled this puppy temperament test the right way, she could do some good. Make things turn out better for the dogs. Still, she had a bad feeling.

Lia stared down the long line of immaculate but empty kennels. The office might look shabby, but she kept the boarding area pristine. Dogs away from the comfort of home deserved to feel safe, and Lia couldn't wait to turn Corazon Boarding Kennels into a state of the art facility. Meanwhile, just keeping them clean was a point of pride with her.

She paused to greet Dolly in the first kennel on the left. The big black dog snuffled her palm through the chain link gate, rubbing her rust color muzzle against the barrier as she slicked her ears back and wriggled a hello. But when the men followed too close, Dolly's hackles rose and she backed away with stiff legs. A bass rumble started deep in the dog's wide, muscular chest.

"There she is! That's Dolly-Danger, the baddest Rottweiler in North Texas." Derek beamed, his expression vulpine. "I guarantee, her pups will be just as ferocious, Coop." He pulled Lia away from the door. "You better not have babied her and let her get all soft. I brought her training collar if she needs a refresher." He banged the wire with his fist. "Go on, Dolly, get fired up. Show us what you've got!"

Dolly bounced forward, mixing snarls with barks, trying to get at Derek through the barrier.

Coop jumped backwards with a frightened cry, and then punched Derek on the shoulder with a shit-eating grin of satisfaction. "If the pups are halfway that badass, you've got a deal."

Lia's stomach clenched and her cheeks heated. *Training collar refresher?* That explained Dolly's sketchy personality. Derek meant a shock collar.

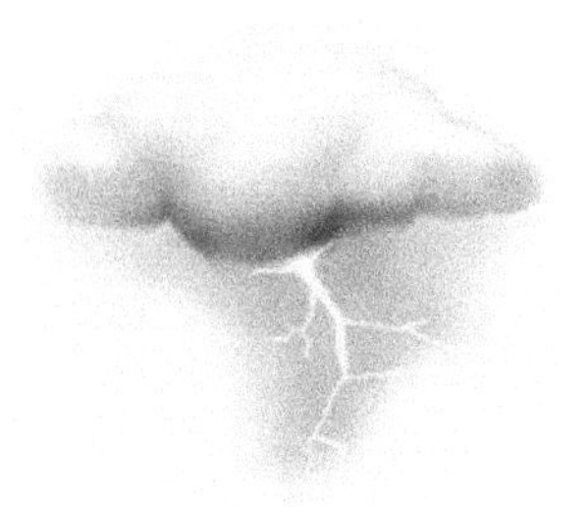

Chapter 6

Karma heard the girl's voice from the office, and wriggled upright from the soft blanket where she and her siblings slept. The fabric smelled good, safe, comforting—like her dam and littermates. Karma yawned and stretched, and couldn't wait to play another game with Lia.

She already took cues from her dam about new things, so she'd know to be cautious or curious. But Karma learned to ignore much of Dolly's suspicious nature when her mother's fear proved unfounded. Humans confused Karma more often than she understood them. She'd been the first of her siblings to learn the girl's presence meant treats, toys, and games.

Two strangers stood beside Lia. One of the men banged the wire with his fist and shouted.

Fear-stink poured off Dolly. The acrid scent stirred up the entire litter even before Dolly snarled and bounded toward the gate. She barked and flailed, doing her best to reach the man through the wire barrier.

The litter squealed in response, and Karma yelped with surprise. Dolly's raging echoed so loud in the cement-floored room, it hurt a good-dog's ears and Karma shrank away. She'd never smelled or heard her mother so distressed. But curiosity overcame caution. After all, Dolly viewed everything with fear. And Karma knew sometimes bravery earned good-dogs a treat.

The other man spoke and laughed. "If the pups are halfway that badass, you've got a deal."

She didn't know what the words meant, but that was okay. She learned new words every day. Understanding the happy, satisfied emotion in the stranger's voice was enough for her.

Karma stumbled away from the safety of the whimpering puppy pile, padded to the front of the doorway, and strained to see Lia.

Nothing scared Karma. At least, not for long. The girl always jollied Karma and the other puppies with happy words when they acted scared and turned the unknown into an exciting game. That didn't always work with Dolly, but Karma had decided the world proved too interesting to waste time being scared. Especially if she got paid with treats to be brave.

Maybe Lia had more of the yummies in her pockets. Karma thought she wouldn't mind wearing her itchy collar so much if treats were involved.

So she stuck her rust-colored muzzle through the gaps in the metal barrier to figure out what had her mother so upset and fearful. The stub of her black tail pointed to the ceiling and her butt wiggled when the girl reached down and touched her cheek. Karma panted and then sniffed long and hard. Her brow wrinkled, recognizing the girl's unease. She wondered why, and concentrated harder, testing the air and reading the scent-names of the two strange men.

"Good-girl, Karma. What a brave puppy-girl."

Karma wagged even harder at the girl's words.

"Derek, you've got Dolly so upset, it'll skew the puppy tests."

The man she called Derek made a snorting sound. "We're not testing the bitch, Lia, just the pups. And that big one you're petting doesn't look rattled at all. What did you just called it?"

"Don't call her an *it*, Derek." Lia's sharp words softened when she stroked Karma's black fur. "I call her *Karma.* She has a nose for trouble. Nothing bad, but it seemed appropriate." Karma wriggled at Lia's affectionate tone.

"Bad-ass puppy needs a better name than Karma." Even though Derek had no hackles to raise, Karma's fur bristled at his mocking tone. "Don't you dare tell me what to do. You're just the hired help,

Lia." He looked her up and down, a sneer in his voice and something worse in his eyes. "Just a tawdry Hawaiian souvenir your tramp mother brought back from vacation."

Karma cocked her head when Lia gasped and recoiled. She pawed the door, wanting Lia to continue scratching her cheek, and then did a paws-up on the doorframe when the girl stepped away.

She smelled anger and a bitter nose-wrinkling aggression spilling from Derek, and her siblings shifted uneasily. But Karma wanted closer. The scent made her teeth ache to bite, and the thump-feeling in her chest sped up.

"What are you waiting for, Lia?" Derek spat the words. "Get your pups ready for the temperament tests." He whirled, and strode away.

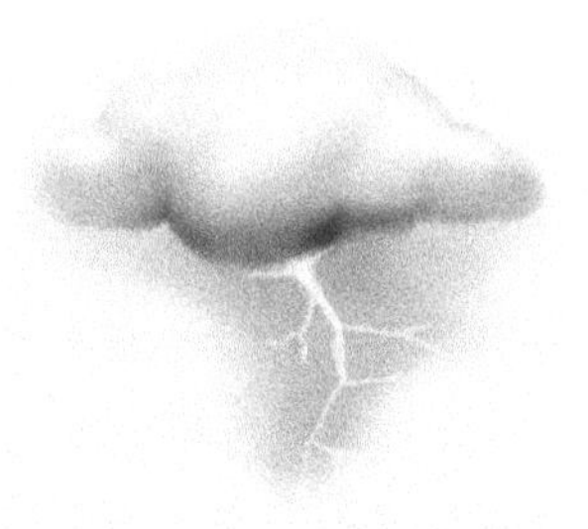

Chapter 7

Lia took two shaky breaths before she remembered to close her mouth. She swallowed past the lump in her throat, glanced over her shoulder where the two men stood whispering, and told herself she didn't care. Derek paid her to do a job, so she'd do it. She didn't have to like him. As for the rest, the scandalous circumstances of her birth were old news.

"Water under the bridge, right Karma-girl?" Her whisper prompted the big Rottie pup to wriggle and jump up against the wire gate.

This was *her* place. *She* was in control. Lia adjusted the bandanna holding her flyaway hair, and crossed to the men, determined to keep the meeting on a professional level.

"The camera's in the far kennel run, like I said. Mr. Cooper—uh, I mean, Coop, you can join me there. I'll show you how it works." She raised an eyebrow and turned to Derek, offering her client an option. "Unless you'd prefer Coop to handle the pups? It's a better comparison if the test person stays the same." She nodded at the pass-through gate to the outside. "The umbrella and other test stuff is in the yard." She couldn't imagine Coop muddying his fine boots chasing puppies through the grass, and wagered Derek would spoil his high-dollar high tops just to make a point.

"Fine. Like before." He didn't look at her as he passed by, so she didn't have to hide her grin.

Distant thunder rumbled. *No time to waste.* It'd take five or six minutes for each pup, and the storm wasn't due to hit for an hour. The building had no storm cellar, so she'd already moved Sunny Babcock's dogs, Buster and Beau, to the kennels that shared walls with the office proper. The safest spot was the center of the building with no windows nearby.

"Coop, are you familiar with temperament tests?" She met his eyes without flinching, daring him to comment on Derek's rude behavior.

"In principle, sure." He held open the kennel gate for her like the door to an office. "Derek says it predicts the best pups, so you know what you get."

She smiled. "That's the theory, but nothing is a crystal ball. We use a series of tests to measure personality tendencies. Based on the results, we can figure out which pups may do better in different circumstances. That helps with placing pups with the right family."

He nodded. "Like the best attack dog, which one's the most alpha." He grinned. "I want the pup that'll turn into the biggest, baddest, most aggressive puppy. And I want a bitch I can breed, to recoup my investment."

Lia took a beat before she answered. "Far be it from me to argue with Derek, they're his pups. That whole alpha dog thing, though . . ." Her voice trailed off at his stubborn expression. Derek had already sold him on the concept, never mind that the most aggressive dog was more likely a fearful dog, like Dolly. But she couldn't live with herself without trying. "It's more complicated. The rank of puppies in a litter changes over time and tests on very young pups may not be accurate. Then socialization and training, even the environment, impact and can change predicted outcomes as the puppy matures." She shrugged. "That's why we test Dolly's litter again today, at four months." She finished in a rush, trying to make her point. "The best protection dogs test middle of the road on temperament." One look at his face and she knew she wasted her breath. He'd believe what he wanted, and Derek fed him what Coop wanted to hear.

Poor puppies.

She escorted Coop to the camera she'd focused on the brown

Bermuda grass just outside the kennel, and pointed out the start/stop buttons. "Derek will get each pup in the frame for the various tests. You just need to start and stop the camera in between, while I record the results and switch out the pups. Work for you?"

He nodded, and moved into place.

Lia left him fiddling with the camera, collected the clipboard she'd previously prepared, and returned to the puppies. She picked up the first puppy, and carried him to the exit and stepped through. "Derek, this is Mr. Green Collar." Each of the pups wore a colorful soft elastic collar to help tell them apart. The color codes also helped keep health records straight, as well as birth order.

Derek waved his readiness.

She set the youngster on the grass. He snuffled the ground, ears flopping and bobbed tail wiggling.

Derek called the pup, clapping his hands and squatting to get the youngster's attention to test "social attraction" and "following." The pup ambled toward him, and jumped up and tried to bite his hands until Derek stood to step away. The little dog followed, getting underfoot and biting at Derek's shoes. Lia recorded the pup's reaction. Next, Derek stooped and gently rolled Mr. Green on his back, to see how the pup tolerated the stress of social or physical domination. Mr. Green whined and struggled and flailed, and Derek had to let the pup go before ten seconds passed.

Lia marked the restraint test score, and frowned. So far, Mr. Green wasn't doing well.

As Derek let the puppy up and began to stroke him, the Rottie pup tolerated a few strokes and then wandered away. The man followed, scooped up the pup and cradled him with cupped hands under Mr. Green's tummy. He held the youngster just above the ground.

Sighing, Lia recorded Mr. Green's growls and struggles. Five more tests to go, but she'd already seen enough. She suspected, though, that Coop and Derek would find this puppy attitude to be ideal.

She'd scored each of the first five test on the standard 1 through 6 scale. Mr. Green Collar scored a 1 or 2 on all parameters. The opposite end of the spectrum—5 and 6 scores—indicated pups that refused to follow or interact out of indifference or fear. The mid-range score of 3 was the ideal for a working dog and indicated a pup eager and willing to engage with people that wasn't too fearful or pushy. The remaining tests with Mr. Green went as expected.

Derek tossed a wadded piece of paper, and then a small ball. Studies had shown a high correlation between willingness to retrieve and successful service dogs and obedience canines. Lia had seen puppy reaction vary from those who stole the toy and raced off with it, pups that brought it back, and still more with no interest in retrieving at all. Mr. Green Collar ignored the toy.

The noise sensitivity test, Derek banging a spoon on a metal pan, brought the puppy running. That was how Lia called the pups to dinner, so the reaction wasn't surprising. But Mr. Green had no interest in the cloth rag or the sheepskin tug toy dragged across the grass. He circled the umbrella with suspicion when Derek opened it and set it on the ground, and then wandered off.

In the final test, Derek grasped the toe webbing of one forepaw between his thumb and forefinger and pressed, slowly increasing the pressure. He stopped as soon as the pup resisted. "That's six seconds on the sensitivity test," said Derek.

Finally, a mid-range score. Lia scribbled and set aside the clipboard. "Okay, we'll get the next pup." Mr. Green scored 1's and 2's which predicted a quick-to-bite extremely dominant dog with aggressive tendencies. He'd require a very experienced and talented trainer.

There should be a similar test for prospective owners. She'd already scored both Coop and Derek. Mr. Green would be out of their league. She could only offer advice, though, and then bite her lip when Derek shut her down.

Taking the struggling Mr. Green from the man, Lia returned him to the kennel with Dolly before selecting another pup. This one, Miss Yellow Collar, scored at the other end with 5s on the test. That indicated extreme shyness that could be crippling, and another difficult dog for an average owner to handle. Miss Yellow wouldn't be a good candidate for protection or police dog training. She'd need lots of help to build her confidence, which could be done with patience. But shy dogs could become fear-biters like Dolly, a danger to the humans around them and themselves.

Lia returned Miss Yellow, and moved on to Mr. Dark Blue, Mr. Orange, Miss Red, Mr. Light Blue, Miss Tan, and Mr. Black in turn, until only Miss Purple Collar—Karma—remained. Lia scooped her up, realizing she'd delayed the inevitable as long as possible.

During her first temperament test at six weeks old, Karma scored at the high end for working dog potential, so Lia assumed this pick of the litter first born would be placed accordingly. She had mixed feelings, though, both wanting Karma to do well on the test but not wanting her to go to someone like Coop.

"What's the hold up?" Derek yelled from the yard, and she saw him look at the clouds when a louder rumble sounded.

No more delays. "Karma-girl, make me proud." She whispered the words into the puppy's soft neck, and Karma wriggled around to slurp Lia on the lips. Not a kiss, not affection, but just polite puppy deference behavior. Still, Lia's heart melted. *Aww...puppy breath!* She set the big puppy on the ground, and Karma jumped, pawing at Lia's thigh for the attention to continue.

"C'mon, here puppy-puppy-puppy. *Karma-pup*, here-here-here!" Derek clapped his hands and waved, beckoning from the center of the grassy area.

Lia's shoulders hunched at Derek's mocking tone. But it got the baby's attention, and Karma whirled, tail up, and raced to reach the man. When he squatted within reach, Karma leaped up to reach his hands, licking and grabbing at them.

Social Attraction Score = 2. *Better than Mr. Green.*

Derek rose, and ran away, calling the pup. Lia had worked on the pup's recall with this exercise, but Derek was a stranger. Much of their training hadn't yet generalized to all situations. The other girl puppies had either refused to come or only reluctantly followed with their tails down or even tucked.

Not Karma. Tail up, she bounced after Derek, grabbed at his shoelaces, and tripped him in the process.

Lia hid a smile. The pup was a fast study, volunteering the behavior on her own without the trigger command. In any event, she scored a 1. The baby-girl learned to chain the cue into a tug game. But Derek didn't have to know that.

The man crouched down, disengaged Karma from growling and gripping his shoe, and rolled her on her back. Karma whined and struggled for about five seconds, then settled. She stared up at Derek's face for a few heartbeats, and began to struggle and squeal again. Ultimately she settled. Karma stretched her neck, straining to look upside down toward Lia.

Good-girl, that's a 3. The score predicted a balanced personality willing to accept leadership.

"Okay, now the social dominance test, Derek." Lia flipped back on her clipboard to see the previous test results, noting that Karma scored a 3 previously with much licking and snuggling. As Karma got older, she no longer liked being held, though. And this time, as Derek tried to pet Karma, the big puppy looked around the yard, spotted Lia and came trotting over to her with a wide puppy grin. Lia circled the 6 on the score—predictive of independence. That could be good or bad, again depending on the trainer going forward.

Karma squealed when Derek hurried to scoop her up, and held her above the grass. Lia feared the man's rush would influence the score. The pup scored a 2 before at the six weeks test, with much struggling and crying. But this time, four-month-old Karma just looked back at Lia and yawned. A solid score of 3, indicating acceptance of human guidance and a commonsense attitude. *Yay, Karma!*

Lightning unzipped the clouds, followed by a delayed rumble. Three heads as one, two human and one canine, checked out the sky. When the distant sirens swelled, the dogs still inside the kennel wailed their answer.

Derek grimaced. "That's the tornado siren. They must have a funnel on the ground somewhere near. Only a few more to go, let's finish before the weather hits."

Lia nodded, but couldn't help the tightening worry. Static electricity charged her hair, creating a halo of frizz, a portent of more lightning to come. She'd rather cut the tests short, and resume when they weren't rushed, but Derek paid the bills. Or he would, once the tests were complete.

They ran the last few tests in less than a minute each, and Karma scored well on each. She chased the paper ball and returned it to Derek, asking him to throw again. Her touch sensitivity tested in the moderate range. She investigated the spoon banged on the pan without a peep, and even climbed inside the umbrella before deciding to use it as a chew toy. She earned a solid 3 on all these tests, except for the last one.

For the sight sensitivity test, Derek dragged the towel across the grass and Karma watched it for just a moment. Then she exploded, attacked the towel, grabbing it and shaking with a ferocious puppy snarl. She only released it when Derek offered a swap with the sheepskin lure.

That's a 1, for sure.

Karma's scores offered an average score of 3 that spoke to willingness to follow a human leader. The 2s and a few 1s indicated independence and tendency toward dominance, not a bad mix for a future police dog. As expected, Karma tested the best out of all nine puppies, and should win a spot for police dog training. *Schutzhund, here you come.*

"That's it, we're done." Derek scooped up Karma, allowing her to hang on to the sheepskin lure, and waved at Cooper to join them. He traded the puppy for Lia's clipboard with the test results. "We can review the scores but I think there are a couple that meet your criteria."

Coop nodded, his grin wide. "Don't need the scores. I want this one." He reached for Karma.

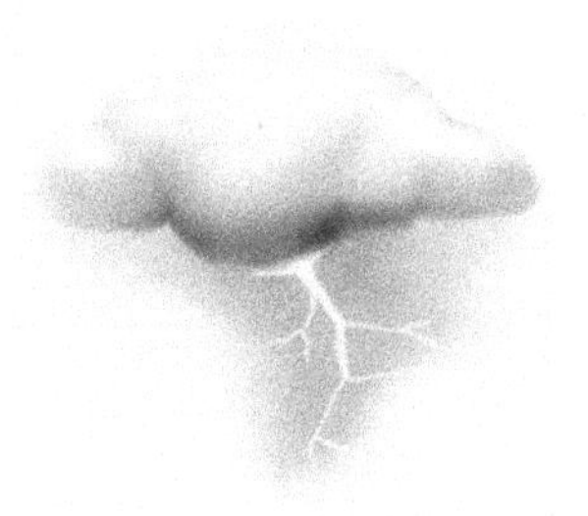

Chapter 8

Karma bit down on the sheepskin lure, braced herself in Lia's arms, and shook it with a ferocious snarl, all the while wagging furiously. Her gums itched and ached, and chewing relieved the discomfort even when they bled. The salty taste and copper-bright smell of her own blood made Karma drool.

When she shook the toy, the soft material flapped and slapped against her muzzle with a satisfying sound. Karma wished Lia would put her down and make the toy move again through the soggy grass. Chasing and pouncing and biting and killing the thing had to be the best game of all. Karma wondered why they didn't play this game all the time.

She only stopped growling and shaking the toy when Lia's arms tightened at the sound of the two men's voices. Karma would have objected to the hug, but the girl's scent changed, from unease to something else. Karma knew that meant something, but wasn't sure what. Nobody told her. She'd have to figure that out herself.

"I want this one, with the purple collar, and the first boy pup we tested. Green collar, I think." The strange man reached out to Karma and she stretched her neck to sniff his hand, wrinkling her rust-color muzzle. She looked at Lia's face for a clue when the girl flinched and pulled her away. Karma growled to cover her own confusion and shook the toy again in a doggy shrug. She smelled no treats on the man, and saw no toy. So he didn't matter. Lia grabbed the other end of the toy, and Karma wrestled back with delight.

The people kept talking, a mishmash of sound with no important words Karma understood, so she tuned it out. Then Lia adjusted her grasp, hugging Karma so hard she yelped and struggled. The girl's arms quivered. That caught Karma's attention.

When she'd first arrived here with her dam and littermates, Lia had been a scary unknown. Dolly's behavior told the litter that all strangers were scary. Puppies learned best from mom-dogs, so at first Karma copied Dolly's behavior.

But with each *good-dog* and treat, with every new game, Karma became convinced Lia was a very-good-thing. She trusted Lia to keep her safe. Not that Karma ever felt afraid, oh no. She would never be a shivery dog like her mother. A good-dog stayed brave and confident even faced with something new, and Karma wanted to be a good-dog for Lia, and for herself. Karma sensed she and Lia were alike even if the girl had only two feet and no fur. Lia also acted ready and eager to face down any threat, to protect what mattered most.

Karma hadn't figured out what mattered most to her. Not yet. But she was working on it. It had something to do with Lia.

The girl's shaking concerned Karma. Dolly shook when she got scared, and she got scared a lot. But Lia had never trembled before, so if the girl was scared, should a good-dog be uneasy, too? Not scared (she was brave, after all!) but concerned?

Karma matched the sharp acrid change of Lia's scent to the girl's body signals; wide eyes, quickened breath, lip licking and turning away from the two much bigger men. She'd remember what this meant. Nobody told her to, she just did it. Karma was smart that way. But she never realized people, especially all-knowing ones like Lia, could be scared. She guessed they acted that way because people couldn't whine and bark, or show their teeth the way dogs could.

The adult dogs inside the kennel howled back at a weird ululating sound that rose and fell on the wind. When the sky boomed again, Karma dropped the toy, and looked up.

Lia looked at the sky, too. "Hey, that was a loud one, wasn't it? Thunder party!" Lia set Karma down, and made the fleece jump and bounce across the grass.

Delighted, Karma forgot about the sky noise, and chased after the toy. It stopped moving and she grappled the toy, growling and shaking it. The thunder echoed again, and the toy skittered and danced. What fun! Sky noise wasn't scary after all, not when it made chase games happen. She'd remember this, too.

"Lia, quit playing with the puppy, so Coop and I can make our deal." The sharp voice stopped the fun and Karma bristled.

"Derek, once your bill is settled you can talk business all you want." Lia jumped when a bright stabbing light unraveled across the sky with the crackling sky-noise. Karma waited for Lia to make the toy move again, but instead, Lia grabbed her up, and ran back to the building where the other dogs howled. She shouted over her shoulder. "Join me, or don't. Just get the hell out of the storm."

Karma saw the two men hesitate. Even over the sky-noise she heard their conversation, even if the words made no sense.

"I can collect the pups tomorrow. I got the big show tonight." The men grinned, and ran to the hulking truck.

Lia's tense shoulders relaxed as soon as the truck drove way. She hugged Karma even harder—dog language for "I'm in control."

But for once, Karma didn't mind someone else being in control. She signaled her deference with an extra-juicy tongue-swipe across the girl's face.

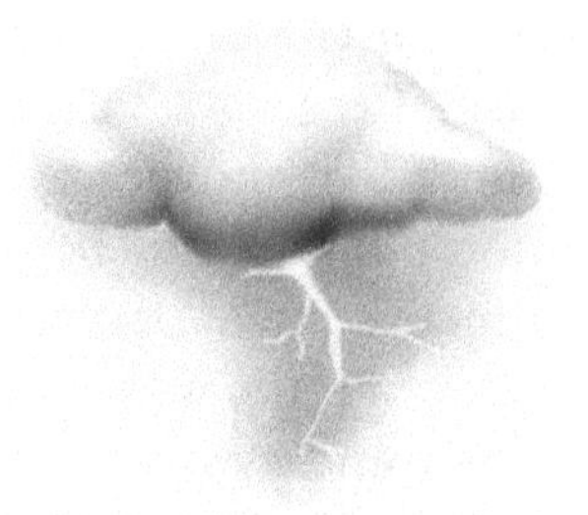

Chapter 9

September struggled to sit upright on the hospital bed when she heard a familiar strident voice arguing with the nursing staff. Mom had arrived, sweeping Dad in tow.

"I'm looking for my grandson, Steven. I want to see my grandson."

Sighing, September's shoulders relaxed, knowing Mom would spend as much time with the boy as they'd let her. Only once satisfied about his well-being would she check September. Several layers of blankets tangled her feet, and IV lines that sprouted from each arm. She'd been lucky, and with a few hours treatment, her near-death hypothermia had abated.

The fallout from the ongoing storm kept both September and her nephew Steven hospitalized on the same floor. The place bustled with visitors and patients. Earlier, Steven's father stopped in to thank her. Their complicated relationship made the visit awkward, but this wasn't the first time she'd saved the boy's life. She first trained Shadow as an autism service dog for Steven. The boy no longer needed or wanted the help, and after the news went out, nobody would doubt Steven's extraordinary talents.

The warm room and clean sheets helped September feel more human despite the scrapes and bruises she'd collected over the past 24 hours. Her body might be warm again, but her heart stayed cold.

As long as Shadow remained lost, her soul cried in silent agony. He'd become more than her PTSD support canine. The black shepherd gave her hope for a normal future. He was family, the one who never doubted and always loved her, no questions asked. So even with the dire situation, September refused to give up hope. She knew Shadow, had to believe he survived the storm to return to her. She couldn't bear the alternative.

Combs strode into the room, and rushed to her side. He wore the dingy, wet clothes from her rescue, needed a shave, and carried an aroma of swamp. He looked wonderful.

"They said you're doing better. You were out of it for a while." He laced their fingers together. "I saw your parents next door with Steven. He's tougher than nails, that kid. Already demanding an iPad." Combs grinned. "I think your Mom brought him one."

Her eyes watered. "I'm glad. Any other news?" Her voice trembled.

His brow furrowed. "Your house is gone. I'm sorry. But it's insured, right?"

She sighed. After renovating the old Victorian, she'd fallen in love with the location and the custom design updates. But yes, insurance would cover the loss. Her lip trembled. "Macy?" Nothing could replace her Maine Coon cat. He had a heart condition, and just the stress of the storm could kill him.

"Guess there's a reason they say cats have nine lives," Combs said dryly. "He's fine. We found him in the rubble, looking for you." His voice caught, and then steadied.

She breathed again and squeezed his hand. "Where is he?"

"The tornado blew out the front windows to Doc Eugene's veterinary hospital, but the rest of his building survived just fine. Macy has a private suite there for the time being. The staff will have Macy spoiled by the time you get out of here."

Mom pushed into the room, catching just the end of Combs's words. "September will come stay with us, of course. Good thing that cat has a place to stay, I'm deathly allergic, you know." The petite blond woman swept into the hospital room as if making an entrance to a gala. She pinned Combs with a hard look until he released

September's hand. "Detective Combs, I'm sure you have more pressing issues to attend."

"Hello Rose. Nice to see you again. Where's Lysle?" Combs kept his expression neutral.

"Mom!" September would have grabbed Combs's hand again in defiance but her mother's dramatic embrace forestalled the impulse.

Rose released September, stepped back from the bed and plunked a small leather overnight case on the chair Combs vacated. "Lysle is with our grandson, Detective. Shouldn't you be with your children?"

Combs smiled. "Nice of you to worry about them. They're fine. Left here two hours ago and are now home with their mom and stepdad." He turned to September. "I'll check back later."

"Wait, don't go!" September raised her voice as he walked to the door, panic resurfacing. "What about Shadow? You have to look for him."

Mom tsk-tsked. "Don't be selfish, September. The police concentrate on more important things." Despite the continuing bad weather, Rose could have stepped out of a photo shoot. With not a hair out of place, flawless makeup and stylish raingear straight from the pages of Land's End, she commanded the room. "You look awful, dear. I brought you fresh clothes and toiletries. And what did you do to your hair?"

"I don't care how I look. Nothing's more important than Shadow." September jutted her chin, and reached for the IV in her arm. She'd mount a search on her own.

Combs knew what Shadow meant to her, but agreed with Mom, regret in his tone. "My hands are tied, September. Emergency services are up to their eyeballs rescuing human victims. Besides, we don't know where to look. That flood could carry him for miles. There's more rain in the forecast."

"Teddy Williams could find him." September allowed Mom to push her back on the bed, and stopped plucking at her fluid lines. "Can't you call him?" The self-described white-hat hacker helped several months ago when Macy turned up missing.

"What can Teddy do?" Combs moved back to September's side, ignoring Rose's sour expression when he again grasped her hand. "That old man must be grieving. You know his wife passed away. I haven't heard from him since, and I think he's out of town."

Rose busied herself opening the overnight bag, and pulled out a brush and comb. "All this nonsense over a missing dog," she muttered, and set to work on the rat's nest tangle of September's dark hair. "Heavens, dear, there's a big bald spot!"

September flinched, and pushed her mother's hand aside. "Later, Mom." Her entire scalp still flamed from Sunny Babcock's hair-snatching grip. "Shadow wore a tracking collar. I lost my phone, but Teddy could get into the computer software and find him. I know he could. It's our only chance to find my boy, Combs." She begged with voice and eyes, not caring what Mom or anyone else thought.

"That could work. If you can reach Teddy, that'd be great." Combs rubbed a hand through his own dirty hair. "The department won't allocate time or expertise for a lost dog, not during an emergency of this magnitude. I'm sorry, September."

A young green-eyed blond boy wearing a hospital gown wandered into the room. Fingers danced over his iPad.

"Steven, what are you doing here? Does your dad know you're out of bed?" Rose hurried to the boy, but knew better than to touch him. Steven had never liked to be touched. He'd recovered enough to begin speaking, though only in weird rhyming phrases.

"Away he washed,
Dog must be found
I find the lost,
I look around."

September stared at the extraordinary child with renewed hope. "You can find Shadow? With the GPS tracking collar. Can you do that?"

Steven never looked up but nodded his head twice. His fingers flew.

Combs watched over Steven's shoulder, eyes wide with surprise and then recognition. He retrieved his phone and made a call, grinned at September, and ran out of the room.

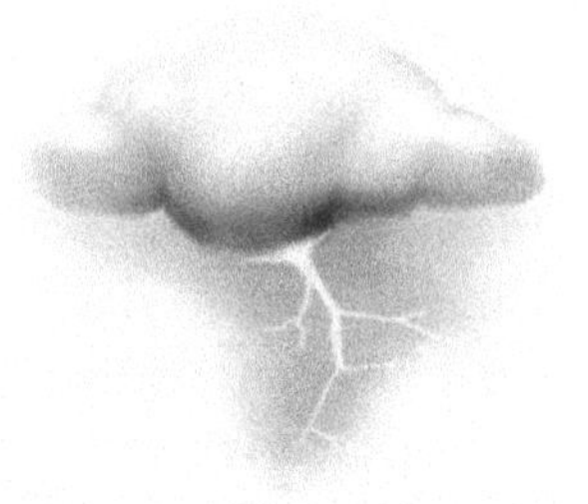

Chapter 10

Lia crouched beneath a solid walnut desk huddled next to Thor in the only room in the cement block building without windows. Thor remained silent, because he couldn't hear much anymore. But the other dogs answered the machinegun rattle of hail on the metal roof with barks, howls and yelps. Lia flinched at each thud, pop and crash when tiny ice balls grew to golf-ball proportions and assaulted the building with window-smashing, roof-buckling gusto.

She checked her cell phone for weather updates. Still no connection. The dogs yodeled, hail hammered, and then an invisible switch shut off the celestial spigot. Lia blew out a breath, and poked her head out from under the desk. The lights flickered back on, and the dogs' frightened yelps subsided. She wanted to cheer that the ceiling appeared intact, but didn't want to get the dogs started again.

She crawled from under the desk, and paused to help Thor's arthritic legs gain traction on the slick linoleum. A change of flooring was on her wish list. The Bouvier shook himself, regained his balance, and then headed for his memory foam dog bed. Thor might be blind but his nosy navigation skills hadn't dimmed, especially when it meant finding favorite sleep, dinner, and pee spots.

A crash followed by a dog's scream made her leap to her feet. The lights went out. She switched on the flashlight, and staggered through the crowded office to the kennel hallway. She levered open the door and speared the light around the narrow length of the interior before wind and wet drenched her face. A felled bois d'arc crushed two of the exterior kennel walls and outside fence.

***

A limb thicker than her body stabbed into the kennel. Karma yelped, crouched and froze. The tree tore a jagged hole overhead, and rain poured through to lash Karma's black fur. This wasn't distant sky-booms and cloud-fire flashes. The sky threw trees at good-dogs!

Karma crouched alone in the cold, wet kennel, shivering. Her mother had dived out the hole in the wall to follow her puppies when they scrambled away from the clawing tree. Out beyond the damaged wall, in the black wet night, Dolly's deep frantic barks beckoned. Before she could help herself, Karma squeezed shut her eyes and allowed whimpers to climb to repeated wails. Suddenly, she didn't feel so brave. She wanted Lia's soothing voice to explain how falling trees could be fun games.

But Lia didn't answer and Karma fell silent. She had to be brave all by herself, without Lia's help. Maybe that's what she was supposed to do.

She stretched her neck so her quivering nose touched the limb, and leaped back when it shifted toward her and slapped the ground. Karma yelped, and her lips lifted to bare fangs against the invisible threat. She was young, but smart. It only took one time to learn the lesson, that booming skies and crackling fire clouds meant trees clawed and jabbed at good-dogs. Beware!

Karma's paws shook but Lia didn't come. She could hear Dolly keening outside in the storm. Dolly was always scared, but she'd bravely gone into the night after her puppies. Maybe being scared wasn't a bad thing, if a dog could still be brave.

She tucked her stubby tail tight, surprised that it somehow helped. She moved closer to the hole in the wall, and in a rush, pushed past the broken blocks. Karma took a big breath, and released a flurry of barks mixed with snarls as she scurried through the breach after her mother.

Once she stood in the yard, she recognized the place they'd played the fun chase-the-fleece-toy games a short time before. Her hackles smoothed, and her ears lifted. Ferocious snarls must have scared away the tree-throwing monster. Karma's stubby black tail lifted higher with interest. Another lesson learned. Dolly's barks sounded again and Karma cocked her head and trotted a few steps in that direction until they stopped. She paused, too, and squinted against the wind that panted like an old sick dog, but she couldn't unravel the tangled thread of scents riding the storm's breath.

A pair of muscular dogs, broad as they were tall, squirmed out of the kennel next to her. Karma flinched away, then squatted and peed to signal "no threat." But the Pit Bulls ignored her, their wide faces set in a permanent grin when one play-bowed toward the other inviting a game of tag. The pair dashed toward the nearby chain link fence, scrambled up onto the massive tree trunk, and leaped to freedom before Karma could untuck her tail.

Maybe they knew where Dolly went? Karma lifted her muzzle and barked a question and then ran to follow.

She put front paws up on the massive tree trunk, and barked again. Small furry creatures that scurried, and feathered fliers that perched on branches traveled trees the way dogs padded grass pathways. Karma had never imagined dogs might also climb trees. She leaped and clawed for purchase but couldn't gain a toe hold to pull herself up and over. The two dogs had already disappeared beyond the fence, following the same scent trail her mother had left behind.

Sniffing deeper, she learned more. Karma put her nose to the spot to find her mother's signature odor. Yes, her siblings had passed this way, but she was the biggest of the litter. If she couldn't scramble up and over the tree, neither could they.

Clouds broke apart and she flinched at the sudden shine. At the same time, the rain slowed and then stopped dripping. The round light in the sky tickled a spot at the back of her throat that wanted to howl homage, but Karma resisted. Instead, she examined the illuminated yard where here and there a well chewed but sopping toy offered temptations. No puppies, no dam, and nowhere to hide.

Of its own volition, Karma's nose hit the ground once more. She found a pool of airborne scent caught in the sheltering lee of the massive tree trunk. Her stubby tail wiggled as fast as her nose wrinkled. Here...and here again. And stronger there.

Karma followed her first trail, tracking her littermates through the fence opening hidden by the tree's crushing weight. Quickly she wiggled through, shook off the mud, and trotted away from the damaged kennel into the woods beyond.

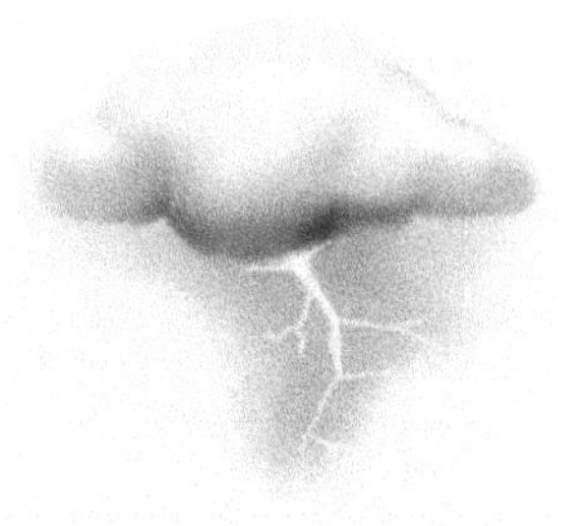

Chapter 11

Lia stared at the rubble for an endless moment before rushing to check the status of the dogs. She'd moved them to the runs away from overhanging bois d'arc but the storm didn't read any rulebook. The massive felled tree, transplanted from who-knows-where, smashed through the flimsy barrier that separated the indoor from outdoor fenced exercise yard.

The wire gate on the first pen screeched against the cement floor when dragged open. Lia raked the flashlight beam over the area, expecting to see Dolly cowering in a corner with her pups. But it was empty, except for the splintered orange trunk. Bois d'arc, also called ironwood, was so hard it destroyed chainsaw blades, and that told her something of the tornado's force.

From the next kennel over, a Pit Bull walked the tree trunk like a balance beam to reach the fence and vaulted out, following his buddy. Damn!

"Beau! Buster, come!" She was so upset, the cry came out half voice. "Dolly, where are you? Hey puppies! Puppy-puppy-puppy!" She grabbed one of the stainless steel food bowls and banged it several times against the cement floor, hoping the sound would carry and lure at least some of the dogs back. The adults knew her, but not well enough for a solid recall, and the puppies were—well, they were babies.

Lightning scratched across the sky a final time and Lia hunched her shoulders in anticipation of the thunder crack, but the storm had moved on and taken the noise with it. Dark clouds split to reveal moon glow that painted the dripping landscape silver and white. She hoisted herself onto the tree trunk, hoping the dogs at least remained inside the yard's fenced boundary.

Hummocks of brown Bermuda grass and winter rye poked through icy drifts of hail, but offered no hiding spots. The tree had crushed part of the chain link fence and created an obvious escape route for frightened dogs. She'd start there, and pray they hadn't strayed too far.

She hopped off the tree, grateful the rest of the runs looked secure. No doubt the roof would need work but she could make do with buckets to catch leaks until able to fund repairs. A building could be repaired. Losing the dogs wasn't fixable. That black mark would follow Lia like a tag-along stray, not to mention the indelible scar it would leave on her heart. She was responsible for their safety.

At least Thor was safe. And his nose still worked.

The old towel the pups used for tug games would serve. She looped it over her neck. Lia stuffed an extra tether into her pocket and grabbed Thor's tracking harness and leash from the wall on her way back to the office. Despite being blind, the Bouvier still tracked like a champ.

Lia rummaged in the mini-fridge for a baggy of pungent liverwurst, and Thor rose from his half doze, licking his jowls. She suspected his deafness was more selective hearing, since the old dog never seemed to miss the sound of the fridge opening. The treats—bribes—would lure the other dogs, but she couldn't refuse offering one to Thor. As he munched, she quickly put on his gear, and then her own. It might be dicey using the Bouvier to find Dolly. The bitch's instinct to keep strange dogs away from her litter might backfire, but Lia had no other option and little time to waste. The longer they stayed out, the greater the chance of losing one or more of the pups to coyotes, accident or weather. The freaky February warmth had dropped back to normal range, and cold could cause hypothermia in young pups.

At the last minute, she grabbed the old lariat, and slung that over her shoulders, too. Better to be prepared.

Thor pulled against the line, always ready for a tracking exercise. The ground squished beneath their feet. She ran the old dog around the perimeter of the fence to where the bois d'arc traversed the metal barrier. Lia offered him the puppies' tug-towel, let him whiff deeply and thoroughly. She took a breath, squared her shoulders—*act with confidence no matter what*—and gave the command, a German word for search."Thor, *such*."

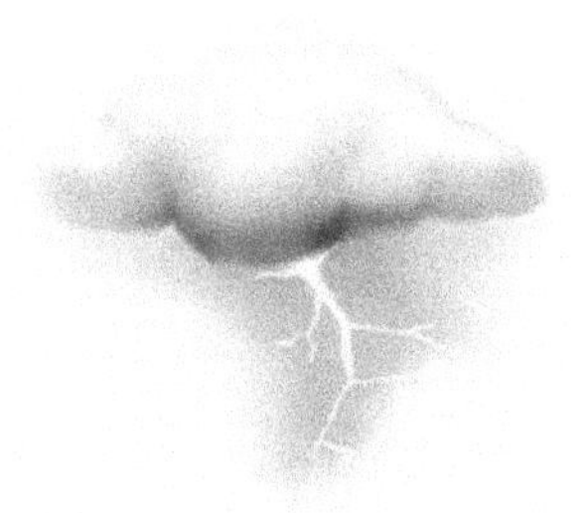

Chapter 12

Karma raced after her mother's spoor. Even with the wind that stirred and scattered the scent like stuffing from a chew toy, the trail shined brighter than moon glow to her discerning nose. She remembered the search games the girl played, hiding trails of kibble with a bonus cache of treats at the end. If she could find treats by following that smell, she'd find Dolly, too. She smothered a whimper. She didn't like being alone. Dogs were meant to be with family, not by themselves. Finding her littermates and dam would be better than a treat.

She had to concentrate to unravel the skein of distracting scents like bugs and grass and even sounds beneath the sod, and focus on the important treat-smell. And sometimes smells disappeared and only re-appeared if she ran ever widening circles to find where they'd hidden. Karma learned to relocate hidden scent by seeking out low spots where smells settled and pooled the way water followed the earth's surface.

The recent rain had washed the ground so that little else offered distraction from the recent passage of her littermates and dam. She loped along, ducking under leafless saplings that whipped and stung her hide as she passed. The trail led downhill, toward the shushing of water runoff that grew louder and louder. Karma didn't let that distract her, though. She kept her nose close to the ground to catch every whiff. Snuffling through the mounds of white ice balls made Karma's nose sting. She liked to nudge them and watch them roll away. She batted one with her rust colored paw, and she bounded after when it bounced ahead.

"Puppy-puppy-puppy!"

Karma's head shot up. The girl! Calling for her!

She whirled, staring back the way she'd come. Her stubby tail wiggled and her cautious stance softened. She could almost feel Lia's small, soothing hands stroking her body, and scratching all her hard-to-reach itchy places. She whined, licked her nose, and glanced back and forth between the girl and her mother's beckoning scent that led the opposite direction.

People could do amazing things her frightened mother could not. Lia made treats rain from the ceiling, provided tug-tag games and toys for good-dogs to chase, and even turn night into day when inside a building. And humans made cars go fast-fast-fast, even faster than a big dog could run. The view and smells through car windows made Karma's heart race. It never rained or grew cold inside cars or the houses. Well, not until someone threw a tree at Karma's sleep spot.

Karma's mother protected and loved all of the pups but feared everything. The girl feared nothing and was all seeing, all knowing, even if scent blind and sound deaf compared to dogs.

Light flashed again across the sky and Karma flinched, and her hackles bristled. The girl would know what to do about the jagged lightning, the way she had taught Karma about the sky-noise. Maybe Lia brought the fleece toy with her, too.

Decision made, Karma whirled and hurried back uphill in the direction of the girl's call. She didn't think to backtrack the scent trail, just arched her neck and cocked her ears for Lia's voice. She pranced forward, mouth parting with each anxious whine of anticipation. She jumped over a toppled tree branch, and landed on a round limb that didn't roll. It recoiled, whipped around, and tried to slither up Karma's leg.

Screaming, Karma hopped backward, shaking her foreleg so hard she fell sideways in her frantic effort to shed the crawly creature. With dismay, she saw many of the slithering things, some with open mouths making hissing sounds. The hole in the ground left by the uprooted tree had filled with water, and out of it spilled more of the long, thin creatures. Some poked out strange ribbon-like tongues or wagged tails like an excited dog. They smelled like cucumber.

She scrambled to her feet, growled and feinted toward the closest one that coiled nearby. It struck at her, head splattering in mud when it missed.

Karma yelped and leaped away, and banged sideways into the fallen tree trunk.

Lesson learned, she'd never mistake it again for a toy, not like a rabbit to chase. Karma tried to dodge past, but the writhing copper-scaled things blocked her way. Now Karma couldn't follow the scent trail to reach her mother. But neither could she backtrack to rejoin the girl.

Plodding footsteps approached and made Karma's ears twitch, but she refused to look away from the writhing serpents. She preferred the soughing breeze in her face even if the cold made her ears numb. Her nose wrinkled, recognizing dog-scent—the old one the girl called Thor—along with clean Lia-smell. Karma wanted to cry out for help but stayed frozen. Motion would make the snakes strike at her again. She enjoyed bite-games with her siblings, but these creatures didn't play.

Thor's paw-sounds drew closer along with the girl's footfalls. Thor must be seeking her dam and siblings, just the way Karma had tracked them. For a moment, her chest swelled with pride that she'd done what Lia wanted, too. But the wet, slick ground made Lia slip and trample with lots of noise. The undulating coil of scaly creatures grew even more agitated, tongues flicked and tails twitched. The triangular coppery head of the nearest turned back upon itself, away from Karma for a moment, as if to target the old dog. Or maybe the girl.

Thor and Lia would tramp right over the creatures. If Karma yelped a warning, Lia would hurry even faster and blunder into the nest. Karma shuddered, imagining the multiple bites, the choking cucumber smell.

Thor was old, blind and deaf. The girl might as well be. Neither knew about the threat, but Karma knew. And Karma could smell, and hear and see, and run very fast with her four paws. She was brave, too, even when scared.

As Thor and the girl came into sight, snakes thrashed toward the vibration of their footfalls. Karma bounded forward and grabbed the twitching tail of the nearest copperhead.

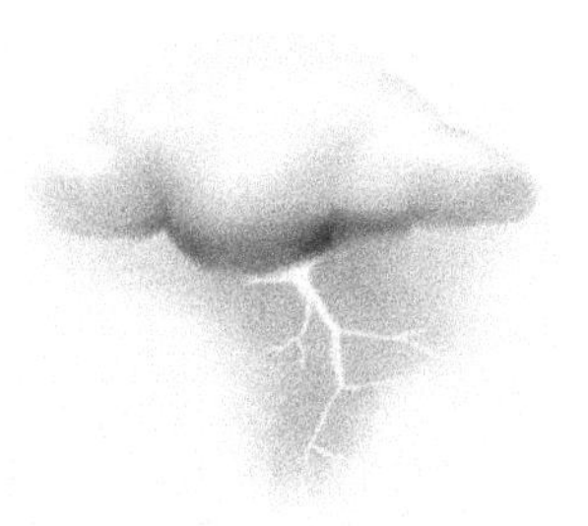

Chapter 13

Most tracking dogs, including Thor, trained to find human scent. But Abe had always played "find it" games with Thor, hiding toys and other items to keep him engaged, and Lia continued the practice. Bouviers were not always dog friendly so she'd kept him away from the others, although he'd been aware of their presence. He'd been interested in the puppies' socialization and she'd staged supervised interactions with the old Bouvier through the fence. She'd been surprised and then delighted when Thor became smitten with Dolly although the feeling wasn't mutual.

Games of "where's Dolly? Find Dolly! *SUCH!*" turned the old dog back into a youngster himself. Lia had to trust that the intelligent canine would generalize the command rather than be confused.

When Thor hesitated, hunching his black shoulders in confusion, rather than repeat the *such* command—Schutzhund training often used German words—she jollied him along. "Want to play hide-and-seek? Thor, find Dolly!"

Thor's shoulders came up with confidence, and his black nose dropped to the ground. Attention zoomed in on the fresh scent. Snout to mud, he nearly yanked Lia off her feet in his eagerness to follow the spoor. Hell, maybe he read her mind. Wouldn't she love to have that connection? Whatever, she'd take it.

The dog dragged her through ragged mounds of winter rye that had volunteered in the scrubby pasture, and weaved between scattered scrubby evergreens and cedar elm. Lia struggled to keep up, not wanting to slow the dog's drive. She ducked under low hanging branches, swatting leafless limbs away from her face as they played thread-the-needle through the overgrowth. At one point, he stopped and cast back and forth for a moment. He barked twice, looked at her with milky cataract-covered eyes before swinging back to the trail and surging on.

In less than five minutes, the old black dog stopped near a stand of burr oak, and barked several times as he plunked down in the mud, his signal of a find. "Good dog, Thor. Wait." She shined her flashlight beneath the slight shelter. The glow of several pairs of eyes met the light.

Relief!

"Dolly? Hey there, good girl." The Rottweiler bitch slicked her ears flat with submission and whined, but didn't move from her crouched position beneath the scrubby protection.

Lia pulled the short tether from her pocket as she continued to talk. "Scary stuff, having a tree fall on top of you. What a brave girl, protecting your babies."

The dog whined again but kept her attention focused on Lia. So far, Dolly didn't seem to mind Thor's presence, but that could change in a heartbeat. She needed to get the tether on Dolly, and get the furry family back to safety. "I brought treats. Treats for Dolly. Want a treat?" She pitched her voice up an octave from her normal contralto into a singsong lure.

Worry lines in the dog's broad brow smoothed as she stood up, yawned wide, and shook herself, the action a physical reset of her emotions. Dolly licked her lips and her stub of a tail began to move when Lia pulled out a chunk of liver and tossed it to the dog. Dolly caught the morsel, and took a step closer. A muddle of puppies stirred around her legs, making it hard for the mother dog to move, but Lia kept the light steady with one hand, while she shook the treat bag with the other.

All reluctance gave way to the lure of the familiar. Dolly hurried to Lia and pressed against her, wanting the contact even more than the yummies. "Poor girl, you took care of your babies, didn't you?"

Lia offered the big dog another of the soft treats, and contemplated attaching the extra lead she'd brought.

Dolly was so strong that the line wouldn't hold her if she decided to bolt. After all, Rottweilers had been used in lieu of horses to pull carts, and Lia weighed far less than a cart. Fear trumped training every time, and Dolly's whale eyed expression—rolling her eyes so the whites showed—shouted fear without saying a word. Another big thunderclap, and treats and the thin line wouldn't be enough. Even if she could get Dolly back to the kennel, wrangling the pups would be easy as herding cats.

Keep Dolly focused on the pups. She'd carry one of them, so Dolly would stay close. And where Dolly went, the litter should follow. That way, she'd have an extra hand free for the tracking lead. Thor at least knew this area blindfolded, literally, and could find his way back to the kennel even without the lead. At the thought, she unhooked the tracking lead and stuffed it into her pocket before scooping "Mr. Yellow Collar" under one arm. Lia shook the treat baggie again. "Puppy-puppy-puppies! Come on, gang. Let's go, Dolly."

She showed Dolly the pup in her arms, and headed off at a brisk confident pace as if Dolly would follow as a matter of course. Expectation made many things happen. She smiled when Dolly stayed glued to her side, while the gaggle of babies stumbled along to keep up.

She glanced back once, and saw Thor still waiting for his release. "Thor, *geh rein.*" He bounded to his feet, and took off for home, no doubt expecting a whole bowl full of liver bits for tracking in the muck. Heck, with a name like Thor, you'd think he'd love storms but he'd always been indifferent to them.

The old boy stood huffing and pawing the office door when she arrived out of breath to let him slip inside. Lia hurried with her puppy burden and canine entourage to one of the still intact kennels.

"Good girl, Dolly, want your puppy?" Mr. Yellow yawned in her arms, ready for a nap. The entire bedraggled bunch acted exhausted. Short puppy size legs had to run twice as fast as Dolly to keep up.

When Lia opened the fresh kennel and swung open the chain link door, Dolly bounded inside and raced to a waiting water bowl. The puppies followed her, exhausted into silence. The entire crew needed a bath. That would have to wait. She still needed to round up the missing Pit Bull pair. Lia doubted they'd follow as readily as the frightened mom-dog and pups, so she needed transportation handy once she found them.

Her truck sat dimpled from hood-to-fender with dings and dents from the hail, but at least the storm spared the glass. Two inches of ice balls filled the truck bed, so she levered open the passenger door and boosted Thor inside. A pair of crates in the truck bed would house Buster and Beau once she found them. And by heavens, she'd find them. Lia shuddered, anticipating Sunny Babcock's reaction to losing her prize hog dogs.

Something, though, wouldn't let her feel relief at finding Dolly and her brood. She checked on them one last time before heading back into the storm. As the exhausted youngsters settled into a messy pile around their mother, Lia counted puppy heads, and came up one short.

Maybe she'd miss-counted. The pups in the dim light looked alike, and the color-coding around each furry neck could be muted by mud. Dolly struggled to get comfortable while a few of the pups tried to nurse. They were weaned, but Dolly was too tired to push them away, and like all babies, they wanted the comfort of snuggling close.

Lia counted again but before she finished, she guessed which one was gone. She tried to swallow past the sudden lump in her throat. She wasn't surprised. The stubborn, courageous attitude necessary for great police dogs might instead get the missing dog-child killed.

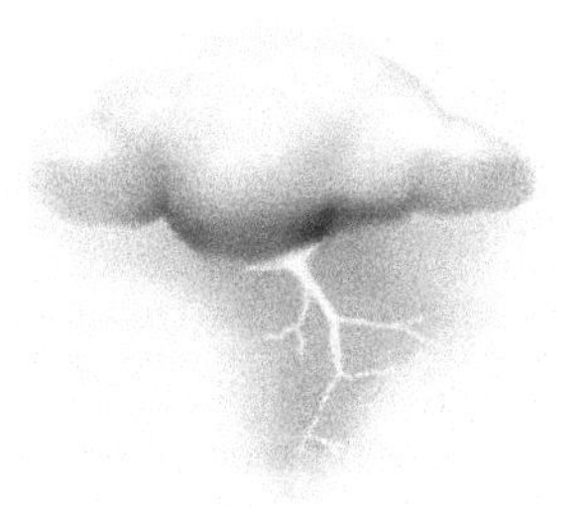

Chapter 14

Karma backpedaled with a squeal to escape the writhing mass of snakes. She still clutched one hissing creature between her teeth, and paused to shake it hard, the same way she shook the tug-toy during games. She shook it again, growling around the mass in her mouth, and took satisfaction in the whip-cracking action until the snake stopped moving. She trembled, not wanting to release the prize and have it slither and chase her. Her heart thu-thumped even harder when the cucumber smell combined with the rusty taste of the snake's blood. After one final shake, she let go and the ropy length fell limp from her jaws. She licked her mouth, wrinkling her nose and showing her teeth at the taste while she tracked the grassy twitches and shudders that revealed the reptilian progress of the others.

"Karma! Puppy-puppy-puppy, COME, where are you?"

The girl's voice rose above the freshening wind, and Karma's head jerked high. Her silent snarls gave way to soft mewls and whines she couldn't suppress, even when she clamped her jaws tight to mute the sound. Crying showed fear, fear that made littermates bite harder. Karma didn't want the snakes to bite so Karma acted brave, she stood tall with her shoulders squared to challenge the threat.

But her ears kept slicking back, and the stub of her tail snugged tight to her bottom, hiding her unique scent the way people covered their faces. She yearned to be far, far away from this wet, strange dark world with scaly smelly creatures. Karma yawned. She wanted her mother, would even welcome the girl's arms, and be brave another day.

"Karma!"

Lifting her blunt muzzle to the sky, Karma called back with a high-pitched warbling howl.

"Good puppy! I'm coming!" Sodden footfalls drew closer, with scrubby branches crashing and switching as the distant figure plowed through the dense vegetation.

She wanted to race to meet Lia. Karma's paws danced forward of their own volition, but stopped short at the sea of snakes that still thrashed in the grass, massing between her and the path. One of the resting creatures, coiled like a leash, sprang forward. Karma spun, crashed through drenched brush, away, away, racing to put many dog-lengths between herself and the snakes, deaf to the strange gushing water sound that grew louder as she drew near.

"Karma! Oh no, Karma wait!"

A snake fell out of the sky and looped around Karma's throat. She screamed, rolled and kicked hard to escape its constriction, and the mushy ground fell away. She slalomed on a raft of mud, bumping and thumping to pinball off trees and rocks, yelping with each blow as the leather snake's tail—a very long one—slithered and chased in her wake. She forgot to be brave and keened a nonstop siren until the sluice pitched her off the collapsed roadway into the air for half a puppy breath. Karma plunged into the rush of a newborn river, and sank beneath the surface.

Water filled Karma's mouth, and slammed her into a broken tree before pulling her back under. The flood tumbled her paws over tail. She clawed and churned muddy sludge to foam until she splashed her way to the surface, gasping for breath.

Motion caught Karma's attention. A small figure chased after, yelling Karma's name over and over.

The girl! Karma thrashed and cried, but the voracious water refused to let her go.

The girl slid to her knees into the deluge, but managed to grab a tree branch and claw her way up out of the flood. She raced the water and soon was ahead of Karma. "Hang on, hang on, baby-dog." Lia grabbed a nearby limb, and shoved the length out across the surface of the water.

Karma's splashing reached the tip of the branch before the flood yanked it out of the girl's grasp and floated it away. Karma followed, barely paddling now, and reserving all her strength just to grab quick breaths. With a final courageous effort, Karma flailed with all four paws and lunged toward a pile of floating debris. She missed.

The water chortled and swept her away.

The snake tightened around her neck, and Karma whimpered and shut her eyes. Sometimes a good-dog couldn't hide her fear . . .

Hot breath warmed her neck when Karma bumped up against the detritus. She never questioned how or why her muzzle suddenly rose above the water, just took grateful gulps of cold night air. She recognized the familiar feel of gentle teeth grasping her neck. Karma relaxed against the fur of a strange black shepherd that held her safe above the flood.

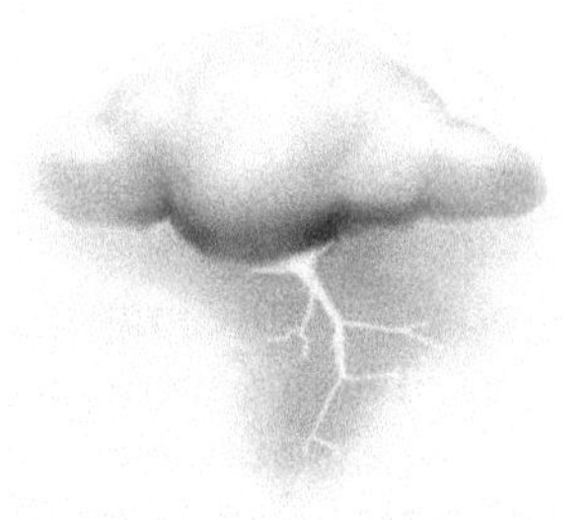

Chapter 15

Lia managed to toss the old lariat over Karma's head before the pup slid into the ditch runoff-turned-torrent. It jerked out of her hands, rope burning her palms when something launched the pup into renewed flight and panic tumbled her into the current. The rope snaked along the bank and moon-glow allowed Lia to track the wailing pup's progress. The thrice-damned flood out-raced anything with two legs. Lia had twice tried and failed to tackle the slithering rope.

With a yell of success, Lia tackled the trailing lasso. The movement slowed and Lia took advantage to gather the slack, looping it around her elbow and palm. She had to be careful not to choke the pup. Even if she pulled Karma out, hypothermia could kill. Karma had stopped crying, and she prayed the puppy still lived.

Lia carefully towed the pup toward the bank. Her brow furrowed at unexpected resistance. The dog-child was just four months old, for God's sake, and shouldn't be that heavy. If Karma hooked on something, pulling could cause more injury than the cold.

"Karma, you there?" Her heart clenched at the thought of losing her. She began to breathe again when resistance gave way. Twenty seconds lasted a lifetime before the Rottie pup blinked owlishly up at her from the water, finally within reach. Reaching down, careful not to slip into the water herself, Lia grabbed the purple collar and leather lariat and lifted, but it remained caught on the black mound of debris. She started when the rubbish moved.

Brown eyes blinked, and white fangs gleamed. A black dog's teeth hooked through the opposite side of Karma's collar.

The puppy twisted, wriggled and whined, and licked the big dog's face. The German Shepherd closed his eyes with a whimper of painful resignation as Karma bathed his sore, battered muzzle where dark blood welled.

He looked like a warrior, a courageous *koa* fighting the storm. He'd risked his own life to save Karma.

She held out her hand to the injured dog, not wanting to spook him. How long had he been in the frigid water? Amazing he'd survived both the tornado and the flash flood. His lips and gums were pale, but his shiver reflex remained intact. Good. Once shivers stopped, it'd be hard to bring him back. Karma would die, too, if the shepherd refused to let go.

"*Aus.*" She tried the German Schutzhund command first. The dog just blinked, so she tried again. "Drop it." Lia spoke with quiet authority, and was heartened when the black shepherd released. His training and discipline had aided his survival and prevented panic that might have killed him. She could see that his paws touched the bottom of the ditch, but he was so weak he couldn't stand for long. And for sure, he couldn't climb out, not without help. She had to hurry.

She dragged Karma out of the water, shrugged off her jacket and rolled her into a puppy burrito. For once, the recalcitrant pup settled without a struggle, wrung out from her ordeal. Or maybe Karma also realized time was running short for the Samaritan dog. His wet fur turned him into a shadowy wraith, but Lia didn't question the shepherd's intent. True warriors, no matter the species, acted brave and generous.

"Shadow-dog, hold on. I'll get you out." She spoke with quiet confidence from habit, then gasped when he confirmed his name with a yelp—and something else. A tickle behind her eyes, deep inside Lia's head made her blink.

What just happened? No time to puzzle it out.

Lia kept her tone low and warm, imbued with as much confidence as she could muster. The Shadow-dog had to trust enough to let her help, and at five foot eight inches and 118-pounds soaking wet, she couldn't get him out by herself.

"No problem. *A'ole pilikia.*" That's what Abe always said. *No excuses*, make it happen. Her hand touched the bracelet, and she stuck out her bottom lip with determination. Buster and Beau were in her truck. One would be enough.

"Thanks for saving my baby-dog."

His ears flicked. Again, a feathery whisper-sensation jittered her nerves, and she knew he understood and recognized something familiar in her words. No, not words exactly, but intensions maybe? Spooky, but a delicious tickle inside her head at the same time. Time enough later to figure it out.

Lia kept up a constant murmur, confident he understood her intent, if not the words. Lia avoided eye contact with the black dog, and thrust one arm to the elbow in the icy water. His warm panting heated her cheek as she threaded the rope under his chest beneath the water. He stayed still, liquid eyes watching her every move. He nosed her cheek and she understood he'd granted permission.

"Good dog. Brave dog." She brought the rope out of the water on the other side of his body, and cinched it into a loop over his shoulders. She secured the tail end of the rope to a cedar sapling so at least he wouldn't drift away. "I'll be right back. Just wait." His yelp of despair cut her to the quick, hurting her deep inside in a way she couldn't explain. Lia raced back to the truck with Karma.

After securing the puppy, Lia unbuckled the tracking harness from Thor. The old dog snored on the front seat of the truck. He'd been through enough and hadn't anything left to give after he tracked down the last two canine escapees. At least she wouldn't have Sunny Babcock coming after her. Lia had kenneled the pair in the back, and now led Buster out of his kennel. She knew Buster's kryptonite. Even now, the Pit Bull carried his rubber chicken security squeaky in his wide, drooly mouth.

Within minutes, Lia harnessed Buster, raced with him to the edge of the flood, and threaded the end of the braided lariat to his harness. She'd have to play it by ear. She didn't know what pull-command the dog knew. But Buster would do anything for his squeaky. It had to be enough.

She lured Buster away from the flood until the lariat grew taut. *Slow and steady, that's what we need.* Jerking the line might further injure

Shadow.

"Hey Buster, love your squeaky? Want a squeaky? Look what I've got." Lia made the toy squeal, and held it just beyond his reach until Buster strained to grab it. "Good dog, Buster, get it!" She tossed the squeaky onto the ground about six feet away, far enough he'd keep pulling but not so far he'd take off and drag the injured shepherd. Or so she hoped.

Lia rushed to the edge of the water where the rope dug into the soupy bank. She shoved a stick beneath the line to serve as a rolling fulcrum for the rope to ride. Buster's eager efforts inched the black dog out of the water. But the rope pulled the shepherd so tight against the bank, his paws had no purchase.

His eyes were closed, his mouth half open, and tongue lolled pale and cold. The rope around his chest cut into his fur, and she worried it impeded his breath.

"Hey *Shadow!* Don't die on me!" She smoothed his cut brow. He blinked, and his tail stirred the water, but otherwise he didn't move.

Lia yelled encouragement over her shoulder. "Buster, get your squeaky. Get it, good boy." Another foot and she could grab the shepherd without risk of falling in herself.

"*Shadow,* you've got to want this, too."

What incentive to offer? Buster loved toys, Karma loved treats, but neither toys nor treats would stir this black dog from death. What would reach this brave warrior, when he'd already given everything?

Then she knew, as clear as a shout on a clear, still day. "Wanna go *home? Home*, good-dog. Shadow, let's go *home*."

He stirred, yelped, and his paws strove to reach for the bank, just as Buster gave one final charge. Lia caught the black dog's front legs behind his elbows, trusting his teeth to stay clear of her face, and pulled as his pistoning rear paws clawed the bank. He collapsed on top of her, both of them safe on the bank, panting in concert with each other.

The black warrior dog stared into her eyes, as if demanding Lia keep her promise. For a split second the image of a cat-eyed woman with white-streaked hair filled Lia's vision. Then Lia blinked, and the vision disappeared.

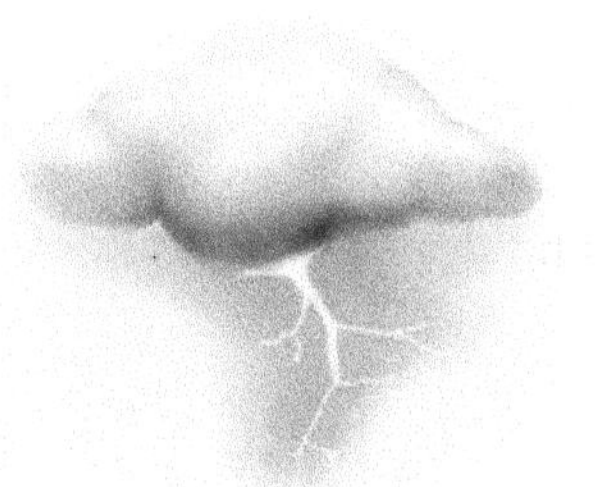

Chapter 16

Combs stood in the rain, shivering with both the cold and excitement. Another call had sidetracked him on his way to track Shadow's GPS collar. September would understand. He hoped.

The dumpster floated in the lee of a flooded culvert. A couple of teenagers challenged the storm on a dare and discovered the green box. They egged each other on to mount the metal box and ride it to glory for a self-recorded YouTube video. They'd joked about the video going viral. Plans changed when they discovered the savaged body inside.

"Gonzales, I'm at the washed out corner of FM 890 and Highway 75. I got four kids found a body inside a dumpster." Combs squinted against the rain, and shrugged his shoulders higher inside the raincoat. It didn't help. "You about done out there?"

"We're still finishing up. It's a mess. We're waiting on animal control. They don't want to get out in this weather, and who could blame 'em." Detective Winston Gonzalez sounded disgusted. He'd drawn the short straw, and had to deal with the dogfight scumbags. "How's September and the kids?"

Combs and Gonzales hadn't been partners for long, but could already read each other's mood. "I owe you. Meant a lot for me to check on my kids. Melinda's shook up, but I think Willie enjoys the celebrity a bit." September had kept all the kids safe while she risked her own life. "I got to see September when she woke up. She's beat up, but I think she'll be okay." He wiped his eyes.

Combs didn't mention Shadow. He had no doubt that Steven's mad computer skills were correct but he dreaded finding Shadow's body. September had enough pain in her life. He feared what the news would do to her.

Meanwhile, he needed to ferry the youngsters back to the station. They crowded together like stray puppies dripping muddy water in the back seat of his car. Combs confiscated their phones as evidence as soon as he arrived, and now waited for the crime scene team to arrive. The unrelenting rain made any forensic evidence moot, though, and he'd given up any thought to staying dry.

"You didn't ask me about the body, Gonzales." He couldn't hide the satisfaction in his voice, and imagined his partner's bright, mustache-framed smile once he heard.

Gonzales didn't even try to guess. "Good news? So the vic had it coming, for a change."

The man inside, or what was left of him, wouldn't care about weather ever again. Some creature attacked and disfigured him, but enough of his face remained for Combs to recognize.

"The Doctor won't be treating kids ever again." He laughed outright at Gonzales' exclamation of satisfaction.

"Drowned? Dead in a dumpster. How appropriate."

"True, that. Don't know the COD, but looks like something chewed him up pretty good." Combs figured Doctor Gerald Baumgarten got poetic justice. He'd created and distributed an off-label drug "cure" that targeted autistic children, including September's nephew Steven. "I'm stuck here until the coroner arrives or the crime scene folks find me. Seems there's a waiting list."

The most horrific case of his career began back in November with the death of his mother. Combs met September during one of the darkest periods of his life—and hers, too. They'd put away Lizbeth Baumgarten, the mastermind, but her son escaped only to resurfaced using an underground dog fight ring to distribute his lethal contraband. With his death, they could close that horrible Chapter and begin a new life.

"Don't get too comfy back at the station, Combs. Cleanup will be a bitch and take days, if not weeks. We've got more perps than places to put 'em. Some are still in the wind."

Combs wiped his face again, and looked up with relief when a black and white rolled up. "Yes, we'll be processing and pushing paper forever. What else is new? Hey, I just got backup. I'll catch up with you later."

He pocketed the phone, and hurried back to his unmarked. Within minutes, a second police car arrived, and Combs released the kids to them. He made a face at the mess they'd left in his car, not that it'd been pristine before. Turning on the heat steamed the windows and made the musty smell worse, so he gritted his teeth. He had a change of clothes back at the station, after his next errand.

With a sigh, Combs took the first turn off the highway and headed to the area Steven's computer identified as Shadow's GPS location. He'd watched on the iPad for several minutes. The flashing dot had never moved. Living dogs moved. "Dammit, I hate this!" He pounded the steering wheel, but continued on. He owed September answers. She wouldn't rest until she knew the truth. And they wouldn't have a life together until she could put the past behind her.

The floodwaters slashed deep scars into the black Texas mud, turning roadside runoffs into white-water rivers. Portions of the blacktop collapsed when the roadbed washed out, and Combs drove with care to stay on solid ground.

The car crept forward around a bend in the road. Water had shoveled debris into gigantic piles of uprooted trees, some scooped out by water and others twisted from the earth by wind. Trash decorated high branches with streamers of tattered plastic, fabric, metal roofing and anything else the storm's fury managed to steal. Old tires, bales of straw and the remains of a car buttressed the growing base. "What a mess." Combs echoed Gonzales's earlier words. Everything about this case turned to garbage.

He pulled the car onto the shoulder and parked, checking to be sure the foundation would support the vehicle. Combs opened the trunk, and pulled out a pair of hip waders he used while fishing on Lake Texoma. The current had slowed, or he'd never risk getting into the water. He needed a closer look before giving up.

As soon as he dragged on boots, his phone rang. He frowned. Uncle Stanley knew better than to call him now, since retired police sergeant Stanley Combs had fielded his share of emergencies back in the day. "Hey there, what's up? I'm up to my hips—literally—in an investigation."

"I know, I know. Wouldn't bother you except an old friend of mine called and arm-twisted me for a favor." Uncle Stanley never gave favors unless he wanted to, so Combs knew the old friend must be someone with leverage. "Two favors, one from you and one from that dog trainer friend of yours."

"September? I can't speak for her, you know that." Combs squinted at the pile, scanning from the bottom and side-to-side, looking for any movement.

"I know that. But you can ask, and coming from you, she might say yes." Uncle Stanley rushed on. "Me and Dub Corazon go way back. He's got that big spread northeast of Heartland, acres and acres of grazing land where he raises some of the finest horses in this part of the world. He's got a storm shelter there, snug as can be, so they have no damage or injury from the storm. I know September lost her house. Sorry about that." He cleared his throat. "Anyway, Dub has a granddaughter, a headstrong young woman as I understand."

Combs couldn't believe it. "I'm in the middle of something here." He had no interest in being fixed up with anyone. Uncle Stanley must be losing it, to interrupt him with something like that.

"Just listen a minute, boy. Won't take you any time at all. See, Lia runs a dog kennel, a training facility for teaching police dogs. But Dub says she's got no call to be doing that. Got no experience. So he asked if I knew someone could show her the ropes, and I thought of September. She can say no, but Dub would pay for her expertise. But he don't want Lia to know about that. Anyway, when you see September, just pass that on to her, if you would."

Combs closed his eyes. For sure, September would need something good to focus on, once she accepted the fact Shadow was gone. Extra funds never hurt, either. "Fine, I'll tell her. What else? You said two favors."

"He wants someone to check on her. See, she wouldn't leave her dogs alone during the storm. Now he can't get a hold of her."

Combs shook his head. Uncle Stanley wasn't a young man anymore, no matter what he thought. "You shouldn't get out in this. They're forecasting another wave of storms." Uncle Stanley's heart condition had forced his early retirement from the police force.

Uncle Stanley bulldozed on. "Don't you dare mollycoddle me. You're as bullheaded as your aunt. She threatened mayhem if I left the house, and hell, I gotta live with the woman. So I called you."

Combs smiled, and finally understood. Uncle Stanley agreed to a favor for his friend, and his pride wouldn't let him take it back. Combs wasn't helping Dub Corazon. Uncle Stanley needed the favor, a man who never, ever asked for help. They'd been close ever since Uncle Stanley and his wife helped raise Combs, only to have a falling out they'd only recently reconciled. So of course Combs would help.

"Give me the address and I'll run by there as soon as I can." He paused. "And I'll pass on the offer to September next time I see her." He disconnected, and returned to scanning the pile of flotsam. When the wind blew, portions of it bobbed gently in the temporary lake created by the overflow.

He found a five-foot branch alongside the road. Combs used it as a walking stick to probe beneath the surface when he stepped off the road into the water, poking ahead of each splashy footstep. So much of the mountain of crap moved and undulated in the current, he knew Shadow couldn't survive stuck inside the morass. So Combs concentrated on the perimeter, slogging past tree trunks, a mattress, several straw bales and—

There! Movement caught the corner of his eye, something outside the motion of windy gusts. He scanned closer, paying attention this time to the water line and above, eyes peeled for telltale black fur.

Again, movement to the right. Not dark fur, though, and not flappy shredded garbage bags caught by the breeze. A pile of clothes slouched atop one of the bales of straw, motionless. Combs drew closer. What had moved?

This time, he saw clearly the soaking wet orange kitten that trembled and cried with wide, silent meows. It clung to the mound of fabric, which Combs now recognized as a coat covering a motionless young man. Shadow's GPS collar looped over the boy's ankle.

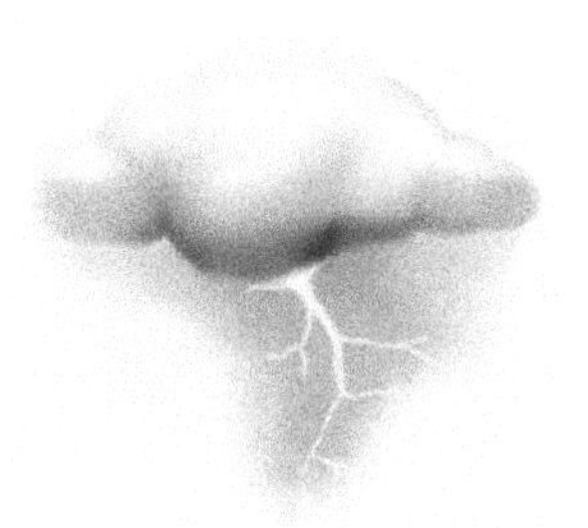

Chapter 17

Karma rested, still exhausted but finally warm after what seemed a lifetime in the cold water. She nosed the empty bowl, and licked up the last drippings of broth.

Lia sat beside her on the cement, stroking her fur, murmuring words Karma didn't know. That was okay, though, she understood the emotion. She was smart that way. Karma's short tail responded with a happy wiggle at the girl's attention. She didn't even miss her mother or littermates—well, not much—and hoped she could stay in the office with the girl from now on. Karma would like that just fine.

"You spoiled your purple collar." Lia tugged the soaked fabric over Karma's head and tried to give her a hug, but Karma wiggled away. So Lia shut the crate and crossed to the door to the kennels. The other dog, Thor, slept on the other side of the room and didn't rouse when she left.

Karma caught the scent of the strange black shepherd who still reeked of filthy water and seeping blood. She'd been half-asleep when carried into the office area, but roused enough to see Shadow lift a lip in silent warning when the girl offered to touch his injured face. Karma wondered why he didn't trust the girl. People knew things dogs couldn't know. The girl had gentle hands and a soft kind voice. She'd pulled them both from the flood. And fed them good things. Karma thought Lia was wonderful.

She wanted to go see the Shadow. Karma pawed and jiggled the front of the crate, and to her delight, it hadn't latched. She pushed her blunt muzzle into the breach and squeezed through. The big black dog intrigued her. He made Karma's tummy flutter and tail go faster when he looked at her. She wasn't sure why.

Karma peeked around the doorway, not wanting to be discovered and shooed away. The nearest kennel housed Dolly and the rest of the puppies, and the shepherd was in the opposite run. He rested on a warm blanket that smelled of many other dogs, but he didn't seem to mind. His black fur was longer than Karma's seal-slick coat, and still matted with mud. One side of his face and neck looked raw and smelled rank. Karma wanted to go to him, maybe lick clean his hurts, but after hanging up the coiled lariat on the wall, Lia crouched beside him.

"Phones work again, and the internet."

His long, furry tail thumped against the blanket.

She stroked his head, and when her hand came too close to his sore cheek, he ducked. "Sorry. Wish you'd let me treat that. Then, I'll find your home."

The black dog whined. He cold-nosed her arm. Karma shivered at the mournful sound, and crept closer.

"You want to go home, I know. I'm sorry, Shadow. You sure understand lots of words. Not everything, I know. But maybe you'll catch some of what I say. If I picture it in my mind." She half laughed. "Makes no sense, I know, but I'm sure you sent me some messages, didn't you? Or did I send my thoughts to you?"

He woofed, and licked her hand. His brow smoothed and Lia's mouth made a surprised "oh" shape like she heard something Karma couldn't detect. Finally she smiled. That made Karma feel better. Shadow recognized that Lia was special, too.

"It's only been two hours. It'll be two weeks or longer before things get back to normal." The girl's voice was calm and warm. "There's no hurry. Besides, you need to get stronger."

Karma jostled against the door, making it squeal, and the sound summoned the girl upright, so Karma scurried out of sight.

Lia hurried toward the office, and then turned back in the

doorway. "I promised to take you home, and I will. If it comes to that, you'll have a home here. With me and Thor." Her voice caught. "And Karma." Her voice broke, and she muttered the next words. "If I could keep her, I'd love her forever. You too, if you'd let me." When she hurried back into the room, the door stayed ajar.

Karma wasted no time. She dashed out of hiding to squeeze through the opening. She hesitated, looking at the shepherd.

Shadow was so much bigger than her, twice as tall even while reclining. Karma turned her head away, licked her lips, and tucked her tail. For the first time in her life she wondered what to do. But then he tipped his head, and his massive tail swept the floor, beckoning her near.

She scrambled to reach him, wiggling her entire body. He nosed her, exploring from shiny wet nose to stubby black tail, and she flipped onto her back and waved rust-furred paws as he learned her scent. Delighted, Karma play-growled and snapped the air, catching Shadow's lip and he winced and stood to get out of range. His legs trembled before holding true. She continued to pounce at him, energy recharged by his attention. Karma leaped high to lick his mouth and slurp his eyes with puppy adoration and respect, signaling deference in the instinctive ritual.

The bigger dog slowly waved his tail, nosing Karma especially around her tail. She wanted to sniff him there, too, and learn his scent-name that shouted louder than any words people used. But he maneuvered away from her attempts to sniff. He lifted Karma off her feet as he pushed her around with his prominent muzzle.

He looked different than her mother and siblings. Where their paws, muzzles and cheeks sported rich contrasting color, his longer fur was black all over. Karma's ears tipped over, like every dog she'd ever seen, but Shadow's ears pointed straight up.

And his tail—oh, his magnificent tail!—it spoke to her in a language Karma's foreshortened version couldn't match, with sweeping, elegant semaphore drawn through the air. Karma's whole body wiggled in an effort to express herself.

The shepherd froze. He lifted his head, ears swiveling as his wagging tail stiffened and raised higher. The fur above his shoulders bristled and a low growl bubbled deep in his chest.

Karma started, and slicked her ears down before she understood his warning wasn't directed to her. She pricked her own ears, standing shoulder to shoulder with the shepherd, and sniffed to discern what he already knew.

There—it came and went, riding the breeze. Her own hackles rose when furtive steps accompanied a familiar scent. An angry man lurked outside.

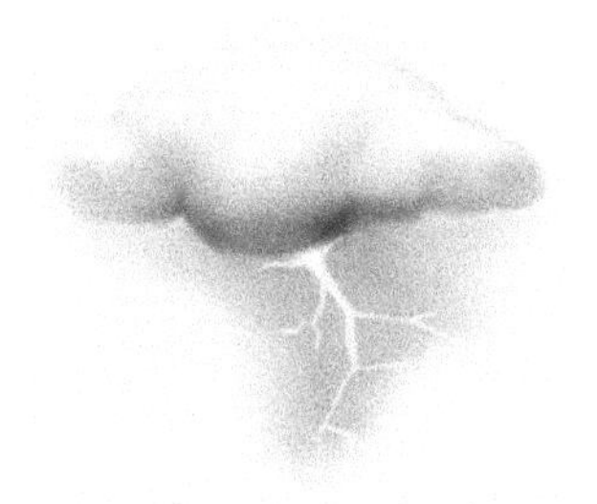

Chapter 18

Lia played with the purple collar she'd taken off Karma. The flimsy thing served more for decoration than function. Now, of course, she could tell them all apart just by the way they entered a room. With the severe damage to the property, Derek would want to move them all somewhere else, not just the two Coop chose.

She'd known this day would come, and knew better than to let herself care. Lia fisted her eyes and looked away from the crate in the corner where Karma rested from her near drowning. The pup needed a vet check before anything else. She straightened. That would be a valid reason for delaying the sale to Coop. Near-drowning victims, both pets and people, often looked fine but collapsed later. Lia didn't want to risk anything with the baby-dog. She knew allowing any puppy to go to Coop would be a mistake. Not that she had any say in the matter.

She sat down hard in the chair, and shoved the purple collar keepsake into a drawer, feeling defeated, angry, and frustrated. Lia already imagined hearing, "I told you so," from Grammy and all of her friends. Grandfather wouldn't say anything, he never did.

The adrenalin rush of finding and rescuing Karma and her

mysterious canine hero Shadow drained away, leaving her legs weak and stomach queasy. She leaned her forehead into cupped palms, wishing for a do-over of the whole day.

On the desk between her elbows rested the digital camera from the temperament tests. She'd retrieved it from the far kennel, a miraculous survivor of the storm's wrath. She sat up, and reached for the cable, and connected it to the desktop to download the video. Lia wanted to watch and remember Karma playing her way through each test, not the terrified soaked puppy she'd fished from the flood.

Lia fast-forwarded through Mr. Green Collar and the other pups until Karma's film debut cued up. On the screen, Derek carried the Black Collar puppy for its close up in front of the camera. He spoke almost too softly to be heard, but Coop's voice was loud and clear.

"Another one for bait? This one has some weight on him, anyway." Derek hefted Mr. Black Collar and the puppy whimpered and hid his face.

"Piss poor showing, Derek. Nothing like you advertised." Coop's voice dripped disappointment.

"It's her first litter. I paid top dollar for the stud service, and I'm giving you pick of the litter." Derek must have squeezed the pup he held, because it yelped.

"Bait's all any of 'em is good for." Coop's voice sweetened when Lia came into the frame and took the puppy from Derek's arms. As soon as she left, Coop continued half voice. "Hell, I'll take all of them off your hands, the bitch, too. Won't wipe all your debts free, but it's a start. Cut your losses, Derek, and start fresh another time. Dolly has some fight left in her. That'll give some of the up-and-comers a good warm up, and she might last a couple of rounds anyway. Can't be too prepared before they go to the big show."

Derek nodded and looked away from the camera before yelling full voice. "What's the hold up?" He flinched and glared at the sky when thunder boomed. Derek straightened, jogged away from the camera back to the middle of the grassy yard, and called, "C'mon, here puppy-puppy-puppy. *Karma-pup*, here-here-here!"

Lia stopped the recording. She sat for a minute. Her pulse pounded in her ears. She grabbed the edge of the desk when the room began to spin. Surely, she'd misunderstood, she had to be wrong. Coop, *Mr. Cooper,* was a respected businessman. Derek came from a high society upbringing. They weren't thugs or uneducated criminals.

Coop never turned off the camera. They didn't know they'd been recorded.

She scrolled back to the beginning of the video before moving forward, stopping to watch and listen each time she'd been out of hearing when the men spoke. She fast-forwarded through Karma's temperament test to the end, and began to tremble and couldn't stop.

How could he? How could anyone conceive such a thing? The bastards! Anyone who would hurt an innocent animal . . .

Checking her phone again, Lia breathed a silent prayer of thanks when she saw a couple more bars. She dismissed the three missed calls and message from Grammy. She started to text a quick answer and then stopped. It would open a conversation she couldn't deal with right now. She knew what *bait* meant.

Instead, she dialed 911 and then as quickly hung up before it connected. The tornado sirens had stopped but the police wouldn't be happy with her diverting emergency personnel from possible injuries. The recording wasn't proof, just indicated criminal intent.

She couldn't let them get away with it. The police needed to know. Dogfights were a felony.

Lia leaped to her feet when Karma's high-pitched frantic yelps joined ferocious baritone barking. She glanced at the puppy crate, puzzled how the baby-dog had gotten out, and hurried to the kennel doorway. She stopped when the bitter voice sounded behind her.

"Put down the phone, Lia. You had to watch that video, didn't you?"

More angry than fearful, Lia punched in a three-character text message and hit send before she turned around.

Then she saw Derek's gun.

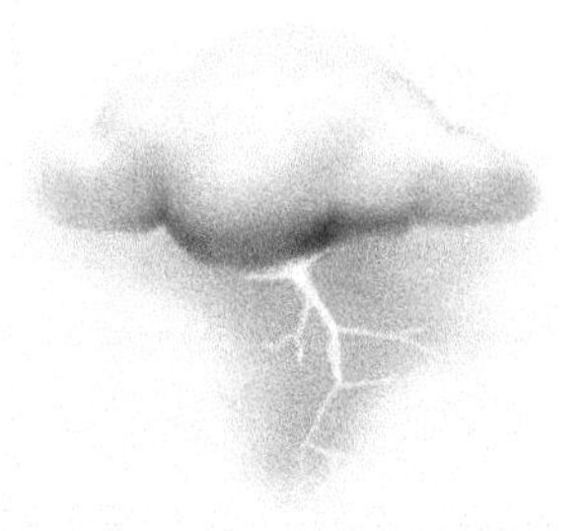

Chapter 19

Karma's ears slicked back as she joined Shadow's alarm bark. She remembered this man and how Dolly reacted to him. At the thought, Karma's bark trailed off into a whine.

She nosed the wire gate at the front of the kennel. When she sneaked into the space to visit Shadow, it swung shut behind her, but hadn't latched. A good-dog could paw it open, just like Karma pawed open the crate in the office. She put a paw on the wire to do just that, but then Karma glanced up at the shepherd.

At his look, Karma backed away, taking a cue from Shadow's alert and cautious stance. She squared her own shoulders, facing forward with arched neck and taut tail, mimicking the adult dog's confident pose.

Raised voices in the nearby doorway prompted Shadow's rumbling growl. The skin along Karma's shoulders rippled in response and her short fur itched. Shadow's defensive pose proved more than enough for her to follow his lead.

"Derek!" The girl's voice sirened up an octave. "Why would you *show me a gun*!"

Shadow flinched at the last few words, and showed his teeth.

Karma wondered what the scary words meant, but trusted the other dog knew more than she did. Her own puppy-pitched rumble erupted. It didn't sound as imposing as she wanted, so she increased the volume.

"Put the damn phone away!" The man snarled like an angry dog.

"Okay, okay." Lia's voice trembled.

In the kennel across the narrow pathway, Karma watched her mother stir and whine at the strident tones. Dolly gave a quick lick to her exhausted puppies mounded about her, and then struggled to her feet and padded to the front of the kennel. She pressed her blunt muzzle against the latched barrier. It didn't move even when Dolly paw-batted the door.

Karma recognized Dolly's hesitancy. People knew and could do amazing things that not even big-dogs like Dolly or Shadow could manage. Why, the girl had pulled Karma out of the rushing water when it tried to swallow and swirl her away. Even a brave puppy-girl like Karma needed a strong leader to follow, and a family to belong to. Karma had decided that Lia would do just fine. So if Lia was scared, there must be good reason.

"Where are they? The bitch and her litter?"

The man didn't bark this time, but Dolly stiffened with recognition. Her lip curled, mimicking Shadow's expression, and she backed away stiff-legged from the kennel door.

Karma tipped her head to one side as soft footfalls approached. The door squeaked open, and the girl stepped into view. She held her hands above her head.

Was it a new game?

Lia made brief eye contact with Karma, and blinked hard, and Karma wondered why water ran down the girl's face. Then Shadow shouldered his way in front of Karma, placing himself between her and the man who followed.

Dolly's caution exploded into a silent attack, and her massive chest banged into the wire barrier, making the metal clang and shudder.

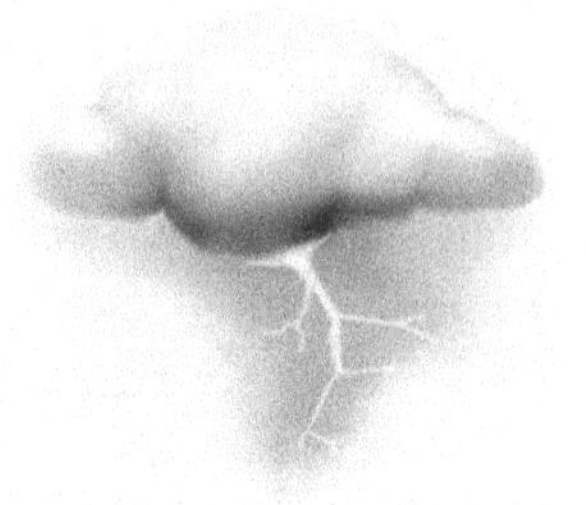

Chapter 20

Lia stumbled into the kennel area ahead of Derek. A spot just below her shoulders itched in response to the gun aimed at her back.

"What's all this about?" *Keep him talking. Maybe he'd take what he wanted and leave.* Her eyes widened when she saw Karma in the right-hand kennel space with the black shepherd. Lia's stomach clenched, knowing what Derek had planned for Dolly and her litter.

As if her thought prompted the action, Dolly attacked, trying to get through the kennel door to reach Derek.

He yelped and grabbed Lia to shield him from the slathering Rottweiler. One arm circled her waist, hand still clutching the camera with its incriminating evidence. His other arm circled her neck, hand leveling the gun at Dolly.

"No! Don't shoot her!" Lia struggled to throw off Derek's aim.

Dolly's puppies awoke. They barked and yipped, surging around her as the big dog leaped and snarled, throwing herself against the wire barrier to reach Derek. Her teeth rattled against the wire, and spittle flew.

Once he realized Dolly couldn't reach through the metal gate, Derek relaxed. He laughed, shoved Lia away, and offered a fake-growl at the distraught dog to egg her on.

When Lia fell against the opposite kennel, she clutched Shadow's kennel door to regain her balance. The door wasn't latched. Derek hadn't noticed. He ignored the shepherd and puppy inside, or maybe didn't care about them.

Shadow's intelligent brown eyes met Lia's own with a calm watchful gaze. That delightful sparkle-tickle inside her mind's-eye returned. *It's you, Shadow? Yes!* Following the surprise, Lia's panted breath slowed, her heart steadied. She embraced the sudden calm determination, and focused her purpose with the extraordinary dog.

They'd get through this. That message came through loud and clear. Though hurt and exhausted, too weak to attack Derek or even defend, Shadow's intent shined clear. *Trust the dog.*

Encouraged, she turned and straightened, her back to the kennel to hide the stoic shepherd. Derek's gun leveled at her. She licked her lips when her mouth turned to dust. "What do you want, Derek?"

"Don't play dumb, Lia." He raised his voice to be heard over Dolly's railing. "Coop got me into the gambling. I needed one big score to get free and clear. This dog deal should have squared everything but the storm screwed everything up. So now I got to get rid of the evidence, in case Coop blabs and sends the cops sniffing after me, too." He pointed the gun again at Dolly. She redoubled her screams, and her puppies wailed. He swung the gun back at Lia. "And the witness."

Her heart stuttered. She stared at the gun, surprised her whispered plea remained steady. "Derek, you can't mean that. Our families have known each other forever."

"That's right. I grew up with your mother." His pinched lips told her she'd said the wrong thing, but she didn't know why.

Dolly raged on, and he banged his fist on the metal door. "Shut up!" He turned back to Lia. "Rather not shoot her, but I will." He cocked his head. "Yeah, I could make that work. Unless you get her under control for me."

"Sure, I can do that. Just don't shoot her." Lia's throat tightened. "I'll do whatever you say." She took a half step across the aisle toward Dolly's run, but stopped short when Derek pulled out the shock collar from his jacket pocket. He thrust it toward her.

"Damn dog never obeys unless I crank up the juice." At her expression, he shrugged. "It's a tool, Lia. It's better than getting shot, don't you think?" Derek tossed it to her.

She caught the leather strap, wrinkling her nose when the twin metal prongs protruding from the attached remote E-stim box brushed her skin. Lia pushed past him, waited until Derek backed away, and then cracked open Dolly's kennel door and slipped inside.

Dolly's focus never wavered from Derek, even though her foam-stained flews trembled, and she'd lost her voice. "Shush, big dog, you're okay, Dolly." Lia held the collar behind her back, not wanting the dog to see and recognize the thing. After weeks to win Dolly's trust, it hurt to betray the dog and confirm Dolly's suspicion about humans. But the collar would save Dolly's life, and give Lia time to figure a way out of this mess. She stroked the short black fur of Dolly's arched neck. The dog's tension thrummed like a hummingbird's wings.

Derek muttered to himself. "You had to buy this old dump. Why'd you have to do that, Lia? Now you're the only witness. Otherwise, it's just Coop's word against mine." His voice rose. "Just like your mother. Sleep with dogs, you're liable to get fleas." He wagged the gun at her.

Poised to fix the repugnant collar about the Rottweiler's neck, she froze. Her shoulders hunched, she held her breath, waiting for the shot.

He laughed at her expression. "Oh, I won't shoot you, Lia. That would just confirm Coop's story about my involvement. I've got something else in mind."

Lia breathed again. "Derek, I see it was all Coop, like you said. Gambling can sneak up on you. It's not your fault." She prayed he'd believe the lie. She knew dogfights attracted big money gambling, illegal guns and drugs. She nodded at the camera he still held. "The camera can be erased. Or just dump it somewhere. Without the recording, there's nothing for the police. It's just Coop's word against yours, like you said. I can back you up." She stared at him, willing Derek to believe, but she sucked at lying. "Let me help you." She nodded at Dolly, who had stopped snarling and now nosed her puppies. "See, she's fine. I didn't even need the collar." Lia hated the pleading tone but couldn't help herself.

He tipped his head to the side. "How about that? You have the makings of a good trainer, Lia. Too bad it's wasted." He glanced toward the end of the kennel where the bois d'arc tree punched through the roof and wall. "So sad. Business blown to hell and gone before it got started. Sort of like my plans." He rubbed his eyes.

"Dog fighting is a felony. I can't be tied to that."

"Should have thought of that before you got involved." As soon as she spoke, she wanted to take back the words.

He threw the camera as hard as he could against the cement floor, and took a half step toward her, fist clenching and unclenching.

She stiffened her jaw and stared him down. Bullies picked on the weak; the strong collected bruises but survived. His hands were tied if he wanted her death to look like an accident. She had to use that, to survive.

With a visible effort, Derek unclenched his fists and smiled, more of a grimace than anything else. "Have it your way, Lia. I have a better idea about the training collar. Use this tie-down and get Dolly secured." He unhooked the braided leather lariat and snaked it through the metal grillwork, keeping the door between him and Dolly closed. "Do it now." His lowered brows warned her not to argue.

Lia nodded and looped one end through the chain link at the other end of the kennel run, then slipped the lasso around Dolly's neck. She stood back, wanting to scoop up one of Dolly's wriggling offspring and lose herself in the scent of puppy breath. No, not just any puppy. She wanted Karma.

She peered past Derek across the cement aisle to the opposite kennel. The black shepherd watched, posed in stiff legged defense. She could still feel the confident calm, a "no-fear" promise from Shadow, an all-enveloping certainty she had no wish to explain. Lia embraced the concept and trusted that somehow this secret communication would save them all. Lia wished with all her being that the tie-down failed. *She pictured bright dog-teeth chewing and gnawing through the leather.* But wishes weren't enough.

"I won't say anything, Derek. You're angry and upset but you haven't done anything that can't be explained away." She took a step closer, threading fingers through the wire grating. "If Coop's talking to the police, they'll be here soon. You should leave."

"Put on the collar, Lia."

"What?" She dropped it, and the collar slapped the cement floor like a reproach. Dolly growled at the sound, recognized the collar, and lunged but the tether kept her at bay.

Derek smiled. "The tie-down controls Dolly just fine. But I know you, Lia, I've watched you for years. I suspect it'll take cranking up the juice, or the threat anyway, for you to do as you're told. So put it on, or I'll shoot the bitch."

With shaking hands, Lia fastened the collar around her slim neck, tightening it to a snug fit when Derek urged her with the gun. The metal conductor tips pressed against her skin, cold as snake's teeth and chilling her soul.

"Good girl. Just so we're on the same page, here's a little taste." He thumbed the hand held remote.

A buzzing itchy sensation at the twin contacts grew to a painful level. Derek watched her while dialing up the stim-level.

She did her best to remain stoic, not wanting to give him the satisfaction, but soon gasped and clutched at the collar to pull it away from her skin. "Bastard!"

"Yes, you are." He laughed. "Time's a-wasting. Like you said, the police will soon be here. And when they arrive, all they'll find are victims of the storm." He pressed the remote again, dialing it even higher.

She screamed, clawed her neck, and fell writhing onto the cold cement.

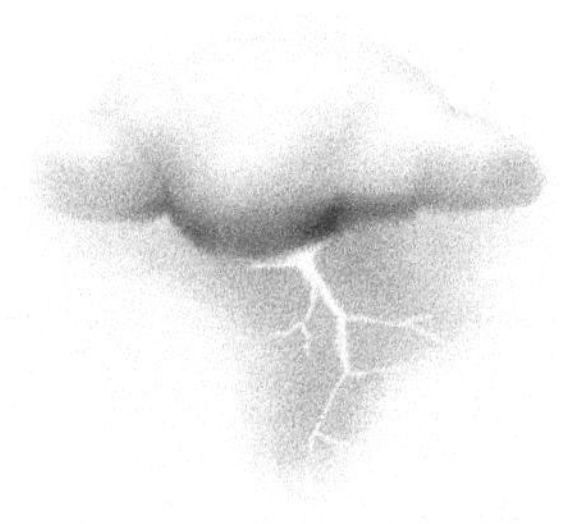

Chapter 21

The girl's shriek hurt a good-dog's heart. Karma pressed her ears flat. Her pulse galloped when Lia fell to the ground out of sight. She had to reach Lia! Karma didn't know or care what she would do once there, just drove forward with a puppy-size roar.

The shepherd still blocked her way, so Karma ducked to squeeze between Shadow's forelegs. But the big black dog shifted and hooked one paw over her back to stop her. The move both restrained Karma and signaled his status.

She submitted with no argument, offering just a weak whimper of frustration. Even an inexperienced puppy-girl like Karma understood that adult dogs outranked her. She obeyed Shadow's *because I said so* command without question. For good measure, Karma licked his muzzle as he stood over her. His legs trembled, and she read his disquiet as easily as her own. He also wanted to leap to the girl's aid, but waited with an adult dog's caution.

Lia's screams of pain trailed off, followed by raspy gasps that mimicked dog-laugh sounds. Karma knew the sound meant the opposite. Lia's fear-stink and the man's anger colored the stale kennel air.

The man opened Lia's kennel and the door squealed in protest, scraping against the cement floor. Dolly, still tied to the back wall, flailed and lunged with silent intent.

"Derek, *wait.*" Lia whispered, but Karma heard it even through all the barking and snarling.

Shadow flinched like the *wait* word hurt. Karma itched to do something, anything, to make the helpless feeling go away. She wanted to be confident and brave again. How could it be, that Lia, with all her extra knowledge beyond the ken of dogs, still couldn't protect herself?

What if Karma protected Lia? Karma had sharp teeth, even if she was little. And Karma wasn't alone.

She cold-nosed the shepherd, urging him to action. Shadow was big. Older. With scars that shouted of battles won. Shadow saved her, and Lia saved him. Now Lia needed their help. She wiggled beneath his heavy paw, and he lowered his head and sniffed her, all without taking his attention from the man. But he still didn't budge.

The stranger grabbed Lia and dragged her out. The remaining puppies cried and squealed, a couple following a few steps before turning tail and running back into the safety of the kennel. The open gate teased Dolly. Powerful shoulders and neck strained against the old leather tether, choking Dolly in her effort to reach the man.

Derek bullied Lia to where the tree poked through the roof and turned the space into a maze of thorny branches. Soon, Karma couldn't see either of them. She whined and struggled against Shadow's paw, but he held her down. She heard Lia crying and yelling, and she yearned to see. People puzzled Karma, and she wanted to understand them. More than that, she needed to help, to stop the bully, to protect Lia the way the girl protected Karma. She just didn't know how. And Shadow wouldn't let her move.

Then the black shepherd removed his paw from Karma's back to take an unsteady step forward.

She bounced to her feet, eager to rush forward, and whined with excitement until a stern look from Shadow silenced her.

Shadow nosed open the door a dog's width, and stepped through on shaky legs. Karma crowded after, dodging the excited sweep of his long, black tail. He growled low in his throat—not at her, though—and paused to scent the air. He gazed both ways before he stepped fully into the aisle. Even Dolly stopped lunging long enough to take in his powerful but injured form before she returned to digging at the cement as if to drag the entire kennel off its moorings.

Karma expected Shadow to go after Lia's attacker. He'd use his bright, sharp adult-dog teeth to help Lia. Karma liked biting toys and wondered what it would feel like to bite a bad man. Make him yell like he'd made Lia scream. She wanted to find out.

But after a brief sniff toward the downed tree and hidden people, Shadow instead stumbled to Dolly's kennel. The other puppies made way, steering clear of the potent male who still smelled of his own blood and pain.

Dolly watched with narrowed eyes, still more focused on the hidden, hated man.

Shadow lowered his ears with respect and cut his eyes sideways. He wagged, low and loose and slow, and stood motionless to allow Dolly to scent his neck and flank. He shifted before she could investigate his tail, nor would she allow him to sniff hers. But she didn't move when Shadow nosed the tether that held her captive. Dolly again surged against the restraint, holding it taut. Shadow licked the leather.

Karma's pleading whine turned to frustrated yelps of disappointment, but Shadow and Dolly ignored Karma. Worse, they ignored Lia. Didn't care about the bad man. Ignored the girl's sobs.

Lia's hoarse voice raised louder than blustery wind and dog noises. Her cries cut deep and made Karma's tummy hurt. Karma was brave, but didn't know what to do. Shadow would know.

Karma ran the few steps to reach him, and barked loud, louder still, a demand so loud it hurt her own ears. But both adults still ignored her. She stopped barking, and stared, her fur bristling all over her body, and stubby tail jerking with determination.

They still ignored her.

Karma leaped forward, and nipped—not a real bite, just a little play nip—on Shadow's hind leg.

He roared. His teeth snapped and clicked within a whisker's width of Karma's nose.

She yelped and spun away, falling on the wet pavement before regaining her feet. Her tail tucked tight she rolled and bared her tummy, even wet herself a little to show no threat before scrambling back to her feet. Karma felt bereft. Dolly couldn't and Shadow wouldn't help.

He didn't care about Lia at all. Maybe didn't care about Karma, either. He just stood close to Dolly, licking, nibbling and grooming her neck.

Lia screamed.

Karma showed her teeth and raced to help her person.

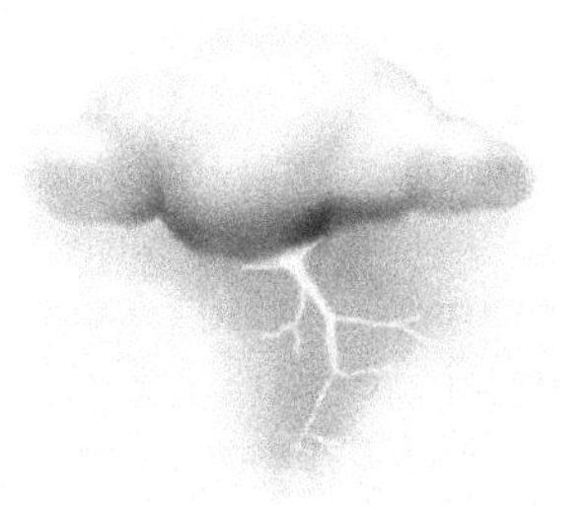

Chapter 22

Lia crouched on hands and knees, and tried to catch her breath. The smell of wet cement clawed the back of her throat. Bare tree limbs rattled like ice in a glass, surrounding her with skeletal fingers.

The loss of control hurt worse than the pain. She offered no physical threat to the bigger man, and after an initial fruitless struggle, Lia conserved her strength. She couldn't outrun him, not when the collar's hornet sting dropped her where she stood, whether a half yard or half mile away. The shock collar kept her bound to him as surely as chains and Lia's sympathy rose even higher for what Dolly had suffered.

Some respected trainers used remote trainers ethically—if there was such a thing—but Derek swung the remote like a club. This went beyond removing a threat. This was personal. He'd already zapped Lia a dozen times, whether she cooperated or not. He punched the button again and again, making her teeth clench, and breath whoosh from her lungs until she lay weak and gasping.

With the ceiling gone and nothing to stave off the weather, the wind tangled her hair into a rat's nest. Lia's wet clothes chafed when he'd dragged her over the rough cement. Derek slung her slight frame beneath the felled bois d'arc that slumped overhead like a brown recluse spider stalking prey.

She bit her lip, determined to silence angry sobs of pain, not wanting to give him the satisfaction. Her throat burned from screaming, and skin tingled and raged where the prongs bit her skin. Each time Derek hit the correction button, dialed to the highest setting for maximum punishment, her muscles contracted from breastbone to chin. Involuntary muscle twitches continued even after he released the button.

"Now what?" Her voice croaked. She needed to distract him, just long enough to tug off the collar. He hadn't tied her up. Hell, if he'd used the lariat on her instead of Dolly, she'd never get free. She braced herself with one hand on a gnarled limb, and rose to her knees. "You can't shoot me, you said so yourself. The police would believe Coop's story and chase you forever."

"Don't have to shoot you." He pocketed the gun, then bent and grabbed one end of a spiny branch that had fallen free. "You were in the wrong place at the wrong time, a victim of the storm. And this big old tree landed on you. Freak storm, freak accident, for a freak who shouldn't have been born." He hefted the branch like a bat, wound up like a Texas Ranger and stepped into a roundhouse swing.

The limb whooshed within inches of her head. Lia flinched and dodged, but it still caught her a glancing blow on the top of one shoulder. She screamed, and scuttled backwards, now using the tree as a thorny shelter. She hissed when one of the spikes caught her back and scored her flesh from shoulder to shoulder. Lia gritted her teeth, embraced the pain. As long as she could feel, she was alive.

He came after her, reaching beneath overhanging branches to flail the limb like a scythe.

She scrambled sideways. Fabric ripped and hot wet soaked her shirt, but she ignored the blood and scooted deeper into the tree's embrace. She'd take a torn up back over a direct hit with the ironwood club. Derek couldn't swing with any force or accuracy as long as the branches thwarted his aim. And he couldn't make the tree fall any further. No, Derek needed her out in the open to beat to death, remove the collar, and stage her body.

Lia panted, and watched with narrowed eyes as he scoped out a way to reach her. She just had to wait him out. Coop's story should have police on the way, sooner or later. When Derek turned sideways to scramble between the massive trunk and limbs, she reached behind her neck to fumble the shock collar's buckle.

"No you don't!"

Lia's mouth opened in a silent scream, fingers grappled at her neck when Derek hit the remote once again.

"Go on. Dammit, pass out already." He hit the remote again and again.

Lia's vision blurred, ears buzzed, and black sparklies danced all around. She curled into a fetal position and prayed it would end.

"Sonofa-BITCH!"

Derek's startled curse overlapped a high-pitched snarl. At the same moment, the pain in Lia's neck abated.

She didn't wait to see what had happened. Despite the muscle tremors and spastic fingers, she fumbled the collar fastener, ignoring Derek's grunts and curses and the soprano barks and squeals that followed. Lia ripped the collar from her neck, sat up, and flung it away.

It slithered across the slick floor, slapping into one of Derek's soaked and ruined athletic shoes.

The yelps and snarls faded to growls. Lia looked up, defiant and triumphant, only to see Derek holding the squirming Karma aloft by her scruff.

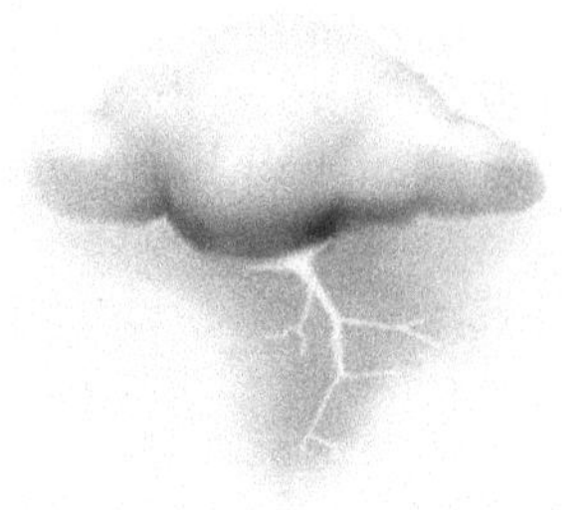

Chapter 23

Karma struggled at first, but that made her neck hurt worse. She keened, hating that he made her squeal. She wanted more than ever to test her teeth on the man's flesh.

"Let her go!" Lia's voice sounded full of gravel, but even the harsh sound made Karma's heart skip with happiness. Karma didn't need Shadow after all. All by herself, she'd made the bad man leave Lia alone, and stopped the girl's screams.

He shook her again and Karma yipped. Her paws flailed the air. "One of the pups got too brave for its own good. Too bad. Could have some potential with Coop's kennel. He wanted a bitch with some drive."

Karma turned the yips into a soprano snarl, making her teeth tingle.

But he just laughed, and swung her in mid-air until brave warning growls morphed back into yelps of panic. Swinging made Karma's tummy feel bad. She'd already vomited dirty water swallowed while fighting the flood, but her body wanted to empty some more.

"Stop it!" Lia clawed her way upright, and clung to the tree. "Such a big brave man to get off on abusing dogs and picking on a helpless puppy." Her sarcasm changed when she spoke to Karma. "That's my brave girl. Hang on, Karma, just you wait."

She remembered Shadow's reaction to the "wait" word, but Karma felt comforted by the promise it held. She yawned and panted, and focused on the girl when Lia climbed onto the massive trunk of the tree, still spitting angry words. She wondered if Lia would use the tree to get away. Karma hoped so.

"This is the pup you call by that special name." He made a funny snorting sound with his nose. "You're starting to piss me off."

His fist clenched tighter on the back of her neck, and he exuded a biting scent not too different from the snakes.

Karma's brow furrowed. The tree rested half inside, half outside, offering an easy slither for snakes to travel. They were bad enough outside, where a good-dog could run away. She whined, but wind blustered through the breached roof, carrying her protest away. Karma kicked her paws again, and tasted the air for snake scent.

Her paws stopped churning at a sudden sound, and she listened hard. There, it came again. This time, the footsteps accompanied a strange smoky smell. Lia didn't wrinkle her nose or cock her head to acknowledge either. Maybe Lia knew that scent? The pungent smell choked Karma's senses.

Karma stared into the girl's face for some clue what to do. She whimpered and turned her head to follow the outside steps, but Lia didn't understand. So she twisted to give the man a hard stare, and risked her rudeness escalating his punishment.

Nothing she did mattered. He just tucked her under his arm, and knelt to retrieve the strap next to his foot. He set her down, but pressed Karma flat to the cement floor while he fiddled with it. The strap smelled like Lia, with overtones of acrid fear-stink from the girl. Karma shivered when he draped it across her neck.

"Let's see how your little favorite likes my style of training."

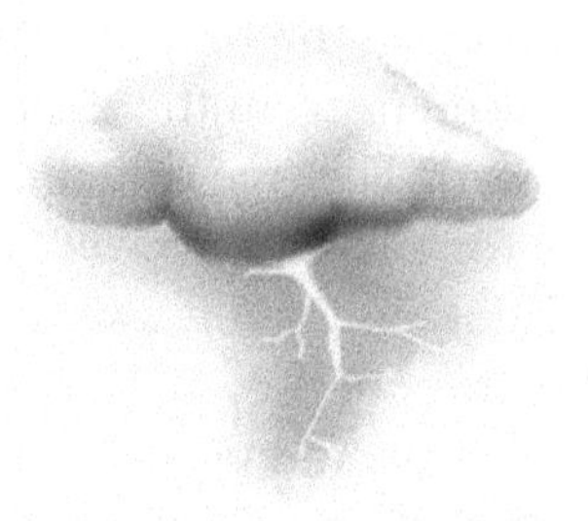

Chapter 24

Lia teetered, braced herself against a massive limb, and then leaped from the prone trunk. She landed in a crouch midway between the felled tree and where Derek stooped over Karma.

He smiled that she'd taken the bait, and released the puppy. Karma snapped at air before skittering out of reach.

She realized he'd tricked her to move too far from the sheltering branches. Lia stumbled away.

Derek stood in one smooth motion, stepped forward and swung his club.

She tucked and rolled, and instinctively held up her forearm. The limb thwacked against her wrist, and Lia's scream came out a croak. She grasped the injury with her other hand.

Karma barked and danced with excitement, trying to reach Lia but had to dodge away when Derek swooshed the club in her direction.

Staring up at Derek, Lia blinked furiously to clear tears. She lay on her right side, and struggled to her knees, difficult to do without using her arms. She couldn't let go of the injury, and knew he'd broken her wrist. The pain radiated to her shoulder. "Why, Derek?

Why do you hate me? What'd I ever do?"

He held the branch like a Louisville Slugger, and offered a couple of taunting practice swings while he watched her. "You look so much like her. Sound the same, act the same." Derek stepped forward, wound up, chose his target and swung. "She made bad choices, too. Went on vacation, and got herself knocked up."

Gasping, Lia covered her head with her good arm and rolled. This time the club thudded against her thigh. At least she still wore the padding from the morning's training session. She gasped, then spoke through gritted teeth. "This is about my mom?" It'd be ironic if she'd learn about her birth, and then die with the knowledge. But if she could keep him talking, distract him with his own anger, maybe help would arrive in time.

"Kaylia." He uttered the name like a filthy word. "Wanted to kill the slut myself when I found out." He swung again. Missed. Braced his feet and swung again.

Karma whimpered, dodged Derek's kick, and scampered to reach Lia. Without thinking, she opened her arms and Karma ran without hesitation into her arms.

"The bitch was my fiancée! If she hadn't died giving birth to you, I would have . . ." He panted, sobbing. "You killed her. You killed my Kaylia. *You* should have died, not Kaylia." Derek grunted, putting everything he had into the club.

Her world spun, the revelation an emotional blow far worse than the thud to her side that numbed Lia from waist to shoulders. She fell over, half-aware of her surroundings.

She couldn't breathe, cement chilled her cheek, her mouth gaped like a catfish. Derek's soaked, ruined high-tops dragged laces within inches of her eyes . . . Lia sucked one fire-laced breath deep into her lungs, fighting to stay conscious, and waited for the next blow that would end it all.

Karma twisted in Lia's limp arms, not leaving her side. She slurped Lia's eyes and then looked down the aisle toward the office.

Lia followed the dog's gaze. After one quick smoke-laden puff—she knew that smell!—the wind died, so the clomping boots echoed in the sudden quiet of the night.

Derek looked from her to the approaching figure, and whispered as he hefted the tree limb. "You get some company under that old bois d'arc." His sneakers made no sound as he hurried to ambush the rescuer.

Lia used very muscle and ounce of will to draw one big breath—*God, it hurts it hurts!*—to scream, "Run!"

"Lia-girl, that you? Thank heavens, thought for sure the storm got you when I got your text." His voice shook with emotion. "Where are you?"

She'd hoped he'd send help. But he came by himself? Been worried about her? "Get out, please get out!" Her voice croak words she could barely hear. The numbness in her torso gave way to throbbing but her good arm still worked. She squeezed the puppy, and Karma squealed.

Derek strode forward, club raised, ready to clock the man as soon as he came through the door.

Then she knew what to do, the one thing left to save herself. To save Grandfather. Lia cuddled Karma, stroked the puppy's face, and whispered in her ear, and then let her go.

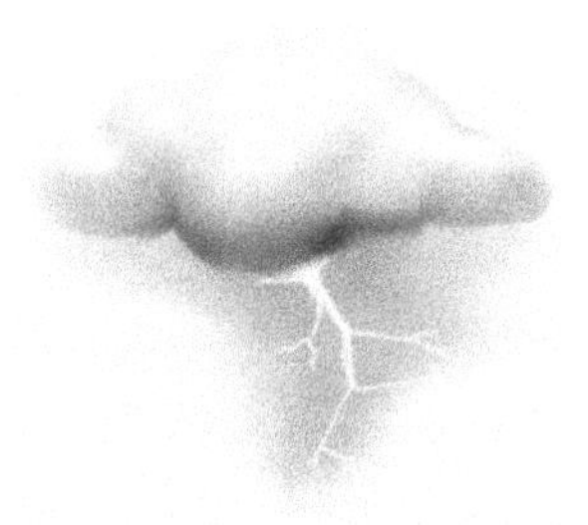

Chapter 25

Karma wrinkled her brow when Lia released her warm embrace. The bad man had moved away. Lia should get up, up UP. Climb through the tree, maybe lift a good-dog so they could leave together. Karma licked Lia's eyes and mouth, and then nose poked her, urging action.

But Lia just lay there, clutching one arm and moaning. Karma could tell she felt bad. Lia's neck looked dark and flushed, and one arm swelled bigger and bigger. Lia's voice sounded wrong, too. So when the girl whispered in Karma's ear, it tickled and she had to shake her head hard to relieve the itch.

"Karma. Be a good-dog." Lia whispered again.

This time Karma concentrated. She needed to pay attention, even if trees plunged through the roof, bad men beat Lia and grabbed good-dogs by the neck.

Derek's soft steps made his shoelaces swish-swish. Karma tipped her head when Lia used a broken limb to point at the man's feet. Her brow furrowed, and then her eyes brightened. No words needed, Karma understood. The girl's eyes rained water. Karma licked the salt away, and wagged her short tail to show she was ready, the way a brave dog should be.

Karma, TRIP! Good-dog, Karma, go TRIP! Lia pointed again, her silent intent as clear as a spoken command.

Her head came up, neck arched with pleasure. She loved this game! Without hesitation, Karma launched herself down the cement pathway, hearing her own claws scrabble for purchase as she bounded forward.

She tackled the bad man's foot, the one with the trailing laces, and bit down hard through pants that had no special padding.

"Son-of-a-bitch!" He yelled, stumbled, and dropped the limb as he fell to a knee. He caught one hand on the nearest kennel gate to steady himself.

A tall imposing man with a shock of white hair and smoky smell stepped through the office doorway. "Why the hell are *you* here? Where's my granddaughter!"

Karma retreated when a canine growl interrupted. She'd known that signature vibration from the day she was born deaf, blind and toothless. Her ears slicked back, and she tucked her tail tight to her body, shouting "no threat!" in every move. Appeasement gestures kept canine peace and Karma bowed to her mother's will. That was a dog rule, at least until Karma reached her majority.

But Derek didn't understand dog rules. He stumbled upright, still clinging to the unlatched kennel gate that swung open, and reached again for the club.

Recognizing the threat, Karma grabbed one end. She couldn't lift the whole thing, but managed to get enough in her jaws to drag the limb out of reach.

Derek pulled something out of his pocket.

"Grandfather, he has a gun!" Lia had crawled out just enough to see.

Dolly strained and lurched against the tether.

Growling as loud as she could, Karma tugged the tree club backwards. Every few steps, she stopped and shook her head as hard as she could.

Good-dog, TRIP Karma, TRIP!

Giving the branch a final shake, Karma obeyed Lia's silent plea and dove again at the man's shoes. She flinched when a loud "pop-pop" sounded overhead.

Shadow barreled out of the kennel. He snarled and leaped toward Derek, but his legs gave way before Shadow made contact.

Dolly lunged again and again. Her growls faded but her focus never wavered.

Derek kicked at the shepherd, and then laughed when Shadow panted with exhaustion, but didn't move. He turned and pointed his hand at the white haired man, and motioned for him to move.

The tall man never flinched. He stood rock steady, with eyes only for Lia. "Police are on the way, Lia-girl, hang on."

Karma padded to Shadow, impressed he'd try to help despite his hurts. She nuzzled his cheek and this time Shadow didn't object. She smelled salt and tasted copper where blood stained his muzzle. She spun into a head up, teeth bared defensive pose, all sixteen pounds ready to protect the spent black shepherd from the bad man. But she didn't have to.

With one final lunge, Dolly's tether snapped. Derek screamed.

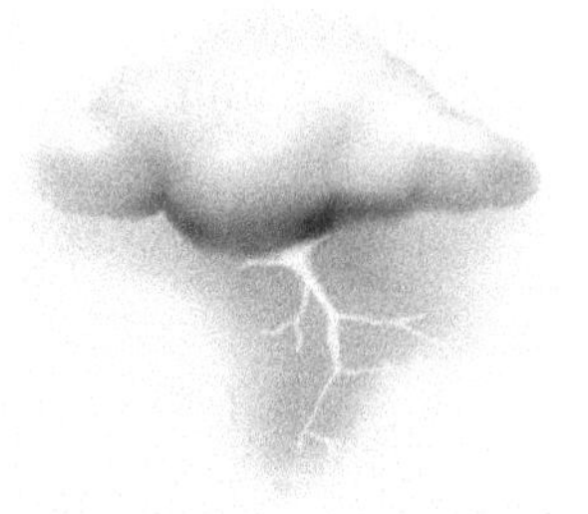

Chapter 26

Lia cradled her injured wrist and peered through the cracked glass of the office window to watch the beehive of police activity. Grandfather stood just outside the door, conferring with a man in plain clothes. One of the ambulances pulled away with sirens blasting, carting Derek to the hospital. Another waited to carry her away, but so far, Lia managed to put them off. She needed to see to the animals first. If the world would stop spinning.

She squeezed shut her eyes, but that made the vertigo worse. The final moments in the kennel were a blur. Dolly's attack proved to be more sound and fury than substance, typical of many dog fights, and ended as soon as it began. She'd been amazed when Grandfather knew enough to issue a stern, "Off!" that shooed Dolly away from the cowering man. He'd shut Dolly up in the run with her puppies, still wearing the bloody lariat that the black shepherd had gnawed through. Just as she imagined. She'd puzzle over that later.

Grandfather tried to keep Lia still until the EMTs arrived, but couldn't stop her from staggering down the aisle to reach Karma. Once satisfied the puppy was safe, she shut Karma and the shepherd together in the kennel. The two Pit Bulls were safe, ensconced in their own kennel space, and Thor had slept through the whole thing. The police arrived posthaste, and a detective soon thereafter.

"I'll give you five minutes, Detective Combs." Grandfather ushered a tall dark-haired man into the room. "After that, she goes to the hospital." He scowled at her, adding, "Whether she likes it or not."

Lia winced when pummeled muscles complained. She slumped into the desk chair he held for her. "I'm okay." She wasn't. Even breathing hurt. But she was alive, and each bruise and scrape proved she'd survived.

Without prompting, she told the detective what had happened, pointing him to the recorded evidence she'd also saved on her computer. "What will happen to Dolly? It's not her fault." Lia looked up at Grandfather, a man she couldn't remember having ever expressed an ounce of emotion for himself or anyone else. "She knocked away the gun. Dolly saved your life." Despite herself, Lia's chin trembled, knowing the most common outcome for dogs like Dolly. "And Karma saved my life."

Grandfather spoke with his trademark just-the-facts clipped tone. "Derek owns the Rottweilers. They're not your problem, Lia." He softened his voice but talked over her protests. "I'll contact Sunny Babcock to pick up her dogs."

Detective Combs interrupted. "You have Babcock's animals here? We're looking for her." He tried to keep his tone neutral, and failed. "She's wanted on several charges in another case. Including murder."

Lia caught her breath. Babcock owed her several hundred dollars in boarding fees for the two Pit Bulls. Any anticipated glowing references from the reality star just turned to crap.

Detective Combs shrugged. "A witness saw Babcock swept away by the flood, too. Lots of people and animals lost in the storm." He paused, and cleared his throat, moved by something he couldn't or wouldn't share. "With the storm damage, and your injuries, best to let the city take the animals."

She hated the thought, but Detective Combs made sense. Thor still waited for Abe to come home, and had little attachment to her. She was in no shape to argue. She had no *legal* claim to Derek's dogs.

Lia didn't care what the law said, though. Karma had already claimed her heart. So had Shadow. And once in the system, it would be months and maybe years before anything resolved. She'd never see them again. The room tilted.

"Detective Combs, she's had enough." Grandfather's hand on her shoulder steadied Lia from tipping out of the chair. "Talk to her later at the hospital, when she's been treated. Go get the EMTs. Oh, and give my best to your Uncle Stanley. We go way back." He ushered the man to the door before returning to kneel by Lia's side.

Grandfather wouldn't listen, he never had. But he'd come for her despite the storm. That had to count for something, right? "Don't let them take my dogs." Talking still hurt, but he had to hear her. To listen this time. "Please, I can't lose them, too." She looked around at the bedraggled office space, her dream crushed.

"Don't worry, Lia-girl, I won't let them take old Thor." His voice caught, and he turned away, and shouted out the open door. "Can I get some help in here?"

"Promise me? Not just Thor. There's three need to stay." She had to push to get any sound past her damaged throat. "The black shepherd and pup, they're together in the same kennel." Karma and Shadow shouldn't be separated. Not like this.

He turned back to her, brow furrowing. "That torn up black dog? He's yours, too? And that fierce little ankle-biter?"

"Grandfather, please. Help me. You won't be sorry." Lia never begged. But she'd do it now, pride be damned. She asked for more than a pass on the dogs, and he knew it.

He stared at her a long moment. "You trained that pup, did you? She did it on command, a young one like that?"

She nodded, and then winced with pain.

"You've got the touch, all right. Kaylia had it with horses, that's how she met your father." He didn't hide his bitterness. "Now you've got the touch with dogs." He scrubbed his eyes. "Never could say no to your mother. Promised I wouldn't make the same mistake with you." His palm cupped her cheek. "You look so much like her, Lia. Sound the same, act the same. So beautiful." His words, identical to Derek's, held wistful longing. "But I lost her long ago to that damn cowboy. And tonight, I almost lost you." He cleared his throat.

"Who is he? My father, I mean. Grandfather, I have a right to know." Her face burned. "Derek said that he and my mom—"

His lips tightened and he took back his hand. "Your father's an ocean away and dead, for all I care. He gave up his rights to you and your mother when he walked away."

For a moment, Lia felt overwhelming relief that Derek had lied.

But that raised even more questions.

Before she could ask, the EMTs bustled into the room and Grandfather stood aside to make room for them. Lia yelped when they moved her to the gurney. The beating had sensitized her entire body so that even untouched areas radiated heat.

Grandfather took her good hand and walked beside the gurney on the short trip to the waiting ambulance. She saw the county panel truck from Animal Control arrive, and she squeezed Grandfather's hand.

"Please, my dogs. Grandfather, don't let them take my dogs!" A lonely howl arose from the kennel area, tickling that mind's-eye magical place. A familiar puppy-girl's falsetto tones joined in. Both pleaded the cause. Or simply serenaded the moon's rain washed glow.

Grandfather squeezed her hand without answering, and watched them load her into the ambulance.

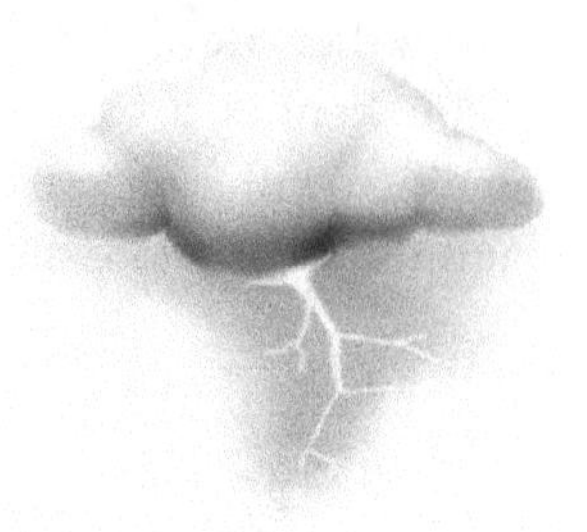

Chapter 27

September crossed her arms, and winced as she lowered herself into the hospital chair. She wore inappropriate clothes her mother had brought, more suited to a business meeting than comfortable recovery. Her bruises would take time to heal, but she had to get out of here. She'd pay dearly for the emergency admittance and overnight treatment that her deductible wouldn't cover. September signed herself out over the protests of the doctors, Combs and her parents. The hospital needed the bed space. And September needed control over her own life.

Mom would arrive any minute. Combs hadn't offered an update on the search for Shadow, and she'd been afraid to ask. Better to find out the truth face to face, when she could read his expression. She scrubbed her cheeks with a sodden tissue, and settled herself when she heard footsteps approach.

A big white haired man clutching a cowboy hat rapped on the doorframe before he stuck his head inside. "Excuse me, ma'am. Are you September Day, the dog trainer?"

She nodded with a wary frown. Notoriety followed her like stink on a skunk, and she had little patience to play nice with strangers today. "I'm expecting someone." She hoped he'd take the hint.

"I won't take much of your time. The name's Corazon, William Corazon. Most folks just call me Dub." He ducked into the room, adding, "Sorry to hear about your troubles." He reached out a hand, adding, "Don't get up, sit easy."

Everyone knew her troubles. She didn't want to shake his hand, but couldn't avoid it. September sighed, wanting to change that. She needed privacy to heal, and reevaluate her life, especially how Combs fit in. "What can I do for you, Mr. Corazon?"

"I'm here visiting my granddaughter, Lia." He nodded toward the door. "She's laid up from the storm and, well, she's got some injuries." His eyes shifted away, and September wondered what he failed to mention. "She's crazy about dogs, wants to train them for the police."

"Sorry to hear about her injuries. I could stop in and say hello before I leave, I suppose." September strained to see around him. "My ride should be here soon."

"No, I'd rather you didn't visit Lia, not just yet." He fingered the brim of the hat, staring at it as though the secret of the universe lay within. "A mutual friend said you'd trained a police dog before, and might could offer Lia some advice. Forgive the intrusion, ma'am, but when I found out you were right next to Lia's hospital room, I had to take a chance and talk with you." He looked up, eyes narrowed. "Make no mistake, I don't support her foolishness. She's got grand opportunities with my business, and a great future. But young people always want to make their own decisions." He growled the last words. "They don't listen and get hurt along the way. This pipe dream landed Lia in the hospital."

She narrowed her eyes. "You want me to persuade her to give up dog training? How old is this girl?" What mutual friend could he mean? She'd told very few people about her days working with the South Bend police. Her heart contracted with remembered hurt at the loss of her first dog. She hadn't been able to protect him, so even more reason to not give up on Shadow. "Combs sent you to me?"

His face brightened at the name. "She thinks she's all grown up, just because she's out of school and on her own."

"She's an adult, Mr. Corazon. She'd resent me butting in. I sure would." Why would Combs suggest she take on this project? He knew she had her own behavior consult clients, not to mention dealing with rebuilding her house. Even if she wanted to mentor someone, she had no facility to train.

"Just consider the idea, would you? Lia won't get out of the hospital for a while. I hope she'll rethink her future all on her own. But if she's stubborn, having someone with experience could shine a light on reality for her. Money's no object, I can pay double your usual fee." He smiled and turned to go.

Combs met him at the door. "What are you doing here?"

September rose from the chair, gritting her teeth with the effort. "Did you find him? Is Shadow okay?" Her heartbeat drummed in her ears. She held her breath, praying for the right answer.

"Just wanted to introduce myself, that's all." He shook hands with Combs, and put on his hat. "Thanks for helping my granddaughter, Detective." Corazon exited the room.

"What did he want? He shouldn't be bothering you." Combs hurried to September's side, and took her arm. "Are you ready to go?"

"You've got to tell me. Did you find my dog?" She couldn't breathe, already knowing the truth. Combs would have shouted good news as soon as he walked in.

"We found the GPS unit. Steven's directions were spot-on. But Shadow wasn't there." He squeezed her hand. "The GPS led us to the missing boy, Lenny. He's being treated. The EMTs say he survived in part because of that orange cat keeping him warm." He smiled. "His folks agreed to keep the cat. Lenny named it Waffles."

"Good news for his parents. I'm happy for them." But she wanted better news for Shadow. At least they hadn't found his body. He could still be alive out there, somewhere. "I have to keep looking for him."

With gentle care, Combs took September into his arms. "I know. I know you do. We can talk about it at home."

September stiffened. She pulled out of his arms. "Mom's picking me up. I told you that." She walked away, putting distance between them to stare out the hospital window. After the many dark days, storm clouds had given way to blue sky. Bright sun reflected on the water-filled parking lot that still resembled a lake.

"I have room at my house, extra bedrooms and everything." He smiled, and when she glanced over her shoulder at him, he held up both palms. "No pressure. We both want to take things slow."

"Why did you send Mr. Corazon to me?" She couldn't stop the accusatory tone. He'd shared private information about her with a stranger. What else had he shared?

"Wait, what?" Combs furrowed brow aged him ten years.

Before he could answer, Mom bustled into the room. "I've got your old room straightened, and your father's waiting in the car—" She saw Combs and her nostrils flared. "Detective. You do seem to spend lots of time away from your responsibilities."

Combs stuck his hands in his pockets. His jaw flexed but he spoke softly. "Rose, I'm here to—"

"You can call me Mrs. January, Detective. I certainly appreciate the help the police offered September, but her father and I will take care of our daughter." She spied the empty overnight bag she'd brought and collected it with a graceful swoop. "Are you ready? We shouldn't keep your father waiting."

September refused to meet Combs's eyes. Mom grasped her arm and led her from the room down the hallway to the elevator. She needed time away from him, time to herself, to figure out next steps. Without Shadow's steadying presence, her brain wouldn't focus. Better to be swept along on Mom's determination, and choose her battles later. She understood Mom. If Combs shared her private past with a stranger, maybe she didn't know him after all.

The elevator opened, revealing a petite blue-eyed blond woman dressed in a matching powder blue suit and blue heels. She startled and her lips drew into a thin, angry line as she stepped into the hall.

Mom's hand tightened on September's arm. "Mom, let go, that hurts!" She shrugged free of the grip, and raised her eyebrows at the two women who faced off like cats ready to spit.

"That's your daughter?" The blond woman sniffed, and looked September up and down. Her lip curled. "She doesn't look a thing like you, does she? But then, I wouldn't expect her to."

"Let's go, September. Your father's waiting." Mom grabbed her arm again, and urged her into the elevator.

"Who is that?" September refused to move. She'd never seen her mother in such a state.

"Nobody you need to know." Mom looked ready to cry.

"She never told you about me." The woman smoothed her helmet of blond hair, the gesture at once familiar. At the sudden déjà vu, September looked sharply at Mom.

"I'm not moving until somebody explains to me—"

Mom whirled, back stiff, and stalked onto the elevator by herself. She faced outwards, ignoring the woman to address September. "Don't keep your father waiting. I'll see you downstairs."

"Oh for heaven's sake." September hurried onto the elevator, but stared back at the other woman's face, noting the resemblance. "Who is that?" The elevator door closed.

Mom wilted. "I never wanted to see her again." She smoothed her hair with the same gesture, the only difference trembling hands. "That's Cornelia Corazon. My sister."

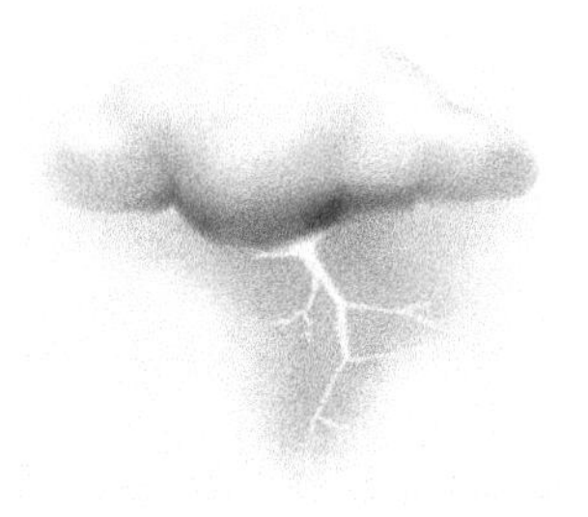

Chapter 28

Lia stared at the computer screen, scouring the "lost pet" postings on social media. Nearby, Thor snored on his bed. He spent most of his time sleeping as if tracking during the storm had drained away the last of his energy. She suspected it wouldn't be long before Thor joined Abe in the heavenly mist over Hawaii. "Rest well, good boy."

Lia's voice still sounded like she'd gargled acid. Grammy said it made her sound sultry, and offered to fix her up with someone suitable. Lia told Grammy she didn't like suits.

Grammy hadn't been amused.

Her wounds healed slowly. Lia still sported peacock-hued bruises, from yellow to green and purple. Her broken wrist remained in a cast, and two broken ribs limited her movement. She'd been confined to bed with a concussion and hated the stern nurses who waked her over and over to ensure she didn't sleep forever. Lia just wished the tinnitus would abate, but the doctors said the ringing in her ears might be permanent. The worst part of the hospital stay, though, was worry about her dogs.

Then Grandfather arrived at the hospital with a deal she couldn't refuse.

Shadow whined, and cold-nosed her arm. Lia hadn't found any listing for the *koa*, the warrior dog. Truth be told, she hadn't looked very hard. She kept expecting to feel that whisper-tickle in her mind's eye, but hadn't experienced anything since her return from the hospital. Maybe she'd imagined the connection, or the life-and-death emotions enhanced a latent talent now gone dormant. Or perhaps her head injuries destroyed the budding ability.

Grandfather had sent someone to care for the dogs. Once home, she'd been forced to take it easy, but could still type one handed for internet searches. She picked up the chewed leather lariat coiled on the desk and fingered the tooled set of initials in the cowhide: W. Tex. She'd assumed that was a maker's mark of some sort, and indicated manufacture in West Texas, but learned that most lariats in the state were hemp rope. This lasso was old, something passed down in a family. W. Tex must be a name, so even if her mother used it, Lia was sure the lariat came from her "cowboy" father.

She fingered bead-letters on the baby bracelet from her mother that spelled out her name, and then turned back to the computer to click on the search icon. She typed in the query:

Cowboy + Hawaii

Her eyes widened at the 800,000+ results. A quick scan confirmed a number of possible established ranches that her mother might have visited and met her *paniolo* father on that fateful Hawaii vacation nine months before Lia's birth. The Waimea possibility made Lia miss Abe even more. He could have answered many questions.

She'd made a start.

Her cell phone rang, and Lia wrinkled her nose at the interruption until she recognized the caller. She'd been expecting this, but had mixed feelings, and hadn't decided how to answer. She hadn't spoken to Grandfather since the argument they'd had when she'd left the hospital. He wanted her to come home. She needed to be here. It's where she belonged.

"How are your dogs?" His inquiry was a pointed reminder that without his intervention, Shadow and Karma would be police evidence still held at the county shelter along with Sunny Babcock's dogs, Dolly and the rest of her litter. He cleared his throat, and added, "And how are you feeling?"

"Fine, getting better all the time." Her false bravado didn't fool him. Hell, it didn't fool her, either. She still felt torn. Lia held out her hand to Shadow, and the black shepherd thumped his tail. Karma took that as an invitation, and threw herself against him.

"You coming home?"

Lia watched the two dogs play, smiling at their antics when the much larger shepherd allowed Karma to maul him. The pair were inseparable, and the puppy-girl was smitten. Hell, so was she.

She sighed. "If you won't loan me the money to fix things, I don't have any choice." She stared out the taped up window, and noticed the broken office door had unlatched itself again. Lia used her foot to scoot a nearby step stool to brace it closed.

With insurance lapsed, and no funds of her own, the kennel dream was blown to hell and gone. Literally. She couldn't board dogs with the place in shambles, and couldn't fix things without money from boarders.

The reservations for spring break loomed. She hated the thought of calling Abe's longtime clients and telling them to find another place.

"Lia-girl, there's always choices. Just have to be willing to live with the consequences." His voice softened. "I want you to be happy, but we've got different ideas about making that happen. It's time you stop playing around and join the family business. You've got the touch, just like your mother did."

"Grandfather, I told you—"

"I know, I know, it's all about the dogs." His deep sigh reached clear down to his boots. "No money in it. But your grandmother and I talked for a long time about this. And I realize," his voice shook, and then steadied, "I can't force you. I learned that lesson the hard way with Kaylia."

What she'd long believed to be cold disdain Lia now recognized as bitter self-protection. Before she could say anything, he rushed on.

"You gotta learn for yourself, I understand that. And some mistakes are good for a person. But I'll be damned if I let you make the same ones she did, so hear me out." The familiar demanding tone returned. Grandfather always got his way.

She sighed, resigned. "I'm listening." He'd never been willing to bend before. Maybe he had changed a little bit. But then, she'd never stopped to listen to him, either.

"I still want you to be part of Corazon Ranch, Lia. But I'll give you six months to prove me wrong. Show me your dog training skills in that time, and I'll rebuild that falling down boarding kennel. At least you won't be an embarrassment to the Corazon brand, and can look like a real professional."

Her jaw dropped open. "You'd do that?" Maybe he had changed. "Wait. What's the catch?"

He laughed. "Always so suspicious. Yes, I'd do that. You get to pick the dog, and I choose the evaluator. Friend of mine recommended September Day. She used to serve with the Chicago PD, but just lost her dog, and needs a new challenge. She's laid up from injuries, too, but agreed to mentor you with a list of commands and skills, since Abe Pesqueira is gone."

"Any dog?" Her pulse sped up as she watched the shepherd and Karma play-wrestle. "Six months? To train a police dog?" *Not enough time for Karma. But the shepherd. . .* Shadow already knew so much that it could give her a head start. "And if I fail the test?" She smiled. No way would she mess this up.

He didn't hesitate. "You put aside that pipe dream about dog training, and join the family business. Oh, and one more thing."

Here it comes. "What else, Grandfather?" She braced herself.

He spat the words. "No more questions about your father. I mean it, Lia. Try to find that *cabrón*, that bastard, and I'm done with you."

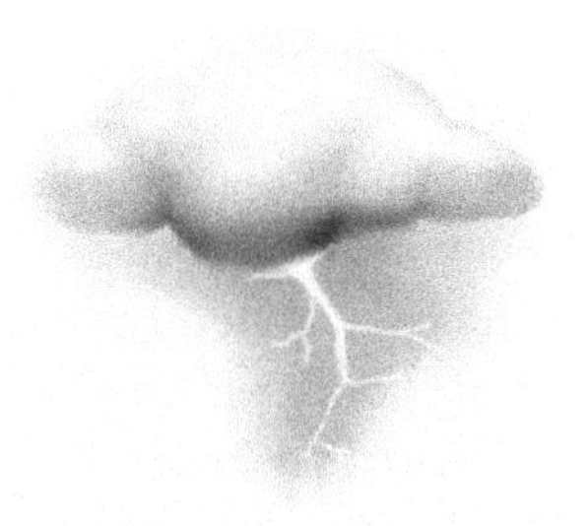

Chapter 29

Karma jumped again at the black shepherd, play-growling and feinting at Shadow's big paws. He pulled one paw away, and then the other, and then stood to get out of reach. Shadow growled, but Karma could tell he didn't mean it by the way his tail moved from side to side and his ears followed her movement.

She looked around, startled when Lia tossed something on the desk, and stood up with an exclamation. "Dammit. Should have known."

The girl's frustration and anger made Karma whine. She loped across the room to Lia, and without prompting, grabbed the girl's pant leg in her teeth and shook her head, hard. As expected, Lia laughed.

She'd figured out all by herself that making Lia laugh made them both feel better. Her short tail quivered and she rolled onto her back to ask for a tummy rub. Karma had become very fond of tummy rubs. The girl obliged, but had to sit in the chair before she could bend over and stroke Karma's chest.

Shadow ambled over, but instead of asking for attention from Lia, he cold nosed all of Karma's tender spots. That was his right, since he was bigger and older than she was. Karma managed to hold still a few seconds before she just had to snap at Shadow's muzzle so that he'd let her up. She might be young, but Karma was brave and in charge, and she let Shadow sniff because . . . Well, because he was Shadow. He'd even let her sniff him. Once. She licked the bigger dog's face.

"Grandfather put us on a deadline, so it's game on." Lia levered herself upright with a groan, and limped from the office into the kennel area.

Karma liked the *game* word, but she followed only a few steps. She whined at the door, leery of the scary place where trees fell through roofs and bad men made Lia cry. Karma remembered biting the bad man. It hadn't been as much fun as she thought.

Hearing *good-dog* was the best. When Lia called her *good-dog* it made Karma hungry to learn more, and more, and more. Maybe she'd learn as much as Shadow! Wouldn't that be fine?

At the happy thought, Karma bounced around the small room, chased her tail for three turns, and then looked up at Shadow. He wagged his tail again, then moved into a sudden forward bow, dancing each foreleg back and forth in clear invitation to play. His hurts had started to heal and his legs weren't shaky anymore.

Delighted, Karma agreed to join the game—dog games were as good as people games, even without treats—and the black shepherd leaped away, dodging her advances. He stumbled into the wooden step stool holding the broken door closed. It jarred a few inches, and the door cracked wider to allow cold wind to whistle inside.

Karma remembered the big yard with lots more room to run and sniff grass and play chase. Outside sniffs painted pictures inside her head of hidden furry creatures that promised contests Karma wanted to win. She yapped and pranced forward, sticking her blunt muzzle into the gap and levered the door open. Karma liked opening doors. She'd gotten very good at it. She trotted outside, head up to drink in the breeze, and noticed the fence didn't reach this far. With no barriers, the entire world of sounds and smells beckoned.

Lia came back into the room, and gasped when she saw Karma outside. "Wait!"

Shadow flinched like the word was a slap, but he pushed his way through the opening to join Karma. They stood shoulder to shoulder, and when Shadow walked toward the road, Karma couldn't resist following for a few paces.

"Please, *wait.*" Lia stood in the doorway. She took a limping step toward them but didn't come any further.

Karma wished the girl would chase them. Dogs could outran people with their pitiful two legs, and Lia still limped from her hurts. Even so, Karma never tired of the game. She looked back at Lia, and barked, tail quivering at the thought of the chase game to come.

But the shepherd kept walking. Even with his injuries, Karma knew Shadow could outrun her. She took two steps after him, but sudden thunder made Karma yelp. She remembered the snakes, the sky flashes, and the hungry flood, and outside adventure lost its appeal. She wanted to squat-and-pee, but didn't.

Because she was Karma! A brave good-dog. So she squared her shoulders, like Shadow, and ignored the prickled sensation of raised hackles she couldn't control. She wanted to be with him, to follow him.

She didn't want Shadow to go. Karma barked again.

He paused. Karma wriggled with delight when he padded back toward her. They nose-touched and she licked his chin. And then he grasped Karma in his massive jaws, and push-carried her back to Lia's feet, and left her there.

Karma let him, relaxed and trusting. Because he was Shadow.

Lia knelt and gathered Karma to her, with her uninjured arm.

No! Shadow couldn't leave her behind. Karma struggled, and yelped, wanting to reach him.

The girl held out her injured hand to him. An invitation.

Shadow stared into Lia's face for a long moment. Her eyes widened, and she half smiled with sad recognition as if hearing a whispered farewell. Then he moved forward for one more nose-touch with Karma. Shadow whirled, dashed to the muddy, flooded road, and limped away.

Lia stood for a long moment in the doorway, staring after the mysterious warrior dog. She called into the night, "*Aloha `oe.* Safe journey home, and *mahalo.*" She sat down in in the doorway and pulled Karma onto her lap with soft whispered words and gentle touches. "My brave Karma-girl, I'm so sorry. But Shadow doesn't need us anymore. He has someone waiting for him, and has to find his own way home. And so do we."

Karma licked the girl's face, tasting salty wet that rained from Lia's eyes. She whimpered, and licked Lia again. It didn't hurt so bad once she realized they shared the same hurt. Because they were together.

This time she didn't struggle. Karma welcomed the girl's embrace. People were confusing, but she'd figured out what hugs meant, when they came from a good-dog's person. Love.

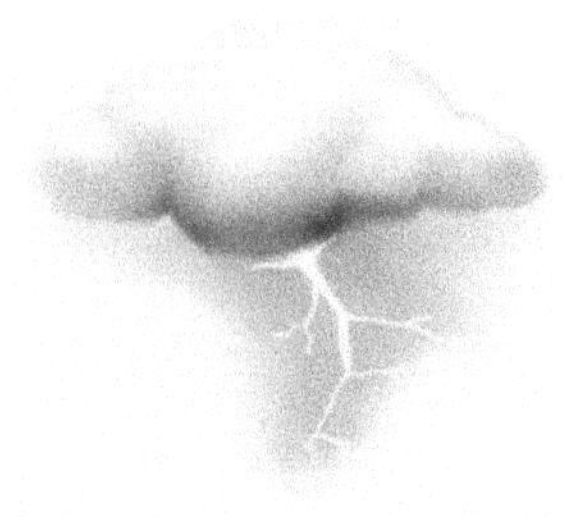

Chapter 30

"Mom, can I borrow your car?" September stood beside the polished marble countertop, feeling about fifteen years old. It sucked not having a car. Or a house.

"Sit down. Eat your breakfast, dear, you're thin as a rail. It's only been a few days, and the doctors made me promise you'd rest." She poured coffee into two delicate china cups, and carried them to the table.

September drank hers in three swallows. She grimaced at Mom's frown of disapproval. "I drink two full pots of coffee every morning. You know that." She retrieved the coffee carafe, refilled her tiny cup, and set both on the table before taking her seat. "I'll get a big coffee mug when I go out."

Little things, like losing her favorite *#1 Bitch* coffee mug, continued to remind her of how much she'd lost. "I need to pick up my cello from the theater, and want to visit Macy at the vet. Since you won't let me bring him here."

Her cat and the cello were all she had left.

"You know I'm allergic." Mom sipped her coffee, and toyed with her eggs Benedict. Rose's allergies excused anything she didn't like.

"I need the car all morning. It's my spa day, and I'm visiting Steven to talk about the newspaper feature. My grandson, the hero! He's so talented, but then all my grandchildren are special." She chattered on, enraptured by the notion he'd saved another boy with his computer skills.

Yes, he found the boy, and not Shadow. She hid ready tears behind another jolt of coffee. She had to accept the painful reality that Shadow was gone.

"I could stop by the theater on the way home, I suppose." Mom took a bite of egg, chewed exactly six times, and swallowed. "Perhaps Steven will want to visit the director. He's so handsome, don't you think? We're very fortunate to have such a talent here in Heartland. It's a shame you'll miss the closing weekend performances." She offered a tight smile.

The old refrain ran unspoken beneath Mom's chatter. September wasn't married. September preferred animals to kids. Two strikes. And she'd denied her musical gifts—well, until Mom convinced her to try again. So count that two strikes and a half.

"Guess I'll ask Dad when he gets home." He'd understand. She'd ask him to take her to get a new car.

That stopped the flow of words for a moment before Mom caught her breath, reset, and babbled on. "He needs his car for work. Really, September, what's your hurry? Heavens, I'd think you'd welcome some downtime after everything you've been through. Might be time to think about getting a real job. After all, Steven doesn't need a service dog anymore." *And neither should you*, she implied.

"Like you don't need a sister anymore?" The words came out of their own volition. "I didn't even know you had a sister."

Mom's smooth brow furrowed, and lips pressed into a thin white line. One fluttering hand went to her throat. "I'm not talking with you about this." She stood, grabbed her half-eaten breakfast, and carried it to the sink.

"Why not?" Hurt fueled her words. September followed, carrying her own uneaten meal. Mom knew she preferred plain Jane scrambled eggs, not these pretentious restaurant recipes. Everything with Mom had to do with appearances. Her home, her family, her looks, all orchestrated to seem perfect to the outside world. September's recent public strife reflected badly, but now a secret sister appeared. Maybe Rose wasn't perfect after all. "What happened between you and Aunt Cornelia?"

"It's none of your business!" Mom grabbed the plate and dropped in the sink, then grasped the edge of the counter, her breathing heavy. "None of it matters anymore. It's a dead issue, and has nothing to do with you." She straightened, smoothing her hair. She painted on a forced smile. "I need to get ready. Please straighten up for me?" Without meeting September's eyes, Mom flounced out of the kitchen, kitten heels clicking on the tile.

September rinsed the plates, ran the disposal and loaded the dishwasher. She drank two more tiny cups of coffee before rummaging in the cupboard and finding a soup mug to use instead.

Her phone rang again. She'd already declined answering the orchestra director twice this morning. September answered without looking. "My mom says she'll pick up Harmony later today."

"Who? Is that you, September?"

"Combs, oh it's you. Sorry." With a clink, she managed to place her makeshift mug on the counter when her hand started to tremble. "My cello, Harmony, is still over at the theater. The orchestra director keeps calling, twice already this morning."

"Oh, right."

"How are you? I mean, have you had any rest at all? The news reports massive damage all over the county." September hadn't been back to her house yet. She needed to figure out whether to repair, rebuild or relocate. Much would depend on the state of the building, and what insurance would pay. "Mom and Dad's house had a couple broken windows and may need new shingles, but otherwise, they were lucky."

September also had to figure out if she wanted to stay in Heartland. Little held her here. Mom would be happier with September out of town, out of sight and out of the limelight that tarnished her family's reputation.

"It'll be months before things get back to normal, if they ever do." He paused, and added, "How's life with Mom and Dad?"

She snorted. "Just as you'd expect." But at least she'd suffered no flashbacks. Stress and memories triggered the attacks, and boy, could Mom pour on the stress. So did Combs, but in a different way. September knew he wanted more from her, but the past made her suspicious of everyone's motives. She wanted to trust him. Until she could get a new car and find a place for her and Macy, she'd grin and bear living with her folks.

Combs cleared his throat. "I've got some good news."

Her heart thrummed, but then settled as he continued.

"They found Sunny Babcock trying to cross into Mexico."

"Oh wow. She survived." The killer escaped the flood, when poor Shadow drowned rescuing the innocent. "Listen, this is hard for me, but I have to ask you something."

"September, I can't talk details about open investigations."

"No, not about that." She pushed coffee color hair out of her eyes. She winced when her hand touched the still tender bald spot at the crown. "It's about volunteering me to train that police dog."

"Lia Corazon's puppy? September, I didn't volunteer you to do anything. But I do owe you an apology." She could imagine him cracking his knuckles as he paced back and forth. "Uncle Stanley found out about your experience with police dogs when we needed his help with that investigation last November."

"Oh." Combs lost his mom—Uncle Stanley's sister—last Thanksgiving in the debacle where she'd first met the detective. "You didn't volunteer me? Then how come Mr. Corazon—"

"They're friends, and Corazon called him for a favor. And then Uncle Stanley called me. I agreed to pass on the info, that's all." His tone turned dark. "Corazon saw you at the hospital and beat me to the punch."

The tension in her neck evaporated. He hadn't shared her secrets with strangers. Working with the police department gave her the sense of worth and purpose she'd needed at the time, and brought her first dog. Everyone had secrets, private horrors they kept locked away.

Before she could reply, Combs spoke again. "Let me make it up to you. Please. I meant no harm. Let me take you to dinner, okay?"

She grinned. "You mean, a real date? A for real, dress-up adult-type date? Why sir, I think we're way overdue." She disconnected and continued to smile as Mom came back into the room.

"Did I hear right? You've got a date? With that nice orchestra director." Mom fairly clapped her hands with excitement.

September laughed. "You heard right, I've got a date." If Rose wanted to keep old painful secrets, then September figured she deserved a happy new secret.

"Well then, hurry up, you're coming with me. It's spa day, and my treat. We've got to do something with your hair."

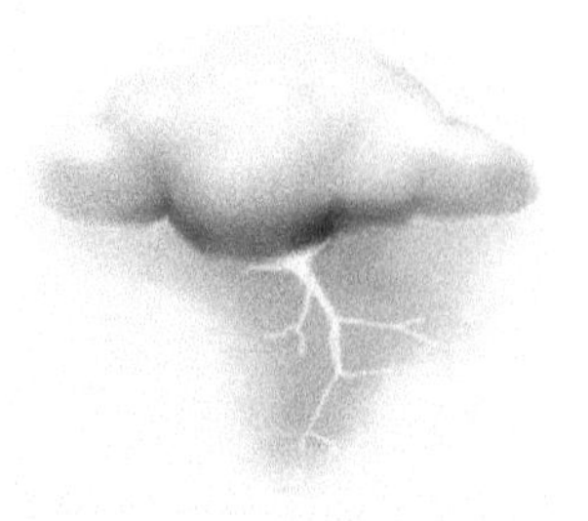

Chapter 31

Shadow limped in fits and starts down the road. His hurts kept him tethered to a slow trudging pace. Moon glow lit the path ahead, and the sky noise had stopped, but water still overflowed pathways that forced detours along the way.

He wasn't sure of the way, just that he must get away from Karma and the girl. Both treated him with kindness, and Shadow felt stronger with food in his belly. He knew that the girl wanted him to stay, and he liked her well enough. But he belonged with September. He'd tried to wait but she hadn't come for him, so he must go to her. September might be hurt, too, so it was up to a good-dog to take care of family. Only by finding her would the achy spot deep inside be soothed. At the thought, Shadow whined low in his throat, and then shook himself, hard, to focus his purpose.

He must pace onward, slow to a walk if needed, but place one paw forward time after time. Head down, tongue lolling, eyes half closed, but moving, always moving onward toward home.

Now and then, Shadow paused to look up at the night sky, and adjusted his path. Shadow didn't think about why, it just felt right. He moved in wide concentric sweeps, in the same way he'd track the missing, and adjusted each sweep deeper toward his goal. By the time the sun streaks chased clouds from the sky, he'd traveled far from Lia and Karma.

No cars met him on the car-path, either. Shadow liked cars. They moved much faster than a dog could run. Many trees along the way blocked the path, though, and Shadow didn't think cars could climb over and around the way dogs could. Strangers sometimes gave tired dogs a ride, but they often took dogs the wrong way. When Shadow heard a car come near, he hurried off the shoulder and hid in the damp underbrush. Men got out, and hooked lines to fallen trees to bully limbs out of the roadway. They ate smelly sandwiches while they worked. Shadow licked his lips at the bacon scent, but he made no sound until they went away. Better that he keep going on his own than risk being driven farther away from September.

He limped a couple of steps, and stopped to lick and nibble burrs from between two toes. His empty tummy grumbled. Shadow drooled at the memory of the treats Lia offered freely, but a different, deeper hunger drove him on. He never rested for long, and pushed beyond exhaustion. Home beckoned.

Shadow stopped to quench his thirst from a roadside puddle. He flushed a flock of birds picking at something, and they scattered in the wind. The birds cursed him, and he hunched shoulders against their static, but wasted no energy returning their cries. September didn't like it when he found dead creatures. He always rolled on them, but September wasn't here to say "drop it." He sniffed the rich leavings, wrinkling his lips.

Before he could gulp down the gift, fur and all, another creature rushed him, snarling and vicious. Before his tired reflexes could save him, the coyote grappled his shoulder and neck, reopening the recent wounds. Shadow screamed, and recoiled, but the more experienced predator scooped up the pungent squirrel and sprinted away. Lesson learned, Shadow moved on, wasting no further energy on the lost cause.

By late in the day, he'd swept back and forth dozens of times in a many-mile zigzag pattern plodding always in an easterly path. The sun had fallen to the horizon when the breeze changed. Shadow's head came up, ears twitching at the familiar sound carried by the wind. There! Again it sounded, pure and real, a beacon he'd sought all along.

The tracking pattern no longer needed, Shadow set off cross-country to reach home as soon as possible. He picked up the pace, forgetting the pain in his bruised paws, and huffed and panted faster and faster. Whines came faster, too. Shadow couldn't help it. He smelled home! He heard home! September waited for him! She'd be at the front door, open her arms, call him "good-dog", and smooth his ears. He cried with longing.

Through the last field, Shadow dodged past regiments of cedar trees that blocked the view of the big house guarded by the strong metal gate. He barked, and barked again, but his voice failed him. He raced to reach the house.

It looked different. He stopped with a whimper, cocking his head from side to side. The moon shine turned the scene to dark and light, and everything familiar turned inside out.

The metal gate hung askew. The roof no longer covered the house, and brick tumbled down one wall and across the front lawn. An open front door yawned like a hungry mouth without teeth, making Shadow shiver when he realized the house stood split in two, leaving the inside open to the weather. The smaller building for the car was gone, too, scrubbed clean by wind and rain.

Shadow crept closer, fearful the clear sky might again throw trees at a good-dog. He sniffed the broken gate, and picked his way with care through the scattered debris. Shivers wracked his body when he climbed the steps to the open front door, testing the air inside before daring to cross the threshold.

Nobody met him at the door. Smells of many strangers teased the air, making the fur on Shadow's hackles bristle with alarm. He padded into the house and up the stairs to the sleep-room he shared with September. But the stairs ended midway up. He scrambled back down, taking another route through the jumbled office furniture to reach the kitchen. Here, three walls still stood, the fourth open into the back garden where the scent of roses floated in the moist air. The clank and clatter of wind chime music, the beacon calling him home, still moved and danced in the breeze.

In this room, he could still detect traces of September, and of Macy-cat. The stale scents, though, told of days gone by. Shadow's home sat empty, abandoned. So he pushed his way past chairs and the stained glass kitchen table that had somehow been moved outside onto the grass. Maybe September waited for him outside in the garden. They'd spent many hours together digging in the dirt.

One of the roses hung down from the sliver of roof that remained, transplanted by the storm. Had September been uprooted and thrown somewhere she didn't belong?

Purpose renewed but energy flagging, Shadow stumbled through the jumble of house parts and tree limbs to reach the fence that enclosed the perimeter of the property. Each morning, he and September patrolled the fence line, making sure no danger lurked. He'd been gone for a long time, and needed to do his job. Maybe once she knew everything was safe, September would come home, too. He'd found his way home and how his job was to guard the house until she returned.

Shadow ranged up and down the fence line, first on the inside and then on the outside of the metal barrier. Where the garden had been dug up, rain turned the ground into muddy slurry that made a good-dog slip. The cold bit deep into Shadow's bruised paws, and he grew more and more frustrated and worried.

He was alone. He howled his grief, the yodel trailing off in the night air. Shadow barked and howled until his voice gave out. When exhaustion overtook him, he curled up in a dry spot beneath a rose bush, slept. By morning, fever set in. He found puddles to drink, but never moved out of sight of the ravaged house, in case September appeared. The third day, Shadow retreated into shivery dreams where September's voice filled his heart with hope.

He awakened a start and struggled to sit up when a man's voice roused him from fevered visions. Guard the house, he needed to protect their home. Another voice, oh joy! September's low voice joined the man's. Maybe not a dream after all?

Shadow tried to yelp, to bark, to announce his presence. His voice failed. Shivers made it hard to move. September was here! His legs refused to take him to her.

"Did you hear that?"

It was her! Shadow again pushed against the sodden earth, but his legs refused to lift him. Breathing hurt, but he sucked in a great lungful and pushed out all the hurt, longing, and love in a gasping hoarse howl. *I am here, here HERE!*

September's familiar footfalls stumbled near, falling and getting up, racing closer and closer. He whimpered and cried, a gurgling strangled plea. She'd come for him, hadn't left him behind, September had returned!

"I'm coming, I'm coming!" Music to his ears, even as her sobs matched Shadow's own.

He levered himself upright, and braced himself against the fence to keep from falling. Tail shouted his joy. And then she was there, only the fence between them. Shadow tried to force his way through to reach her, and warbled his happiness with garbled, heart-breaking gasps.

September dropped to her knees as close as she could get. "Oh baby-dog, my sweet boy." She pushed her arms through the fence, trying to hold him, to touch him, but the bars kept them apart. Her hand came back red with blood. "He's hurt."

Combs grabbed her waist and lifted her, and she struggled. "No, no, no I can't leave him; we have to get him help." And he set her down on the other side of the fence.

Then her arms were around Shadow. He burrowed his head into her neck, licking her face, tail bruising them both. Bliss.

And Combs had leaped the fence. "I'm not leaving either of you." His strong arms encircled them both. "You're my family. This is where we begin."

PART 2 TRAINED to SERVE
(*August*)

Chapter 32

Lia Corazon squinted against the bright August sun as she watched Karma fidget near the gate. She slapped at mosquitoes that haloed her frizzy goldenrod hair, but Karma didn't seem bothered. She grinned, knowing the *bleib* (stay) cue posed one of the greatest challenges for the ten-month-old Rottweiler. Karma's stubby tail stood erect, and she already had begun distance scenting in short, staccato bursts. "No cheating, baby-girl. *Bleib!*"

They'd trained each day for the past six months, and the young dog enjoyed every minute. Lia not so much. To Karma everything was fun and games, treats and sniffs. But Grandfather's deadline loomed, and how they performed in three days for the test—Lia's training, and Karma's skill—would determine their future.

K9 service dogs trained forever. She'd learned that Rotties weren't a common choice for the police, but their versatility, strength, drive and devotion made them adaptable and a good match for the right partner. The athletic breed, descended from ancient Roman cattle dogs interbred with Swiss and German mastiffs, could hunt bear or play with the kids, guard cattle and then share a beloved human's pillow. Only the elite with the best temperament and physique were suited for the rigors of protection, military or police work. Karma was one in a million, at least in Lia's eyes.

The rash of freak tornadoes last February derailed Lia's dream of opening Corazon Kennels. Injuries from her run-in with a client selling dogs to a fight ring delayed her return to work. She'd contacted September Day, the dog trainer Grandfather recommended, but they'd both sustained injuries and property damage, which delayed collaboration. Their interaction had been limited to emails and Skype conference calls since Lia's broken wrist took weeks to heal, impeding her ability to train the powerful dog. She still had intermittent problems with tinnitus from the concussion, but at least her broken ribs no longer hurt. Well, not unless she bumped them the wrong way.

Losing income from the spring break boarding fees put another nail in the coffin. Most of her clients agreed to a last-minute pet-sitting arrangement with Lia trekking several times a day to each individual household. That left her exhausted, and the funds still weren't enough. Without income or insurance to rebuild, Lia had no choice but to accept Grandfather's challenge: train a dog to police K9 standards in six months and he'd fund her dream. Fail, and come home to work for him.

"Good girl, Karma. We'll start the game soon."

Karma trembled with excitement, and whined under her breath at the "game" word, but didn't break her seated position. Extra challenges kept Karma engaged, and delaying the scent game made her eager to start. Nothing killed training faster than boredom.

Her success rested with Karma. The mother dog and Karma's siblings were evidence and had been confiscated by the police with the arrest of the dogfight ring principals. The last she'd heard, September conducted temperament evaluation on them, in the hopes they might be rehomed, but Lia was afraid to ask what had become of them. At least Grandfather had pulled strings to let her keep the pick of the litter. When Karma's training helped save Lia from Derek's attempt on her life, Grandfather's disapproval thawed enough for him to at least make that possible.

The glamor of belonging to the Corazon dynasty wore thin with the hobbling demands of her grandparents. She'd her fill of mucking out horse stalls by the time she graduated to training yearlings. In between Grandfather's character-building work demands, Grammy smothered Lia with society commitments. Of the two, she preferred mucking out stalls. The older she got, the better Lia understood why her mother ran away from home.

Nevertheless, she'd stuck to the family's plan until two years ago, and dropped out of college to pursue her passion. Her first mentor, Abe Tesquiera, sold his business to Lia before he died. He'd had faith in her, and Lia's success training Karma honored his memory as much as it validated her dream.

In the nearby corral, Fury kicked up his heels and cantered around the perimeter, dragging a long rein on the ground. He'd pulled the line free, telling her in no uncertain terms he wanted attention and needed a good run. "We've already been out once today." Early this morning, she declined the daily ride with Grandfather and Grammy to instead set up Karma's practice track in the test field. She'd enjoyed the slow amble with Fury and tied him nearby to offer more distractions for Karma to overcome. But not like this.

Lia smiled. Abe used to say, "Use every situation to train. Dogs learn constantly." And if you didn't guide the smart ones, they'd learn to do stuff you didn't want them to do.

Abe trained his Bouvier, Thor, to herd cattle, and Lia inherited the dog along with Abe's kennel. Thor lived only a few weeks after they moved to the Corazon homestead, but they were happy days for the old guy. Thor switched "on" around livestock and the years fell away. He lived to round up and bring in the horses. Grandfather liked the dog so much, he asked Lia to look into getting a ranch dog for the stables. The place was already thick with cats.

When Thor brought in the horses, Karma had watched with great interest. Lia hadn't pursued the dog's herding skill. Maybe she should refresh the notion.

"Karma, come." Karma's pent up excitement exploded into motion. Her rear paws left deep gouges in the loose dirt beside the arena gate. She skidded into a sit in front of Lia, panting and whining with excitement for the next cue.

Lia kicked herself; she'd not used the German command employed by most police K9 teams. She needed to be consistent with cues but forgot herself more often than not. She hoped trainer error wouldn't penalize Karma's performance. Maybe they'd get points if Karma was bilingual.

The precocious pup mastered the basics by sixteen weeks: sit, down, wait, come. Lia transitioned the dog to German and now

Karma understood and responded to three forms of verbal cues: English, German, and hand signals. Abe used whistles to train herding, and Karma was reliable with the whistle recall. Today, they'd practice yet another type of cue, until it became automatic.

Lia smiled at Karma's eagerness and ability. Most dogs didn't have enough concentration for effective police training before at least a year old. She'd planned to train the mysterious shepherd she'd rescued from the flood, but Shadow had other ideas. Lia hoped he'd found his way home.

So she trained Karma. To be this focused at ten months gave her hope. Given the time constraints, Lia concentrated on patrol training. That included obedience that every dog should know, plus agility—police dogs needed to be athletes—and now tracking. Further scent discrimination skills would be important for evidence searches, including the ability to match a potential suspect to a weapon or other object used in a crime. Some police service dogs were adept at finding lost people like children or Alzheimer's victims, or specialized in narcotics or explosives detection. They trained dual-purpose K9 officers, the "super dogs," to excel at everything.

She couldn't yet tell Karma's best fit. Her youthful energy and innovative problem solving kept Lia smiling, though.

Karma's mind worked in unexpected ways. Every once in a while, Lia got just a glimpse of the whispery mind-tickle insight she'd first experienced with Shadow. Maybe, just maybe, the special talent resided within her rather than the *koa* warrior dog, but she hadn't a clue how to develop it further. Or if she should. Abe used to say that trainers got the dogs they *needed*, not the ones they *wanted*. Special gifts must be the same, since she'd learned as much or more from Karma as she had taught the dog.

It helped that Karma lived for treats, but the pup responded even better to Lia's approval. Smart dogs challenged the best trainers because they often "knew better," but those also were ideal dogs for service fields. Sweet and biddable dogs obeyed without question. Dogs like Karma needed to know when to use their own judgment. Selective disobedience could save a human partner's life or get the job done.

But first, a new challenge. Lia couldn't wait to see what the dog would do—Karma always had her own way of doing things. "Karma, *bring*!" She waved at Fury.

Chapter 33

Karma sprang to her feet, leaped forward and then slowed her gait as she neared the corral where the big animal lived. She had great respect for the creature. Horses were much bigger and faster than dogs. Even faster than Karma. She'd never met another creature that ran so fast.

She knew immediately what Lia wanted. It was a good-dog's job to please Lia. She wondered, though, why Lia didn't just tell the horse to *come*, the way she did Karma. Maybe Fury didn't know the *come* word. Karma knew lots of words, though, and *bring* was a favorite. It meant the same thing as *fetch*.

Karma reached the fence, and squeezed under the lowest rung. She had to duck since she'd gotten so big, and watched when Lia trotted to the gate and cracked it open to squeeze through.

Fury wore a heavy leather pad on his back, and long flappy things bounced on each side. He tossed his head, dancing and prancing around the area when he saw Karma. A second long line fell from the harness on his head, dragging in the loose soil.

Karma knew about harnesses. She wore a harness and special collar during scent tracking games, and Lia attached a long tether to her shoulders. Karma noticed a coiled rope hung on the fence rail right next to Lia's perch. Maybe after she fetched Fury, Lia would play the tracking game. Wouldn't that be fine!

Now, though, Karma had a job to do. She trotted out to the giant animal, keeping her ears tight to her head and out of horse teeth range. The big feet had hard sharp edges that could hurt a dog, too. Karma knew Fury wouldn't run over her, not on purpose, but didn't want to give him a chance. She'd watched old Thor move horses the same way dogs moved each other, by claiming space. Every creature, from dogs to horses and even the skittery cat creatures Karma liked to chase from the barn, all had personal space surrounding them they needed to protect. Move into that private bubble, and dogs adjusted away from the encroachment.

Horse space, though, was different than dog space, or cat space. Or people space. Karma wanted to puzzle more about it. Not now, though. Doing her job meant fetching Fury to Lia.

Karma stepped into the pathway Fury trod. She stood steady, staring at the creature and waiting for the horse to finish his circuit. As the animal approached, Karma play-bowed, the stub of her tail wiggling while her front paws danced in the dust.

Fury slowed, stopped and whirled, snorting and rolling his eyes. The reins flapped free.

Following at a lope, Karma pressed closer to the horse, not physically touching him but encroaching on personal space. As expected, Fury reacted, shying away and turning the other direction. Panting with happiness, Karma enjoyed the game, making the animal go fast or change direction. She got so caught up in the fun she forgot the original fetch request.

"Karma, *bring*! Quit playing with him!" Lia's reminder brought her up short.

She loved to make Fury move back and forth. Karma's forehead creased with concentration, scoping out what position to press so the horse would go to Lia. The reins flapped again in the dirt, and her forehead smoothed with sudden understanding.

Why waste time and energy running circles around a silly horse that didn't even understand the word *come*? Karma waited for the moving horse to lap the corral again, and this time when he came close, she grabbed the rein.

What fun! Karma congratulated herself when her grip caused Fury to stop and whirl. She backed way, turning the fetch-cue into a tug-game. The horse stretched out his neck, blew out loud breath, and only then gave way and followed the dog.

Karma led the horse to where Lia sat perched on the top rail of the fence, mouth open. Karma sat, signaling completion of her task as she held the rein in her mouth and waited for the release word.

Two riders cantered up to the fence on their own mounts. Lia wobbled, and grabbed for balance, but Karma never dropped the rein, even when Fury reared back and dragged her a couple of feet. She just dug in her paws.

"What the hell you doing there, Lia-girl? And what's that dog doing with Fury?"

Chapter 34

"Grandfather!" Lia jumped off her perch, and hurried to collect the rein from the dog. "Karma, sit. Stay. I mean, *bleib*." Dammit, Grandfather always left her flustered. "Back early from your ride? Where's Grammy?" She breathed again with pride when Karma complied. She raised questioning eyebrows at the stranger riding Grammy's old chestnut. He white-knuckled the saddle horn to keep from sliding off.

"Cornelia has a hair appointment for the big shindig tonight." The stately man with snow-white hair sat his champion bay stallion with the pride of a Spanish conquistador.

Lia hunched her shoulders. She'd forgotten about the party.

"Hey Dub, could I get a hand here?" The little man began to tilt, and she saw his feet weren't even in the stirrups. He managed to right himself before he fell.

"Oh, this is Mr. Kanoa, a possible future business associate. He's visiting from out of state. Antonio, that's my granddaughter, Lia. And her police dog." Grandfather removed his straw cowboy hat to mop his brow before replacing it.

Kanoa lifted a hand to wave, and then dropped it to clutch the saddle horn again. Lia hid a smile.

Grandfather swung off his big bay, and held the chestnut mare's head while Kanoa scrambled to dismount. But he directed his words to Lia. "Tell me again why your dog's messing with Fury? That can't be part of police dog training, and I won't abide a dog chasing livestock for fun."

"No, she wouldn't do that. Karma just, well, she improvised when I asked her to fetch the horse." When she heard her name, Karma closed her panting mouth, and tipped her head as she looked from the big man to Lia and back again. Lia fidgeted, playing with her bracelet out of habit. "We'll get back to training now. Mr. Kanoa, nice to meet you."

"Pleasure, Ms. Corazon." He retrieved a shiny cigarette case before noticing Grandfather's scowl, and slipped it back into a pocket without lighting up. "Right, I'll meet you back at the house." He scurried away, shiny shoes kicking up dust in his wake.

Grandfather stared after. "Funny little guy. Friend of a friend asked me to host him while he's in town. Kanoa is in the import-export business and has clients interested in horses." He smiled, and his face lit up. "Not that he'd recognize a quality horse if it bit him." When he smiled, Lia could see a shadow of the dashing brash immigrant who, with his Spanish bride, started an equine empire more than fifty years ago.

"Want me to take care of them? So you can have some quality time with Mr. Kanoa?" She dared to inject a teasing lilt, and grinned at his barking laugh.

"Thanks, Lia-girl. But you got work to do yourself." He held out his hand for Fury's rein, and then led all three horses to the nearby barn. She knew he enjoyed the after-care of brushing, cleaning hooves and simply communing with the animals as much as riding them.

She loved horses, too. Just not as much as dogs. "Good *bleib,* Karma! Ready to get back to work?" Lia waited a moment, delighted when the dog didn't make a move from her stay-position. Karma wriggled in place, but waited for the release word. She'd chosen something unique, so Karma wouldn't be miscued by an inadvertent uttering of something like *okay* used so much in everyday language. So she used thank you, but in Hawaiian, a nod to her own roots. "Karma, *mahalo*!"

The dog's powerful haunches launched her into the air, and Lia laughed at Karma's antics. The word fit Karma's personality. The big dog ran a full circuit of the corral before returning to Lia's side, and then surprised her by leaping up and grabbing the coil of rope suspended from the gate. She tugged, loosened one end, and continued unraveling the line on her way back toward the practice paddock.

Karma often used the ploy to get her way. She wanted to move on from the confinement and structure of the paddock drills, and work on the longline, tracking. Lia smiled, delighted by Karma's eagerness. But the drills were still important.

During a tracking exercise, Karma knew to lie down, or "*platz*," to indicate she'd found the item. Lia needed the action to be automatic, and triggered by scent.

They hurried back to the paddock, Lia put Karma back into a sit-stay, and again coiled the tracking line. More than a dozen different objects sat around the arena, but only four—a glove, a rag, a shallow bowl, and a shoe—were targets. She didn't want to use the same search item each time, or Karma might think the prize was always a glove, for example.

Her training mentor specialized in tracking. September told Lia the object wasn't important, just the scent mattered, so she'd worn gloves to place all the objects except the targets. Those she'd handled and even spit on to imbue them with her scent.

Beneath each of the four targets, September told her to place a dried liver treat. "They don't smell too strong, and you want your dog to focus on human scent, not finding treats," she explained. The treats reinforced the notion that scent cued Karma's "successful find" signal. Eventually, the scent of the find would prompt her to lie down, no treat reminder needed.

Lia took a breath, offered Karma her hand for a scent to match, and then gave the search command. "Karma, *such*!"

Karma took off, running from box to ceramic pot, around to a coiled garden hose and on to a stack of bricks with a glove on top. Her first *platz* announced the glove's find. Karma nosed the glove off the bricks, and slurped up the liver treat without breaking her position.

"Good girl, Karma!" Lia encouraged her, but didn't offer the expected release word. The dog was used to a single target, but during trials there might be many such finds. Lia needed to keep Karma focused and her drive revved up, to continue beyond the first target. "Karma, *such*."

Karma sprang to her feet, and again hurried from spot to spot, snuffling and testing each for the next scented target. She quickly found the bowl, balanced on a fence rail. She knocked it over to collect the treat and in the same motion she lay down. Karma looked over her shoulder to Lia, and before *such* escaped her lips, the dog took off. She alerted to the rag and the shoe each in turn, and completed the exercise in less than three minutes.

The accelerated training schedule wasn't ideal, but so far, Karma hadn't missed a paw-step. "What a good-dog, you're so silly. *Mahalo*."

Karma bounced up from her final find, tossing the shoe in the air, and then racing around the paddock as she had with Fury. Once again she zeroed in on the long tracking line looped over the fence, pawing and mouthing it with determination.

"Okay, okay. I get it, you want to keep going." Lia knelt beside the pup, smoothing her silk-soft coat and marveling at the muscles. "Let's get you watered first, and then I've got chores to do. It's already hot, and I don't want either of us stroking out. Patience, baby-dog, we'll run the course this afternoon once it cools off."

***

Lia glanced overhead, grateful for the shade that knocked ten degrees off the temperature, even if the overhead leaves looked more brown than green. Wind made a rattlesnake sound through the brittle vegetation. She'd need another water break soon, Karma more than Lia. It had taken them much longer to get to the start point than when she'd ridden Fury out to set up the trails earlier in the day. She wished she could afford a cooling vest for Karma.

After the test, once Karma passed and proved her worth to Grandfather, funding extras would be available. They could continue training with better equipment, while she rebuilt her business. Lia licked her cracked lips and smoothed long flyaway hair the wind combed free.

The big pup tugged the tracking line in Lia's gloved hands. The 102-degree August weather argued against gloves, but Lia had learned the hard way to protect her skin from the powerful dog's pull. Rope burn on your palms took forever to heal.

Wearing a bright purple collar with built-in GPS as well as the tracking harness, Karma led the way. She towed Lia's slender form, weaving through lush stands of Johnson grass and the canopy of cedar elm and bois d'arc. Lia reminded herself to do a tick scan once they finished today's exercise. North Texas swarmed with too many disease-causing parasites that sickened both dogs and people.

Karma hesitated, and cast back and forth, sniffing deep and wiffering the air in and out. Lia held still, not wanting to offer an inadvertent signal which direction the track continued. She hadn't said a word since giving Karma the *such* command at the beginning of the course, but now offered quiet encouragement. "Good-dog, Karma. Good *such*."

The dog turned and proceeded forward at a right angle to the previous route and Lia couldn't quell a grin. The first object, a ball cap, rested behind a massive cedar tree just over a slight rise and to the left. Karma made a beeline for the cap. Lia trotted to keep up, letting the dog tug her forward. Lordy, it was hotter than chili peppers in Grammy's special sauce.

The Rottweiler ran to the ball cap, sniffed once, and flopped onto her belly.

"Good girl, Karma! What a smart girl, good *platz*, you're so good!" Lia hurried to reach Karma, smiling again when the young dog flipped the cap and snarfed up the hidden liver treat. Karma looked up at Lia, panting with a wide Rottie grin, but not at all relaxed. Her muscles bunched and twitched beneath tight black fur, and she whined under her breath. She was ready.

Lia retrieved the ball cap, brushed the cedar needles and bugs off, and put it on. She'd hidden the last object, one of Karma's favorite toys, only a short distance away. Lia wanted the dog to end on a high note, so beneath the Frisbee she'd hidden half a handful of liver treats. She gathered up the long line and repeated the cue Karma trembled with eagerness to hear.

"*Such*! Karma, *such*!"

Powerful haunches propelled Karma forward, and the explosive motion caught Lia by surprise. The energy, the drive, everything she wanted in the Rottweiler came alive. But Karma drove in the wrong direction.

Hiding her deep disappointment, Lia trotted to keep up. She didn't want to dampen Karma's drive or delight. Lia remembered Abe's words. *"Trust the dog. Dogs always know things we don't."*

Like a squirrel, she thought.

Karma stopped and flopped to her belly so fast that Lia tripped over her. The dog looked at Lia and whined. She didn't bark. Rotties "grew into" their voice, and some didn't become alert-barkers before two or three years old. But her wrinkled brow signaled Karma's unease, as if she knew she'd disappointed Lia in some way. Karma turned back to her find and nosed the bundle of half-buried rags tangled in the space between her paws.

Lia tried to stay upbeat, but couldn't deny her frustration. "Good girl, Karma. You've had enough for the day." She'd rushed the dog, couldn't blame the pup. *At least she gave me a platz.* Then Karma lifted her nose, and howled, sending chills down Lia's sweaty neck.

When Karma shifted, Lia saw the human hand.

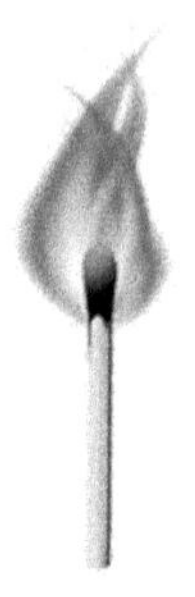

Chapter 35

Karma whimpered again and nosed the cold hand. She flinched when Lia cried out, but didn't move from her position. Lia hadn't said *mahalo* yet, so she knew the game wasn't done. A good-dog worked hard to please her person. Treats were good and she knew treats awaited at the end of the other trail Lia meant her to follow. But this scent, this trail, this find compelled her to follow, and trumped any amount of treats. Now Karma wondered if she'd made the right choice. She'd trade them all for a smile and *good-dog* from Lia.

She licked her jowls and panted, but the heat made it hard to cool off. Karma's hackles still bristled in response to the scent around the body. The clothes reeked of girl fear, but also early changes of decomposition. She'd found dead animals before. Amazing rich and enticing scents clung to the road kill Karma retrieved as treasured toys, or even rolled on to perfume herself with a dead possum's essence. She'd been the one to find Thor when he died. But this was different. This was people.

People could stop breathing and die, too. The thought confounded Karma, and she whimpered again. She remembered when a bad man hurt Lia. If Karma hadn't protected her, Lia might be like this dead girl. Karma didn't want Lia to be dead! She whined at the weight of new responsibility. It was a good-dog's job to protect her person. Protect and serve Lia.

Her brow wrinkled again when Lia shuddered. Had she done the right thing, finding the dead girl?

"*Mahalo,* Karma. Come away, good-dog. Yes, you're a good girl." Lia's voice shook.

Leaping to her feet, Karma raced to Lia. She'd been right! Lia's gasp just testified to her surprise. Karma filed away the experience for the future. People could die. And sometimes a good-dog knew more than people. Karma leaned against the girl's thigh, relishing the comfort of Lia's hands.

Lia sank to her knees, trembling and voice shaking. "Got to call the police, baby-dog. Tell them somebody died." Karma tipped her head from side to side when Lia fumbled in a pocket for the phone she liked to talk to, and then slurped the girl's face. That always made Lia laugh. This time it didn't.

"Stay with me, girl, no more games. Settle down. Need us both to stay calm." Lia poked the phone with one finger, and waited.

Karma glanced over her shoulder and then back at Lia. She wanted some water from the bottle Lia carried. But more than that, she wanted Lia to say *such* again. The game wasn't finished. Maybe Lia didn't know? People couldn't hear all the wonderful sounds surrounding them, and missed out on delicious aromas good-dogs sniffed. Sometimes Karma felt sorry for people. Her ears twitched and nose wrinkled. Over there, in the brushy thicket only a few yards away. . . Karma could feel the other's eyes watching them.

The game wasn't done. Lia called Karma good-dog for finding the dead person, even though it made her upset and Karma tracked the wrong trail. Karma whined. The dead girl couldn't be helped. The other, though, watched and waited. And Lia didn't know. Just like ignoring the Frisbee and choosing a different trail, Karma had to decide.

Karma stood, shook herself, and bounded forward past the dead girl's body to reach the watching stranger.

"*Mai ho`opā mai ia`u!* No, no!" The watching girl screamed, tried to run. With delight, Karma played the *trip* game to stop her. It just seemed to be the right thing to do. Then Karma assumed the *platz*-down position, announcing her find.

Chapter 36

Lia whirled as the long tracking line snaked through brittle grass past her feet when Karma dashed away. What now? Unflappable and stoic, Karma rarely broke a cue until released. Granted, these were unusual circumstances. And she hadn't asked her to stay. Mixed signals weren't fair to the dog.

"*Mai ho`opā mai ia`u!*"

Lia didn't understand the words, but the terror in the scream needed no translation. "Hurry, send the police ASAP. There's someone else here." Lia disconnected from the 911 operator. "Karma, *come*!"

When she ignored the request, Lia went to her. She found a cowering girl not much bigger than Karma herself.

Karma slicked back her ears and lowered her head in a classic appeasement gesture, the "guilty" look designed to diffuse Lia's disapproval. The dog yawned and looked away from the hysterical child, as if the gesture that calmed other dogs would do the same for the girl.

The child—young woman?—shuddered in a fetal pose, her long black hair curtaining her face. She wore a shiny pink sports bra, and skin-tight bicycle shorts. No shoes, though, and Lia winced at the raw crisscross wounds on her callused brown feet. Her arms sported fingerprint bruises, sticker-vine slashes stitched her legs, and bug bites polka-dotted her back. A high-pitched keening whispered from her lips as she rocked back and forth in the dirt.

"Hush, you're safe. My dog, she won't hurt you. It's okay." Lia didn't know what to say or do. She reached out a hand, then withdrew it without touching the girl. Those bruises said touch meant pain, not comfort. "Karma, *come!*" The big pup instead scooted closer to the girl, ignoring the command. Yawning again, Karma settled her big head on the stranger's bare, bruised thigh, and let out an audible sigh. Almost magically, the girl's shudders calmed.

Lia knelt beside the slight figure, and brittle weeds crunched beneath her knees. "I'm Lia. This is Karma." She placed a gentle hand on the girl's shoulder. "Are you hurt?"

Stupid. Obviously she's hurt. And doesn't speak English.

But the girl shook her head. She opened her eyes, peering through the dark curtain of hair, and slowly sat up. A silver heart pendant bordered with flowers glittered at her throat. "He kill her."

Lia sucked in a breath. *Murder.* "She was your friend?"

Again, a head shake. "She make me do things. She bad. But Boss make her do it." She fingered the pendant.

Lia struggled to make sense of her words. She didn't recognize the accent, although her dark complexion and hair suggested a Hispanic heritage common to North Texas. None of that mattered. The police, when they got here, would take care of the details. If Karma hadn't found the girl, she would have died in the heat.

At that thought, Lia reached for her water bottle. "Thirsty?" She unscrewed the top.

The girl stared at Karma's big head, but didn't try to pet her or move away. She reached past the dog for the water bottle, fingers trembling. "*Mahalo.*"

Karma raised her head. Her stumpy tail twitched as the girl drank deeply.

"You're Hawaiian." Lia recognized the plumeria flower design on the girl's pendant. She stopped her from chugging the entire bottle. "Not too much. What's your name?"

"Boss call me Melanie. Don't like it." She tossed her head with defiance, and for a moment, the girl she was born to be shined through. "I'm Mele."

"How old are you, Mele? And who is *Boss*? The one who hurt . . ." She looked back over her shoulder toward the dead woman.

"I old 'nuff to make a man happy, Boss say. Boss is jus' Boss. Vicki, she show me what t'do."

Lia's stomach lurched. "You'll be safe now, Mele." Her cell phone rang, and she saw 911 calling back. "The police are on the way."

"No!" Mele bolted upright to her knees. "*No māka`i*! Boss say no cops. I get dead like Vicki!"

"Mele, the police will protect you from this Boss person." The phone kept ringing. Lia needed to give them directions.

"No, no, no, no!" Mele struggled to her feet. The whites of her eyes shined, her nostrils flared, and the pulse in her throat thrummed so fast Lia expected the girl to pass out.

Karma sprang to her feet, dancing around the pair. Her tracking line swished in the grass in a herky-jerky rhythm.

Lia grasped the girl's arm and Mele screamed and yanked free. She ran, waist-length hair a tangled cloud, covering the uneven terrain quickly despite her limping gait.

"Dammit!" Lia thumbed her phone to answer the 911 operator.

"Don't hang up again. Are you still with the body? Stay on the phone and wait until the police arrive."

"I can't talk. There's another victim here, a Hawaiian woman, a kid. Dammit, she's running." Lia stamped on the end of the track line to keep Karma close. The dog trembled, eager to give chase, but conflicted about what to do.

"Stay where you are. Do not pursue. The police are on the way."

"But she's hurt. Says she knows who killed the other woman."

Karma's whine turned into a warble of concern.

"Settle! Karma, *platz*." The dog downed, but continued to complain.

Lia's frustration rose as Mele tried to disappear into the brush. It wouldn't be hard. The sun-blasted stands of winter rye stood higher than the girl's shoulders, with encroaching native cedar trees giving way to occasional bois d'arc and mountain ash. "She's going to die of dehydration or heatstroke if we don't get her help. How soon will the police get here?"

"Ten minutes out. Sit tight. And stay away from the body. You understand, you are not to disturb the area any further." The dispatcher spoke by rote.

Lia bit her lip. Ten minutes? Mele would be who-knows-where

by then.

Karma rolled onto her side, pawing the ground, maintaining the letter if not the intent of the cue. Her whine turned into an escalating Rottie grumble of discontent.

"Okay, right, *I* won't move." Lei bent to unhook the tracking line. "Graduation day came early, baby-dog. Keep her safe, Karma." She pointed the direction Mele ran. "*Achtung*!"

The massive dog sprang to her feet, nosed Lia's hand, and raced after Mele. Lia watched, praying she'd made the right choice by telling Karma to guard the girl.

Chapter 37

"Macy-cat, time for your meds." September rattled the bottle, and the big Maine Coon raced to reach her. Little chirrup-mews erupted as he rubbed back and forth against her ankles, and then seemed to levitate onto the top of the dresser. He opened wide, accepted the heart medication without a fuss, and then paw-grabbed her hand. "Yes, okay already. I owe you a treat. How about two treats?" She laughed when he sat without prompting and offered a paws-up.

At the treat-word, Shadow came to attention. "Okay, you can have one, too." She tossed the yummy to where he reclined on the bed, and he snapped it out of the air.

She stroked the cat's long, mahogany fur the same color as her own. Macy placed his paws on September's shoulders, and they enjoyed a mutual cheek-rub session, green eyes that matched her own slitting in pleasure before Macy leaped onto the bed to stalk Shadow's waving tail.

It had taken Dad's intervention to bring Macy home. The Maine Coon stayed mostly in September's room. His heart condition, controlled with the medication he accepted on command, meant he shouldn't overdo, but September felt guilty Macy didn't have more room to play. Whenever Mom wasn't around, she gave the big cat run of the house and if Dad saw or suspected, turned a blind eye.

September watched the pair wrestle, the big cat pulling his claw-punches and Shadow mouthing his feline buddy with wide, careful jaws. She felt heartened at the return to a semblance of normalcy. Visible injuries had healed, but she remained vigilant for signs of the hidden hurt. They all had more than their share.

Shadow took much longer to recover than expected. September pretty much lived at Doc Eugene's veterinary hospital trying to get him well. Infection and Shadow's own worrying at the injuries, delayed healing until September decided to cut their losses. Literally. Shadow came through his final surgery three weeks ago, and was back to himself.

His cheek now sported a jagged slash of white fur that arrowed toward his bullet-notched ear. Mom allowed Shadow in her house, recognizing he held the key to keeping her grounded and her PTSD at bay. More important in Mom's eyes, Shadow had saved her grandson's life more than once.

She'd changed, too. A haircut sheared more than a foot off her dark mane. She had to admit the style offered cooler comfort in the wicked Texas heat. Mom's stylist worked magic, and nobody could see the bald patch that slowly shrank. September refused to color the white streak that grew from her temple. She'd had it since childhood, and now it mirrored the white mark near Shadow's brow.

Today, she wore her new work hat, a gift from Combs. He'd had it custom-embroidered with the words *Crappiocca Happens*. September smiled every time she saw it. Mom was appalled, of course. That made it even better.

"Macy, guard the room and the house." She smiled when he meowed back. "Yeah, you always want the last word. But sorry, you can't come." She and Shadow had their weekly lunch date with Combs. The cowboy dive welcomed Shadow as her service dog. "Prejudice against cats, Macy. You should start a social media campaign." She laughed again, and called Shadow to her side. They galloped down the stairs, and hurried out the door.

"Like our new car, Shadow?" She grinned when he woofed approval, and again stuck his black muzzle out the rear window of the SUV. They'd had the car two weeks. September checked to be sure that the childproof window lock remained engaged. Shadow never forgot a lesson, and he'd already figured out the windows rolled down like they did in the old car.

It had taken months for the insurance settlement, and even longer for appraisals on the damaged house. The new car returned September's freedom so she could escape her folks' house whenever stress grew too great.

She pulled into the gravel parking lot and parked beneath the shade of a live oak. Nearby grass would give Shadow safe passage up to the restaurant's entrance. In this weather, the sunbaked dirt could blister a dog's footpads.

September gathered the paperwork in the passenger seat beside her. She wanted to discuss the house repair appraisal with Combs, but didn't see his car in the lot. Sighing, she got out and opened the rear door for Shadow. They had a standing date every week here at Hog Heaven, and other times as work allowed. That was the problem. Work trumped everything. Just when she'd opened up and stopped pushing Combs away, he'd become distant.

"Shadow, wait." She pushed through the scarred barn door to check for people before inviting the big dog inside. Shadow didn't wear any service dog vest, as it wasn't required, but she preferred to avoid any questions. And she didn't want to startle others when the impressive black shepherd came inside.

September waited to be seated and returned the greeter's smile. She and Shadow were escorted to their usual table at the far end of the bar. The whole staff knew and loved Shadow.

A new waitress approached with silverware and the menu. "I'm waiting for someone." September waved away the menu. "Water bowl for Shadow, please. It's three digits outside."

"How 'bout some barbecue short ribs, specialty of the house here at Hog Heaven. Sweet tea for you?"

She gulped, and wrinkled her nose, but didn't explain. "Not a fan of barbecue. Unsweet tea, please." Near sacrilege in the South, she knew, but September had spent many years in Chicago. That experience changed her taste, in many ways. "Oh, and please bring a second glass filled with ice."

Once they arrived, September added the ice to Shadow's water. He drank, and then leaned against her leg before settling beneath the table.

She sipped tea and stared out the window, wondering what Combs would say. Finances made demands, forcing unpopular choices. "It is what it is. Right, Shadow?"

He thumped his tail against the swayback floor and then stood when Combs arrived. Shadow pressed hard against her leg again.

"How's my favorite people?" Combs strode across the room, and leaned down to brush September's lips with his own.

The unfamiliar but welcome fluttery feeling in her stomach made September smile. It had been so long since she could allow, and even welcome another's touch. "I got the estimate from the contractor." She gestured to the folder.

The spindle-back chair scraped against the wooden floor, and peanut hulls crunched beneath his boots as Combs took his seat. "Good news, I hope?" The waitress returned with another huge glass of iced tea, along with a basket of yeast rolls and honey-sweetened butter. "You want the usual?" She nodded, and he ordered for them both.

Without a word, September handed him the folder and waited. His brow furrowed as he read, flipping pages. He closed the file, and handed it back to her. "The insurance won't cover the replacement cost. I'm not surprised. The house was old." He sighed. "I'm sorry." He reached out and took her hand. "But my offer still stands—"

She cut him off. "We've been over this. I can't move in with you." She pulled her hand away, dropping it to caress Shadow's soft ruff. "I love you, but I can't rush this. Please understand."

His jaw clenched, but Combs held his tongue. Better than anyone, he knew her past, knew her inner demons and the damage that still reared its ugly head. She needed healing on the inside, too. Besides, with his ex-wife so sick, Combs had to think about his kids first.

"Most of my savings went into the renovation. It'll cost that much and more to pull the house down and start over. And take months, if I decided to rebuild."

"You willing to stay on with your Mom for months?" He cracked his knuckles, and gave a low whistle. "Good luck with that."

She shrugged. "I'll rent an apartment."

"Shadow might want more room to stretch his legs. I have a backyard—"

"Stop! Just stop. I'll rent a house. We'll find a place that works for us, until I figure things out." This time she reached across the table to take his hands. "Melinda and Willie need you now more than ever. You talked about getting full custody."

"You love my kids!"

"Yes, I do. But they're hurting right now. They're losing their mom. They don't need me butting into their lives." His wife suffered from a devastating brain disorder similar to Alzheimer's disease. Their stepfather's focus was on his wife, and the kids needed their dad. She squeezed his hand. "This can't be just about us. It has to be right for them, too."

Real life sucked, but she had to be honest with him, and with herself. No matter how much she loved Combs, she couldn't play mom to his kids, or wife to Combs until she could trust her own emotional health.

Their food came, but neither had much of an appetite. When his phone rang, Combs looked relieved. "I've got to go. Will catch up with you later."

He didn't kiss her goodbye.

Chapter 38

"The police are here." Lia disconnected the 911 connection. She noticed three missed calls, four text messages and one voice mail, all from Grammy. Damn! Probably about the fund-raising gala tonight. Hosted by her grandparents, and benefiting CASA (Court Appointed Special Advocates for children), Grammy supervised every detail, including Lia's appearance. Grammy would have to wait.

Lia shifted from foot to foot, frustrated by the delay. It had been closer to 20 minutes since she'd sent Karma after the runaway. "Here! Hey, over here!" She waved her arms to help them see her over the tall weeds, then hurried to meet the police. Her step faltered when she recognized one of the men.

Detective Jeff Combs raised one eyebrow, but otherwise didn't react. He'd been the lead investigator back in February. She'd been too sick at the time and distracted over worry about losing her business to pay much attention to anything, including his striking looks. The detective's tanned face and sun-bleached hair wouldn't be out of place on a beach. Heat rose to Lia's face at the thought.

"You found the body? Trouble follows you around." He motioned her to join him. "Let the techs do their job while you catch me up, Ms. Corazon. Can I call you Apikalia?"

"Just Lia, Detective Combs." She walked beside him. He must be over six feet. She'd inherited Grandfather's imposing height, but her head barely reached his chin.

"So call me Combs." He stomped back the way they'd come, glancing around the scrubby field with its islands of native trees. "This property belongs to Corazons, correct?"

Lia nodded again. "There's more than 4,000 acres."

"How'd you happen to stumble across one body in 4,000 acres?" He didn't look at her. "What're you doing out here in the back of beyond anyway? With that kind of luck, you should play the Lotto."

She pulled up short. "I'm training Karma. This is our test track."

He turned to her, light brown eyes laser bright. "How often do you train? And why this place?" Smile lines creased his cheeks, despite his current serious expression. "I take it this is the first body you've found."

"And the last, I hope! You don't think there's more?" He didn't answer, just waited for her to continue. "It's a short hike from the barn and paddocks where we train. The house isn't far, either." She shrugged. "There's an access road a quarter mile that way, past the body. I don't lay track on the same route every time. Got to mix it up for the dog. This is the first time I've been out here in a while. And yes, this is the first body." Karma wasn't trained to be a cadaver dog. Lia much preferred finding the living.

"What's *a while*? A week? A day?" That sun-bleached eyebrow quirked again.

"A week, maybe." She couldn't look away from the body. "What about the Hawaiian girl? She's barefoot, and so young." She fingered the tracking line she'd coiled and slung over her shoulder like a lariat. "Karma is with her, so at least she's not alone. If they get too far, though, don't know if my recall will work." It hurt to admit that, but she needed to be honest. The dog already ignored Lia's signal to come away from Mele, and that didn't bode well. Besides, the whistle might not carry far in this wind.

"Karma? You had a kennel full of dogs, last time we spoke."

An ache settled in her throat. The beat up shepherd—a true warrior/protector—had come and gone quickly yet made a huge impact. Shadow appeared like a furry guardian angel, but Combs hadn't seen him that night. He'd focused on Derek, not on the dogs. "Karma is the Rottweiler pup."

The smile lines deepened. "That the ankle-biter I heard about?" He retrieved a chocolate-colored kerchief that matched his eyes to mop his face and neck.

In three days, Karma's police dog future would be tested. Sweat trickled down her back, too. Lia lifted the long ponytail that stuck to her skin, pulling it through the back of the gimme cap to keep it off her neck. "Could we continue this conversation in the shade?" She motioned to the nearby stand of burr oak.

He followed her to the drooping trees, ducking to get beneath the umbrella-like canopy. "Take me through what happened." He pulled a digital recorder from his pocket and thumbed it on before he spoke into it. "Detective Jeff Combs. State your name, please."

"Apikalia Corazon. Lia." She leaned forward to talk into the device to be heard over gusting wind. "What about the girl?"

"Speak normal. And let us worry about the investigation, Lia." He dabbed his brow again. "Take it from the top."

Her shoulders tightened at his dismissal. *Fine, be that way.* The sooner she gave her statement, the quicker she'd get out of here, and could go after Karma herself. The dog wouldn't let just anyone near Mele.

"This morning, Karma and I drilled for half an hour in the paddock. That's up near the house. I can show you. She nailed it, so I decided to up her challenge here. I'd already laid a track, just in case."

He scratched his nose with the recorder. "This was what time?"

"Paddock drills at 8:00 this morning, before I fed Karma. Then I had chores to do." Nothing like mucking out stalls in the heat to make you appreciate dogs even more. "Didn't want to heat-stress her too much, so waited until late afternoon to run her here."

"You set the track a week ago?"

"One of the tracks, yes. Dogs can still scent a week later, depending on the dog, terrain, and a bunch of other things."

"No doubt. I know a dog like that." He smiled.

She added, "I set the second track this morning, about sunrise around 6:30 before I started working Karma. It's cooler that time of day." She glanced at her phone when another text came in, then pocketed the device. "Karma nailed the first find in less than five minutes. My hat." She tugged the brim. "I had a second track going west and up that rise, back toward the house." She pointed. "Instead, she led me here and alerted on the body." Lia felt goose bumps but not from the cold. Furnace-hot wind had picked up even more, and rattled the spindly oak branches like bones in a barrel.

Both of his eyebrows climbed toward his hairline. "Twice today. See anyone either time?"

She shook her head. "But that doesn't mean anything. I wasn't anywhere near here. The dog's toy is 400 yards that way. It's not like there's a clear sight line, with all this overgrowth." Her phone buzzed in her pocket. The fundraiser started at 8:00, in another 90 minutes. She had a good excuse to ditch the event, though she'd pay for it later.

"You touch the body? Disturb the surroundings in any way?" He paused, adding, "We need to exclude any trace you may have left behind."

She swallowed hard. "All I saw was her hand, and stepped away. Karma was right next to her, though. I didn't know if it was a man or woman until the girl referred to her as Vicki."

He nodded. "Tell me about this other person. She's on the run? A woman?"

"A child. She looks about twelve years old, Combs." Lia couldn't help the trembling in her voice. "I think she's Hawaiian. At least, she said *mahalo*—I recognized that word anyway, and she told me her name. Mele. That's Hawaiian, too. Her skimpy clothes won't protect her in this weather." She swiped her wet brow with one forearm. "I'd already called 911 when Karma found her. When I mentioned the police, she panicked, and ran off, barefooted."

"Barefoot? She won't get far." He slapped at a mosquito. "That's right, you're part Hawaiian, too."

Everyone knew about her heritage. Lia was a bastard mix of aristocratic Corazon Spaniard and a villainous Hawaiian father nobody knew much about. At least, nobody would share her father's details with Lia. Her grandparents hated the mystery man who abandoned Lia's pregnant teenage mother.

Two months ago, Lia sniffed out Kaylia's death certificate, and confirmed her mother's death coincided with her own birthday. Grandfather and Grammy didn't come out and say it, but Lia knew they blamed her for Kaylia's death. If Grandfather found out Lia had been looking, there'd be hell to pay.

They tried to make her ashamed of her Hawaiian heritage. Now she'd found a Hawaiian child who boasted with pride about her skill to please men. Lia's stomach churned.

"Combs, Mele knows who killed Vicki. She called him *Boss.* I think he's her pimp." The foul word even tasted bad. "She ran because he'd *make her dead like Vicki.* If she can identify this Boss person, she's in real danger."

"Bet she helped move the body," he mused, looking around. "I don't think Vicki died here. Girls like Mele do as they're told."

Lia hated his phrase, *Girls like Mele.* "It's not her fault. She's a child, for God's sake! It's time someone protected her." The wind lifted hair from her sweaty forehead, but didn't cool. It tasted dusty and bitter. A haze on the horizon spoke of distant fires.

He switched off the recorder. "Stay available. We'll have more questions for you." She started to argue, but he cut her off. "We'll look for Mele, I promise. Show me where you found her, and then you can go."

"It's about time." She muttered the words, but saw him hide a smile when he heard. Lia parted the slumping branches of the burr oaks and gave a wide berth past technicians and Vicki's sad corpse.

Combs spoke quietly with the investigators before following her. They had turned Vicki's slight body. The dead girl's long hair spilled all around, clotted with leaves and dirt. Earrings shined in her delicate ears, dried vomitus spilled down her front, and her mouth glowed an odd deep purple color. Lia averted her eyes.

Her phone buzzed and again Lia ignored it. Grammy would be beside herself. "Combs, it's just up this rise. See, Mele hid here, crouched down behind this cedar. And when she saw us—that is, me and Karma—she scrambled forward a few yards before she fell right here. Actually, Karma tripped her." Teaching that *trip* cue to the puppy came in handy last February. Karma never forgot a lesson.

The grass crunched beneath her tracking boots. It would be needle sharp on the child's bare feet. "Karma *platz*—that is, she lay down—right there. For a pup, she's very intuitive, and I guess wanted to be less threatening. It seemed to calm Mele, at least for a short time." She waved and pointed as Combs approached. "The access road runs about another hundred yards that way."

"So you sent the dog after her? Does he have protection skills?"

"She. Karma is a bitch. And yes, she's trained for protection." Lia couldn't help the pride coloring the words. Maybe he understood more about dogs than she expected. "Karma won't let anyone but me get close to them. You need me there when you find them."

He smiled. "Nice try, Lia. But we've got our own resources." He pulled out his phone.

"What? Wait, you have a dog handler?" She'd planned to make Karma available on a contract basis to the local police. With an average purchase price of $8000 for a quality dog, plus another $25,000 training fee, most local departments couldn't afford a K9 unit.

"Will your dog stay with the girl? No matter what?" Combs scrolled on his phone, looking for a number.

"Well, yeah. That's what Karma's trained to do." She hoped so, anyway. "Take me along. I won't get in the way." Karma's protective nature could save Mele's life, especially if the Boss showed up. But it could get Karma shot if she wouldn't allow the police to rescue the girl.

"Great! If Karma stays with the girl, we're good." He spoke into the phone. "Yeah, Gonzales, it's me. The team is processing the body now. And we've got a runner, an underage girl. Fits the profile, too." He nodded at something Lia couldn't hear. "Right, and I got tentative confirmation the runner's Hawaiian. Don't know yet about the vic."

Lia interrupted. "Both of them wear matching jewelry. Mele has a heart pendant with plumeria blossoms. Like these." She showed him her bracelet. "The dead girl's earrings look the same. It's a popular Hawaiian flower."

He mouthed "thanks," and shared her information. "The dead girl, first name Vicki, may be Hawaiian, too. Right, I'll get our consultant up to speed, soon as I come in. This could be the break we need."

Lia stared at the ground, angry she'd be cut out of the hunt for Karma.

"One more thing. The runner has a protection dog with her, a Rottweiler." He looked at Lia, and grinned. "I know, how convenient is that? Soon as I hang up, I'll call her." He disconnected, and turned back to Lia. "I happen to know someone with a dog that tracks lost pets."

"Karma tracks people. She's going to be a police dog." The wind tore off her hat and spun it away, swirling her hair free of the elastic band into an amber halo. An acrid scent rode the heavy air, tickling the back of Lia's throat. Grudgingly she added, "I've heard of pet tracking services. Guess that's good news for Mele."

"How bad was Mele hurt? That must be from her feet." He

winced, pointed out bloody stains in the grass Lia hadn't noticed"

"Not that I could see. Her feet weren't bleeding badly enough to drip red."

Combs squatted to collect a sample. "Poor kid. That's gotta hurt."

"Anyway, that's where Karma lay. Mele was over there." She pointed to a spot three feet away, where scuffed dirt and stubbled grass marked the spot. "You've got to let me handle Karma when you find them. She's *my* dog. I can help, just let me." She added a final word. "Please."

He packaged the sample and stood. "We'll call if we need you." He gave her his card, and made a note of her own cell phone number. "Go home, Lia."

Lia whirled, grabbed up her hat, and stalked back the way she'd come. For her, the stakes had gone up. She knew the blood wasn't Mele's. So it must belong to Karma.

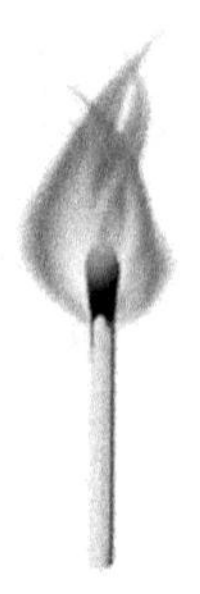

Chapter 39

Karma trotted beside the young girl, panting but not yet feeling the strain of the heat. The sun threw long shadows against the ground. Whispery critter rustling made way when big dog paws and small girl feet crunched through the scorched vegetation.

The new game both puzzled and excited Karma. She knew the *Achtung*-watch cue, and had practiced with objects before. Other than Lia, she'd never guarded anyone. So Karma shadowed the girl, keeping watch all around as Mele trotted across the field. She enjoyed the freedom from the tracking line, and ran back and forth, fast or slow, without the impediment. She felt an odd, new yearning to range far in search of…*Something*, she wasn't sure what. Maybe she'd discover the elusive *something* as they raced away from Lia's structured drills.

They found a paved road. The girl stopped behind a massive tree trunk, and peered around to check both directions. Karma thought that was smart. Cars and trucks ran fast on these smooth paths, faster than a good-dog could run. Karma didn't want to be chased by a strange car, either. She liked riding inside cars, though.

The girl darted from behind the tree to reach the paved car path.

Mele hissed when her feet touched the surface. She hopped and skipped across, and stopped on the far shoulder, sitting for a moment to rub her toes. Karma padded over to her, but didn't flinch at the superheated asphalt, despite the burn. Her paw pads, extra thick, withstood higher temperatures than bare girl-feet, at least for the short term. Besides, Rottweiler pride pushed Karma to remain stoic during guardian duty. Lia expected no less. She'd been trained for this. And Karma wanted more than anything to earn Lia's "good-dog." And maybe a treat. Liver would be nice. Bacon would be better.

She paused beside the girl, waited the way a polite dog should, and sniffed the girl's hand when she placed it on Karma's neck.

"Nice *īlio*, good-dog." Mele pushed to her feet, making a face and hissing between her teeth again. "Boss come, I no go. Okay? You help me, yeah?"

Karma wagged her back end, not understanding the words or caring what Mele said. She recognized "good-dog" and that was enough.

Mele limped from the road. Karma started to follow until the girl held up her hand and made noises the dog understood to mean *blieb*. So she waited. Karma tipped her big head one way and then the other, watching from the distance when the girl stripped off her tight shorts and squatted.

Karma took the cue and found her own spot to take-a-break. She made the mark more obvious than usual. After finishing, Karma sniffed the spoor, her jaw chattering at the pheromones signaling her state, and then for good measure, she scratched the ground with both front and rear paws. She pretzeled herself to check out and clean herself as well.

Toilet done, Karma waited until Mele stood and adjusted her clothing. Karma was glad dogs didn't wear clothes. The girl's tight shorts looked uncomfortable and even hotter than Karma's short fur coat. The clothes smelled, too, like Mele hadn't been able to clean herself the way good-dogs did. But Karma relished the aroma. It helped her learn more about the girl, just as Karma's own scent revealed information to other dogs about Karma. She wasn't sure why people covered up their self-scent with lotions and perfumes, when people-smell explained so much more.

She bounded to catch up with Mele, and paced beside her. She enjoyed the weight of the girl's hand when Mele steadied herself against Karma's broad shoulders. Karma knew that meant the girl trusted her to keep Mele safe, just like Lia did. Some things a dog just knew without being told. Karma was smart that way.

The wind panted hot breath into Karma's face, and her nose twitched with concern. It smelled bad from a long way off. Not yet scary-bad, but it could get worse. She licked her lips, wishing Lia had shared the drink. When the wind shifted, Karma turned toward the more welcoming aroma—water. A lot of it, with pungent horse scent mixed in.

Mele trudged forward, but stopped when Karma didn't follow. The girl frowned, but didn't say anything.

Lia said to watch and guard. That didn't mean a good-dog must *follow*. Maybe Karma could *lead* for a while, and Mele could follow, especially if it meant water. Karma licked her lips again, and continued panting. She needed to tell the girl somehow. With Lia, Karma grasped a pant leg or sleeve and tugged, not as much as the *trip* game, but enough to explain. Mele, though, had tender, bare girl skin.

Karma whined, and trotted to the girl and first licked and then mouthed Mele's wrist.

Alarmed, the girl snatched it back, grabbing it with her other hand. She stumbled backwards, brow furrowed.

So Karma offered a play bow, forelegs stretched out in front of her and butt in the air, wiggling her tail. She whined again, showing she meant no harm.

Mele peeked from beneath a curtain of dark hair and smiled. Karma let her tongue loll out her wide muzzle, and rolled onto her back. She wriggled in the weeds and grass, scratching her back and baring her tummy in an ultimate no-threat display that always made Lia laugh.

The girl laughed, too. Mele reached down to rub Karma's tummy just the way she liked it.

Karma rolled over, sprang to her feet and pranced away. She looked over her shoulder, taking several steps toward where the distant water beckoned. She knew Mele couldn't see or smell the water. People were scent-blind, so a good-dog had to show Mele the way to the water.

"Want to go that a-way? Okay, *īlio.*" Mele smiled and braced her hand once more on the black Rottie shoulders.

Before they took half a dozen steps, Karma heard the car on the road, and looked back. Would Lia drive them now? Karma liked car rides. She could stick her head out the window and taste the smells riding the wind.

But no, the sound wasn't Lia's car. Mele kept trudging forward, so so so slow. Cars traveled fast, even faster than good-dogs could run. Even a strange car could take them faster to the water.

Karma licked her lips, and wrinkled her brow when someone climbed out. The car door slammed. Mele whirled, gasped and froze. "Boss?"

"Get your ass back in the car, girl, before the cops see you!"

Mele screamed, and ran.

Chapter 40

Grammy met Lia at the door. "Oh Lia, you're an absolute mess." Her nose wrinkled. "And you smell. Dear heavens, girl! You should have been home an hour ago. I've got your party dress picked out. Quickly, run upstairs and put yourself together." Grammy's helmet of blond hair, always perfect, matched the understated elegance of her gown and aristocratic features. Cornelia Corazon would look like a queen in sackcloth.

"I can't stay. I'm sorry Grammy, it's an emergency." Lia raced past the tiny woman, and bounded up the stairs. She needed her car keys and overnight gear. Whether Detective Combs authorized her help or not, she had to go after Karma.

Grandfather stood at the top of the stairs. He glowered, blocking Lia's access to the second floor.

"Let me by, Grandfather."

"You promised your grandmother, Lia. It's time to live up to your responsibilities." More at home on horseback than in a cummerbund, he still cut a dashing figure. One gnarled, work-worn hand stayed her protests. "I know, you've got the dog test tomorrow—"

"No, in three days." She wouldn't let him shortchange her.

"Okay fine. In three days on Monday. But tonight you keep to your word, and make an appearance. People expect a lot from you, Lia. We expect a lot. Don't disappoint us." He stood back, and released her arm to let her pass. His tuxedo, accented with a sterling and turquoise bolo tie and cufflinks, echoed his roots.

Unspoken words, as always, pointed how Kaylia disappointed her family. Lia remained a constant reminder of her mother's shame.

The 4000-acre spread had been in Cornelia's family for six generations. Corazon Stables bred and trained champion cutting horses. They hosted the annual gala as a way to give back to the community, and as a networking event drawing movers and shakers from all over the state and beyond. Bankers, attorneys, investment brokers and politicians mixed with salt-of-the-earth ranchers and manufacturing executives.

Grandfather gave free tickets to the ranch hands as thanks for their work ethic and loyalty to the Corazon empire. Of course, they knew better than to presume to date Lia. Never mind that Grandfather himself started in a low position, and married up, wooing Cornelia and charming her parents. No, her mother Kaylia's tragic story trumped anything else. Even Detective Combs, who looked more California surfer dude than boot-scootin' Texan, knew.

"You don't understand. Karma and I . . ." She debated telling Grandfather about the body. Grammy would hate the unsavory nature of the experience. She didn't understand Lia's penchant for training "nasty dogs" over "elegant horses." Worse, though, any mention of Hawaii would set Grandfather off. She didn't need extra drama when Monday's deadline loomed near.

Grandfather's newfound interest in Lia proved more burdensome than she'd expected. As a child, she'd catch him watching her from a distance, always with a scowl painted on his rugged face. Grammy tried to curtail Lia's wild streak, setting strict curfews and supervision, and hired home schooling tutors to keep Lia segregated from other kids her age. Lia suspected similar restrictions led to Kaylia's elopement at age fifteen with a Hawaiian cowboy. She'd never risked saying that to her grandparents, though.

"You've known about this for months. Go get ready." Grandfather clenched an unlit Cuban cigar between his teeth. His signature aftershave reminded Lia of new-cut hay.

Easier to agree now, make a quick appearance, and duck out later.

The gala got going by 9:30 and would last until the wee hours of the morning. Since police stayed at the dumpsite, she'd go in the back way. The sun set late, after 8:30 and she'd also have the full moon in her favor. That, and Karma's purple collar. She smiled. A success tonight for Karma could tip the balance in the Rottie's performance score, and her own. She had to find Karma and Mele before the tracking team did. Besides, she couldn't wait to see Detective Combs's face when she trumped the outside expert.

"All right, I'll get ready." She brushed past Grandfather on the way to her room.

Lia had no interest in being Grandfather's "do-over" project. She was no Kaylia, no golden girl to carry on the Corazon family name and traditions. They had to accept she was Apikalia, a Corazon through her mother. But also Hawaiian. Someday she'd find her missing father, whether Grandfather approved or not.

Lia shucked off dingy tracking gear—she'd don them again soon enough—and brushed twigs and sweat out of her hair before she jumped into the shower. The cold spray soothed the bug bites that stippled her skin. After drying, she donned the simple tea-green slip-dress Grammy had chosen. Lia brushed wavy hair until the dark gold tresses spilled past her waist. It was her best feature, and another day she might have left it unbound to float over her bare shoulders. But to save time for the "after party" of tracking, Lia braided and coiled her hair, and fixed it around the crown of her head. She finished with a decorative comb of stylized plumeria blossoms, still wearing the matching baby bracelet she loved.

The bracelet's dainty flowers framed her name spelled out in tiny individual letters. She'd looked it up. *Apikalia* meant *My Father's Delight.* Someday she'd find her father, whoever he was, and ask if the name was his idea or Kaylia's choice. And why he'd abandoned them.

Before she stepped into her future, Lia wanted to discover her past. She had a premonition that Karma finding Mele might be a first step in unraveling that mystery.

Chapter 41

Karma squared her shoulders and lowered her head toward the stranger. Her ears twitched backwards as she tracked Mele's footfalls when the girl raced off across the field. Dogs ran much faster with four feet than people, so she could catch up to Mele with no problem.

The *problem* stood on the road, the one Mele called "Boss." Karma could smell Mele's fear-stink in the girl's wake. Karma must guard Mele until she heard Lia's release word. She stood solid and proud between Mele and Boss.

Grass higher than a tall dog's head rattled and shuddered in the hot wind, so tall it hid Boss from view. She couldn't get a clear sniff either, what with the wind stirring and whipping everything around. Even so, Karma tracked the man's progress once he stepped off the high paved road, stumbled down the ditch and hitched along through the weed-choked field.

Boss couldn't see Karma either and didn't know she stood guard. Boss just shouted hard words at Mele, words a good-dog didn't need to understand to know they hurt. If Karma were less brave—and she was very brave, as a Rottweiler should be—she might be fearful, too.

Karma's job meant to be brave despite the fear, and protect people from scary people like Boss. She'd done it before.

At the thought, a deep, impressive rumble vibrated deep in Karma's chest. She stared in the direction of his approach, and raised the volume of her warning. She gathered her haunches, in case he didn't stop. Muscles tensed and rippled beneath shiny black hide.

"Told you to wait for me." The man's strident voice hurt Karma's ears. "The cops will throw you in prison forever. You won't like prison. Come with me, girl. I got someone to take you far away, where you'll be safe."

Mele yelled back. "Done what you said. An' you hurt Vicki."

"Texas kills little girls like you for being wicked." Boss took another step, and fell, cursing in the weeds. "Get back here! If I got to catch you, it'll be worse than prison."

Five more steps and Boss would be within bite-range.

"Go 'way! You liar. I tell ev'rybody."

"You little shit—"

Karma bounded forward with a roar, short fur bristling over her shoulders.

"Whoa-whoa-whoa. Where'd you come from?" Boss scrambled backwards, hands out in a warding off gesture. "Dammit, Melinda. Where'd you get that police dog?" His head whipped around, looking for something or someone.

"Not yer business. I got frens better 'n you fo' hep." Mele sing-songed the words, then yelped when Boss again reached for her. "*Īlio*, make him go 'way!"

Growls turned into snarls. Karma stiffened, gathered her haunches to spring forward. She eyed his forearm, a good bite-hold place Lia taught her to grab. Her tail jerked back and forth with excited anticipation.

"You *got frens,* do you? Talked to someone?" Boss mocked the girl's patois. "What'd you tell them?" Boss backed away, steps slow and careful, but stared with hard eyes at Karma all the while.

The direct eye contact increased Karma's resolve. She'd meet his challenge, and didn't need Lia to tell her. She stalked forward, growls continuing to bubble nonstop. She signaled her intent, and waited for Boss to show deference and turn away, or face the consequences.

"You're not worth saving. You're a dime a dozen, I'll find another *wahine nani* to satisfy my client. Don't know what he sees in you island girls." Boss turned and strode back through the weeds to the road.

"Should've done you the same as Vicki." He spat on the ground.

Karma relaxed, and glanced over her shoulder at Mele. The wind gusted the water smell, and the stub of her tail wriggled. She told herself *good-dog* for facing down the scary Boss. She preferred hearing Lia say the words.

"No-no-no!" Mele turned, and ran. "*Īlio*, run! Run fast!"

Karma whirled, on alert to see what so frightened the girl. But Boss stood too far away to be a threat. He lit one of the smoke-sticks some people liked. He blew three long puffs of white before flicking it away in the weeds.

Karma didn't know what that meant but it scared the girl. So she dashed after Mele, and the pair raced away across the field. Karma's thirst and unerring nose guided the girl toward the water that beckoned from more than two miles away.

Chapter 42

September disconnected the phone call from Combs. "Mom, I've got to go. I'll be late." She hurried upstairs to collect tracking gear from her room. Shadow raced up the stairs behind her. Once he saw her pull out tracking boots, he danced and vocalized his excitement. It had been weeks since they'd worked a trail. They both needed this.

Macy trilled and wound about her feet, nearly tripping September as she gathered work clothes. She dumped the heavy gear on the bed while Shadow jittered in front of the door, impatient to be on their way. Macy immediately hopped onto the bed and curled up on top of the pile.

She shed her shorts and pulled on heavy jeans. "Macy, move. I need that shirt." Meowing his aggravation, the Main Coon allowed himself to be dumped, but clung for a moment to the fabric. He wanted her to tow him across the bed, one of his favorite games. "Sorry, kitty, another time."

September shrugged into the heavy long-sleeved shirt over her tank top. She sat on the bed to pull heavy socks up over the bottom of her jeans cuffs, and secured the fabric with tape before shoving feet into leather tracking boots. Bug repellent sprayed on top of clothing added an additional protection from ticks and the diseases they carried. Both Shadow and Macy got monthly preventative. Long sleeves offered a shield from sunburn, but would add to the debilitating heat.

Mom had followed her upstairs. She stood in the doorway, lips pursed with disapproval. "Can't it wait? Your father planned to take us all out to dinner tonight. He'll be home anytime."

"Sorry. I'll make it up to him—to you both. Apparently it's an emergency." Otherwise, Combs wouldn't have called so soon after their disagreement.

Tsk-tsking disapproval, Mom stood with arms folded tight across her chest. "Are you meeting with the contractors again? I don't understand what takes so long."

September pulled the gimme cap onto her head, squinting out the window. The sun wouldn't set for hours yet, so she'd need the protection. She gathered her tack bag with gloves, treats, water bottle and first aid kit. Shadow's harness and tracking line were in the car.

"Oh. A tracking job. Really?" Mom shook her head and prissed back into the spotless living room—or rather, parlor, as she called it. "Somebody loses his precious pet, and calls you to fix the problem. Heavens, September, how can you stand tromping around getting bug bit for no reason?"

"Plenty of reason, Mom. It's part of a police case." She gave Macy a fisted hand signal, and he sat on cue. She owed the cat some quality time. As she shut the pet gate that kept Macy confined in her bedroom, she promised herself they'd spend the evening playing laser tag. Shadow raced ahead of them down the stairs. She asked him to sit at the door, using the same hand signal, and he contained his delight with effort as she looped a soft lead about his neck.

"It's that Detective called you, isn't it? The one made you cry today. I saw you, I'm not blind." Her voice dripped with disapproval. "He's divorced, and a disgraced cop. You can do so much better." She perched on the futon, and stared up at September with deep disappointment.

"He was exonerated!" With exasperation, September dropped the old argument. "My relationships are my business. Besides, this has nothing to do with Combs."

"Don't the police have their own dogs? I know you're coaching someone to train a police dog. Then they can take over all this." Mom waved her hands to encompass the "all this" aspect of

September's work. "At least giving behavior advice through your website avoids all the sweat and bugs." She shuddered.

September didn't answer. The consults had picked up since the February crises. Being famous—or notorious, as Mom called it—had benefits.

"At least tell me where you'll be. Do you have your phone?" She stood to follow September and Shadow toward the front door. "You're still my daughter, however independent you get. I worry, you know."

Shoulders scrunching, September braced herself. "I'm tracking the police dog, she's gone AWOL. They want me to meet the investigative team out at Corazon Ranch."

Mom gasped, her blue eyes widened. "At the ranch? What happened, is Cornelia all right?" She jumped up from the futon and grabbed September's wrist to stop her from leaving.

Mom offered no clue about the two sisters' estrangement. But clearly, feelings for family survived, even if they'd not spoken in years. "Not your sister, no. It has something to do with the dog's trainer, Lia Corazon. Her granddaughter. Guess she's my cousin?"

"You're coaching Apikalia?" Her face darkened. "No, you can't go out there. September, I forbid it! You'll ruin everything, and destroy that poor child. I forbid it!"

Shadow offered a low whine as September twisted her wrist free. "It's a job. They're counting on me to help. Give me a good reason to stay away . . ." She waited a moment, until Mom bit her lip. "Like I said, we'll be late. C'mon, Shadow." September hurried from the house with the dog in tow.

It took more than forty minutes to arrive at the entrance to the Corazon estate. Her shoulders relaxed when she didn't see Combs anywhere around. His partner, Detective Winston Gonzales, came to her car and she rolled down the window.

"Park your car out here, we need to hike in. The family has some big gala planned for later, and you'll get blocked any nearer the house," he told her.

She nodded, found a shady spot beneath a giant live oak, and let Shadow out of the back. "Settle, Shadow. You'll wear yourself out before we get started." September gave him a drink of water, peering overhead at what looked like darkening clouds. She wrinkled her nose. "Smoke?"

Gonzales nodded. Small of stature but powerfully built, he had to look up to meet her eyes. "It's that time of year." He wiped sweat from his brow and smoothed his neat mustache before striking a brisk pace toward the house. Once they came abreast, they cut across the pasture and stable. A narrow path circled up a low hill into trees and disappeared. "Over there." He pointed, and explained along the way what he needed.

Shadow wore no collar, a calculated decision because of his former neck injury. Putting pressure on his weakened trachea could impede his breathing, and the harness connection signaled him to track. So they'd wait until they reached the place where the child witness had run away to don the tracking harness. The soft leash looped about his neck kept him near, but Shadow hadn't willingly left her side since their last separation.

"Quick thinking on Lia's part to send Karma after the girl. As long as the Rottie pup stays with her, Shadow can find them. The trail's dry and fresh. Easy-peasy."

"I hoped you'd say that." He grinned, and smoothed his neat mustache with one hand. "We need to avoid the immediate area. It's still a crime scene, and they've not finished processing yet."

"Okay. I'll have Shadow track ahead of the origination. He should pick up the trail pretty quick." She grinned. "Then we're off and running." She thought for a moment. "I don't suppose you have anything scented with the dog? A toy or something?" She sniffed the air again. The smoke grew thicker. They better start soon, or she'd need to call it off. She wouldn't risk Shadow again.

"Lia left behind one of the dog's toys. A Frisbee, I think. It's up at the site."

They trudged into the shade of a stand of trees, and September wiped her brow. She offered Shadow another drink, but he refused, too excited by the anticipated track. She took a drink herself to wash away the taste of smoke making her tongue feel gritty and dry.

One of the uniform officers came forward and handed her the dog toy. Smiling her thanks, September knelt beside Shadow and offered him the toy to sniff-explore. She removed the short lead looped over his neck. "Shadow, *wait.*" He whined as she unlooped the long tracking line from over her shoulder, and jittered forward out of reach. "Shadow, *wait*, good-dog. I know you're anxious, but let's get hooked up first. *Wait.*"

The wind shifted. Smoke clogged the breeze, making her eyes water. September jumped up to reach Shadow, but he stutter-walked another few steps, testing the air.

With a barely heard woof, Shadow whirled and raced off toward the fire, leaving September behind holding the empty harness.

Chapter 43

Combs dreaded leaving the AC in his car, and ran his hand through hair already wet with sweat. He stared at his cell phone with frustration. September's anguished recriminations still echoed in his ear. She blamed him, and rightly so. She'd never forgive him if something happened to Shadow. Hell, he'd never forgive himself if the big black shepherd got hurt. What was he thinking, involving her? With their relationship turned rocky, anything could tip the balance in the wrong direction. Combs loved her, but trouble followed September in everything she did.

His attention shifted to the petite police officer waiting outside on the road. Officer Pilikia Teves intrigued him. Her square face boasted a natural tan. A few freckles on her bare arms matched the soot-colored curly hair that framed her strong features. Tiny gold turtle earrings offered the single nod to fashion. Slim jeans and a tank top hugged her compact 5'4" athletic build. She cultivated a hard-as-nails attitude, but he sensed she hid something more fragile underneath. None of that mattered to him at the moment. She was here to consult on the missing Hawaiian girls.

She crossed to Combs when he climbed out of the car. "News?"

Her oval, slightly tilted hazel eyes gave her an exotic look.

"A complication. The tracking dog we sent after Karma—that's the Rottweiler police dog—just spooked and took off. Now I got two pissed off handlers, two dogs and an abused kid in the wind." At least Gonzales kept September from going after her dog.

"A dog named Karma? Hope it's not the bad kind. I've had enough of that." She offered a tight smile. "Pilikia is Hawaiian for *trouble*."

"You're here to help, but you follow my orders, understand? I don't need more trouble, Officer Teves." He wasn't in the mood for eager beaver banter. A sudden gust blew so hard he nearly lost his hat. At least it kept mosquitos at bay. Mostly. He slapped his neck. Despite sundown, triple-digit temps elevated tempers and boosted bugs. The intermittent wind made his eyes water and feel gritty.

"Understood, Detective Combs."

"Just call me Combs."

She nodded. "Back in Chicago they call me Tee. I only cause trouble for bad guys." She dimpled again, and then turned serious. "I'm here to learn, and help any way I can."

They needed a breakthrough on the case, and Combs would take it any way he could, even from someone as green as this officer. "I got a tentative ID on the body. She's Vicki Kala, seventeen years old but with a long history of arrests for solicitation. The vice guys say she's a bottom girl used to recruit and train the newbies."

Tee sucked in a breath. "She's a minor, too. Using kids like that, making them sell themselves. There's a special hell for pimps." Her nostrils flared. "Let me guess. Vicki pays for the rooms and delivers the girls to get a little extra something from her pimp?"

Combs could tell the subject struck a nerve. Made him want to punch a wall, too. His daughter was a couple of years younger than Vicki. "Yep, bottom girls put a layer between the pimp and prosecution. He's got deniability while she goes to prison."

A lot of underage girls fell into the life as runaways from foster care. Someone rescued them with a place to crash, food to eat, maybe even drugs. Shortly thereafter, the kid finds out it's payback time. She figures, why not get paid for what she used to give away to a stepdad or mom's latest boyfriend.

He shook his head with disgust. "The system's broke. We're supposed to help these kids, but CPS can only do so much with the funding cuts. Once they age out of the Child Protective Services system or just disappear on the streets, they're easy pickings for the vultures. Time ran out for Vicki. With her last arrest, she would've pulled some real time."

"Instead, she's dead from—?"

"Probable OD. Blue fingernails and purple mouth point to fentanyl spiked with something else." He slapped at another bug, and eyed the threatening orange glow on the horizon.

Grass fires to the south and west continued to plague North Texas this time of year and the fire department, including volunteers, was stretched thin. He could taste the ash, and his eyes watered from smoke blown hundreds of miles away.

"Vicki agreed to testify for a reduced sentence." He pulled out a stick of gum, offered her one, and she declined. "But before it got tied up all neat with a bow, somebody bailed her out."

"Let me guess. Her pimp?" Tee rubbed the inside of her arms, tracing the pale scars that marked her olive skin.

"Or someone higher up. This wasn't a typical local yokel running a couple neighborhood girls for extra bucks. I'm ashamed to say Texas has one of the biggest sex trafficking problems in the country."

"Illegals? They'd be vulnerable." She crossed her arms, eyes narrowed, uncomfortable but playing the stoic cop card.

Combs appreciated that. It took time for new officers to earn the thick skin that allowed them to function yet remain human. She'd been a police officer for eighteen months, just reassigned from Hilo, Hawaii to Chicago. Had to be a culture shock last winter. She aspired to become a detective. "Some of it has to do with illegals, sure. They do what they're told to keep from being turned in to ICE." He rubbed his eyes, and cracked his knuckles.

She stuck one hand in her pocket, perhaps to stop the fidgeting. "Maybe they get trapped in a situation they never asked for. The damage done to kids is permanent. Some never get over it." Tee looked haunted, as if she had a personal stake in the situation. "They targeting Island girls?"

He nodded. "If that's what a client wants, yes. Special requests command higher fees for those willing to take the chance, especially for underage girls. Penalties skyrocket with kids. The Hawaiian angle might be coincidence. No offense, but I hope it's part of the profile. That sort of detail could nail the head of the snake, whoever's calling the shots."

"Yeah, well I'm still pissed I got grounded at DFW. Supposed to go visit my Auntie Isabella."

He snorted. "No accounting for air travel these days. Turned out lucky for us, when you contacted Dallas PD."

She smiled. "While I'm here, figured a quick tour would add to my education. I'm working on my bachelors in Criminal Justice. So, I make one call and the next thing I know, I'm in a squad car screaming its way to the Oklahoma border. Sorry I had no time to change into something more appropriate." In addition to her vacation attire, she wore spanking new cowboy boots.

"They wear those in Chicago?" He smiled.

"Gift shop at the airport. They're for Auntie Isabella, sort of an apology for delaying our visit. Funny, she seemed excited for me to be in Texas. Said I shouldn't argue with karma, and it's where I need to be." She dimpled again. "Anyway, hard to argue with Auntie. Happy to help." Tee motioned with her own phone. "I already sent the picture of your body, Vicki Kala, with a close up of the plumeria heart earrings to colleagues back in Hilo. Good call on that."

"Yeah, I'm not much on jewelry. Lia Corazon, the one discovered the body, she recognized the design. Lia said the runner wore a matching pendant."

"Right. Very popular in the Islands. Why would a Texas prostitute, two of them, wear Hawaiian jewelry? Gift from a client? Or a link to her heritage." She paused when her phone rang. "I got to take this."

Combs needed to make some calls, too. First to September, he owed her that. Then to Lia. She'd insisted she could help, and maybe the two dog ladies could partner. He got the feeling Lia held back information, and that irked him.

Before he could dial, the radio broadcast the code for fire. Damn. Mele's risk just increased tenfold. Combs climbed back into the car, cranked up the AC and used the dashboard laptop to find the online site that tracked grass fires in the area.

"Hey Detective, you're not going to believe this." Tee's grim expression told him the news wasn't good. "My guys recognized your victim. Vicki was her nickname on the Island, too. Wikolia Pa'akaula disappeared five years ago during a vacation with her family in San Antonio."

"Runaway?" Same age as Mele.

She shook her head. "Nope. Happy family, they saved up for the vacation. That earring and necklace set was special order, and the last Christmas gift Wikolia got from her family."

Her voice shook. "They target Island girls. Wikolia wasn't in the foster care system. She was kidnapped."

Chapter 44

Lia stood far away from the band, close to the door, but the noise still aggravated her tinnitus, making her ears ring. How anyone found enjoyment in the ear-bleeding level defied logic. She'd been here twenty minutes and figured another twenty would satisfy Grandfather. Grammy had her hands full directing the caterers and schmoozing with other North Texas glitteratti who lived for such events, and wouldn't miss her when Lia ducked out.

Grammy spent the first twenty minutes introducing Lia to every eligible bachelor in the place. She might as well be a horse at auction. Lia wondered when a would-be suitor (or his mother) would ask to see her teeth.

She recognized some of the ranch hands and smiled as they passed by, all decked out with their best boots and Sunday duds. Wives and girlfriends on their arms showed whitened teeth, hair teased and done up "proper," batting eyelash extensions and showing off designer nail-claws that clutched stems of wine glasses with studied poise. No plastic cups for Grammy's event, only real glass would do. Lia hid another smile, though, noticing that most of the men—even the high society guys—chose long neck beer, taking their cue from Grandfather. Lia sipped iced tea, no sugar, thank you very much.

She fingered her bracelet like worry beads or a rosary. Abe had challenged her to find ways to honor her heritage. So she used the bracelet as an acronym and meditation focus. It helped especially during times of stress. Like now.

"A is for Ancestor," she whispered, and touched the first letter in her bracelet. "P is for pride." Whenever she needed courage, she recited the litany to spell out Apikalia. She whispered the words three times: *Ancestor Pride, Intelligence and Kindness, Act in Love with Intuition and Attitude.*

She'd need all that and more to go against Grandfather, the police, and Detective Jeff Combs. For some reason, it mattered what Combs thought.

She debated calling him. She should have told him about Karma's tracking collar. It wasn't right to put another handler and dog at risk for her own stupid pride. Besides, Combs might have news by now about Karma and Mele. She'd give anything to figure out how to switch on that elusive whisper-connection to touch base with Karma the way she had with Shadow.

Lia sent Combs a quick text. "Any news? Ready to help." She told herself she'd give him ten minutes to answer—no, make that five minutes. He owed her an update, after all. She'd found the body, and on Corazon land. Combs should be grateful she'd kept quiet, or Grandfather's attorneys would complicate everything.

Her phone vibrated announcing a one-word answer. "No."

Her cheeks burned. There must be more news by now. She texted again. "Find Karma?" If he wouldn't share police updates, she had a right to know about her own dog.

Again the phone buzzed. "No."

Lia grinned. She still had time. Pulling this off would impress Grandfather and make Combs and future police departments treat her with respect.

Sudden nerves fluttered her stomach as she prepared to leave the ballroom. The massive area made up more than half of the ground floor of the Corazon family home, which was an ostentatious relic of the past. Across the way, open veranda doors allowed overflow to spill out onto the green carpet of specialty St. Augustine grass Grammy preferred. It needed far more water than the native and hardier Bermuda grass that turned brown at this time of year.

Several of the ranch hands and their dates headed out to the yard, with Grandfather and some of his cronies in tow. He had a smoking area set up, far enough from the house to satisfy Grammy, where he could offer special guests the imported cigars he enjoyed. The veranda had a clear view of the family garage. Maybe he'd be done smoking before she made a dash for her car.

It would take at least five minutes to reach her room in the west wing, another five to change clothes, and maybe ten more to drive to the access road. Her phone application synchronized with Karma's GPS tracking collar once she got within range. She'd never risk sending Karma after the girl without a way to retrieve them.

She had a good idea where Karma would guide the girl. After being in the heat, she'd want to find a cool resting spot, like a horse tank. There were dozens. She'd start with the one nearest Mele's starting point, and go from there.

Without a backward look, Lia slipped out the massive ballroom into the reception hall. She handed her empty tea glass to Grammy's caterer, and pulled the stylish man aside. "There's a very important visitor Grandfather wanted to meet as soon as he arrived. I have to run but could you give Grandfather the message? Tell him Mr. Kanoa waits in Grandfather's office with a deal to discuss." Nodding, the caterer hurried away.

She smiled, satisfied. That should get Grandfather back into the house long enough for her to collect her car without him seeing. That is, if Kanoa wasn't already out there with the rest of the smokers.

As she passed other staffers, Lia held a finger to her lips in the universal sign to keep her secret. Used to Lia's antics, they didn't look surprised when she slipped off the high heels Grammy had chosen, hiked up her skirt, and took off at a dead run.

Her suite of rooms remained as she'd left them. The staff no longer tried to pick up after Lia, and respected her wishes for privacy. She agreed to stay here until her kennel became livable. She didn't agree to give up her independence.

The clothes she'd worn earlier slouched in a heap on the bedroom floor where she'd shed them. Lia peeled off the party clothes and tossed the glittery shoes and dress across the rumpled bedclothes. She pulled on a fresh tank top and long work socks, followed by heavy jeans and a loose-fitting long-sleeved canvas work shirt that kept stickers and mosquitoes at bay. Work boots gave more ankle support for hiking and navigating in the dark. Finally, she grabbed her training pack with assorted tools including a flashlight, and stuck in two full water bottles, an extra leash, training treats, her cell phone and her mother's lariat for luck. You never knew when a rope would come in handy.

Lia left her braids but tied a bandanna around her forehead as a sweatband, and grabbed car keys on the way out of the room. She sprinted down the stairs and out the front door, and stopped short in surprise.

The front drive plus the area surrounding the nearest barn and the family garage overflowed with cars and trucks of every persuasion. They blocked any easy escape for her old ramshackle car. Now what?

A pause in the band music offered respite for her ears. In the sudden quiet, she heard a whinny. A horse would get her where she needed to go without having to hike in and out.

Decision made, Lia threaded through the sea of parked cars to reach the horse barn. She dismissed Grandfather's prize bay stallion. Some lines she knew better than to cross. The chestnut mare at age eighteen wasn't a good choice, either, and barely had the stamina to carry her petite grandmother.

The flashy young buckskin gelding snorted and trotted over to nuzzle Lia's matching hair. "Twice in one day, how about that, Fury. You up for an adventure? Want to make up for Karma teasing you?" He pawed the ground, and she took that as a yes.

She'd beg forgiveness later for borrowing Grammy's saddle and tack. Within minutes, she mounted and cantered away, grateful for the moon's weird orange glow as bright as early twilight. She clucked soothing noises to keep her horse calm when coyotes yodeled a duet with a distant siren.

Lia traveled less than a mile when her phone vibrated. She checked the message, giving Fury his head to continue along the trail toward the practice track. He knew the way, since they'd set the track that afternoon.

Three texts waited, arriving within seconds of each other. The first came from Grammy. Lia groaned. Busted! The other two came from Grandfather, one angry on Grammy's behalf and the other demanding why she'd taken Fury.

How had he discovered Fury gone so soon? The guests wouldn't leave for hours. It made no sense for Grandfather to check the barn.

Before she could answer, yet another text buzzed in, this time from Combs. "Call me."

She dialed. "Did you find them?"

"Where are you? Your grandfather just contacted my boss. Said you disappeared from that big dance on one of his horses. Please tell me you're not hunting your dog."

"What if I am? Did you find them?"

"Not yet. Lia—"

"What about that fancy tracking expert?" He couldn't tell her what to do. She was a Corazon, on Corazon land riding a horse that belonged to the family. Karma was her dog, and she had every right to look for her, and for the poor little girl she guarded.

"Lia, there's a fire, a big one. The dog sent after Karma . . . I don't know, something happened, the dog spooked maybe from the fire and went AWOL. Had a hell of a time keeping September from going into the fire after 'em."

September? She should have guessed. Lia's heart ached for the woman's separation from her dog. Her worry for Karma and Mele ramped up ten-fold now that the orange glow and sirens made sense. As if to punctuate the knowledge, Fury shook his head and snorted. Lia cleared her throat. "How close?" Lia grabbed the reins, tightening her grip, and the horse sidestepped with a hopscotch gait in reaction.

"Not sure. We retrieved Vicki's body but they're still collecting evidence. Had to suspend until we know the status of the fire. With this wind, we've got to leave it to the firefighters. So should you. Get the hell out of there, before the fire catches you."

She shook her head, even though he couldn't see. "Mele's just a kid. And Karma will try to protect the girl, but she won't know what to do with fire." Fury neighed and tossed his head again, as if agreeing with her. "If what you say is true, there's no time to argue. I'm not searching blind, Combs. I know how to find them."

Chapter 45

Karma snorted and coughed foamy saliva between deep-chested panting. Her tongue hung from one side of her square muzzle, thick and sticky-dry. Even though the sun no longer stood high overhead, the heat made it hard to breathe. She longed to wade in cool mud, belly flop into pungent water, and drink her fill. The horse tank beckoned.

Along the way, Karma stopped to "take-a-break" several more times, even though she had little urine left to spend. She wasn't sure why, but it seemed important.

Mele favored one foot, hobbled by a shambling gait, and finally slowed and stopped. Karma drew close and leaned against the girl's bare thigh.

"Ua `ālina au." The girl's whimpering tone communicated more clearly than any words. Mele hurt.

Karma wanted to stop, too. Her eyes hurt, and she blinked away grit from the dusty air. She lifted her muzzle into the wind, and sniffed long and deep. Water. Not far now.

Smoke colored the air. Karma couldn't tell if fire stalked from behind or raced from the front to cut them off. Gusts tossed and shredded scent-cues, making it hard to read. She dropped her nose to the ground, where spore pooled in the dips and valleys between grass hummocks, trying to get her bearings. But Karma knew water in the tank didn't move. It stayed in one place. She knew the way.

Whining, Karma nosed the girl's hand, panting hot breath against her skin. Mele pulled away and took a step forward. Licking her thigh, and poking with her blunt muzzle, Karma again urged the girl forward. Karma herded the girl in a stop-and-go progress, until Mele saw the stand of trees with glittering water below.

With a cry, Mele broke into a staggering run. Karma loped alongside, thwarting her own impulse to reach the water as quickly as possible. Lia told her to watch and guard. That meant staying with Mele, even though the girl ran slower than a puppy.

Mele stumbled across the cracked muddy border where the tank's level had dropped to half-normal capacity. She collapsed, sitting in the mud. She splashed dirty water up her legs and down both arms, trying to cup mouthfuls to drink, ignoring the green scum coating the edges of the tank.

Karma relished the squishy sound and feel of black clay between her toes. She liked the smell of it, too, and waded up to her knees. The sluggish warm water cooled her skin, relief from the furnace-hot air, and Karma lapped and lapped as fast as she could, gulping and swallowing every third or fourth scoop. It would taste better cold, but even warm water tasted delicious.

The pair sat in the wet for a while, enjoying the mud. Mele even scooped water and tossed it at Karma with a giggle. Startled, Karma dodged and yelped before realizing Mele meant to play. Karma shook herself, hard, and flopped forward when she stepped into a hidden hole beneath the water. Her head submerged until she flailed upright and regained her footing.

She didn't like water in her face, not at all. A good-dog couldn't trust water to stay quiet and still. It might rush along and sweep her away, like before. Dogs drank water. Water cooled hot paws. Anything else could be dangerous.

Karma splashed her way to the shallows, and flopped in the shade of a tree, panting happily when the young girl joined her. Mele drew up her knees and leaned against the tree, resting one hand on Karma's neck, rubbing gently. Bliss!

A sound and then a scent bristled Karma's hackles. She shook off the girl's caress, and stood, square and powerful between Mele and potential danger.

"Please no, no, no." Mele reacted to Karma's alert with a whimper. She scrambled behind the massive trunk of the tree.

But this wasn't Boss. The one Mele feared walked on two legs, not four paws. Testing the breeze, Karma recognized a scent with a weird thrill of anticipation. She trembled with excitement when the familiar black shepherd stepped into view.

It had been a long time since her near drowning, many more days than Karma could count since he walked into the night and out of their life. Now Shadow, the *Koa-warrior* had returned.

Karma danced forward, bowing and prancing, with half-muttered joyous exclamations bubbling from her throat. Shadow followed the scented signposts she'd left along the way, marks announcing her status. She'd yearned for *something*, never knowing he would answer.

They'd both changed. His wounds had healed, and Shadow puffed his powerful chest and arched his neck. She was no longer a puppy.

Shadow paced forward. Karma sidestepped to meet him with a flirtatious gait, flagging her tail to one side, but only a moment. She allowed a brief sniff before teasing him to join her in the dance as old as time. Karma spun, racing away in a butt-tuck joyous romp around the perimeter of the tank, splashing mud in her wake.

The black shepherd accepted the invitation. The pair play-bowed and pranced, taking turns who chased who, which sniffed and returned the sniff, testing boundaries, relearning their scents, discovering what each needed, expected and demanded.

Long-ago days as a four-month-old pup, Karma begged for Shadow's attention with muzzle licks and bared tummy. She'd showed proper deference to the potent, adult shepherd, as was his right. But now, by the light of an orange moon, Karma directed each move. When he paused the dalliance to drink, she chastised him, egged him on by mounting his side before dashing away with Shadow in eager pursuit. Finally, Karma allowed her suitor to catch her.

Mele watched from behind the tree, in awe as the lithe black shepherd wooed the flirtatious Rottweiler maiden. The joyous ritual filled with such affection was strangely, achingly beautiful. Mele touched the heart pendant at her throat, and wept for all she had lost.

Chapter 46

Lia gave Fury his head for the moment, waiting for Combs to come back on the line. He'd already given her an earful. Maybe she deserved it.

Now he wanted her to give him Karma's location for him to find. She wished it were that simple. The GPS on the phone only worked within a limited area of about two miles. So far, Karma didn't show up. She'd already explained her theory about the water tanks. Fire complicated everything. Riding blind into a blaze could at best delay the rescue, or leave Lia and Fury hurt or worse. Karma and the girl might have already been caught in the fire—

No! She'd trust that Karma would keep Mele safe. As much as Lia wanted to kick Fury into a frantic gallop after the pair, she agreed to allow Combs's technology to steer her clear of the fire.

He came back on the phone. "Okay, I've got an online aerial view of wildfires on my laptop. Two new hot spots just appeared in the past hour. One erupted not far from where you found the body."

She flinched at the news, and Fury jittered forward. Had it become harder to breathe? Orange glow turned the horizon to blood, and wispy tendrils played tag across the moon's face.

"Lia, you there? Send a screen shot of the cattle tank locations in relation to the access road." He paused, talking to someone else, maybe his partner, before adding, "We can overlay your map with the fire and figure out safest rescue paths."

"Okay, but I have to hang up to text. My old phone can't text and access the application at the same time." The nearest tank sat a quarter mile away. Once within whistle distance, she could reconnect with Karma even without the GPS.

"Wait, before you hang up, where are you now?" Combs's grim tone raised her own concerns. "A third fire just broke out along the access road. Either the wind drop-kicked embers in unexpected directions, or we've got an arsonist in the mix."

"Must be the route the killer used to dump Vicki. I'm maybe a mile the other side of the road. It's a shortcut we use, my horse knows the way." In fact, Fury had picked up his pace, probably smelling the water. That, or getting spooky about the smoke. Maybe both.

"Hot spots send out arms and circle around, can catch and trap you in minutes. Wind gusts measure 40 mph last I heard, so stay alert. Now, send me your text, then get back on the line. Best we stay connected." He paused. "Lia, I don't want you doing this, and I'd stop you if I could. At least let me help keep you safe."

A good guy, after all. But she disconnected without answering, and fiddled with the phone until able to cut-and-paste and send the ranch's schematic to his number. He was right. A fire pushed by a strong wind could outrace a horse. Lia hit redial, and gathered the reins as she waited for Combs to answer.

Smoke enveloped her face, and Lia coughed hard, surprised by a blanket of gray blocking all light. Fury reared and whirled. Lia lost her phone.

"Dammit! Settle, whoa boy. Calm down, Fury, I know, I know, it stinks bad. Brave boy, hold up." The smog thinned enough to see again. She had to find the phone. She couldn't find Karma without it, and relied on Combs's breadcrumb directions around hot spots and through the smoke. Fire was bad enough, but disorientation from the smoke or just inhaling enough of the stuff, could kill.

Lia swung off the big horse, reins clenched tight in one fist. Fury pinned his ears. He snorted with unease and held his ground but just barely. She looked for the glow of the phone's face blinking from somewhere amid the tall grass.

Combs's tinny voice shouted her name during a brief lull in the wind, and she pinpointed the phone's location. But a rush of bright fire crested the nearby rise with a roar.

Fury screamed, and yanked the reins from her hand.

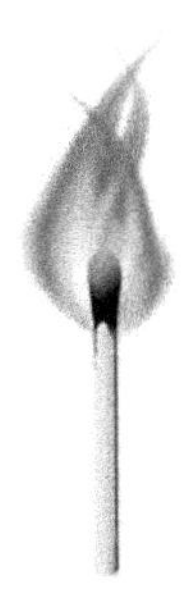

Chapter 47

Karma woke when Shadow nose-poked and then licked her face. They snugged each side of Mele beneath the largest tree, and Karma sighed, not eager to move from the close contact. She yawned and stretched before she returned Shadow's nose poke. She settled her head on Mele's thigh, ready to sleep the night away.

But Shadow whined, stood, and shook hard before lifting his face to the wind. An unsettling yodel of many voices ululated from the distance, speaking of coyote concern and fear. Shadow tipped his long muzzle to the sky and answered with a long, aching howl of his own.

Mele mumbled. She hid her face on one arm.

Now Karma smelled it, too. Haze that stung a good-dog's nose grew stronger. She sneezed to clear her head, but the choke-smell remained, and grew stronger. Her skin twitched, and the fur along Karma's spine stood erect.

Shadow's hackles also bristled, and he howled again, and then barked, dancing forward with warning toward the invisible but advancing threat. Still, it hurried on, and they could hear it threading its way through the dry prairie land, leaving behind superheated air and ash, all with a cackling, chuckling crackle like an old hag laughing. Wind blew, but didn't clear the smoke or cool a good-dog's face.

Leaping to her feet, Karma stood shoulder to shoulder with Shadow to face the enemy. She growled and snarled, showing her teeth when the shepherd's tail lashed her side as he pounced forward and then immediately retreated.

"Īlio?" Their noise roused Mele.

Karma raced to the girl and licked her face, urging her to get up-up-UP! Karma had to protect Mele, the way Lia said. Show teeth and stand against any threat, as she'd been trained. Bite, if need be.

Mele jumped up. "Ahi-ahi-ahi!" She ran from the waves of advancing heat, following the muddy shoulder of the tank's perimeter. Karma followed, happy to put distance between them and the fire.

But Shadow continued to bark. He bounded back and forth in a line parallel to the advancing blaze, as if to herd the flame away. Still it jittered on, blustering and muttering, only to pause and puzzle before letting the wind decide which way to run next.

As they reached the top of the embankment, Mele stopped. Karma ran into her legs and nearly toppled the girl. Below and as far as they could see, a moving blanket of fire came for them, black smoking char in its wake. Mele screamed, fell silent, and froze, too frightened to move.

Karma mouthed the girl's wrist, tugged to turn her back to the tank below. The relative cool of mud on a good-dog's paws beckoned. Could fire drink water the way it ate grass and wood? Karma didn't know. But they would burn up if they waited in the tinder-dry brush.

Smoke and bright flame jigged closer and closer still, and sent out teasing bright fingers ready to gobble anything in its path. A narrow untouched lane offered the only hope for escape. Shadow saw it, too, and paused his noisy defense to slink closer and see for sure.

Karma nosed Mele's hand, and the girl stumbled back down the slight incline. With four fast paws, good-dogs like Karma and Shadow could race the fire and dodge through the narrow flame-free path to safety. Fire would soon cut off even that slim chance.

Shadow stared hard at them, and barked. He barked again, using all his herding heritage to press into Karma's personal space, urging her to move-move-move and run with him, run away to safety, out into the last fire-free trail. His invitation was clear.

Mele never looked up. Her gaze remained focused on the fire-monster now following them down the steep embankment they'd just abandoned.

Karma's paws stuttered in place, yearning to join Shadow and race away, dodge past the hungry bright monster. It scared her more than anything she'd ever seen. She was fast, though. Her four paws could outrace the fire.

But Mele couldn't. The girl's bare feet barely kept her upright. Karma's training demanded she stay, guard and protect this vulnerable child. Karma wasn't sure how to do that, but a good-dog didn't run away, even if afraid. Karma was brave, and trained to serve. It's who she was, even if Lia hadn't asked.

Karma barked a hoarse, tortured cry when Shadow bowed her way, acknowledging her decision. She knew that another held his loyalty, just as Lia held Karma's heart. Shadow whirled and raced away, disappearing into the wall of smoke.

Now, everything was up to Karma.

Chapter 48

Combs yelled into his phone. "Pick up! Lia, pick up the damn phone. You there?" He still had a connection, but nobody answered.

Beside him in the car, Tee waited impatiently. "That can't be good."

He shook his head and punched off the phone. "Something happened."

Tee adjusted the tie keeping long hair from frizzing over her face. "Didn't she say the phone application wouldn't work while you talked? Give her time. She'll call back. I get the idea Lia does things her own way." She smiled. "Like me. Hawaiian girls got minds of their own."

"So do Texas women." He sighed, and turned back to the laptop coordinates. "I know her approximate location. Here's where she cut out." He pointed to a spot midway down the access road, and then compared it to the ranch schematic she'd sent. "That's maybe a mile and a half away." He pointed again. "There's a tank right there, a half mile in the other direction."

"Tank? Like, a fire truck uses? That could be handy."

"No, in Texas a tank is a manmade reservoir, a pond. It fills up with rainwater or sometimes is spring fed. Big spreads like the Corazon's sometimes drill wells to keep them full. Tanks water the livestock. Wildlife, too."

"Still handy in case of a fire." She squinted at the screen. "So Lia figured the dog would take the girl to the closest water, and that's where Lia's headed. Half a mile? Shouldn't take a horse long to get there, even in the dark and walking slow." When he looked surprised, she added drily, "Hawaii has horses too, you know." She sniffed. "My father was a *paniolo* on the Big Island, learned to cowboy from his father."

Combs raised his eyebrows with surprise. Based on her scathing tone, he figured the story wasn't particularly happy.

"Don't suppose your PD has a mounted squad? We could canvas the area from our side, meet Lia in the middle and cut the search in half." She looked at the car, musing. "Take a while to get horses here, though. Don't suppose you've got four-wheel drive on this thing?"

She had a point. With the fire hopscotching everywhere, an ATV would be ideal to stay ahead of any hot spots. That wouldn't happen, though, even if they had the equipment. Like he told Lia, they'd leave it to the fire fighters who lived to eat smoke.

Being so new to police work tempted Tee to go superhero, especially with a missing child. That was admirable. But even firefighters knew to stand down when the risk grew too hot. He had a responsibility to his own team. His partner, Detective Winston Gonzales, coordinated from town while Combs worked onsite. Rushing in at this point, without knowing where to go would get more people hurt.

"A lot of officers have horses, or at least know how to ride. They bring 'em in for parades and special occasions, but we've no official mounted division. Besides, horses get testy around fire." Combs wasn't a fan of horses, either, after being thrown as a kid and breaking his collar bone. His daughter pestered for a horse all the time, and he'd leave it to Melinda's stepdad to handle that argument. Combs preferred smart men and women partnered with technology, rather than temperamental animals. That had become something of an issue with September. If she lost Shadow after he'd asked her to risk the dog, it could finish their relationship. He pushed the hurtful thought away, telling himself the big dog had survived worse.

"Come on, Detective. How much time does that little girl have, if she gets caught by the fire?" Tee shoved open the car door, slammed it, and paced back and forth in front of the hood, getting more and more agitated. "How's a dog protect against fire? Flame bites back. Fire has sharper teeth."

He sighed, and rubbed his eyes, angry because she was right. "Pray the tanks haven't gone dry." By August, many turn into cracked and crumbling empty mud flats. He rolled down his window. "Lia grew up here, knows her way around. Acts like she knows what she's doing, anyway." If not, it could get her killed. "We got to let the firefighters do their job."

"We can't just sit here." Before he could argue, she added, "You asked me to help, not just observe. I'm a police officer, too. Protect and serve, Detective." She breathed hard. "There must be something we can do."

A screaming neigh split the night sky. Combs jumped out of the car, and aimed his flashlight. The sound of hoof beats grew louder until he spotlighted the wild eyes of a rider-less horse.

"Watch out, Tee! Out of the way." He could see the fancy "C" embossed on the side of the saddle, the Corazon brand, as the horse galloped by. Combs grabbed for loose reins, but missed.

"Put down the light!" Tee stood in the middle of the road, and held her arms out to each side, hands fisted, to block and slow the frightened horse. She acted like the horse wouldn't run her down. And he didn't.

When the buckskin stuttered to a stop, Tee darted in, ducking beneath the animal's arched neck to gather the reins in one hand. She spoke in low soothing tones, the words for Combs but also designed to calm the animal.

"I'm guessing he's Lia's mount. So she's out there on foot now, in the middle of the fire. Bet she lost her phone when this big guy spooked." She murmured something like a lullaby under her breath to the horse, patting the side of its neck and jaw, waiting for the blowing breath to slow. She grinned. "I like Texas. Make a wish, and a horse appears." In one swift motion, she vaulted into the saddle.

"Hey, what the hell you doing?" Combs ran toward her, expecting she'd pitch off. He hated green cops, always showboating and as unpredictable as this horse.

The stirrups were far too long, adjusted for Lia's much longer legs. That didn't seem to bother Tee. She stuck tighter than a tick to the saddle, and tossed her own dark mane to punctuate her words.

"I can't sit still and wait. You know what they say about gift horses." With some signal Combs couldn't detect, the horse whirled, and cantered back the way he'd come.

Chapter 49

Karma growled and showed her teeth at the encroaching fire. She nudged Mele's side with her nose, and licked the girl's hand. But Mele didn't react and again stood frozen, just her head swiveling to and fro as she watched the flames surround them and draw ever nearer.

What to do? Where to go? Heat blew against Karma's face, hotter than a good-dog could stand. Her eyes watered and she squinted, dropping her head low to get beneath the bitter scent. Mele followed her lead, and bent double in a coughing fit.

Spooky shadows danced against the gray-white curtain that swirled all around. Karma wished Lia was here. Lia knew what to do. She always explained so Karma understood.

But Lia wasn't here. And Karma didn't understand. But Lia must believe Karma could protect Mele, even with fire all around. It sparked and danced, throwing up starry shoots of flame so that the wind caught and carried firefly-bright embers high, high, high into the sky. Only the placid black water remained free of the spit and spread of heat.

Mud still caked Karma's paws. Now dry, it sloughed off when she pawed the cracked ground. She took half a dozen steps forward until the mud squelched between her toes again, and one big forepaw splashed in the shallows. Warm, almost hot, but wet. Wet wasn't fire. That was a good thing.

The nearby tree that had shaded their slumber continued to make hissing cat-spit sounds, leaves blackened and flew away until the flaming trunk and limbs remained alone. A clot of glow-bright leaves landed on Karma's back and she screamed, twisted and dodged away, running into Mele and knocking the girl to into the shallows. Mele curled into a ball, keening and shivering in the muddy water. The smoldering leaves floated for a moment in superheated air, coasting above the pond surface and then dropped into the water. Flame sizzled as it extinguished. The remainder floated, black, no bright fire or embers, just ashen twigs buffeted back to shore by the windy breath.

That was the answer!

Karma licked Mele's face, cold-nosed her ear and even jabbed her muzzle in the girl's bare armpit. That worked best to rouse Lia up in the morning. Up-up-up, Mele had to get up, too! Karma licked the girl's eyes until Mele tried to push her away. So Karma took the girl's wrist in her massive jaw, and tugged.

When the dog's teeth closed on Mele's skin, her eyes flew wide and she instinctively pulled back. But Karma kept up the gentle, tugging pressure, pulling Mele toward the water. If gentle didn't work, Karma had to act.

A loud CRACK! sounded. A big branch fell off the flaming tree, and rolled, hissing, into the water where it sizzled, charred branches below and flames still riding the upward twigs. Karma saw sudden understanding in Mele's expression.

Together, they stumbled into the water, Mele falling to her knees after a couple of steps. Karma also struggled to keep her balance on mud-slick that coated the floor of the tank. Mele's small hand gripped her harness and collar, so Karma took another strong stride into shoulder-height water, tugging the girl with her. Water soothed her body. But bits of fire rained from the tree, stinging a good-dog's head and the girl's bare skin.

Karma whined. She remembered the rushing flood from that long ago time, when water filled her eyes and mouth, choking away air. Shadow saved her then, reached out and snagged her collar the way Mele grabbed it now. But Shadow was gone.

Karma didn't want to go deeper. She was brave, but wanted solid ground beneath her paws.

Another CRACK announced more flaming rain. No time for fear. Karma lunged, yanked Mele along.

The bottom of the tank fell away. Karma sank, head swallowed beneath dirty warm water, and she flailed with all four paws, fighting the treacherous liquid. Breathe! She couldn't breathe. Karma choked on a mouthful of brackish tank water before her toes touched the muddy bottom. Mele above scissored the water to froth with thin girl-legs, thumping toes into a good-dog's head and back.

Mele's foot struck Karma's nose, and Karma emptied half her lungs in a bubble-filled snarl. She couldn't see. Couldn't smell. Couldn't hear. Black, silt-filled liquid clogged her nose, mouth, ears. And no air. Karma had to reach the air! Another string of bubbles escaped as she struggled to find the surface.

With great effort, Karma pressed muscular hind legs into the muddy bottom, springing her massive body upward. She burst up-up-up out of the water, pummeling the water with her front legs to keep her face in the air while she gasped and gagged. She tried to shake water away. The liquid muffled every sense.

"Karma! Karma-pup, you there?"

Whimpering, Karma's ears twitched with hope. She paddled, frantic, neck straining to find the familiar voice.

Mele's arms snaked around Karma's broad neck, and they both went under once again. This time, Karma relaxed and let herself settle to the bottom, ignoring the girl's throttling grip around her throat. Once all four paws touched the mud, Karma propelled them back to the surface. She gasped in two great lungfuls of tainted air, and struggled not to choke. The girl helped this time, kicking her legs to keep them afloat, even though the superheated air scorched a good-dog's nose and ears.

Again came the cry. "Karma! Please be here. Karma? Mele!" Lia's silhouette appeared at the far side of the tank, backlit by bright flames. She staggered toward the water.

Karma's happy yelp of recognition couldn't be heard over the next CRACK from the burning tree. It shivered once, tipped, and fell, reaching with burning limbs toward the center of the tank. It somersaulted on top of where Karma and Mele trod water.

Chapter 50

Lia staggered to the edge of the tank, flinched as the mountain ash tree splashed into the water. She saw a seal-slick dog head duck down just before it hit.

"Karma! Mele? Answer me!" Hot wind scalded Lia's back through her thick shirt. She stumbled to the tank's edge, and splashed belly down into the water, and then rolled. She welcomed the stink of rancid but lifesaving wet, and came up from the four-foot dunking, sputtering. The braids came loose with the bandana. Lia took it off, dunked it in the water, and tied it over her nose and mouth as she cried out again, "Please, are you there?"

A flash of something—a Karma whisper-tickle message!—filled her mind's eye a split second before Mele's shout. "Here here, we here!" Mele's frightened voice cut through the cacophony. "*Īlio* here, too."

Thank you God! "Hang on, I'm coming." Lia shouted encouragement and prayed she hadn't lied. She didn't question the return of her fickle mental "gift" that appeared during life-and-death struggles.

The inferno surrounded the water tank, all but a narrow passage on the south-west side she'd been fortunate to find. Wind blew from that direction to the northeast, and might keep fire at bay in that one spot. Lia made a mental note. Maybe they could make a run for it.

Conventional wisdom said to stay beneath the smoke. Inhalation of the gases killed more fire victims than burns. Water helped fend off heat, but the smoke remained an issue because it flowed in thick eddies even over the water surface. Lia took a careful breath through the bandanna, before she dove and swam toward the sound of Mele's voice near the smoldering tree.

She surfaced amid blackened witchy fingers scraping her face. Mele screamed, and Lia saw the girl's long hair caught in a smoldering branch. The submerged tree impeded swimming while the uppermost branches dribbled embers like a volcano raining fire. Lia weaved through the watery obstacle course to reach Mele.

"Hold still." She splashed water onto Mele's head and hair. No time to untangle the mess, she just broke the branch and left it in the tangled tresses. "Where's Karma? My dog, where's my dog?" She felt Karma's comforting presence, but needed the confirmation of her eyes. Then Lia couldn't bear the heat any longer, and watched blisters erupt on Mele's forehead. No time to wait. "Under! Under, now!" and as one accord, both Lia and Mele let themselves drop below the surface.

A furry body brushed against her. Lia wanted to shout with joy at the physical confirmation that Karma survived. On her other side, Mele rose to the surface, and Lia followed the girl up, grateful for the wind's brief respite.

A doggy whine greeted her. Karma paddled hard to keep her head above water. Her scorched muzzle and blistered nose looked bad but she lived!

"Good-dog, Karma, you're so smart and brave. My good girl." The Rottweiler whined and huffed under her breath, and Lia could imagine Karma's tail pin wheeling like a propeller beneath the water. The poor dog looked exhausted, though. Lia found a sturdy branch just beneath the surface, and guided Karma's forelegs to rest across the floating ledge for buoyancy.

The stopgap mattered little, though. They wouldn't survive another blast if they stayed above water. Fire incinerated anything combustible. The sheltering tree would turn to ash, and them along with it.

"Mele, listen to me. We have to breathe, but the fire or smoke will kill us. So we must stay underwater until the fire goes out. You've got to do exactly what I say. No questions, can you do that?" She waited for the girl to nod. The fire offered stark illumination that transformed the scene into hell on earth. Tears streamed down Mele's face, but her eyes shined with resolve. "You need to help me with Karma, too, okay? I'll show you what to do."

The girl's lip trembled and then steadied. Made of grit, this girl, or Mele wouldn't have survived this long.

"I'll be right here with you. Be right back." Lia smiled, and let herself sink into the dingy water. She shed her billowing work shirt. This one shirt had to do the job for all of them. She kicked back to the surface.

The wind blustered, building up to another firestorm. No time to spare, Lia gathered a branch dipping down and up in the water. "Help me, Mele. Take that side, yes, that's right." She handed the other edge of the soaked shirt to the girl, and showed her how to drape the sopping fabric over the rake-shaped limb. The shirt formed a shallow tent, enough to filter out the worst of the smoke. She prayed it would provide some protection from the fire. Otherwise, they'd cook. Two human faces and one Rottweiler muzzle must fit beneath.

With a rush, the wind egged on the fire, a banshee-scream boiling toward them.

"Now! Mele, under the shirt, go-go-go! Hang on to my belt!" Lia clutched the submerged tree trunk with one hand, and looped her other arm around Karma. She pulled the dog under. She saw red-rimmed canine eyes brim with tears, and felt Karma lick her own eyes. Lia filled her mind's-eye with calm, with trust, with love, imagined it surrounding them all in a blue-cool safe bubble…and neither Karma nor Mele offered any struggle, trusting that Lia knew best.

Chapter 51

Karma gasped with relief when Lia held her underwater just a few seconds. She blinked but couldn't see anything. Her nose, still clogged with smoke, could only scent musty water, Mele's fear, and Lia's comforting smell. They breathed the same stale air, cocooned beneath a sweat-impregnated cloth. The choking taste of ash diminished, even as fire roar grew deafening.

She tried to stay brave, but couldn't help a whimper. She peed, too, the warm rush a strange sensation under the water, grateful Shadow didn't know. She wondered where he'd gone. Had the fire made him dead? Her whimper became a sob.

Lia's arm tightened around Karma's neck. "Good-girl, Karma, you're a brave good-dog, you know that?"

The crooning litany made Karma feel better. She licked Lia's face again to tell her so. But nothing seemed to help Mele. On the other side of Lia, the girl sobbed and her shaking made the dark water ripple.

Lia shouted when fabric overhead sizzled, and a bright spot appeared where fire nibbled through. "Under again, now!" Lia shouted again, and Karma didn't understand the words, but intuited the action when Lia's arm tightened around her neck. Mele and Lia took big breaths, so Karma also filled her lungs with too-hot sooty air, and let herself be dragged down, down, down.

They huddled together for more heartbeats than Karma could count, until a good-dog's chest ached with the need to gulp air. Lia's arm drew her closer and closer, trembling with tension, and Karma knew she also struggled to deny herself breath. Finally, Karma could stay still no longer. She'd risk fire rather than let water end her life. She twisted, tore from Lia's grasp, and thrashed until she broke the surface several yards from the sheltering, smoldering tree.

Gasping and choking, Karma had to blink many times before sore eyes could see. Fire had passed their meager shelter, devoured everything, and left blackened twisted trees and smoking ground everywhere. The prone tree Karma had escaped still puffed dark clouds high above, but gusts of hot wind broomed clean the air below.

She twisted, paddling in a tight circle, watching for Lia. With fire roaring away into the distance, they could safely leave the shattered tree. Maybe Lia didn't know? Underwater muffled sounds, and people couldn't hear the same as dogs.

Mele popped up, choking and sputtering. "*Piholo, piholo, piholo*!" She screamed the strange words over and over as Karma paddled to her, still expecting Lia to appear. When Mele grabbed her collar, Karma lengthened her stroke to tow them both to the shallow edge of the tank.

"Hey there. Lia Corazon, you there?" A horse thundered up to the edge of the tank. Karma recognized Fury, but not the athletic woman riding him.

She swung out of the saddle in one smooth motion. Black mud and soot colored the horse from hoof to flank, and the rider's bandanna covered her nose and mouth so Karma couldn't read her face. She ran to reach Mele when the girl struggled out of the water. "*Aloha Mele*. And you must be Karma."

Karma tipped her head when the stranger called her name. She stared, brow wrinkled, waiting for the black water to give up Lia.

Mele launched herself at the stranger. "*Piholo, piholo, piholo*!" She jabbed a finger at the half-submerged tree.

"Drowned? Not today, she won't drown!" The woman scooped Mele into her arms, carried her to the waiting horse, and set the girl high on the creature's back.

Karma didn't trust the big animal. They smelled different than dogs, and ignored a good-dog's invitation to play. But when Karma followed Mele out of the water, she recognized Lia's lariat looped and hanging from the saddle.

Lia made magic happen with the rope. She'd whirl it around and around her head and tossed the lariat far away to catch and fetch. Would this stranger use the lariat to fetch Lia? Karma danced with excitement, eager to make something, anything happen so Lia would come out of the water again. She could feel Lia there, under the water, knew it because of the itchy-odd sensation inside her head.

But the woman just talked into the phone that people always seemed to carry.

Time, no time! Karma's lungs still ached from holding her breath, and Lia had been under far longer. She danced forward toward the horse, signaling "no threat" with averted gaze and oblique approach, but Fury sidled away. Another reason to distrust the confusing creatures. Karma yelped—she couldn't help it—and that made the horse shy even more. Karma couldn't reach Fury's reins this time to stop him and the horse jumped sideways. Mele squealed, grabbed for purchase, and knocked the lariat from the saddle.

Yes! Karma bounded forward, and grasped one end, and shook it like a stuffed toy.

"What're you doing, dog?" The woman scowled, and took a step toward Karma. She paused when Mele spoke.

Karma paid no attention. She didn't understand the words anyway, but Lia's anguish cried out to her from the hidden spot under the water directly into her mind. Sometimes dogs knew what to do better than people. She shook the end of the rope again, and backed away, dragging her end into the water.

It was up to her. Get the rope to Lia, so Lia could make magic happen and save herself. At the thought, Karma spun around and splashed into the cattle tank, ignoring the shouts of surprise from Mele and the stranger.

Chapter 52

Lia took shallow breaths, conserving the oxygen bubble still held by the canvas shirt. The tree had settled further in the water, trapping her in a prison of branches she couldn't escape. Spending the last of her energy breaking through the barrier would speed her death, and the thought of burning terrified her more than drowning. Besides, Mele was gone, as was Karma. She could no longer feel the pup's presence in her mind's eye, and the absence left her bereft. She feared both had already perished in the fire.

Tears welled. Her fault, all her fault. She should never have let Mele run away in the first place, or sent Karma after her. Fury killed, too, all because of her stupid pride. She didn't bother wiping away tears. She couldn't see anything anyway. Soon the fire would consume all the oxygen, leaving carbon monoxide and other gasses that could send her to eternal sleep. She'd join Karma and the others. And her mother. All her questions would be answered . . .

Something hit her leg, and Lia flailed in reaction, only by chance avoided deflating her makeshift bubble. It hit again, and she felt Karma's fur. She grinned in the darkness. The fire must have blown through. Either burned out or moved on. Maybe the girl had survived, after all!

Karma's domed head surfaced beside Lia. The dog cried happy little noises past the rope she clutched in her jaws. She pushed it toward Lia, insistent, in the same way she demanded games.

Lia recognized the feel of the lariat, the familiar texture an old friend. Her breath caught. Someone had found Fury. Help waited beyond the watery sanctuary. Time to leave, before it became her tomb. "Good-dog, Karma." She hadn't taught this. The Rottweiler, like a true police K9, improvised for the situation.

Her chest tightened, and black sparklies danced before her eyes. If she didn't make a move, she'd pass out. "Karma, go out, *vorhaus!*" The *move forward* cue was the closest approximation she could offer to get the dog back to safety. No reason to risk Karma any further. Besides, there wasn't room to maneuver alone.

With a final slurp across Lia's face, Karma sank beneath the water and disappeared. Lia prayed the dog could again weave through the confining branches. At ten months, Karma hadn't yet reached her full size, while Lia's frame couldn't squeeze through. She'd tried until her healed ribs screamed in protest. Lia hoped whoever held the other end could pull her out.

She looped the end of the rope around her upper chest, and hung on with both hands. Lia sucked in several more breaths of stale air, feeling dizziness begin to claim her, and yanked three times on the rope.

The slack in the line grew taut. A steady tugging ensued, and Lia took a final breath before sinking beneath the water. She threaded her head and one shoulder between the widest, most spindly span of branches. Pressure on the rope increased, pulled with bruising force as Lia twisted sideways until her upper torso squeezed through. She kick-kick-kicked with both feet, and reached behind to press apart the scissor grip now tightening around her waist.

Bubbles streamed from her lips as scraping pain flamed over hipbones. But with a final twist, the tree gave her up, birthing her into an open passage. The rope towed her to the shallows. Lia could hear Fury whickering with excitement as he pulled her out, while a woman's calming voice spoke lilting words Lia didn't understand.

Groaning, Lia braced herself on hands and knees, retching and coughing to rid herself of the sludge and soot. An ecstatic Karma splashed around her, and having found her voice, barked with joy at the reunion.

"You must be Lia Corazon. That's some dog you've got there. Makings of a great K9 officer." The small woman held out her hand to help Lia up. "I'm Officer Tee Teves." She hesitated.

"You're Hawaiian!" Lia wiped her face. "Sorry, that was rude. I wasn't expecting you, is all. Where's Mele?"

Tee nodded over her shoulder and Lia saw the girl astride Fury's broad back. "Some horse you got, too. Seems to know Mele needs gentling. She's been through a lot." She didn't look at Lia as she took care to coil the lariat, treating it with respect, or something else. Caution, maybe?

Lia took the coiled rope when the officer handed it to her. "Did you call for help? I lost my phone. Don't think Fury can carry all of us. And I don't want Karma walking in that hot mess. She's already burned."

"Yes, Detective Combs has rescue vehicles on the way. He's pissed I went all Lone Ranger when your horse showed up." Tee hesitated, then added, "Where'd you get it? The lariat, I mean. It's old. Looks like, anyway." She still refused to meet Lia's eyes.

"Belonged to my mother. Part of it got chewed off in another rescue, but I had it repaired. I think it may have been a gift from my father, but I haven't been able to find out much about it. See, I think that's his mark on it right here." Lia rubbed the embossed lettering, showing the *W. Tex* brand to the other woman. "I've not had much luck yet getting answers. Hey, since you're from the Islands, maybe you could help me out—"

Tee's eyes widened when she saw the mark. She made a noise as though punched in the gut, and staggered a couple of steps backwards.

"You all right? Hey, Officer . . .?"

The smaller woman folded in on herself, and sank to the ground.

Mele called from her nearby seat on Fury. "*Maka'u, weli.* She scared, ghost from past. I seen it, she one like me."

"Let me be, leave me alone. Just need a moment." Tee buried her head in her arms, shuddering.

Lia stood by, helpless, not knowing what to do. The fickle blue-aura of comfort had left like so much mist.

But Karma knew. The big dog padded to the officer, and pressed one black, warm shoulder against the woman's side.

With a sobbed gasp, Tee twisted and gathered the Rottweiler into a frantic hug. They were still entwined ten minutes later when Combs arrived with EMTs.

Chapter 53

Combs took a calming breath before entering the room. Previous encounters with Dub Corazon hadn't been easy, and he didn't look forward to this interview.

At least he'd gotten a reprieve with September, when Shadow came back. The black German Shepherd had more lives than a cat. They still had things to work out, though. He thought September might be the most aggravating, stubborn woman he'd ever met.

Lia ran a close second. She sat next to her grandfather, fidgeting, and her face brightened when he entered. Combs tried to ignore how that made him feel.

"Please, Mr. Corazon, stay seated. This is just an informal talk, that's all." Combs closed the door behind him, and took a seat on the opposite side of the table. "Ms. Corazon. How're you feeling?"

"It's Lia, remember? And I'm much better, thanks." She turned to her grandfather. "See, I told you we don't need an attorney."

"We'll see." He smoothed his white hair and fussed with the straw cowboy hat he held on his lap. "Could we move this along? Lia has an important appointment later this afternoon to test that police dog of hers. Of course, that's assuming the pup gets released from the veterinarian in time."

Lia's jaw flexed, and although she looked at Combs, she directed her pointed remarks to her grandfather. "You'd think after everything Karma did to keep Mele safe, not to mention rescuing me, that a test would be moot."

"Deal's a deal." The older man's knuckles tightened on the hat.

"You've already given your statement, Lia, we just need it to be read and approved." Combs opened a folder and gave her several pages. "Please make any necessary changes or clarifications, initial them and sign." He watched as she went through the formalities, scribbling a couple of notes but otherwise leaving the statement as prepared.

"How's Mele? What's going to happen to her?" She shoved the completed paperwork back to him.

"She's with CPS." Combs put Lia's statement in the folder. The girl had run away from her last foster home, and been plucked from the streets in Hawaii by…they hadn't figured that out yet. Combs wasn't thrilled about sticking Mele back in foster care, a situation she'd run from before.

According to national data, eighty-six percent of missing children suspected of being forced into sex work came from the child welfare system. In Texas, the vast majority of young victims had some contact with Child Protective Services. "Here in Texas, we focus on the pimps. Wish we could do more for the victims."

"Girls like Vicki are victims, too. Didn't you say she was kidnapped? And yet, if she lived, she'd be going to jail." Lia's righteous indignation made her voice shake. "Vicki wanted to testify, and she ended up dead. Now you want to put Mele in the same no-win situation. How do you keep her safe?"

"I know, I know. You're preaching to the choir." He noticed someone outside the room, and paused for a moment. "Mele knows who killed Vicki. But the only name she has is *Boss*. Says it's the same person who set the fire that nearly killed all y'all. Not to mention the property damage done to Corazon holdings." He nodded to the older man, face solemn. "Glad you got the alarm in time to move your horses, sir."

"Appreciate that, Detective. And I appreciate you rescuing my granddaughter." He didn't look at Lia.

Lia's face turned rosy and she looked away as well.

Combs cleared his throat. "As it happens, we're lucky our

Hawaiian consultant has a knack for getting Mele to talk." He motioned with one hand, inviting someone to join them. "In fact, she wanted to talk more with you, Lia, and is staying on for a while as part of the ongoing investigation."

She tugged on his sleeve. "Grandfather? You don't have to stay. I'm fine, if you want to go ahead." Lia looked more nervous than embarrassed. Even fearful. Combs wondered why.

He shook off Lia's hand and stood when the petite dark-haired young police officer entered the room and held out her hand. "So you're the one who fished Lia out of that tank. I'm William Corazon, ma'am, but you can call me Dub. Very pleased to make your acquaintance."

"Nice to meet you, too." She took his hand, and offered a firm handshake. "Officer Pilikia Teves. You can call me Tee."

He dropped her hand as if snake bit. "This some kind of joke?" He towered over Lia. "Did you put her up to that? Have you been digging in that mongrel shit, when I ordered you to stay away?" His other hand crushed the brim of his hat.

Combs frowned, and took a step forward. "Mr. Corazon, I don't understand. Let's stay calm. What seems to be the trouble?"

"I won't calm down, Detective. And if you're part of this, I'll have your badge, see if I won't!" He jammed the hat back on his head, stormed to the door, turned, and offered a parting shot at Lia. "Forget about testing that mutt of yours, I'm calling it off." His lips whitened, breath came in gasps. "You lied to me, did the one forbidden thing I can't forgive. You're no better than that Teves bastard who killed my girl!" His voice rose to shouts, face purpled and a vein throbbed in his neck. "You're not part of this family, not anymore. You made your choice. So pick up your stuff, and clear out. You hear me!" He slammed the door.

Lia stood silent, face white, mouth agape. She played with a bracelet on one delicate wrist.

Tee folded her arms tight, jaw working. She looked ready to bolt, too.

Combs stared at the two women, a tall Texas beauty and a petite exotic cop, one light and one dark. But they had the same eyes. The same smile. The same hair, except for the color. "What just happened?" But he had an inkling.

"I lost my home." Lia knuckled tears away and squared her shoulders. "Need to find a place to stay. For me and for Karma."

She gathered her small bag, and hunted for car keys. "We'll be camping over at Corazon Kennels if you need us. Who needs electricity or running water?" Lia tried to smile, but it faltered. "I have to go get my dog."

Tee took a breath, and uncrossed her arms. "I like dogs. Been thinking about getting one."

"That so." Lia didn't look at her.

Tee addressed Combs. "Karma could identify Mele's *Boss* just as well as the girl. Dogs testify sometimes, don't they, Detective?" She didn't wait for an answer, as if she'd made a decision. "The department's putting me up while I work the case but I need a ride." She nodded at Lia. "You got a car. You need a place to stay, and I got a room. Maybe we can help each other out. Maybe we can share, you know, resources." Her hesitant offer anticipated vehement objections.

Surprise, anger and suspicion chased across Lia's face in quick succession. Finally, she nodded stiff agreement. "Appreciate the offer. Karma and I will help any way we can."

Tee turned to Combs. "What do you say, Detective?"

He had no reason to object. "You want to share the room, that's up to you. If management has objections about the dog, have 'em call me. Police dogs get special consideration."

Lia smiled her thanks, and followed the smaller woman out of the interview room.

Combs called after. "Tee! I'm still lead on this investigation. No more running off without backup, you hear me? Lia, that goes for you double." He sat heavily and dropped the file on the table. One of 'em alone was trouble enough. Teaming a Texas firebrand and a Hawaiian volcano? He predicted fireworks in their future.

Chapter 54

Lia drove faster than the speed limit, but didn't care. She had a cop riding shotgun, after all. She glanced sideways at Officer Pilikia Teves, and didn't know whether to be angry, or relieved.

Grandfather never lost. He'd set Lia up to fail. So in a way, this woman had done her a favor. "We need to talk."

"We will. Just not now, please." Tee kept her eyes focused out the window, taking in the North Texas landscape as the city streets made way for pasture. "It's not easy for me, either." She played with something—looked like seashells—in one hand, and they made a whispery sound like waves at the beach. "You the one emailed my Auntie." It wasn't a question. "That's why she talked about fate, me being in Dallas."

There, she confirmed it. Lia gripped the steering wheel so hard her hands hurt. All those emails she'd sent, so careful to keep them secret from Grandfather, even hiding her name. She'd received zero replies. Now, this. Heat flushed her face. She wanted to scream at the woman, make her talk, explain, give details about the man Grandfather blamed for everything. Lia had only suspicions until Grandfather's reaction confirmed the connection.

"What does the *W* stand for? His first name, give me that at least." Tee had answers to the questions that had plagued Lia her whole life. She'd let the woman dodge most for now, not wanting a repeat of the woman's meltdown.

"Wyatt." The officer spit the name. The shushing of the seashells grew agitated. "Don't we have to get your dog?" She changed of subject without apology.

Lia nodded. *Wyatt Teves.* The old worn leather made the letters look like *Tex* rather than *Teves.* With the name, she could dig deeper to find out more about her family history, even if Tee—her half-sister—refused to help. Maybe the woman's Auntie would be more forthcoming.

"The vet kept Karma for oxygen therapy, same as us. She had some superficial burns on her muzzle and paws, but nothing serious."

"Good." Tee turned from the window since conversation moved to safer ground. "What happens now? With the police dog training, I mean." She slipped the shells back into a pocket.

"Don't know." Lia rubbed her bloodshot eyes that still stung from the after effects of the fire. "Even if Karma passed the test, Grandfather wouldn't come through with the financial support."

Tee frowned. "Sorry I barged in. I should've waited until he left."

Sighing, Lia pulled the car into a nearby lot, and parked in front of Heartland Veterinary Hospital. "You couldn't know." Her eyes narrowed. "Or did you?"

The derisive snort spoke volumes. "If it had to do with Wyatt Teves, yeah, I'd expect a toxic reaction. But I didn't know it was you." She looked out the window again, anywhere but at Lia. "Your last name isn't—"

"Like you said, we'll talk later." Lia sat for a moment, wanting to rush in and collect her dog but worried what she'd find. Dogs could have PTSD, just like people. Only time would tell if Karma suffered fallout from the fire or water. That could disqualify her from police dog consideration. Her breed already counted against Karma because of overheating concerns. In Texas triple-digit heat indexes, Karma wouldn't be a top K9 no matter how well she performed. She'd do better in a cooler climate.

Only one hurdle stood in Karma's way. If Doc Eugene gave the okay, Lia would sign those papers, get it done today, and pick up the big girl tomorrow. "You want to wait in the car, or come in?"

"I'll wait. We can put my suitcase in your trunk to make room for Karma in the back seat." Tee started to get out.

Lia shook her head. "It's fine for now. Karma may need to stay an extra day or so for surgery. I'll let you know."

"Surgery? I thought she just needed oxygen. You said she wasn't seriously injured." She sounded more concerned than Lia expected. Tee and Karma connected out at the tank. Karma knew what to do, to cut short the woman's flashback.

"You can come in if you want, but the baby-dog's fine." Lia smiled as she got out of the car, too. "She's just getting spayed, that's all."

"Wait. You're getting her fixed? But you can't." Tee looked panicked.

Puzzled, Lia tried to calm the cop's concern, and explained. "She can't be a police dog unless she's spayed. Girl dogs go into season, and that's a distraction for her and any other dogs she encounters. It's a safety issue. To perform at peak levels, female dogs are spayed." She started toward the clinic. "Karma won't even notice the difference."

Tee didn't look convinced.

"Look, it's usually done at a much younger age, and safe. I shouldn't have waited so long, but got caught up in the training, and Rotties don't often go into heat this early. Jeff—that is, Detective Combs, found blood trace that didn't belong to either victim." She shrugged. "I always figured we could get Karma spayed after Grandfather's test. Now that won't happen, so it's as good a time as any."

"You don't understand." Tee grabbed Lia's shoulder, stopping her. "Mele told me a story. She said Karma had a lover." She smoothed her dark curls, clearly upset. "She called him a *Koa, pu'ali īlio.*"

"That can't be true." But the words rocked her. Six months ago, an injured shepherd appeared to help save them, and then vanished just as quickly. And now, he'd reappeared when Karma faced her trial by fire? On top of that, September's tracking dog had gone missing during the fire. "What else did Mele say?"

"She said they slept together, all three of them. Mele says *Koa* warned them of the fire, he barked and held it at bay until they were safe in the water. Then he disappeared into the smoke." She laughed uneasily.

Lia shivered, still not willing to believe. "She must have dreamed it."

Tee shook her head. "No, I saw him, too. When I galloped after you, I planned to ride west to the nearest pond. Instead, a big dog appeared like a smoky shadow, and drove Fury the other direction. That's how I found you."

"A shepherd? Like a shadow?" Lia whispered the question. She'd never asked September about her lost dog, believing the topic and questions too painful.

Tee nodded, eyes wide. "I'm not into all that woo-woo mystical stuff, but still. Lia, do you have to spay Karma today? I mean, what if . . ." Her voice trailed off. The corners of her mouth twitched into a hopeful smile.

The past six months overflowed with anger, stress, heartbreak and even death. Karma's future as a police dog already teetered on the brink. Now with Lia's future shot to hell, and Mele's past offering little hope, didn't everyone long for—and deserve—a happy ending?

"No, the surgery doesn't have to be today." Lia nodded at the car. "Make room for the baby-dog. Let's take Karma home, and see if that Shadow-dog's magic is real."

PART 3 CALLED to PROTECT
(*October*)

Chapter 55

The chilly October wind pushed gusts that rattled bare branches against the windows. Karma woofed under her breath and levered herself upright with effort. Her black brow furrowed, and her short Rottweiler tail quivered. She clawed the soft bedding with low mutterings before settling once again, but immediately stood, unable to find a comfortable position.

Her head cocked to one side and she eyed the nearby sofa. It smelled of Lia, her favorite person. Lia taught her important things a good-dog needed to know. Strong and bold, but always fair, Lia gave Karma fun games to play.

Lia slept here, on the sofa. The other girl, Tee, slept in the other room.

Karma hadn't known Tee for very long. She wore uniforms and carried a gun, but had a hidden hurt inside, one that Karma kept trying to heal with face-licks and snuggles. Tee pretended to be strong, but a good-dog could sniff out hidden broken pieces. Karma wondered how humans could look one way but be something very different. They tried to pretend but could never fool a good-dog.

Dogs never pretended. Dogs always looked and smelled and acted like dogs, no matter what.

Karma loved making Lia happy. Being close to her made Karma happy and feel safe, too. Sometimes, not nearly often enough, they shared feelings so strong that a dog might burst with the sensation. Karma made herself small, so she fit in the curve of Lia's knees, and they slept that way all night long on the sofa. Until recently. Now, Karma couldn't curl herself tight enough to fit.

She whined again. Lia and Tee had been gone all day. Karma begged to go with her girls, but no amount of paw-dancing or butt-wriggling requests changed their minds. She'd been left behind in this stuffy two-room hideaway, all alone, all day long. It made Karma want to howl. So she did.

Karma wondered what she'd done wrong. A good-dog stayed with her people, no matter what. She used to go everywhere, even to visit Tee's other uniform-wearing friends. But now, she had trouble jumping into cars, or running as fast as before. Her body had grown clumsy and didn't move right.

She missed playing her favorite games. Karma loved playing the "*achtung*" game to stop people who raced away. But Karma yearned to stretch into a flat-out butt-tucking run and feel the wind in her face. Even her adored ferocious tug contests with Tee—for a little girl, she was strong!—were better with grass beneath her paws.

Karma's stubby tail quivered at the thought of mauling a padded sleeve until Tee gave up and fell down laughing with joy. Tee didn't laugh enough, and Karma had decided that should be part of her job, to make the girl laugh. That was the best! Lia would give the command, and Tee would yell and hold out the sleeve, and squeal when Karma bit down hard. Oh, so much fun! Tee didn't know the proper words, like "*such*" to search, or "*achtung*" to guard, but Karma still understood. She was smart that way.

They still played the hide-and-seek "*such*" games but finding treats and toys hidden around two rooms bored her. Nothing remained hidden from her nose for long. She remembered tracking the young girl Mele, despite the twists of smoke and swirling fire. Her breath quickened at the memory, and she licked her burn-scarred paws. She wanted another challenge, but maybe one not so dangerous, please. She'd run through long grass, head down and nose following neon-bright scent, until she found the hidden, and flopped down on her tummy—*platz*—to announce the find.

But now, a tummy flop hurt. Her body no longer obeyed. Karma worried her girls wouldn't let her play the best games anymore.

Wind teased the tree outside the window so it scratched the glass like cats clawing their way inside. Karma barked at the thought of cats, so much fun to sniff and chase. She barked again, even though she knew no cat-scent was near. But sometimes barking made strangers come to the door. She cocked her head to listen, but no neighbor responded. She was alone, and she didn't like it.

Grumbling to herself, Karma left the window, caught up her stuffed bear-toy, and carried it to the sofa. It took two tries to climb onto the soft cushion. She scratched and scratched the fabric, not sure why, but needed to rearrange the surface before settling down. With a sigh, she sank into the softness, but immediately reared back up and dismounted. It felt wrong. She grabbed her bear-toy again, whining, and paced from the sofa to the window and back again.

The open door to the closet caught her attention. A handful of clothes swayed overhead, and Lia's tracking boots littered the floor with dirt. Boot-smell comforted Karma. It also meant her girls weren't tracking without her. She lay down again, snugging one of the boots and bear-toy close to her swollen tummy.

A sudden sharp pain made her scramble to her feet.

With another grumbled whine, Karma padded into the bedroom to Tee's bed and hoisted herself up. She wasn't supposed to hop on furniture but couldn't help herself. She grabbed one end of the fabric covering, tugged it loose, and walked backwards while pulling it after her. Karma gathered the spread into a messy pile at the head of the bed. Then she nosed the pillows, paw-thumped them into submission, and settled with care in the new nest.

Karma hadn't felt normal for many days. Always hungry, she got sick every morning. A gnawing feeling filled her middle now, not hunger, but something akin to that yearning. Karma whined again and scrubbed her face against the sheets with a satisfied moan. She liked the smooth fabric better than her own floor-level pillow. Tee-smell was different than Lia-smell but was the next best thing to her girls being here. Karma sighed, and settled her big head on her paws to wait.

She yelped and jerked. Pressure in her tummy became a sharp, unrelenting pain that came in waves. Different than anything she'd ever experienced. Karma was brave and strong, she'd trained to face down scary people, survived flood and fire, and would protect her family no matter what. But how could a good-dog fight a hurt on the inside?

Showing her teeth didn't frighten the pain away. She drowned in the burning sensation she couldn't escape.

Karma whimpered and shivered, no longer the brave, proud Rottweiler girl. She wished her family would come home. Lia always knew what to do.

Chapter 56

Lia pulled into the narrow parking space outside the shabby efficiency apartment. Her petite passenger bolted before the car shuddered to a stop and slammed the door. *Typical.*

The sun painted long shadows across the parking lot, and wind swirled dead leaves against the windshield. Fall in North Texas meant brown trees and yellow grass and rushed by in an eye-blink. Lia knew the 60-degree temps would drop once darkness fell.

She watched the smaller woman hunch against wind that tangled her brown hair into a messy halo. Lia adjusted her own goldenrod tresses, tightening the ponytail to keep the sheath out of the way. She sat for a long moment, and stared daggers at her half-sister.

Not that anyone would guess they were related. Tee's petite stature held surprising strength despite glimpses of vulnerability and a brooding pain she refused to acknowledge. Her oval face framed by curly mahogany hair offered a sharp contrast to Lia's fair complexion and dark gold mane. Lia's slender frame mirrored an aristocratic Spanish heritage on her mother's side that she wore with stubborn pride. She'd only uncovered her father's identity two months ago, the same day Grandfather disowned her.

Tee turned back to Lia, hands on narrow hips. "You coming, or what? I left my key." She hugged herself before the battered door, not used to the fall weather. She wore plainclothes, not officially on the clock, and that was the problem. Tee acted like she knew better than anyone how to run the police investigation that brought them together. She'd already been reprimanded once. That didn't stop her, though, and now she wanted Lia to help—and get sideways with the police, too.

For the past two months, Lia had shared an uneasy truce and living space with Officer Pilikia "Trouble" Teves, on loan to the local PD as a Hawaiian expert working on a sex-ring kidnap case. When Tee offered to share the room in exchange for transportation, Lia jumped at the chance. After Grandfather kicked her out for digging into her Hawaiian background, she needed a place to stay, plus thought it would be an opportunity to find out more about her heritage. Besides, if Tee hadn't spilled the beans about their shared parentage, Lia wouldn't have lost her family. But after living in close quarters with the prickly young woman, Lia wasn't any closer to knowing the truth.

Grandfather believed Wyatt Teves got his beloved sixteen-year-old daughter pregnant and abandoned her when Kaylia died giving birth to Lia. Considered a shameful, nasty secret, Lia committed the unforgivable by researching her heritage and trying to find her father. Getting back into Grandfather's good graces required proving her father wasn't the devil Grandfather believed. To add insult to injury, the mere presence of half-sister Pilikia Teves poured salt on the wound.

Any thought of sister-to-sister bonding evaporated within the first two days of living together. Lia would have bailed if she'd had any other options. Tee drove like a maniac—Lia didn't trust her to bring the car back in one piece—which meant chauffeur duty at all hours. That turned into a lot of off-the-clock police work that could get Tee fired, Lia arrested, them both hurt, or worse.

At least Tee loved Karma. And the feeling was mutual. Lia couldn't help feeling a twinge of jealousy.

The cop hugged herself again. Lia guessed Hawaii breeze didn't carry the same bite as the fall Texas wind. Just wait until she returned to Chicago for her first winter and she'd be nostalgic for the Texas weather. "Open the door, Lia, I'm freezing!"

"Quiet, you'll have Karma barking and get the management after us again." Lia climbed out of the car, and fished the key from her pocket. She wondered why the Rottweiler hadn't woofed her usual greeting.

Tee owed her some answers. Instead, she stayed close-lipped about their shared history. Lia could still hear Grandfather's gravelly voice, shaking with venom:

"You're not part of this family, not anymore."

It hurt more than she wanted to admit. Sure, she'd bucked their rules, wanting them to let go of the reins so she could run her own race. But Grammy and Grandfather were the only family she'd ever known, and without them in her life, she felt adrift. For so long, she'd felt smothered by a secret past they wouldn't share. She'd never belonged, and now she knew why.

Now, she had no family—except a sour, argumentative half-sister—and still had no answers about her father. The sooner she said goodbye to Tee, the better.

Repairs on Corazon Boarding Kennel were almost done, though. Grandfather co-signed the loan before he'd kicked her out, but with the business closed and no income, she'd already fallen behind on payments. The kennel had to be ready in six weeks, before the Thanksgiving rush. She'd missed Labor Day bookings but had several reserved for Thanksgiving and Christmas. The pet-sitting door-to-door visits provided stop-gap funds but Lia needed a substantial payday for her winter nut.

If she couldn't win the lottery or get an extension on the loan, the bank would foreclose. Grandfather would win. Again. Getting away from Tee before she strangled her was the least of her worries.

Of course, the woman's supervisor, Detective Jeff Combs, just might beat Lia to the punch.

"Combs won't be happy, you know." Lia's words stopped Tee in her tracks.

The athletic policewoman rounded on Lia. "Who's going to tell him? You got another hot date?" She grinned. "September won't like that."

Lia's face burned. "It's not like that."

She hadn't spoken with September since August when Lia's actions nearly got Shadow killed. Lia wanted a sit-down with September at some point. There were things she wanted September to know about her dog Shadow, and Karma.

"Combs just offered to help me with my bank stuff, that's all."

"Bank stuff?" Tee stood to one side as Lia juggled the key to open the door. "You behind on payments or something? Wish I could help, but my finances are worse than yours." She grinned, and a dimple appeared. "So, is Combs going to float you a loan?"

"Hardly."

"Didn't realize you're that close. Or that he's that flush. You know he's got child support, right?" Tee grinned again. "September won't be happy."

Lia ignored Tee's teasing, and shouldered her aside to get to the door. Yes, she liked the man, in part because he didn't seem impressed by her Corazon name. And yes, she knew he had two kids living with their stepdad and his disabled ex-wife. And she knew about his relationship with September, a woman she'd rather have as a friend than consider competition. Detective Jeff Combs had a complicated life, and she needed simplicity in hers. Enough said.

But he'd become a friend. It irked her that Tee went behind Combs's back as if a new-minted cop knew better than an experienced detective. Still, this was her sister, the only family that still claimed her, so of course she'd stay mum.

"You're so gung-ho running your own investigation, he's sure to get wind of it. Combs is a detective, you know."

"Not likely, the way they're dragging their feet." Tee jutted out her chin, eyes flashing. "The clock is ticking. My partner says they want me back in Chicago soon, or I could lose my job. But I owe it to Mele and all the other girls that SOB destroyed to get the scumbag caught and put away."

Lia swung open the door and let Tee storm inside ahead of her. Combs would be here soon, once his shift ended. She hoped his friends at the bank would give her some breathing room.

She'd barely shut the door when Tee yelled from the bedroom.

"Something's wrong with Karma!"

Chapter 57

Karma looked up from her nest amid the bed pillows when the door opened. She struggled to sit up as Tee strode into the bedroom, then gave up. She offered a wide doggy grin of apology and slicked back her ears.

"Something's wrong with Karma!" Tee sat on the edge of the bed, and smoothed Karma's brow. "What's wrong, baby-girl? You're not supposed to be on my bed, you know that." Worry filled her voice, and Karma licked the girl's hand.

The tummy pains had stopped, allowing her to nap. Now, Karma feared moving might make the hurts start up again. And besides, the fluffy clothes surrounding her soothed a good-dog's swollen tummy. She wouldn't move at all, unless Tee frowned at her again. Karma didn't like it when her girls frowned, it made her tummy hurt in a whole different way. Tee put on a brave front but Karma could tell how inside-fragile she was. And lately, that made Karma feel even more protective.

"What's up, Karma? On the bed?" Lia turned to Tee. "Nest building, that's all." Her face smiled, so Karma knew she wasn't upset. With a grunt, she managed to roll up into a sit, and half closed her eyes with bliss as the two women petted her.

"Don't scare me like that." Tee cooed, scratching under Karma's chin, and then turned to Lia. "I came into the room and she didn't move. Are you sure it's safe to leave her alone?"

Karma tuned out the voices. She didn't understand the words and had more important things to do. She whined, and struggled to climb off the bed, paced to the door and paw-thumped it.

Lia followed. "Need to take-a-break? Bet you do, and some food, too."

Karma wiggled her stumpy tail and waited for the door to open. She hurried to a familiar-smelling spot, and squatted for immediate relief. She flicked an ear toward the two women's raised voices. Hurrying back into the cramped room, she stood between them, wanting to jump up on each in turn to move them apart, but her bulk wouldn't allow. Instead, she yawned, wide and loud. She pawed Lia's leg, and then leaned against Tee, and yawned again.

"I'll get the thermometer." Lia brushed by, crossed to the bathroom, and quickly returned. She knelt beside Karma and stroked her throat. "I know you don't like this, but it'll be over quick. Karma, stand."

Karma rose to her feet, but tucked her tail in protest of the rude intrusion. She relaxed when Tee knelt at her head-end and rubbed her ears.

Lia removed the stick-thing and Karma woofed and shook herself with relief. "Her temp's 99-degrees, just as I thought. It'll happen in the next 24 hours." Lia stood, grinning with excitement.

"All right, you win. I'll stay while you go to the bank with Combs. But you better be back in time. I'm no midwife." Tee rubbed Karma's ears again, and Karma returned the favor with a slurp across her eyes.

Chapter 58

Tee dodged Karma's kiss, but couldn't stop smiling. "Do I taste good, or what?" She looked up at Lia. "Am I crazy, or does Karma get upset when we argue?" She stood, removed her gun, and set it on the bedside table.

"Yep, it's called splitting behavior when she barges between us. Dogs do it to each other, and also with people." She shrugged. "It's a way to calm down interactions and prevent fights." She crossed to the closet, peeked inside and laughed. "Karma has been in here, too. She rearranged all the shoes." Lia traded her ragged windbreaker for a less shabby jacket and tied back her hair. "I'll be gone a couple hours at most. A dog's first stages of labor can last six to 18 hours, so I should be back well before she whelps." A car horn blared outside. "That's Combs. Gotta run." Lia bent to smooth Karma's brow, and planted a kiss on the dome of the dog's silky black head.

"Wait, I don't know anything about dogs. Or puppies. What am I supposed to do?" As a cop, she should be stoic and unflappable. She'd even taken training to help with unexpected births, but that was human babies. The thought of Karma in distress left Tee breathless. "What if something goes wrong?"

"Just keep Karma quiet, and chances are she won't deliver until late tonight. She'll do all the work." Lia grabbed her phone and keys, hesitated, and turned back. "Just in case there's a problem, I'll text you Doc Eugene's phone number, and you can use my car to get to his clinic." She dangled the keys. "But only for Karma, if it's an emergency. Got it?" The horn blared again.

"I know how to drive. Give it a rest, already." Lia wouldn't let her forget that tiny ding in the bumper of her precious car. She shooed Lia to the door with waving motions of her hands. "Go on, me and Karma got this, don't we, baby-girl?"

Karma woofed and wriggled, leaning hard against Tee's thigh. The warm presence made her feel invincible with the dog by her side.

Tossing one last worried look over her shoulder, Lia left the efficiency apartment. Tee exhaled and her shoulders loosened. She stayed on guard around other people. Having Lia as her driver, meant to be a convenience, instead became a burden, especially with her sister's constant disapproval. But nobody else could pull off this undercover sting and it could close the case. Sometimes the ends justified the risks.

No worries keeping secrets from Karma, though. Tee could be herself.

"You hungry?" She grinned at the dog's paw-dance response. "Lia only gives you that gravel she calls dog food. I got some veggie burritos." Better forego the hot sauce, though. She'd learned that dogs liked veggies, too. Karma liked raw carrots and broccoli. "Bet you'll love burritos, with sour cream, yum. After all, you're eating for two now. Or maybe more."

The veterinarian predicted one puppy, which apparently wasn't unusual for a first litter. But a single Shadow-pup made the impending birth even more special. "Do you miss the warrior dog? I wonder." Karma tipped her big head from side to side and licked her lips as Tee stuck the food in the microwave.

The young Hawaiian girl that Karma rescued in August swore she'd seen Karma mate with the mysterious black shepherd. Tee would have discounted the tale as fantasy born of the dramatic situation, but that same warrior-dog appeared and led her through the flames. Karma saved the girl Mele that day, but the black shepherd rescued Lia by showing Tee where the three sheltered. Something beyond common understanding must direct such things.

Tee never thought much about animals until the past two months with Karma. Go figure, she preferred dogs over most humans. "What will a Karma and Shadow baby become? A police dog like you?" A dog like Karma sure would come in handy back in Chicago, especially once she became a detective. But she'd never be able to afford a trained dog, not when the price tag started well over $20,000.

Besides, if she were Lia, she'd never let Karma go. And, there'd never be another dog like Karma.

The microwave DINGED, and Karma pawed her leg and whined, ready for her burrito. "Okay, hungry girl. But you know the rules, right? Gotta work for your food."

Tee might fudge on what she fed the dog but agreed with Lia's rationale about earning rewards. A police dog had to stay sharp and practice tracking and protection skills every day. Pregnancy compromised Karma's agility and stamina, so they'd cut back on physical activity and increased mental exercises.

She placed the food on a plate and broke off a piece. She never bothered to learn all the German commands Lia taught. Hell, half the time Lia forgot and used English anyway, except for "*mahalo*," the release word. Tee thought that appropriate.

"Karma, sit." She snapped her fingers, and the dog plopped her behind to the carpet, dewlaps drooling with anticipation. She snatched the tossed treat out of the air, and stood, licking her lips for the next bite.

"Karma, bring bear."

The dog whirled and ran faster than Tee thought possible given her girth, into the bedroom. She frowned, listening to Karma's grunts and whines, then remembering the bear's placement in the mussed sheets. Jumping up on the bed wasn't a good idea in her condition. Before she could amend the command, bedsprings squeaked, followed by a thumped landing. Karma reappeared clutching the toy in her massive jaws, her whole rear end gyrating with pleasure.

"Drop the bear. Good girl, Karma." Tee tossed another third of the burrito and watched as Karma didn't bother to chew before swallowing. Then she focused, attentive once more, waiting for Tee's next request. "One more, okay, let's make this one count." She thought for a moment, and remembered Lia experimenting with the dog's ability to combine commands. Lia called it a chained behavior. The "bring" command Karma recognized as a fetch-game. But others were reserved for her work as a police dog. Only one way to find out. "Find gun, Karma. Bring gun."

The dog's happy panting mouth snapped closed. She cocked her head first one way and then the other. Karma nosed the hand with the remainder of the treat, and then dropped her head to the floor. She took deep breaths through her nose, whiffing them out her mouth, and cast back and forth a few times, before lifting her head. Questing the air, she padding around the room and paused to snort likely spots: the sofa where Lia slept, along the edge of the kitchen counter, the windowsill beside the door.

Tee tried not to smile or offer any encouragement or clue. She got a rush watching the dog work, and cautioned herself to stay silent. Lia never repeated the command, unless the dog wavered. So far, Karma performed exactly as trained, searching the perimeter of the front room before heading to the smaller bedroom.

She heard Karma bulldozing through the pile of shoes in the closet. Worried the dog would again try to leap on the bed—and maybe hurt herself and the unborn puppy—she followed to watch from the doorway. Karma glanced back at her, big brown eyes bright with intelligence, and then turned in a circle testing the air. With sudden decision, she trotted to the other side of the bed, nose-poked the tabletop and then fell to the floor in a "down" position, her signal for a find.

When Tee didn't respond, Karma woofed, stood and again nose-poked the gun on the bedside table before assuming the down position.

"Karma, find gun. BRING gun." Tee understood the confusion. Lia had another way to explain to the dog, but now they'd started, she needed to finish the action. "Bring, Karma."

Karma rose and mouthed the gun Tee had placed there. The gun thumped onto the floor when Karma lost her grip, and Tee stifled her gasp. The dog's big head dipped low, and immediately came up with the gun in her mouth. She hurried to Tee with the prize, sitting before her with ears slicked tight and tail stirring the dust on the floor.

"Good find, Karma! Good bring, you're so smart! Drop it." She took the gun from Karma's massive jaws, careful not to bang the dog's teeth, and gave her the rest of the food.

Her phone pinged with an unexpected text. "Dammit!" Good news for the case, but the timing sucked. She couldn't put off this meeting, either, or risked blowing the whole scheme. "Lucky for me,

Lia left her car keys." She sank onto the sofa, gun in one hand and keys in the other.

If everything worked as planned—and it would, it had to!—all would resolve in two or three hours at the most. She told herself she'd be home before Lia returned.

Karma finished licking her lips, padded to Tee, and rested her chin on her lap. Brown eyes looked up into Tee's face. She stroked the big dog's thick neck until her heartbeat slowed to a more normal rhythm. "We've got no choice, Karma. Let me get ready, and then we're going for a car ride."

Chapter 59

Lia's nails dug into the palms of her hands, and she forced herself to relax her clenched fists. The loan officer's ultimatum replayed in her head. Pay off the loan by end of the month—less than a week—or the bank would take possession of the boarding facility. She slid into the passenger side of Combs's car and slammed the door.

"Wish I could help." Combs took his place behind the wheel, his low baritone sympathetic and brown eyes concerned as he started the car. His faded jeans, boots and hat, and canvas jacket made him look more cowboy than police detective.

"I appreciate you spending time on your day off. But you heard him. They want the whole thing paid a month early." She pushed flyaway hair out of her eyes and aimed a weak smile his way. "Unless you know someone with the whole amount to loan, I'm screwed."

She got the line of credit back in February after the freak tornado damaged the kennel. Lia planned to pay it off with the money from placing Karma with a police department. Obviously, that didn't happen. Now they'd called the loan. She gritted her teeth. She'd bet anything Grandfather instigated the demand.

Combs cracked his knuckles. "I'm sorry, Lia. I don't have that kind of money, not on a detective's salary. Neither does September, and even if she did, you'd have to ask her."

"Hey, I know that. She doesn't owe me anything." Lia wanted to apologize to September for putting her dog at risk. More than that, she'd been anxious to confirm September's black shepherd was the same as the Shadow-dog that kept appearing in Lia's life. After learning more about the challenges September survived, the woman's reluctance to meet disappointed Lia but made sense.

He pulled out of the parking lot. "Can I at least buy you lunch? That I can afford. I'm meeting September in half an hour, and you're welcome to join us."

"Are you sure?" Lia didn't believe the other woman would be pleased. She'd avoided meeting with Lia for weeks.

He shrugged, and then added, "What have you decided to do about Karma?"

Breath hissed between her lips. She didn't want to think about that, but she managed to keep her cool. "Just take me home. I don't have much of an appetite."

The payment for a trained police dog would more than pay off the loan and set her up for the next six months until Corazon Kennels regained some traction. September's plan to place Karma with a local PD would have given her visiting rights, but after Grandfather pulled his support, that option evaporated. Just as well. Lia wasn't sure she could let Karma go, not after all they'd been through.

The beautiful Rottweiler girl had saved her life twice, as well as the young Hawaiian girl caught up in the sex-trafficking ring. Combs and Tee continued to butt heads over the investigation. Compared to the countless victims, her own troubles weren't worth spit. "How's Mele doing? Have they found her folks?"

"Nope, and we may never find them." Combs adjusted his hat, frowning. "CPS placed her with a foster family, and she's getting some counseling." He cut his eyes toward her, and grinned. "She misses Karma. That big ol' dog of yours sure makes an impression."

Lia laughed. "I'm sure Karma misses her fan club, too. But she's big as a house and due today or tomorrow. I don't want her traveling. That's why I left Tee with her. Maybe in a few weeks, Mele can visit."

"What will you do with the puppies? I mean, if you don't have the kennel anymore . . ."

She gritted her teeth. "Don't know. Can't think about it right now." She turned away to stare out the window at the gray day. "Rotties often have 8 to 12 puppies in litters. But the vet only palpated one or two puppy bumps early on, and first litters often are small."

Karma's romantic encounter with the mysterious shepherd happened under traumatic circumstances. Planned matings often put the prospective parents together several times to ensure conception. Under the circumstances, she was surprised any pups resulted. Her pups might be candidates for police dog or other training, depending on how temperament tests shook out. Any funds garnered from them, though, would be months to years down the road.

Combs was right. Without a place to house and train them, several dogs would be a challenge. Once Tee returned to Chicago, the temporary lodging they shared would go away, too.

Any way she looked at it, kennel plans had hit a wall.

"Hang in there, Lia. What's that old saying? Things always look darkest—"

"—before crap hits the fan?" She nodded at the cloudy sky. "Had my fill of storm clouds, Combs. If anything, it taught me you can't outrun a tornado or stop a flash flood. You just hang on for dear life and pray you'll come out the other side." The temperature had dropped. She pulled on hot pink gloves, a gift from Grammy, but at least the silly looking things kept her hands warm.

"You've got puppies to look forward to. Nothing brightens a mood like puppies. Or neon pink hand warmers." He grabbed her hand, squeezed, and let go to navigate the turn back toward the efficiency where Karma and Tee waited.

Her neck and face warmed. She turned away to look out the window. Damn! It didn't mean anything, she knew. She fought back tears. All the stress had her riding an emotional roller coaster.

They pulled into the parking lot, and Combs stopped outside her door. "Will you be okay, Lia? The lunch offer still stands. A good meal would make you feel better. I'm so hungry I could eat a horse and chase the cowboy."

She snorted a laugh. Maybe a meal would help her think. And she'd finally get to meet September. Come to think of it, a first meeting might go smoother with Combs there. Lia started to agree, until she noticed her missing car. "Dammit, what now?"

Combs started at her sudden exclamation and called after her when she jumped from the car. "What? Something else wrong? Lia!"

"Tee took my car. I told her not to leave Karma alone. To use my car only in case of emergency to go to the vet." She rattled the door to the apartment. Worry grew when no bark answered. "Why didn't she call me?" She juggled a coat pocket for her keys.

He tipped his head and resettled his hat. "You know Tee. Besides, Karma doesn't bark unless it's a stranger, right? I bet she's inside snoozing with your shoes again. Tee took your car for one of her off the wall ideas." He sounded pissed, but not surprised.

Lia pushed open the door. "Karma? Baby-dog, where are you?" The place felt empty even before she confirmed it.

They must be at the veterinarian. She had to be there, needed to be there for Karma. Combs would take her.

Lia ran back to the open door in time to see his car speed out of the parking lot, leaving her stranded.

Chapter 60

The car hit a big bump, and Karma grunted and winced.

"Sorry." Tee looked at her in the mirror but didn't slow down. "I've got to meet a lady about a very bad man and can't be late."

Karma braced herself to stay balanced in the swift car. She wanted to stick her nose out of the back window, and drink the smells that gushed past. But each time she stood on the back seat, the car lurched. At least the strange ache inside her tummy had subsided. She still wanted...something, she wasn't sure what. Karma scratched at the blanket covering the back seat, scrunching it up into a more acceptable bed. She grabbed the bear-toy, pulled it close to her tummy, and sighed with satisfaction.

"Almost there. This should happen quick, Karma. I already texted Combs, so he'll have the cavalry ready on my signal. We'll be home in no time." Her words came fast, high pitched with excitement.

Karma's ears pricked at the *"home"* word, but Tee's excitement and her underlying fear-smell made Karma's hackles bristle. She wagged at the thought of the shabby kennel building she shared with Lia. That was home. Karma missed the home-place, and often wondered why they stayed away.

Staying with Lia and Tee in two tiny rooms made Karma's fur itch and paws yearn for wide open spaces where a good-dog could sniff and roam, run and roll in grass and mud to her heart's content. Her muscles ached to race, throat longed to bark and howl without hush-demands, and claws wanted to dig up some dirt. Home meant adventures, search and sniff games. And comfort. Safety. *Home.*

The tiny rooms they shared smelled stale, and lately, she'd been restricted even more. Lia kept her on leash for the few steps outside to take-a-break. Tracking games in two rooms offered no challenge. Karma's boredom made her want to chew and tear and break things, even though she shouldn't. So she couldn't wait to see what happened on this ride. She loved car rides! But she wished the lurching-bumps would stop.

Maybe they'd drive home? Wouldn't that be fine! Karma wondered if Lia waited for them at the home-place. She couldn't help wriggling at the thought.

The car slowed and pulled off the road. Tee stopped the car behind a very large sign surrounded by trees that hid them from the road. Karma leaped up with happy anticipation. It wasn't home, but that was okay, especially if she got to run outside in the nearby field with Tee. It had been many many days, more days than a good-dog had paws, since she'd been allowed to run with Tee. Karma panted happily when her girl turned around to stroke Karma's face and scratch under her chin. Karma leaned into the caress, and half closed her eyes.

Chapter 61

"They'll for sure take my phone. And gun, if they see it. But maybe you can help, baby-dog. Can I borrow your toy?"

Talking to Karma helped Tee focus her thoughts, and the dog's happy personality kept Tee in a good mood. For some reason, talking to Karma helped keep her calm, too, and she'd not had an "episode" since August, when Karma's presence grounded her and brought her back from the trance-like state she occasionally suffered. Half the time, she didn't remember she'd been "gone" unless someone nearby noticed and told her. God, she hated that! Damaged goods, in so many ways, that's what she was. Just her bad luck that Lia witnessed her weakness.

She picked up the bear. Karma woofed softy and nosed the stuffed toy. "I'll bring it back, I promise."

Tee got out of the car, shedding her jacket and leaving it on the front seat. She shivered in the brisk October breeze, her bare arms and thudding heart homesick for the warm breeze of Hawaii. But their informant insisted her undercover ruse required the skimpy outfit, to convince the Boss she was a street-wise runaway. They knew Boss still wanted a girl to replace Mele. As a cop, Tee wanted to catch the Boss, but also the lowlife scum who solicited such human merchandise.

Her cell phone rang. Combs, calling back. Tee braced herself for his disapproval and slipped back into the front seat of the car, switching the heater on. "Like I said, Momma Ruth sent a text. The plan's a go." She worked to loosen the stitching of the stuffed toy as she talked.

"You can't go in by yourself. There's a procedure, you know that. We got no backup in place, and you're not experienced enough—"

"Then get backup out here ASAP." She rattled off the location, ignoring his angry tone, and countered with her prepared argument. "We knew it'd be a now-or-never opportunity whenever she gave the go. I texted you as soon as I got the call. Not my problem it's your day off. Sorry to interrupt your meeting." She couldn't resist the dig, knowing Lia's feelings for him even if Combs seemed oblivious.

"This is my operation, and there's more at stake than you cow-boying it alone. Hold on."

"What the hell does that mean? You're the cowboy." He looked more like one of the haole surfer dudes from the Island. But she spoke to dead air. He'd switched lines to speak with others on the team, giving them details of the unfolding operation.

None of the other female detectives could pass for Hawaiian. Tee was older than the youngsters Momma Ruth recruited, but her small frame could pass if she just acted the part. Karma's toy bear would help the illusion. And according to Momma Ruth, the Boss was desperate to satisfy a specific buyer's Hawaiian hunger so beggars couldn't be choosers. She tugged the form-fitting short-shorts to a more comfortable position, wondering how anyone wore such outfits in public.

If all went well, they'd nail the mysterious Boss, and cut the head off the sex trafficking ring that left Vicki Kala (aka Wikolia Pa'akaula) dead and Mele traumatized last August. It had taken six weeks before Momma Ruth took the bait Combs's team set up. Vicki's murder and Mele's escape ratcheted up the probability the Boss would run. Momma Ruth would come sooner or later, and the woman seemed to fear the same thing. Combs offered a deal with protection and possible reduced sentence, but only if Momma Ruth worked with them.

Combs came back on the line, chewing his words in his hurry.

"We're scrambling from this end. Chances are you'll be moved. We need a way to track you. And for God's sake, ditch your gun and phone or they'll make you and it'll be all over. Damn, why did you have to rush this?"

"Already covered. Put the tracker in my boots." She figured the over-the-knee boots would be the last place they'd look, at least right away. And she had to take the gun. No way would she go unarmed. She checked the time. "I got to walk to the meet spot in the next ten minutes, or we're done. Momma Ruth sounded on the edge, and I don't want to give her an excuse to rabbit."

"Okay, go. Make this work, Tee, and the public will call you a hero. Fail, and your police career is over—and maybe your life." His tone softened to add, "In other words, don't die."

"Glad to know you care, Combs." She grinned and ended the call.

***

Karma tipped her head first one way and then the other as Tee manipulated the bear-toy. She pawed the front seat, then stood up, short tail jerking with excitement when the car door opened again and her girl got out. The front door slammed, and she panted with short interspersed whines of anticipation when Tee walked to the back door. But instead of opening it so a good-dog could go with her, run in the grass and feel wind in her face, Tee just stuck her hand through the partially open window. Karma licked the hand and raised her head to accept the chin-scratch.

"Back as soon as I can, Karma. People know where we are and will be here soon. Wait here." She tucked the bear-toy under one bare arm, turned, and strode away.

Wait? Karma hated that word. It meant being left alone. Whining, Karma pawed the door again. She woofed softly, and then more sharply but her girl didn't look back. She kept walking, until out of sight.

Karma stuck her nose into the crack of the window, huffing the intermittent breeze for her girl's scent. Concerned whines grew more and more strident when the sound of a stranger's car drew near, slowed, and stopped on the hidden road where Tee disappeared.

Tee screamed.

Karma howled and threw herself against the window.

Chapter 62

Lia stood, mouth agape, watching Combs peel out of the parking lot. "Son-of-a . . ." She grabbed her phone, dialed his number and disconnected when it went to voice mail. She typed an angry text instead, and then bit her lip, wanting to take it back. After all, he'd offered and she'd declined the invitation, so why should he stick around? September wouldn't appreciate Lia horning in on their regular lunch date.

She closed the door, still fiddling with the phone until she found the vet clinic number. If she couldn't be there, at least knowing Karma's status would lessen the worry.

"This is Lia Corazon, I'm calling about my Rottweiler, Karma. Is she there? My sis—" She cut herself off. Her relationship with Tee wasn't anybody's business. She didn't need to fuel more gossip. "Has my roommate, police officer Tee Teves, brought her in yet?"

"Oh hi there, Lia. No, they're not here. Is there a problem with Karma?" The receptionist sounded concerned. "When's her due date?"

"Not for another five days. But her temperature dropped this morning." She swallowed hard. "I had an errand, and left Karma with Tee. Now they're both gone, so I figured . . ."

The girl tsk-tsked. "I see. Well, they're not here, but I'll give Doc Eugene a head's up. Are you on your way?"

Lia sank into the computer chair, shaking her head. "Tee has my car, so I have to catch a ride. Could you please call me as soon as they get there? And keep me posted?" She disconnected.

The trip to the animal hospital took about twenty minutes, so they must have left minutes before she'd returned. Lia thumbed her phone, opening the Uber app. She bit her lip seeing it wouldn't arrive for another 40 minutes. There wasn't much call for taxis and the like in Heartland, and she lived several miles out of town.

On impulse, she dialed another number. September answered on the first ring. Maybe she could still reach him.

"Hi Lia. Is Combs still with you?"

"No. He just left, heading your way for lunch." She paused, then added with a rush, "I had another quick favor."

"Guess he's running late. How'd the bank meeting go?" September sounded sympathetic. Everyone knew everyone's business in a small town. "We keep missing each other. I've been meaning to ask about that big police dog wannabe." She added dryly, "Never mind what your Grandfather wants."

Lia gathered her thoughts, and spoke with care. "I thought you were avoiding me after I put your dog at risk with the fire . . ."

September laughed, but Lia detected a bitter note. "Combs asked, and I answered. When kids are in trouble, people respond first and think later. At least, I do. Anyway, you didn't do anything wrong, Lia. Shadow put himself at risk." Her voice caught. "I don't think I could forgive myself if he didn't come back."

She understood the feeling. The brief but intimate connection she'd shared with Shadow changed her life. "I only had him for a short time, but Shadow's special. His pups will be, too. That's why I'm calling. I need a ride to the vet. Karma is in labor."

Dead silence.

"September? Are you there?" Surely, she knew.

But she spoke with sharp edge. "When did you meet Shadow? What are you talking about?"

Lia's grip tightened on the phone, not sure what to say. She took a chance. "September, what do you know about animal communication."

No hesitation at all. "It's crappiocca. Hold on." A long pause, and then September came back. "Combs just texted me. He's not coming, got called to work."

Only the one word registered. She blinked back tears. "Crappiocca?"

"Made up. Pretend. Scammers prey on gullible folks. Don't tell me you had an animal communicator do a reading on Karma, after she got bred? Oh Lia." She spoke as though to a child.

She couldn't disguise the hurt and disappointment. "You don't believe in—"

"I didn't say that. I'm sure there are talented individuals able to communicate on levels beyond the norm. I just never met anyone legit." She sounded exasperated. "The wannabes do so much damage, I end up with the fallout in my behavior caseload." September was kind, but firm, and offered an olive branch. "Since Combs can't come, I'm happy to give you a ride. That way, I can finally meet Karma and you can tell me your Shadow story. Sounds like quite a tale."

"Okay, thanks. I do need the ride." Lia figured if September didn't want to know the truth, she wouldn't waste time trying to convince her.

September spoke gently. "Don't get me wrong, Lia. My Shadow would make some lovely puppies. But he had some injuries that wouldn't heal from the frostbite back in February. So a couple of weeks before that August fire, Shadow was neutered."

Chapter 63

Lia sat silent and stunned for a long moment after September disconnected. She jumped when her phone sounded an alert for an incoming Skype call. She'd used the app to speak with Tee's Auntie Isabella, but she wasn't expecting a call. She'd had two conversations, scheduled when Tee wasn't around. Her sister got prickly about family history.

She accepted the call, wondering why it came from a different account. "Auntie, I can't talk for long." Lia stopped speaking when the live image loaded on the phone. A man, a stranger with intense eyes and an odd familiar look, stared back. "What do you want?" She started to disconnect.

"Wait, Apikalia. Don't hang up."

Lia's breath quickened when he used her full given name. Her Hawaiian name. She fingered the baby name bracelet that she never took off. "Who are you?"

But she knew.

"You look just like your mother. But you have my eyes." He cleared his throat. "Isabella gave me your number. She insisted I should call, make amends. But there's no way to do that."

"You're Wyatt Teves." She couldn't bring herself to call him father. After years of wondering, she finally faced the man who abandoned her pregnant, unwed mother. So many questions to ask, yet now she struggled to voice a single one.

"You're how old? Twenty?"

"Twenty-five." Her dry mouth turned the words into whispers. She had to steady the phone on the counter to stop from shaking.

"So long ago. A lifetime." He paused. "You have questions, and so do I. They give us 20 minutes for these calls, so you first." Wyatt smiled, and Lia could see more of herself in the expression. Somehow, that made the hurt worse.

"Who is *they*?" For the first time, she noticed his surroundings. He sat in a plain chair, bare walls behind him, and wore a nondescript uniform.

"Apikalia, I'm sorry to tell you I'm in prison."

"Call me Lia." She whispered the correction. Though not surprised—being in prison explained a lot—she couldn't help feeling shocked. "They let you Skype?"

He smiled again. "The latest thing in prison visitation, Lia." He tasted the name and nodded his approval. "They set it up so we call the local Skype number and the call is forwarded to a phone or computer anywhere in the country. Most inmates hate it, prefer a real face to face. Of course, works out good for long distance." He spread his hands, indicating their situation. "Isabella gave me your number weeks ago. Finally got up the nerve."

Her shock gave way to anger, and heat spread from her throat to her face. But she'd start slow, she told herself. She didn't want to give him an excuse to hang up before he explained...tried to explain away abandoning them. "How did you meet my mother?"

"At a line dance in Pukalani, after the Makawao Rodeo. A bunch of us rode in the Paniolo Parade. I thought Kaylia was just a rich haole on vacation. Boy, did she set me straight." He grinned, the memory bittersweet.

Lia nodded. That fit with what she'd managed to ferret out. "The Corazon's used to make annual trips to the Big Island, buying and selling horses, I think." That stopped after her mother died.

"Your mother was an expert horsewoman. She proved it in competitions, beat me bad." He laughed. "She won my lariat off me, too. Hurt to give that up, been in my family forever. And I fell for her, hard. Imagine me, a poor kid from Waimea, in love with a

Spanish princess. And, Lia, your mother was a princess to me."

"Then why'd you leave us?" The cry came from years of anguish. "You got my mother pregnant and disappeared!" She blinked back tears, vowing not to give him the satisfaction, but couldn't keep the pain from her voice. "If you loved her so much, how come you married another girl and got her pregnant not even six months later?" She was six months older than Tee. Her half-sister remained closed lipped about her family, but she knew they both shared the ache of losing mothers early in life. Auntie Isabella had adopted and raised Tee, so Wyatt hadn't been around her sister, either.

He looked away, and then back into the camera with a stricken expression. "Kaylia told me she was 18. I didn't know otherwise, until too late. I was a kid, too, but that's no excuse." Wyatt's expression hardened. "I didn't abandon you. Wasn't my choice. We loved each other, and I married your mother before we found out you were on the way. We even decided on your name together. Apikalia. It honors your mother Kaylia, and also your Hawaiian heritage. Do you know what that means?"

She didn't say anything, but a lump clogged her throat. She looked up the name years ago and felt confused by the meaning. Lia figured her mother's choice of Apikalia—*my father's delight*—had been wishful thinking, not a reality. "You were married? Then why—"

"I was arrested for statutory rape. By the time I got out, our marriage had been annulled, and a restraining order issued. I never saw your mother again."

Chapter 64

Karma drummed her paws against the car door, barking and snarling with frustration. She pushed her blunt face through the open part at the top but couldn't get more than her muzzle through.

A strident argument ebbed and flowed out of sight but not earshot. Tee's distinctive voice increased in pitch and volume, alternating with a stranger's insistent words, words a good-dog couldn't understand. But the emotion told Karma everything she needed to know.

Anger. Fear. Danger!

When threats appeared, she needed to act. The instinctive drive for self-preservation extended to family. And Tee was family. The urge to protect overwhelmed Karma's heart and mind, until all thought and effort crystalized into one, single imperative: out, get OUT, drive away the threat. Get out-Out-OUT!

Her barks and snarls gave way to whines as she backed away from the futile paw-battering of the barrier. She sniffed the door and window top to bottom, turned, and tried the other side. A puff of warm air from the front of the car caught her attention. Karma shouldered her way between the front seats, huffing with effort to squeeze her burgeoning girth through the narrow passage.

Tee squealed again, and Karma's hackles bristled. This time, though, she managed to stifle her barks to concentrate on escape, although she couldn't stop a deep-throated vibration that set her ear tips aquiver. Barking and bullying didn't work to open car doors. Lia and Tee opened car doors all the time without any noise or fuss. What did they do?

Something with their hands. Not battering but grabbing. Karma's paws didn't grab, though. She grabbed with her mouth.

Nosing the side of the barrier, she found a smooth lever that moved a bit when she gripped it but couldn't manage a secure hold. Her broad nose prevented upper teeth from hooking over the lever enough to pull. She growled louder, as if the warning would make the lever do what she wished, still conscious of the loud argument that continued outside.

A car door opened and slammed, muffling Tee's angry shout. They would drive away, and leave Karma alone, trapped, with no way to protect family from the threat.

With an anguished roar, Karma again resorted to paw-battering the door. This time, the glass scrolled down.

Karma didn't pause to wonder what had happened. She gathered her haunches, and sprang from the front seat through the window, and sprinted to reach Tee.

Chapter 65

Tee huddled in the back seat of the SUV. She clutched the stuffed toy, trying to still the shivers she told herself arose from cold, not fear. She couldn't escape with the childproof locks engaged. She told herself that nerves made her sharp, not scared. Better to have that edge than be overconfident.

She'd expected to meet Momma Ruth. Instead, this gopher showed up, with as much muscle between his ears as his biceps. She tried to get answers, and confused him. Made no sense, unless Boss found out and hired a delivery boy unconnected to the full operation.

Was Momma Ruth still alive? Tee couldn't retreat now, she had to brazen it out. Play hard-nose whiny street kid—a little soft in the head needing her toy for comfort—and pray she'd give an Oscar-caliber performance. She screamed when he tried to take the toy, and it hadn't felt like play-acting, either. Tee would be dead if he discovered what was inside.

The muscleman stood outside, speaking into his phone with emphatic gestures of his other hand. She made mental notes of his appearance—hulking build, buzz cut hair and gray eyes, DIY prison tattoos that disfigured rather than enhanced. His distinctive appearance made him easy to track, either a stupid mistake on his part or a calculated move by Boss to deflect blame. She wondered how many were involved in the trafficking scheme.

She'd marked him, too. Tee wiped her mouth, grimacing at the taste of blood. Sure, he'd hit her when she bit him, but nobody put hands on her without permission, nobody. And she never gave permission.

"What the hell!" He scrambled back toward the car.

She twisted in her seat to see what had him on the run. Her stomach flip-flopped. "Karma. Oh no."

The Rottweiler drove toward him in full attack mode. Tee's horror mounted when he drew his gun.

"Stop, don't, please don't shoot!" She needed no acting skills to communicate fear and desperation. Dear God, what had she done? She'd left the dog safe in the car and couldn't fathom how Karma got out. But the dog's clever escape would get herself killed.

She could stop him, but that would blow the operation. Yet she couldn't bring herself to sacrifice Karma, either.

"Please, leave her alone. Karma, *WAIT*!" She screamed the command, praying it would be enough to diffuse the situation.

Karma stopped on a dime, but kept her massive head lowered, threat clear.

Tee breathed again. Maybe, just maybe, she could salvage things. "Please mister, don' hurt īlio, she good girl."

Ears pinned tight, hard eyes drilled the man and his gun. Karma's snarling barks spewed saliva as she fought the urge to complete the attack. But she held true to the wait-command.

The man's attention flicked from the dog to Tee, but the gun's direction never wavered. "Your dog? Mighty fine mutt for a homeless party girl."

"My dog, yes. She go lost, no home like me. We stay t'gether." Tee fell back into the pidgin that defined the character she played. She'd known many young girls on the Island, homeless or one paycheck away from worse. She'd come close herself, after her mother died and father sent to jail. If not for Auntie Isabella, she might not have escaped that world. That early life spurred her determination to help by being the best damn cop possible.

If she didn't die trying.

"Trained good." He eyed the still-slathering Karma with consideration. "Okay, Missy, here's the deal. Momma Ruth told me to collect and deliver the merchandise. That's you. Nothing about an attack dog. I should shoot you both and be done."

She squeezed the bear-toy, fitting her hand inside to what she'd hidden within. She'd never shot someone but wouldn't hesitate if he made the wrong move. Dammit, she should never have brought Karma. This would kill her career, even if they survived the man's threats.

Tee turned on her wheedling little girl voice. "No shoot, she good dog, the best. See? She stop, no bite. I go wit you, like Momma Ruth say. Jus' let dog go, see?" *Please let him just get in the car and leave Karma alone.*

He pursed his lips. The wheels turned slow before she saw the mental click of decision behind his squinty eyes. "She's a beauty. Too nice to shoot and I bet Momma Ruth could use her. Maybe get me some bonus time for bringing you both." He kept the gun trained on Karma but looked at Tee. "I'm gonna open your door, and you're not going to move a muscle. Nope, you're gonna tell that well-trained dog of yours to hop into the car with you. One wrong move, and I shoot the dog first, and then you. Got it?"

Tee nodded, biting her lip and squeezing the bear even harder.

"First, though, so's you don't get any idea about making a break for it and siccing that bad-ass dog on me, you're gonna take off your boots." He grinned. "Boss likes 'em barefoot so we'll just get that out of the way now. Go ahead, shed them high tops, and shove 'em up over the front seat. Do it!"

Karma growled louder and took a couple of shuffling paw-steps closer the threatening man.

"Wait! Karma, good girl, jus' wait!"

Had she given something away? Why shed the boots now? Tee remembered that both Vicki and Mele had been barefoot when found. She unzipped the boots, mentally kicking herself she hadn't thought of a better place to stow the tracking bug. She peeled off the first boot and stuck it through the narrow opening. As she skinned off the left boot—the one with the device—she fumbled with it to try and palm the bug. How else would Comb's team find her?

"Hurry up, quit stalling, or I'll shoot your sweet puppy and come in there and strip off more than your fancy boots."

She shoved it over the front seats. If the boots and tracking device remained in the car long enough, the digital breadcrumbs could still work in her favor.

"Okay, that's good, real good." He clicked the fob on the car key, and Tee heard the door unlock. "Open your door real slow and call that dog. Make it quick, we already wasted too much time."

She swung the door wide, and then backed away to the far side of the SUV when he motioned with his gun.

Karma didn't look at her, though. She kept her focus steady, ready to sink fangs deep with Tee's command.

Tee was tempted to give Karma what she wanted. But taking custody of this errand boy wouldn't yield the top players they wanted. Besides, her pride wouldn't let her. She could still salvage the operation, and prevent her personal disgrace.

"Karma, *come!*"

With a final aggrieved look at the threatening stranger, Karma turned and leaped into the car and Tee's arms. The door slammed behind her.

The locks engaged, and he spoke into his cell phone. "I got the merchandise, just like Momma Ruth said." He grinned, picked up the boots, and tossed them out on the road before shoving the car in gear and speeding away.

Chapter 66

Lia braced herself as the car took the turn too fast. "I appreciate the ride, September. And great to see Shadow again. I worried whether he ever made it home." That is, until she'd learned about his reappearance during the fire.

Lia turned in her seat to address the stunning black German Shepherd. A white stripe on one furry cheek testified to the now-healed injury that she'd seen last February. She also learned his notched ear came courtesy of a bullet, when the brave dog saved September's nephew, Steven.

September smiled. "A car ride is nothing, Lia. I still owe you for saving Shadow's life." Her voice trembled, and the big dog woofed softly in response.

Both women laughed. Shadow slicked back his ears and thumped his tail against the seat. Even though the special shivery communication failed to whisper a single message, Lia knew Shadow was the Samaritan dog.

"I thought you wanted to go see Doc Eugene?" September smiled when Shadow woofed again. "Shadow loves the vet clinic staff, don't you boy? He's been there enough."

She shook her head. "They know to call me. Karma is in excellent hands. I've got something to do first." Her mouth tasted sour and tongue turned dry as they took the turn into the drive to the Corazon estate. It felt like a lifetime since she'd been here, and a strange sense of deja vu shivered the back of her neck.

The Skype call with her father left her reeling. No wonder Grandfather and Grammy forbade any questions about Lia's father. She'd always assumed they wanted to protect her from reconnecting with the man who'd treated her mother so shabbily. Instead, the secrets they kept protected their own actions.

The car stopped outside the house, and Lia saw movement behind the front door sidelight. She took a breath, bracing herself. Silently, for strength, she repeated the mantra she'd created, fingering each letter on the baby bracelet in turn like the beads of a rosary: **A**ncestor **P**ride, **I**ntelligence, **K**indness, **A**ct in **L**ove with **I**ntuition and **A**ttitude. She wouldn't be buffaloed this time.

"You want me to stay? I can wait for you." September watched as Lia climbed out, and then quirked a grin. "Your Grandfather won't be thrilled I'm here, though."

Lia shook her head and waved her off. Grandfather would be pissed enough without a stranger witnessing their conversation. She wouldn't leave without answers and had 25 years' worth of questions that September didn't need to hear. Grandfather's angry bluster wouldn't silence or chase Lia away, not this time. Despite the brave assurances, her stomach roiled like a million butterflies danced inside.

Grammy met her at the door as September sped away. She stood, arms crossed, voice stiff as her posture. "How dare that woman bring you here! Call back your car, Lia. Neither of you are welcome here."

Lia pushed past the smaller woman, noting that as usual, she looked ready to host a high society tea. Not a hair stirred on her tightly coifed upsweep and little makeup was needed to enhance her striking looks. She was queen here and knew it.

"Call Grandfather. I have questions for you both."

"He's in a meeting. He won't see you." She jutted out her chin, nostrils flaring. "You made your decision when you defied our wishes."

"Grammy, I'm an adult. Neither of you gets to decide what I think, say or do." Lia closed the front door behind her, making clear her intention to stay. "Is he in his office? We can go there together." She took two quick steps into the entryway.

"No!" Grammy grasped her arm, then released her grip as if the action was beneath a well-bred woman of her station. "You will not disturb him. I'm warning you, Lia."

"Or what? How can you stop me, Grammy?" Her brow stitched two parallel lines. She ignored the older woman's pinched mouth. "I found my father."

Grammy winced, and she took a step backwards. "Then you know what he is." She fairly spat the words. "Worthless, a shiftless nobody. A criminal, who defiled my little girl." She whirled, and strode down the wide hallway, heels click-clacking on the hard surface.

Lia followed, pressing her advantage. "I spoke to him."

Grammy froze. She turned, manicured nails clenching like claws at her side. "He's a liar. Whatever he told you, it's not true. You can't believe anything criminals say." She took a breath and repeated the tale she'd told every year since Lia grew old enough to ask. "He treated your mother like dirt, took advantage of her innocence, and that killed Kaylia as sure as I breathe."

"Don't you mean that *I* killed her? That's what you've always thought, isn't it?" Lia couldn't control the tremolo in her voice.

"Of course not." Her voice dripped acid. "Don't be dense, Lia. It was that man, that Wyatt Teves that caused all our troubles."

"He didn't abandon my mother. He told me what Grandfather did, had him arrested for statutory rape."

The smaller woman sniffed and paced. "He deserved it." Her fingernails stabbed and sliced the air in a staccato counterpoint to her words. "Your mother was a child. That *paniolo* took advantage, had eyes for our money. He used her, and when he learned he'd get nothing from us, he threw her away like garbage."

"They were in love!"

"Love, bah. She was 16, she knew nothing of love. I had—your grandfather and I had spectacular plans for her. All ruined, and for nothing." She sniffed again. "You can't expect anything good to come from those people."

"What people?" Somehow, Lia wasn't surprised at the illuminating comment.

"How dare you! I am not a prejudiced person. Your father was common, an opportunist. Raised that way, not like decent folks."

She continued to pace. "We did what any responsible parents would do to protect our child."

"Yeah, and that worked out great."

Grammy's head jerked as if slapped.

Lia bared her teeth. "They got married. My father picked out my name. Apikalia. Do you know what that means?" She shook the baby bracelet in Grammy's face. Her throat ached for all the years she'd missed not knowing him, and all the lies for the sake of bitter prejudice.

Grammy barked a laugh, and ice-blue eyes narrowed, shining with malice. The angles of her face sharpened and she spat like a cat defending territory. "They didn't have the right to marry. Your mother needed our consent, and we wouldn't give it, so she ran off to play house, that's all. Your Grandfather set her straight, and we all came back home. Where we belonged." Her expression softened. "She didn't tell us about the baby until we couldn't do anything about it."

Before she could digest the implication of the comment, a door opened and closed nearby. Grandfather spoke in muted conversation with another man.

All color drained from Grammy's face. Her mouth opened and closed but no words escaped, and hands plucked at Lia's coat sleeve to detain her. Lia realized not all secrets had been revealed.

Lia strode past the older woman to intercept Grandfather as he left his office, knowing he'd be less likely to verbally attack with a business client present. For the Corazon's, everything came down to public perceptions. Reputation was all, and disowning Lia hurt their standing in local society. Everyone already knew what she was. But spilling Grammy's secrets would damage the Corazon name beyond embarrassment.

"Appreciate your time, Dub. If you change your mind, I don't head back to the Big Island for two days. My associates have a few more product orders to fill. My clients are very particular."

The slight man shook Grandfather's hand. He looked familiar.

"Sorry I can't help you, Mr. Kanoa. I stopped doing business in Hawaii years ago. For personal reasons." He noticed Lia standing in the open archway, and a frown carved trenches into each side of his mouth. He'd lost weight, and his imposing stature looked gaunt, a shrinking shadow of his former vigor.

Grandfather turned his back and spoke through gritted teeth.

"Cornelia, get her out of here."

Mr. Kanoa glanced Lia's way, and his face brightened. "Oh, what a pleasure. Lia, isn't it? We met at the gala in August. Antonio Kanoa, remember?" He offered to shake, ignoring the tension, or perhaps relishing it. She gripped and released his delicate, damp hand, and forced herself not to wipe her palm against her shirt. She remembered he ran an import/export business, acquiring unique merchandise ordered by high-paying clients like Grandfather.

Kanoa chuckled, looking back and forth between the two. "Some family issues, I see? Good luck, young lady, I know from experience what a difficult man your Grandfather can be."

"Call me Apikalia." She stared at Grandfather. "That means, *my father's delight* in Hawaiian. Did you know that, Grandfather?" She paused, and added, "My *father* told me he picked my name out special."

"Get out, Lia. You don't belong here, not anymore." Grammy hissed a warning as she grabbed Lia's wrist and tugged.

Lia shook it off.

"You're Hawaiian?" Kanoa's smile widened. "What a coincidence. I have business dealings there now and again."

Grandfather's face flushed beet-red and his voice growled from deep inside. "You *spoke* to him? You have the gall to say that to my face, girl? Get out!"

"They were *married!*" She pointed a shaking finger in his face. "Grammy's ashamed I'm a bastard, but that's on you, isn't it? You fixed things, thought you'd make the problem go away. How dare you lie to me all these years?"

He slapped away her hand. "I never lie." Grandfather glared at Kanoa, and nodded at the door. "This is private, see yourself out."

The small man nodded, grinned even wider, and pulled out a fancy cigarette case as he walked to the door.

Lia stuck her hands in her coat pockets, fidgeting with the pink gloves, when she wanted to flail and hit back at something, or someone. She blinked hard, refusing to give Grandfather the satisfaction of her tears.

"I never lie, Lia-girl. Wyatt Teves promised to marry her, but he lied. He disappeared instead. Broke my poor Kaylia's heart." Grandfather took a step toward her, and she couldn't help but retreat. "That evil man didn't have the cojones to ask for my daughter's hand like a decent—"

"He was the same age as when you married Grammy—"

"Jailbird, a convict. I checked up on him later, you know, when we found out Kaylia was pregnant." He glared at his wife. "Tell her."

Grammy looked away, and Lia knew. "It was you!"

Chapter 67

September pulled into her usual parking spot at Doc Eugene's veterinary hospital. In the back seat, Shadow whined with anticipation. He loved the staff, in part because they offered bacon-flavored treats.

She hadn't wanted to leave Lia alone at the Corazon estate but had no choice. September felt protective of the younger woman, but had no right to offer any advice, even if they were cousins. Lia didn't know about the relationship, though, and September wouldn't dare overstep to say anything, especially after Mom's warning. Some family secrets were best left hidden.

Lia's stories pushed the boundaries of belief, though. "What do you think, Shadow?" He barked, paw-dancing on the back seat and anxious to go into the building. "You recognized Lia, didn't you?" She'd often wondered how he'd survived the flood. Coincidence followed September, and despite earlier misgivings, she felt drawn to the younger woman. "Let's see if you recognize Karma, too."

Although the Rottie momma wouldn't be interested in anything except her babies for the foreseeable future, September's curiosity prompted the visit. She'd coached Lia by phone and Skype call for months, but barely caught glimpses of the young dog. Now, with the fantastical story fresh in her ears, and Lia otherwise engaged, she wanted to meet the police dog. And ask Doc Eugene a couple of pointed questions, besides.

"Hey September. Hiya Shadow, how's the big boy?" The young receptionist grinned when they entered, and then frowned with worry. "Is Shadow okay?"

Shadow woofed his own answer, and pranced to the front desk for a paws-up greeting over the counter. His tail wagged double time.

"How's that for an answer." September laughed, and shrugged an okay for a treat. "Can you tell me if Karma had her puppies yet? That's Lia Corazon's Rottweiler."

The girl wrinkled her nose, and fished out another treat for Shadow. "Lia called earlier. Nobody's brought her in."

"Is Doc Eugene around? Love to bend his ear for a minute." While Shadow munched and the receptionist hurried to the back, September leaned on the counter.

Doc Eugene bustled in, drying his hands on a towel. "Busy day here, September, what can I do ya for?" One of the best veterinary cardiac specialists in North Texas, Doc Eugene also ran a general practice. He held a special affection for Shadow, since he'd come from the last litter bred by the veterinarian's wife. "Macy doing okay? The staff still misses that kitty." He came around the counter into the waiting room and took a knee to interact with Shadow on the dog's level.

"Macy hasn't had a fainting spell in months. The medication has him back to his bouncy pestering self." She loved watching Shadow turn into a puppy at the man's attention. "Macy teases Shadow into chase games, and they run laps around the house. I worry it's too much for Macy, not to mention driving my Mom nuts." The cat knocked over a stained glass lamp during a recent romp, and also liked to bat at pictures on the wall. Mom had not been amused.

The veterinarian gave Shadow a final pat on the dog's tummy, and stood up. "You know the prognosis as well as I do. Macy's already outlived most cats with the condition, so he may buck the odds." He softened his tone. "If he tolerates exercise well, let him have some fun. As long as further signs don't develop, aim for quality of life. We can adjust the meds as we go."

"Okay." She'd suspected as much, but hoped for better news.

"Have you contacted Macy's breeder? They should have done

testing. We talked about this."

September ran a hand through her hair, still getting used to the short bob. "Macy came from a breeder in Chicago." Actually, the cat had been a gift from a man she hoped never to see again. Because of the bad associations, she'd put off any follow up.

"Any responsible breeder will want to know." He turned back to Shadow. "This boy looks good. Finally healed, and I bet he's a whole lot more comfortable now."

She hesitated. "I've got a hypothetical for you, Doc."

"Oh goodie." He smiled and rubbed his hands together like a cartoon character relishing a treat. "Asking for a friend, I take it?"

She laughed. "Let's say it's for a couple of friends, including Lia Corazon."

His eyebrows lifted. "Karma's due to whelp anytime."

"Right. So if canine gestation takes 63 days—"

"More or less, yes." He waited.

"That means she bred back in August, right about the time she got caught in the fire." September waited for his nod. "The thing is, Shadow nearly got caught in the fire, too. And there are witnesses that saw him and Karma together."

"Witnesses? Together, how. Oh, you mean?..." He grinned widely.

She held out her hands, with a "what can you do?" gesture. "Lia believes Shadow fathered Karma's pups, but that can't be true, can it?"

He rubbed his chin, then strode to the counter and looked at the paper appointment book. He flipped back several months, and pointed. "Here's the date Shadow had surgery." He flipped forward a few pages. "And here's when we admitted Karma for smoke inhalation, two weeks later." The corners of his eyes crinkled, and he spoke to Shadow. "You dog, you!" He laughed.

Shadow woofed and wagged, looking very proud of himself.

"So it's possible?" September wasn't sure how she felt about it, but couldn't wait to tell Lia.

"Viable sperm remain in the system for up to a month following castration. So yes. It's unlikely, but possible. If they were together, Shadow may have fathered Karma's puppies."

Chapter 68

Karma whined deep in her throat as the car jittered and swerved over the country road. She leaned hard against Tee, appreciating the girl's soothing hands and low murmurs, but her girl's fear-scent choked a good-dog's nose.

She'd played countless games to learn dozens of commands and skills. Often, she bit down on Tee's padded arm, but that was a game, too. Afterward they snuggled and shared treats. Karma wanted to bite the man, though, even without the padded sleeve. He smelled wrong, smelled of danger and sour blood, and wet feathers. Like the dead bird Karma found one time, and Lia threw away.

Her uneasiness grew, but respect for Tee ran deep. Even though the girl lacked sharp teeth like Karma, and had only two legs to run, Tee's fierce attitude rivaled Karma's own. Getting into the car was wrong, but she did as Tee asked because humans sometimes knew things that good-dogs couldn't understand. Karma had to trust her girls. She knew Lia and Tee would never wish her harm.

Still, people missed out on many things that a talented dog understood. Together, Karma and Tee made a good team, each adding to the strength of the other. Karma nestled close against her girl's bare arms to show that a brave dog would protect, no matter what, even from the hidden dangers people couldn't detect. As long as they stayed together, all was fine.

The car slowed, turning off the paved country road onto a dirt pathway that cut through brittle stalks of spent vegetation. The stalks flipped and flapped against the sides of the car, every once in a while punctuated with a "thump" that made Karma growl.

"Shush, it's just on old cornfield." Tee whispered soothing words she didn't understand, but Karma felt better anyway. Her girl sounded excited but brave, like she planned and expected this very strange car ride. Maybe this was a new game Karma needed to learn?

Her ears pricked and brow smoothed. Karma pulled away from Tee, staring first one way and then the other out each side of the car windows. Within minutes, they stopped in a clearing well hidden by the spindly field corn and parked in front of a weathered building. Its rusty metal roof creaked in the wind, and Karma noticed other dilapidated outbuildings. But more interesting by far were a dozen or more wooden A-frames sprouting from the dusty yard like giant fire ant mounds. Karma cocked her head when first one, and then several more disgorged noisy birds. Big birds, as big as bear-toy! Karma wondered if they squeaked when bitten, too.

The driver climbed out and slammed the door. He trotted to the house, stomped up shaky stairs and banged on the porch door until it cracked open.

Tee hugged Karma again, and smoothed her black ruff with trembling fingers. "Didn't mean to get you into this. Can't pretend I'm sorry you're here, though. Just be brave, watch me, and do what I say." She smiled, and a dry laugh escaped. "You always do, though, such a good-dog."

Karma wriggled at the praise for only a moment. Her jaw snapped shut and hackles bristled when the man returned to the car with a tall, thin woman. She made no sound, but stared hard, making Karma growl louder. She gave orders the others jumped to obey.

"Put these on." The driver shoved three lengths of rope over the back seat into Tee's hands. "Two on the dog, one on you. Be quick."

When Tee looped ropes around her broad neck, Karma whined but accepted the leashes. Her brow furrowed when the girl pulled the other rough loop over her own head, cinching it tight. She watched with growing unease when Tee followed instructions to thread her own leash through one window and Karma's out the other narrow opening.

The man gathered up the ends of Karma's leash. The woman grabbed Tee's rope, opened the car door, and yanked hard. Tee's startled yell squeezed off in a squeal of pain as her air cut off. She made a frantic grab for the bear-toy on the seat and missed.

Karma didn't think. She lunged to attack without need of command, teeth snapping at the bad woman who dragged Tee from the car. But Karma's own leash, anchored by the man outside her window, kept Karma in place as she thrashed and struggled to protect her family.

Tee clutched at the rope to relieve the painful pressure. She managed one final command before he dragged her away. "Karma, guard bear. Guard bear!"

Without pause, Karma grabbed the toy, but that didn't stop her outraged, toy-muffled barks. She only fell silent when Tee disappeared into the house.

She turned her attention to the bad-man outside the window. Karma growled, pouring her soul into the sound, intent clear in a hard-eye stare.

"Hey, need some help here." His voice stuttered with fear, and that pleased Karma, so she growled louder.

The woman reappeared without Tee and seized the second rope. The two strangers moved apart, each holding a rope taut when Karma's door swung open.

Karma roared, dropped the toy and leaped at the man. Jaws snapped closed on empty air, though, when the woman's rope yanked Karma back.

Together they dragged Karma, howling and snarling, toward the house. At the last moment, Karma remembered to snatch up the bear-toy before they heaved and yanked, and then tied her to a stake in the ground by the front porch and left her there.

Karma yelped, and jerked this way and that way. The noose tightened around her throat until her voice rasped raw and tongue dried with foam. Finally, she paused to draw the toy closer to her tummy, obeying her girl's final command. Karma curled up in the dirt beneath the strange house.

It was a good-dog's job to protect her family. But she'd failed. Tee was gone.

Chapter 69

Combs stared at the boots they'd found discarded beside the country road. The tracking device remained secured inside the instep. They'd also found Tee's abandoned car, parked behind a nearby billboard.

He wanted to strangle the cop and was ready to send Tee back to Chicago. She'd offered initial help back in August, but since then, she'd been a thorn in his side. Rather than following direction, she always had *better ideas* than the experienced team of detectives. Reining in her impatience and boundless energy exhausted his patience.

Once they made the connection with Momma Ruth, the team put next steps in place involving an undercover officer. Tee volunteered, and he had to accept. Combs preferred a more experienced officer, but the only other officer able to pull off the masquerade was on maternity leave.

He knew this case had personal implications for Tee. She hadn't shared what, but he could tell. Granted, they all took it personally and wanted to nail anyone connected to abuse of minors. Those engaged in child pornography or sex trafficking of children deserved eternal damnation. Combs shuddered, thinking of his own kids. He'd almost lost Melinda and Willie in the random storms last February, but having a child caught up in this sort of evil must be a special kind of hell.

His partner Detective Winston Gonzales returned from searching the car. "Find anything?" Combs asked. Tee was resourceful. If they'd taken her boots, she'd find another way to leave behind a trail.

Gonzales shook his head, smoothing his neat mustache with one hand. "Nothing helpful. Car's clean. No gun, no phone. It's registered to Lia Corazon, though, not Tee."

"That's right. Tee doesn't have a car, and Lia was pissed her car got taken. And her dog." At least Lia hadn't been pressed into playing chauffeur, though he suspected Lia knew more about this than she'd admit. One sister at a time took his breath away, but two at once caused more ruckus than a Texas twister. "Sure her phone isn't there? She called me ten minutes ago. She must have ditched it or hid it somewhere."

"Too risky to call her." Gonzales had already jumped ahead to the next logical step. "Bet she shut it off, too."

"If it's on her person or in the vehicle she's in, the ring tone could give her away. You're right, we can't risk it. But we can get an order to track it."

He smiled. "On it. Sounds like something Tee would do."

Combs hoped she'd not pushed safety boundaries too much. They'd planned to have Tee wired before she went in, but maybe they could still make this work. "What else you got?" He took out a stick of gum, offered Gonzales, and he demurred. He'd given up smoking ages ago, but at times like these, he needed something to stem the urge.

"Lots of slobber marks inside the windows, some still tacky. From the police dog?" Gonzales shook his head, puzzled. "Did Tee take the dog along for some reason? How's that play in the sting?"

He didn't know. He'd rushed away from Lia's place before finding out. As long as Lia had no car, she'd be out of the way without a way to go after the dog. Combs unwrapped another stick of gum. This might turn into a five-stick operation. "Go on."

"They're collecting any trace they can find. If they took Tee and the dog out of the car, there's sure to be something." Gonzales hesitated, and added with relish, "Hope Karma nailed 'em."

Combs grinned, and silently seconded the notion. Everyone at the station knew and loved Karma. They spoiled the gregarious

Rottie every time she showed up. The dog's heroics during the fire last August were the stuff of legend, and all agreed she'd make a spectacular K9 officer. That is, if Lia ever turned her loose. They had a running bet on the dog's delivery date, and number of pups Karma would whelp—and who got first dibs to claim one. Gonzales said his kids wanted a pup.

"Tee does a lot of stuff spur of the moment." But Combs couldn't imagine she'd take Karma, especially in her condition, and for sure not without Lia being part of the decision. Dammit! He should have talked to Lia before leaving. She couldn't lie to save her life. God help them all if the two sisters cooked up their own plan to trap the sex ringleaders.

He'd ignored Lia's angry text long enough. He sent a quick answering text: *Car found abandoned. Tee & dog AWOL. U holding out on me?*

He waited. She typically replied immediately, so when nothing happened, he called and left a similar terse message, with an urgent demand that she call back ASAP.

Combs also wanted to dial up Momma Ruth, but that could make her run if she thought Tee hadn't played straight with her. Or, it could tip off Boss that something was amiss.

He pocketed his phone, heading back to his car. "Tee's laptop may tell us more. That's back at her place." He'd talk to Lia there, too, and get some answers, so they could put this ugly case to rest, before any more girls got hurt.

Chapter 70

Lia stared at her grandparents as if seeing them for the first time. The shock and betrayal in one expression met the guilt and stubborn defense in the other.

"Cornelia? What's she talking about?" Grandfather's ashen face aged him another decade.

Grammy refused to bend. She lectured Lia, voice growing ever more strident, and spots of red hectored her high cheekbones. "Listen to your Grandfather. That man wasn't good enough for Kaylia." She rounded on her husband, the tiny woman vehement in her defense. "We had *plans* for her, she had a *place in society*, after we fought for years to be taken seriously here. The Corazons are somebody in this community. And she wanted to throw the Corazon name into the trash." Her chest heaved.

"What did you do?" He steadied himself with one hand against the wall, braced for a hurtful punch.

"I did what you wouldn't! I protected our daughter. You pretend to be macho, the strong father, but always you encouraged Kaylia's defiance. So proud of that headstrong Corazon blood. It's your fault she ruined herself!" She whirled, this time throwing the bitter words at Lia, still justifying an anguished confession. "Yes, I had that paniolo boyfriend trash arrested, got their so-called marriage annulled." She smoothed her throat, playing with the strand of pearls, and aimed another shot at her husband. "You weren't strong enough to do the hard thing. The right thing."

Grandfather stared at Grammy for endless seconds. That seemed to spur her on.

"She had prospects here, don't you see? A place in the community. That no account wouldn't fit in here. He wanted to keep her in that Godforsaken island place. So I had to smooth things over, for her own good. For our family's sake." Grammy grabbed Lia's hands, held them tight. "Nobody knew about you, and we had to keep it that way. To protect your mother."

Lia dragged her hands away and staggered several steps backwards. Grammy followed, tottering and clacking on her high heels that now seemed ridiculous rather than stylish.

"All that changed after you were born, Lia. You have to understand." Grammy held a pleading hand out to her husband. "Your Grandfather agreed. Tell her, Dub. And we would have convinced your mother to see reason. Tell her!" Grammy appealed to the man, who still seemed rocked to his soul.

"Agreed to what?" Lia looked between the two.

He rubbed his face and spoke in a hush. "It was the only way to give your mother a fresh start. Without painful reminders."

Grandfather meant her. *She* would be the painful reminder, a reminder of love gone wrong. Of love derailed by meddling parents.

"My mother didn't want to give me away, though, did she?" Her voice filled with wonder. Her stare pinned Grammy, still hungry for details. "But you had already made the arrangements to keep the dirty little secret. That's why I was born here, and not in a hospital? So the inconvenient baby could disappear, and your society snobs would never know?" Her tears finally overflowed. "That's why my mother died, with no doctor nearby to intervene. Isn't that right!"

"What? No! We never planned for you to be born here." Grandfather held up both palms toward her, as if fending off a blow. "You came early. I was gone on a buying trip so her sister stayed to help. Cornelia called to tell me. You came too fast to get to the hospital. Tell her, Cornelia. For God's sake, tell her!"

"Why do you think I haven't spoken to Rose in more than 20 years? It's all her fault," Grammy crossed her arms tight across her chest, turned her back, and stalked away, making surreptitious swipes at her eyes. She bowed her head. Her shoulders shook.

Shocked understanding turned his features dusky. Grandfather sucked in a ragged breath before his attention returned to Lia. He looked broken, proud carriage stooped and bent, and his rough voice trembled. "When your mother died, I couldn't bear to lose you both." He held one gnarled hand out to her.

She knocked it away, choking on a sob. "You were right all along. I *don't* belong in this family. You lost me a long time ago." Lia whirled and ran out the door.

Chapter 71

Tee squinted against the single bare bulb swaying high overhead. It painted stark shadows in the smelly bathroom. She flexed achy wrists, zip-tied by the silent red-haired woman—Momma Ruth?—who dragged her through the shabby cowboy diner and down the narrow hall, to lock her in. She suspected a back room in the building played host to cockfights, if the birds in the yard were any indication. The smell of chicken poop added to the miasma.

With quick efficiency, she searched the tiny room. In the last of the three stalls, a figure cowered, squatting between the nasty commode and the wall in an effort to be invisible. Dark hair curtained her face, making it hard to judge age. "Hey, are you hurt? Come on out." Tee gestured with her bound hands. "We're locked in. But not for long." She imbued the promise with as much conviction as possible, knowing Combs and the team would find them. Without the tracking device, it would take longer, but he'd figure out her backup plan. She had to believe that, anyway.

The delicate form unfolded, and Tee helped her up. "What's your name?"

"Alana." A child, maybe ten or twelve at most. Scarred skin.

Haunted eyes.

Tee looked away, seeing too much of herself. "Pretty name, Alana." In Hawaiian, it meant *offering.* Tee wondered what sicko had made an offering of this child. "How you stay? You okay? My name is—"

Karma's distant barking stopped her words. Alana shivered and retreated again to the stinky stall.

"It's okay, that's my dog, my ilio. She on our side, Alana." Tee drew close to the locked bathroom door and pressed her ear to the panel. Muted shouts from the driver and the redheaded woman made her smile. Karma wouldn't do their bidding.

She turned back to the child. "How long have you been here? Momma Ruth bring you here, child? You the only one? All Hawaiian girls?"

Alana shrugged. "Boys, girls, from many places. We come, then we go. Boss teach what t'do, so mens come pick ones they want. Some go 'way, never come back. Boss say I'm for special someone." She shuddered, knowing what that meant. Her little hands flitted like hummingbirds to smooth waist-length hair.

Tee's stomach clenched, and for a moment, her vision tunneled. She pinched her bare thigh, and the stinky surroundings returned to focus. "Who da boss?" Couldn't be the muscle man who drove her here. "Big man? Small man?" Hell, anyone would be big from this girl's viewpoint. "He haole, or maybe Hawaiian? What he like?" She fell into pidgin to better connect with Alana.

But Alana's lips pressed tight. "I no tell, or Boss gi' me to Tony." She shuddered.

"Tony, he work fo' Boss?" Must be the driver. "What about Momma Ruth, she treat you good?"

Alana burst into tears.

Tee moved to hug the child, despite her hobbled hands. But Alana shrank away, leery of any touch.

She'd pressed too much. Alana knew few details anyway, not any more than Mele had known. But this place looked deserted. Boss must be planning to move on soon, if only a single child remained in their sick inventory. Why, then, had they taken the bait she'd set up with Momma Ruth?

Momma Ruth had answers. And so did the mysterious Boss. They'd be more willing to gloat and share incriminating info in front of her, the merchandise. *Play the part, and meet the Boss.*

Tee returned to the locked door and banged so hard on it the plywood cracked. Given time, she could break through the shabby patched barrier. For now, though, everything she did should prime her captors to talk. Momma Ruth drew a hard line about revealing details, and only agreed to get Tee inside to find out firsthand. Tee wanted the Boss and everyone else involved put away for good. Combs and his team needed to hang back so nobody ran too soon, before she got the info needed to put them all away.

She banged on the door again. "Hey! Let me outta here. You got no right t'keep me. Hey! You talk t'me, what you doin' here. An' leave īlio—my dog alone. Hey there, hear me? Hey! Hey! What you doin' here anyways?" She banged again and again until her fist bruised. She'd wear them down. They had to answer eventually.

***

Outside, beneath the porch of the tacky building, Karma lay in the dirt. She chewed the rope tether that kept her confined. She heard Tee's muffled voice, a clarion call for a good-dog to protect. She'd been trained to serve those she loved and respected, and Tee was chosen family. Her girl was in danger! Karma whined, and redoubled her efforts, pulling against the strong rope to test progress.

A strident mewling made her ears twitch, and she twisted around to look. Something stirred in the far reaches of the makeshift shelter. Despite the crazy rooster crowing that hurt a good-dog's ears, and dusty-feather smells of stale nests and dead critters, this life-affirming sound made Karma's stubby tail wiggle despite other worries.

She stretched her broad neck as far as she could reach, and whined low, low in her throat to keep from scaring the creature. Karma wrinkled her muzzle in the effort to sift scents and find this one's signature odor amid the multitude of smells. She whined again, detecting the unmistakable stink of decay. Others hadn't survived.

But this baby toddled closer, questing with tiny pink nose, mouth agape with ever more strident cries. With a low woof, Karma scooted nearer until able to grasp it by its blond scruff. She settled the three-week-old baby next to her tummy beside bear-toy, and set about washing it nose to tail. She stiffened with surprise when it purred and latched onto her nipple, and then she relaxed. For a moment, as the kitten nursed, Karma sank into a peaceful doze.

Then a mechanical sound, something no human ear could detect, vibrated deep inside bear-toy. Karma paused, tipping her head, and nudged the stuffed toy with one paw.

"Hello? Hello? Where the hell are you, Tee, and what have you done with my dog?"

Chapter 72

Lia ran from the house, tears blinding her, the revelations from Grammy beyond anything she could have imagined. All she'd been raised to believe turned upside down. Winded, she stopped halfway down the long drive in the shadow of a huge bois d'arc tree she'd played beneath as a little girl.

Her father had a name—Wyatt Teves—and he was alive. He hadn't abandoned her mother. Lia had been wanted and loved, and her parents married. They'd been driven apart by the whims of controlling parents who wanted to erase the embarrassment of Lia from their lives. Only her mother's death, caused by Grammy's desire to hide the shameful secret, left her to be raised by grandparents who clearly despised her.

That explained a lot.

She'd tried to fit into the box they wanted until she'd had to rebel or lose herself. Grammy wanted a do-over to make Lia into the daughter-replacement she'd lost. Grandfather, unbending and unforgiving, believed his wife's manipulations, maybe because he couldn't stomach the alternative. In Lia's eyes, that made him just as culpable.

Training dogs and opening the boarding kennel was the first thing Lia ever wanted just for herself, and not to please someone else. As expected, her grandparents did everything possible to quash Lia's desires, and remake her in their image.

Fisting her eyes, Lia straightened her shoulders and her resolve. She'd thought finding the truth would make things right. She'd prove to Grandfather that her father wasn't the villain, she'd have a new sense of her heritage, and everyone could go back to their prickly relationship—but still be part of each other's world.

All that ended with no going back. Wyatt—she couldn't bring herself to call him Dad—provided more truth in their brief Skype conversation than she'd had in 25 years. He'd been honest about his mistakes, too, including that he'd hurt her sister Tee in some terrible way, and wanted to make it right.

Lia debated calling September but couldn't bring herself to impose again. She'd missed messages from Combs. He'd found her car, but not Karma or her sister. Dammit!

Doc Eugene should have called by now about Karma. That meant the other option turned the awful, horrible, terrible day into an even worse nightmare. She'd bet a year's salary that Tee took Karma with her to meet Momma Ruth, and didn't tell Combs, either. She further bet he found out about it, and that's why he took off like a buckshot coyote.

Lia didn't bother listening to voice mail. Time enough to call Combs back once she'd reamed out Tee. She dialed her sister's number, shivering in the brisk breeze. She pulled on her gloves and didn't notice the car's approach until it stopped next to her. Lia scrubbed at tear-stained cheeks before turning when the driver rolled down his window.

"Need a ride? I couldn't help but overhear—"

"Thanks a bunch, I appreciate it. Just a second." She held up a pink-gloved hand as Tee answered the phone, but when she heard heavy breathing, Lia grew exasperated. "Hello? Hello? Where the hell are you, Tee, and what have you done with my dog?"

Barks erupted on the other side of the line, followed by a cacophony of crowing roosters. "What? Do you hear that?" Incredulous, she climbed into the car. "Something's wrong. Take me to the police station, I'll explain along the way." She slammed the door.

"Oh, I'm sure it's quite a story." Antonio Kanoa smiled, shoved the car into gear, grabbed Lia's phone and tossed it out the window.

Chapter 73

Combs waited while the office manager unlocked the door to Tee and Lia's efficiency apartment. He'd hoped Lia would be waiting when he arrived but the place was empty. She'd still not returned his call or text, and that worried him.

"Where's your uniform? You sure don't look like a cop." The manager stood aside, grumbling.

"Detectives don't wear uniforms." He'd shown his badge, but still hadn't changed from his off-duty clothes, so he looked like a refugee from a rodeo. He didn't wait for response and closed the door behind him.

The place looked bipolar, but he wasn't surprised. Tee kept her space tidy, if not immaculate, but Lia couldn't be bothered. Part of that, he knew, had to do with sharing space with a 90-pound pregnant Rottweiler. Karma's frustration with confinement prompted all sorts of destructive behavior, so the folded clothes spilled off of the sofa, shredded burrito wrappings, and tipped over wastebasket weren't surprising.

He hurried to the tiny kitchenette and found Tee's laptop. Thankfully, she hadn't locked the machine, and he found the file he wanted. They file-shared, so he'd seen most of it before, but she'd updated since his last review. Combs scanned the document, paying particular attention to the most recent entries made less than an hour ago. "Bingo!" God bless Tee for being anal.

The snitch made contact and set the sting in motion. Tee also noted the phone number changed from previous Momma Ruth communications. She'd used at least three other phones before, but this wasn't a text, but an actual phone call. A landline, not a cell number. *Interesting.* On top of that, Momma Ruth said the "merchandise" moved out today, pushing the sting to go-status.

His own phone buzzed. Before could answer Lia, the call cut short. He return-dialed, but she didn't pick up. Weird and worrisome, but his most immediate concern had to be Tee.

He called the station. "Get someone to track down this number." He read the landline from Tee's file. "Yeah, I'll wait."

He'd gathered as much information as he could. Without more, he'd rejoin Gonzales and the rest of the team back at the station, compare notes, and figure out next steps. Maybe they had a line on Tee's cell phone by now. He headed back to his car, when the station came back on the line.

"That number's for a hole-in-the-wall diner way up north, over the Oklahoma border. They've had some raids out that way on account of cockfighting and gambling. There's an order to disconnect the line later today. It's out of our jurisdiction. You want me to contact PD over yonder?"

"Do that. We have an undercover cop in the mix, so tell 'em to tread careful. And get someone to light a fire under whoever's tracing Tee's phone." He disconnected.

As long as her phone stayed on, and the battery didn't run down, they had a chance. Combs hoped she had the sense to mute the thing so calls wouldn't give her away. Damn, he wanted to call her, but didn't dare.

Before he could start his car, Momma Ruth called, again from the landline.

"She no here. Where your lady cop, spoze to come hep me. Where she be? We had a deal!"

"You contacted Tee this morning to set up the meeting."

"But she not here. They gwon kill me! You promise get me outta the biz, if I hep. Now, Boss smells somfin wrong, got long reach. So I go 'way. Far 'way, you no fin' and Boss no fin' me."

"Wait! Where's the Boss now? With you at that diner in Chicapee?"

Dead silence. "What diner? No diner, no Chicapee, I nevah tell you dat! Boss come by me to Dallas, where I tell your girl-cop meet wif me. I hear tell about big boat they take in Houston, too. You gotta get Boss, so I go home Hawaii, okay? Leave me be!" She hung up.

He didn't buy it. The call didn't ring true. Still, Combs made two calls; first, to his counterpart in Dallas County to check into known cockfight operatives. And second, a call to Gonzales to gather the team and meet at the Chicapee diner. He'd make the forty-minute drive in record time.

Chapter 74

Lia cradled her aching jaw, still not understanding what prompted Antonio Kanoa to coldcock her. While dazed, he'd secured her wrists. She wasn't sure how long they'd driven when he turned off a narrow farm-to-market road onto a pig path that cut through a spent cornfield. She roused enough to peer through the window, taking in the ramshackle property ahead. He threaded the car through chicken coop shelters, and when the colorful birds began to crow, Lia roused in startled recognition at the sound she heard on Tee's phone. Dog barks joined the crowing cacophony, and she recognized the bass howls. "Karma!"

Kanoa backhanded her. "Shut up. You say nothing, do nothing."

The car stopped, and a slim red-haired woman exited the diner's door. "You're late. Who's she?" Her attractive features turned ugly. "Momma Ruth gave us up. I just talked to some detective, tried to steer him Dallas way, but I don't think he bought it. Now you pick up some random girl? She's not even your usual flavor, and we already got merchandise to liquidate—"

"But I thought—"

"Thinking is my job."

He licked his lips. "Right, Boss. Of course. If your guy won't take delivery—"

"Everything's blowing up, nobody will do a deal now. I'll make up the loss later."

"Give me Alana." His eyes gleamed.

"You keep her, it's your funeral. Changing your name won't help for long, not without better planning." She tossed her long hair. "I got a special order to deliver Pilikia Teves. Momma Ruth did us a favor, luring her in. The stupid bitch still has no clue we know she's a cop. I paid off the delivery guy, he knows nothing, even if they pick him up."

Kanoa gestured at Lia where she slouched in the car listening with growing horror. "She's a Teves, too. Half-sister to the cop, one of Wyatt's bastards. Should be a bonus for your client if they've got something against him. This one won't be missed, either, she just cut ties with the Texas branch of the family." He grimaced at the noise. "What's with the mutt?"

Karma's barking grew to hysterical proportions. Lia's throat ached in sympathy, hearing the dog's hoarse sound. Karma's presence meant her sister was in trouble, too. Lia eyed the car door latch. If she could reach Karma, they couldn't touch her.

"That's the cop's dog. I thought we could use it as leverage. If we had more time, fun and games for me to see what my knives could do to its shiny black fur." She laughed, and added, "Never got the chance when I worked at the vet clinic last year." Karma redoubled her barking, as if she knew they discussed her. "Shut up! Shut up, dog, or I'll shut you up!" Boss screamed, taking a few steps toward the dog.

"About that barking." Kanoa nodded at Lia. "She called someone. Nobody answered, but I could hear crowing and that dog." He looked around at the cackling flock. "Tee has a phone hid somewhere. They can trace those, can't they?"

"Son-of-a-bitch!"

The pair turned away, and Lia unlatched her car door, slid out and pushed it closed. She crouched, keeping the car between her and the couple, and scuttled to where Karma stood shaking and barking with aggression. When she noticed Lia, her barks morphed to squeals and howls of delight. Karma slicked back her ears and wriggled with happiness.

Boss narrowed her eyes, swinging attention back from Karma to the car. "Where's your merchandise, Tony?"

Lia sprinted, reaching Karma in less than ten seconds, and rolled beneath the porch overhang. Her zip-tied wrists prevented hugging the warm, black neck, but she welcomed Karma's frantic lapping face-kisses before pushing away. Now what?

Kanoa screeched and started toward her. Karma's growl warned him away.

"Leave her, she's not going anywhere. Help me put the merchandise on ice, and we'll come back for her. I've got a date with a plane, and a new passport." Boss whirled, and Lia heard her feet thump overhead as the woman ran back into the diner.

"Good girl, Karma! What a good-dog. Let's get you loose." Karma's teeth offered their only defense. She pulled off her pink gloves, and struggled for long minutes to untie the rope.

Karma grabbed something soft and pushed it against Lia's bound wrists.

"Yes, I see, you brought your bear. Hold still, Karma." But the dog repeatedly thrust the toy at her, hampering her efforts. "Karma, no! It's not playtime." What was wrong with her? This wasn't like the dog, not at all. In exasperation, Lia grabbed the toy to fling it aside.

The weight of the bear made her pause. Karma looked at her with a wise expression, cocking her head from side to side. Something was inside. And Karma knew it.

Tee! Leave it to her savvy sister to offer a back door for rescue. Lia smiled. That explained the noise when she called. Tee's phone was inside the bear, and somehow, Karma answered the call.

Overhead, she heard more screams, and loud voices. Soon, Kanoa and the woman would return for her. She needed to call Combs and get the police out here before something awful happened.

Lia found the open seam in the stuffed toy, reached inside, and pulled out the phone. But something else remained inside. She stuffed the phone into her pocket and drew out Tee's gun.

Her heart thudded. The only gun she'd ever fired was Grandfather's shotgun. He told her as a Corazon, she needed to respect firearms, and know how to use them. She wished she'd paid closer attention.

Karma whined and licked her face as if to say, *we're in this together.*

"Good girl, Karma." Lia didn't like guns. She'd get over her distaste, though, if it meant defending herself and Karma, and the rest of the *merchandise* inside.

Chapter 75

Tee waited inside the bathroom, prepared to continue the masquerade. She'd heard a car leave—her driver?—and another arrive—maybe, finally, the Boss. Now at least two pairs of footsteps echoed down the small hallway toward their smelly prison.

Alana cowered. Tee winked at her. "Like I told you, I'm here to protect you. Don't be scared, even if I pretend to be hurt or frightened. It's all pretend, okay?"

"Pretend." Alana repeated the word, but didn't believe her. To the child, pretend wasn't valid when she lived a real life of horror.

A loud banging sounded on the door. Alana tugged Tee's bound wrists, and the pair backed way.

"Coming for you, sweet Alana, my little damaged goods!" The man's voice made the child whimper. Tee's nostrils flared, and goosebumps shivered her flesh. His voice scratched some secret dangerous memory deep inside, and sudden terror clutched her gut.

The door screeched open, and Tee no longer had to pretend. Tony Kanoa reached to grab Alana and drag her out. Tee did nothing to stop him. Couldn't. She was helpless, just like all those years ago.

Her vision darkened, and she slipped away from the hurtful *now*, welcomed the black, wanted to go away and not come back. The boogeyman of childhood nightmares, foggy memory keeping her safe, shined real—not pretend at all—with evil embodied in his flat face and fervent eyes.

"No, Mr. Tony no no no!" Alana screamed.

Tony Kanoa.

Tee fell into a black abyss and welcomed the nothingness.

Chapter 76

Lia heard a young girl squealing and blubbering. She peered from beneath the porch as Karma continued to growl. "Shush." She whispered the command, and the dog fell silent, but Lia could feel the muscular shoulder pressed against hers trembling with pent up energy.

"Your choice, Tony, but consider the merchandise your payment in full." The woman's strident exasperation was clear. "When you're caught—and your habit will make that happen—you say nothing."

"I'd never say anything, Boss."

"Yes, you would, Tony. I know you. Just don't forget I have a long memory, and longer reach."

She couldn't hear his answer. Lia saw him shove a tiny girl into his car and drive away. Lia remained silent, holding her breath as the woman paced back and forth on the wooden porch overhead.

Mele didn't know the Boss's name. But Mele never said if Boss was a man or a woman. Antonio Kanoa, if that was his real name, took orders from this woman. She called the shots.

"I have your requested merchandise, and a bonus package that's closely related to the merchandise. You understand? But delivery isn't possible. How would like me to dispose of said merchandise?"

She strained to understand the one-sided phone conversation. Tee had been suckered into going undercover, when in fact she'd been targeted. Lia thought she'd been a drive-by casualty, but instead, Kanoa also targeted her. She couldn't figure out why. Lia juggled the gun with her bound hands, prepared to defend herself. She half-expected Tee to burst out of hiding with guns blazing like a super-cop. Her sister must still be okay, or Boss wouldn't ask her client for instructions.

"Understood. Yes, it will be painful. You shall have the honor of informing their father. And I expect payment to my account in the name of Dr. Robin Gillette, though I'll be changing things again very soon. I will text you the transfer instructions." The call ended, and the Boss walked down the stairs to peer beneath the boardwalk. "Come out, before I shoot you, kill your dog, and burn your sister to death."

Lia braced both hands on the gun, closed her eyes tight, and began to shoot.

A scream of anger greeted the half dozen gunshots.

Pulling the trigger, not trying to aim, kept the woman at bay. Lia didn't know what else to do and had no plan beyond that. Boss knew the police would show up. Maybe she'd cut her losses and go, rather than risk waiting Lia out.

The woman scrambled back up onto the porch, so Lia rolled onto her back and shot overhead through the rickety wood. Splinters hit her face, and mud dobber nests shattered and sprinkled her face with dirt. "Go away, go away, leave me alone!"

"You've seen my face now. You and your sister, both. And my payday and escape depends on you both going away." The voice taunted her. "I've got plenty of new names ready to go, so take your best shot."

She'd never been so scared or angry. Lia pulled the trigger again, and nothing happened.

Boss tromped down the stairs, voice gloating. "All out of bullets? Figured it was the cop's gun, so I counted to 15." She bent low to stare at Lia, and didn't flinch when Karma roared at her. "Amazing what tools one can find rummaging about a country kitchen." She held a cylinder in her hand, flipped a trigger, and the blowtorch spewed blue flame, licking at the tinder-dry structure.

Karma screamed, and backpedaled from the fire. The dog's tether caught Lia across the throat, knocking her head sideways against the bois d'arc support beam, leaving her dazed.

Boss reached a hand tipped with blue lacquered fingernails and aimed the flame to sear Lia's face. But she recoiled and dropped the blowtorch and it rolled out of reach when a poof of fur hissed and clawed blindly at her skin.

"Dammit! Thought I got rid of all of you filthy things." Boss flung her hand, and the orange tabby hissed and spat, sailing past Lia's head.

Lia blinked, sure a kitten hallucination meant very bad things for her brain. She struggled as Boss grabbed her by the neck, and dragged her out of the shelter, leaving the flaming torch, bellowing dog, and screaming kitten behind.

Chapter 77

Karma dodged the flame-spitting demon when it rolled toward her. The area under the building restricted a good-dog's movement, and she struggled to gather her feet. Her job was to protect, but the rope kept Karma from reaching Lia. She checked on the kitten, and it hissed and spat with startled aggravation, then purred when it smelled and recognized Karma.

Hands reached under, grabbed and pulled Lia away. Karma snarled and bucked hard against the rope, powerful Rottweiler haunches bunching and claws digging into the soft soil, but the tether held. She howled, bugling her anger and frustration. How could she protect her girls when she couldn't leave the cubbyhole beneath the house? Karma wanted to bite something, especially the bad-woman who stole a good-dog's family.

It was her fault. She failed the test. If she hadn't flinched from the fire to protect the kitten, she could have lunged and snapped at the thieving hands and kept Lia safe. Karma licked her burn-scarred paws, whimpering, remembering. Fire hurt.

But losing family hurt worse. She nosed the kitten and its fluffed fur smoothed as it purred very loud, a self-soothing lullaby.

Get away, she had to get away from this place, and go to her girls. She'd snarl and threaten anyone in the way, and Lia and Tee would call her "good-dog, Karma" and they'd go home together.

She wanted to go home. Not to the cramped rooms, but back to the kennel-home where she could run and sniff, and roll in dirt, and have her girls nearby to scratch hard-to-reach itchy places.

Karma pulled the kitten close to her tummy and went back to work. She growled as she gnawed, every so often tugging to see if the tether still held. When clattering footsteps tromped down the stairs, Karma bounded toward the fire-threat woman, and the rope snapped.

Something was wrong! Her tummy ached, and constricted in that hurty-strange way it had done off and on all day. She'd ignored it, to better serve her girls, but now the pain demanded Karma's attention. It would not be denied. Karma whimpered, and half fell in the drive. She watched as the bad-woman climbed into a car and drove away, leaving Karma alone in the dirt.

Dragging herself upright, she struggled back to her sleeping kitten. The pain came in waves and wouldn't stop. She settled herself, ignoring the chicken smell and decaying dead things. Something new had begun, something strange and scary and wonderful all at the same time. Something Karma had to finish.

She wished her girls were here. But she was a brave Rottweiler girl, and smart. Lia and Tee told her so, and she believed them. Karma would manage by herself.

And then she'd go rescue the rest of her family. And they'd go home. Together.

Chapter 78

Tee blinked when the door opened and brought in a whoosh of warm air. How had it become so cold? She moaned, wondering how long she'd been out of it. Her bare feet tingled and burned. She shook and shuddered from the cold, and one bare thigh felt hot where it made contact with the icy floor.

A figure fell into the room, and the door slammed shut, plunging them back into darkness. She'd caught a glimpse of gold hair. "Lia?" Tee struggled to her feet and hugged her still-bound wrists to her chest. Lord, the cold hurt. Where were they?

"Yes, it's me." Lia fumbled in the blackness until a dim light bulb came on overhead.

Tee gasped. It had been better in the dark.

Ice crystals covered the walls and door of the walk-in freezer. A young woman with long dark hair sat frozen to one corner of the room. Icy tears on her cheeks glittered. Tee looked away. But a glass thermometer at the door sparkled like crystal . . .

Like the Lucite butterfly night-light in Tee's childhood bedroom where, at age 9, Tony Kanoa turned her into damaged goods.

Her vision darkened again, chest tightened, and then Lia's hands clutched hers. Tee fought, struggled, crying to escape the faceless fog-demon from her past, but Lia wouldn't let go. "I've got you, you're safe. We're together, and we'll get out of this together."

Tee took a big cleansing breath, puffed it out, and nodded as the room swam back into focus. She pulled away from Lia's bound hands and took turns standing first on one foot and then the other. "A freezer? Hell of a way to die." Two women, hands bound, with no tools to escape. They'd be *pau*—finished, dead if they were ever found at all.

The freezer measured 6-by-5-feet. The temperature registered 5 degrees Fahrenheit. If standard issue, the walls, ceiling and doors, were four to six inches thick. No way out.

"Aha! Look what I found!" Lia held up a box cutter, grinning, and cut off her zip-tie and then Tee's as well. She shrugged off her jacket and held it out, and Tee didn't hesitate. No time to be a hero. She slipped it on but it offered little relief. Even with heavy clothing, they'd both soon succumb to hyperthermia, if they didn't suffocate first.

"Aren't these things supposed to open from the inside? Some sort of emergency switch?" Lia pushed through the swaying plastic curtains at the entry and banged on the door, searching the walls nearby for an emergency switch of some kind.

"Even if this one does, I've a feeling that Boss made sure we're not getting out." Tee dumped a carton filled with frozen mystery meat—maybe chicken?—and watched them hockey-puck across the slick floor. She used the blade to break down the box, then pressed the cardboard flat to the floor to stand on. The barrier gave much needed respite to her bare feet that might as well be dead. Her blue toes had icy white tips.

Lia noticed the body for the first time. "Oh my God! The poor woman."

Tee spoke through her shivers, her voice a herky-jerk staccato. "My guess, that's Momma Ruth, but doesn't matter at the moment. Lia, we don't have much time. Walk-in freezers are airtight. One this size gives a single person maybe four to six hours of air, and that's with no exertion. Divide that by two for both of us. And we need to cobble something together for shelter. I wouldn't count on more than a couple hours at most, before we're breathing carbon monoxide or worse."

Chapter 79

Combs rolled into the yard minutes behind Gonzales and the rest of their team. He climbed out, and hurried to the front of the ramshackle diner, meeting one of the officers stationed at the front door. On the way here, they'd gotten confirmation that Tee's cell phone was nearby. "Anything?"

Gonzales shook his head. "They're still looking, but no vehicles in the vicinity. Appears to be deserted." He nodded behind him. "Except for all those chickens."

"Roosters. Fighting cocks. Sort of pretty, except when strapped up with razors and slashing each other to death." He'd never understand the attraction, how anyone could enjoy watching. Money fueled the blood sport through gambling—always accompanied by drugs and illegal guns. As soon as law enforcement squashed one, two more operations sprang up.

He'd first met Lia when she had a run-in with a guy out to make a quick buck breeding and selling fighting dogs. He smiled at the memory. Karma would have had a very different life, if Lia hadn't intervened.

He couldn't worry about Lia now. He guessed she'd caught a ride to the vet clinic, and by now was up to her neck in Karma's new puppies. At least something happy might come out of this shitty day.

Combs squinted and stuck another stick of gum into his mouth. He took in the nearby barn and a lean-to shed. "We need to go over the outbuildings top to bottom. If we can't find Tee, they have her and the sting's still in play." He hoped so, because if she'd been made, they'd dump her body somewhere they'd never find. "We're chasing ghosts," he muttered.

His cell phone rang, and he answered without looking at it. "Combs. What've you got?"

"I don't have my granddaughter, that's what." The deep voice shook with anger and fear, and it took a beat for Combs to recognize Lia's grandfather.

"Mr. Corazon? I'll have to call you back. I'm in the middle—"

"You were just on a date with Lia. My buddy saw you at the bank. So you should care what happens to her. She just took off and I'm afraid I..." He cleared his throat. "Some harsh words were spoken. I'm worried, she got a ride with someone—"

"You'll have to excuse me." They weren't dating. His ears burned. Small towns loved gossip, and he'd had enough drama dealing with September's adventures, not to mention her mother.

"Dammit, boy, she went off with that Antonio Kanoa character. Wouldn't trust him as far as I could toss a horseshoe. He's crooked as a crik."

Kanoa? Why did that name ring a bell? "Okay, hold on. Lia got in a car with this guy? What make car?" He made a note. Finally, a lead he could get his teeth into. "Will get back to you soon." He hung up before the man could make any further protestations or demands.

Combs couldn't resist a satisfied smile. Lia wouldn't believe it. But the concern he'd heard sure didn't sound like someone who hated and disowned their blood kin granddaughter.

One of the officers waved from the barn, and Combs held out his hands with a *"what'd you find?"* gesture. The headshake made him want to spit with frustration. They were too late. If Momma Ruth and Tee had been here, they were long gone.

He turned to walk up the steps to check the inside of the diner, and noticed a bloodstained rope sticking out from under the porch overhang. Combs bent to look closer and saw the hot pink gloves.

Lia's gloves.

She was here, too, or had been! And, he'd be willing to bet, so was Tee.

He reached for the glove. Low growls turned to snarls and stopped him dead in his tracks.

Chapter 80

Tee's teeth chattered so hard, she bit her tongue when she tried to speak. Lia wasn't much better.

"Oh God." Lia looked around, stamping her feet, and flapping her arms for warmth. "What do we do?"

"Don't move so much. You'll use too much oxygen." Tee's nose ran, then froze as she inhaled the subzero atmosphere. Her nose hairs crackled. "Then again, we'll be unconscious before we freeze to death."

"Not funny." Lia looked around. "We need a shelter to conserve body heat. The plastic works." She used the box cutter to rip free the curtain barrier of heavy plastic. Designed to keep cold in, it would just as easily contain their body heat.

"Good idea. Boxes build a scaffolding for plastic over top. Plus we need something to sit on so our butts don't freeze to the floor." Snuggled together in the tiny space, their body warmth would keep them from freezing the same way an igloo made of snow became toasty with enough bodies inside.

In theory, anyway.

They hunkered side by side beneath the flimsy plastic canopy. Tee folded her legs and pulled Lia's borrowed jacket over top of her knees. The pair hugged each other, not out of affection, but necessity. As long as their teeth chattered and shivers shook them, they were good. No shivers signaled severe hypothermia and impending loss of consciousness. "Let's hope Combs is smart enough to track my phone. I put it inside Karma's bear."

"Of course!" Lia pulled the phone from the coat pocket with a "eureka" flourish.

"Great! Don't suppose you have my gun, too?" Tee dialed Combs.

Lia shook her head. "I used up all the bullets but didn't hit anything. Sorry."

Tee glared at the phone when nothing happened. "Shit, it's out of juice." She dropped it with disgust. "Had it muted so a call wouldn't give me away. Must have left it on auto-answer by mistake."

"Huh? Auto-answer, you mean like blue tooth?"

"No, it's a setting for hands-off automatic answering. I use it when I run." The plastic crackled when her shoulder bumped it, and she shifted away from its icy surface. "Somebody must have called. It answered but didn't hang up and that ran down the battery.

Lia looked stricken.

"What. Oh, don't tell me, YOU called?"

"What was I supposed to do? You ran off without a word, took my car and my pregnant dog with you. So yes, I called. And I heard Karma barking her head off and a bunch of roosters crowing." Her arms loosened, as if she might flounce off.

Tee tightened her grip. "Don't you dare leave. We can't survive alone." She sighed. "They can still find us if they started the tracking procedure early enough. We'll just have to put up with each other."

"Until we pass out, right?" Lia loosened her hair tie, so her tresses spilled down both sides of her face and covered her neck. "I can't feel my ears."

Tee grimaced. "Don't suppose you messaged the police? We've been running an investigation into cockfighting in the region. Bet it's all tied together."

Lia glared. "I wanted to do more than message the police. I wanted to report my stolen dog. Before I could, I got grabbed, too. And it's your fault." Her lip stuck out, making her look all of twelve. "And it's your fault Karma is out there, maybe hurt by that maniac, instead of home having her babies. Wish I'd never met you!"

"What are you talking about?" Tee stiffened. She always poisoned relationships. Something tainted in her spoiled things sooner or later. She'd kept Lia at arm's length, not needing one more person in her life she'd disappoint, or the hurt sure to follow when the relationship ended. Tee's relationships always ended.

"I heard Boss talking. You had to run off halfcocked without calling Combs or even telling me. You thought your plan would catch 'em and make you a hero." Lia's shivers combined with angry shaking, her breath panted, and Tee could feel her sister's heartbeat go from canter to gallop. "All the time, somebody knew all about you, and made a deal to get rid of you. And me, too, because—oh happy day—Wyatt Teves is my dad, too."

She'd left Hawaii in part to distance herself from a bad situation. Now its tentacles reached clear across an ocean into Texas. "Wyatt's in prison for his part in killing a very bad man named Simon Wong." She'd heard rumors Mrs. Wong took over the Island Mafia after her husband's death. She held grudges. "We didn't tell anyone about us, that we're half-sisters." Neither of them wanted to advertise the relationship, for various reasons.

"While you were out running around with Karma, I got a Skype call from our father." Lia whispered the admission. "I confronted my grandparents. They wanted to give me away for adoption, can you believe it?"

"There are worse things." She pinched herself hard to keep focused. "Auntie Isabella adopted me. She saved me. You don't know how good you have it, girl."

Lia scrubbed her face. "They lied to me for years."

She rolled her eyes. "They lied for the right reasons, to protect you. Didn't they?" She yawned, getting sleepy. "There's lies, and then there's lies." Like the way her memory lied to protect her from hurt. "Besides, whatever they say about Wyatt Teves, he's worse."

"At least he told me the truth!" Lia's shivers had subsided, so perhaps their combined body warmth made the plastic atmosphere more livable. The tip of her nose had turned white, though. She blinked, slower and slower, and her words slurred.

"Truth's over-rated. Sometimes it's better not to know." Tee couldn't feel her feet, or her nose or ears. Her eyes watered, and tears froze and turned to fairy dust when she blinked. Despite the cardboard seat, her butt tingled like it had gone to sleep. If she looked anything like Lia, Tee guessed most of her own extremities had taken on the ghostly pallor of chalk. She yawned again. Remembered the notecard she'd saved from therapy back in Chicago, a touchstone to keep her grounded: *Trust Your Heart.*

And trust the dog . . .

A nap would be nice. Yes, a nap. And a dream...dream of misty volcanic peaks, plumeria blossoms perfuming the air, surf lapping her ankles, toes digging into hot sand beaches, a special dog's warm kisses on her cheeks . . .

Chapter 81

Karma roused from a doze, still worn out from her recent labors. Nuzzled against her breasts, four furry beings suckled with enthusiasm next to her deflated bear-toy. She nosed and licked each clean, top to bottom, as if counting the babies over and over again, reveling in the new emotion that overflowed within.

The temporary peace shattered when cars with screaming sirens tore into view.

She growled, and shifted further beneath the sheltering overhang, squinting to watch scrabbling activity as strange men and women poured from cars. Karma stretched her neck as far forward as she could, tasting the smells. The uniforms were familiar—sometimes Tee wore similar—but she didn't recognize anyone by sight, scent or sound.

In the past, she would have bounded forward with ferocious barks to announce a brave Rottweiler girl stood guard. But now, she preferred to stay unnoticed, but vigilant, ready to guard and protect her offspring to the death.

Bathed in a flood of chemicals including prolactin, estrogen and the "love hormone" oxytocin, she considered the puppies and orphan kitten no differently. All belonged to her. Karma, now a creature of pure instinct, obeyed a single imperative: *survive.*

Ignoring the shouting voices and stomping feet, Karma dozed as her newborn family nursed. A nagging worry wrinkled her brow. She'd not heard anything from her girls, but wished they'd come get her soon so they could all go home.

At the thought, she inhaled the comforting Lia-smell on the pink gloves her girl had left behind, and Tee-smell on the bear. Oh, how she missed them both! She'd seen bad people leave by themselves, so Karma's girls were still here. Somewhere.

But Karma couldn't risk leaving her babies to find them. Home, the boarding kennel with acres of grass to play and secure walls with warm places to sleep, that would be the safest place for them all.

Another car drove up, one without annoying sirens, and a familiar man got out. Karma cocked her head with interest. She knew him. Lia and Tee knew and trusted him. Sometimes when Karma visited the place with uniforms, Combs fed her treats from his sandwich. She licked her lips. Bacon would be nice!

She kept an eye on Combs when he walked close to where she lay hidden, but he didn't speak and Karma didn't make a sound, either. Sometimes, humans couldn't detect even the most obvious things. To her, the scent of birth remained strong in the air, despite her best efforts to clean up. Once the police left, she'd move her family away from the stink, or the smelly beacon would draw danger to her litter.

Again, she dozed, then started fully awake when a hand reached in to take Lia's discarded gloves. Karma snarled and bounded forward, shaking with aggression. The babies, unceremoniously dumped, squealed and cried with high-pitched sounds that elevated her emotion. She didn't look at them, though, but kept her attention trained on the face now lowered to stare into her own.

"Damn! Is that you, Karma? Settle down, girl, don't you know me?" Combs backed away, his voice a soothing singsong. "There's a good-dog. Where's Tee? How about Lia, is she here?" He turned away and shouted to someone before again speaking to her.

Her ears flicked, and Karma whined. She licked her lips, trying to calm herself as much as any perceived threat, and glanced back at the mewling babies.

"Nobody's gonna hurt your babies, Karma. But we need your help to find Lia and Tee, if they're here."

The only words she understood were the names, and "find." She knew it meant the same as the *such* command to search. Her ears slicked down, and a distressed yawn turned into a yodel of concern. Karma wanted to find Lia and Tee, too. They belonged to Karma and were her family as much as her new babies.

But she couldn't leave the litter. Blind, deaf, helpless and fragile, only Karma stood between them and death. She trusted her girls, but they weren't here. She barked at Combs, licked his offered hand, but didn't dare come out.

He withdrew his hands, taking Lia's gloves with him. "Lia's here somewhere, these are her gloves." He yelled over his shoulder at one of the officers. "Have you found sign of Tee yet? She would've found some way to bring her gun."

Bring gun. Karma woofed, remembering the new game from that morning. She snuffled in the dirt nearby, found the discarded gun, and picked it up to show Combs. Maybe he'd take the stinky, noisy thing away, and leave her alone with her babies.

Combs gasped, and gingerly reached out to take the gun. "Good-dog, Karma. So both of them were here. Hope to God they're still around. I need your help, Karma."

Chapter 82

Combs dialed the number by memory, never taking his eyes off Karma. He held his breath, praying she'd accept the call.

"September, don't hang up. Please."

She sighed. "I'm not angry anymore, Combs. I'm fine." Her tone said she wasn't. "Everything's been said, and I just can't do this anymore."

He closed his eyes. Maybe he deserved that. He risked everything and anyone to close a case. That argument was for another time, one he swore he'd win. He wasn't ready to give up on September, on them being together. But now wasn't the time.

"I need your help. You have every right to be mad, and I'll keep apologizing forever if you'll forgive me. But right now, just listen. Lia and Tee are in trouble."

"In trouble, how? I just left Lia at the Corazon estate."

He didn't have time for long explanations. "Tee tried to execute a sting on her own, and Lia got caught up in the crossfire."

"My God, Combs, is she okay?"

He hesitated. "We can't find them."

Dead silence. Then, "Combs, Shadow doesn't track people, you know that." Her tone included *how dare you ask.*

"Karma tracks people, and she's here, too. But I can't reach her. I don't know how to get her to track. September, she's had her babies, and I can't get close." He described the situation.

And September told him what to do.

***

September stared at the phone for long moments. Her throat ached with the effort to focus, focus, stay in the NOW and not fall into the abyss of a flashback. Just the thought of sending Shadow out again made the room spin.

Shadow nudged her with his nose. She buried her face in his black ruff, breathing deeply of the essence of dog-savior-friend.

Not to be ignored, Macy pushed his way under one arm. The trio held fast to each other, purrs blending with breaths, wags timed with tears.

Chapter 83

Karma cocked her head, mystified, when Combs put Lia's gloves on his own hands and slowly shoved a box under the crawl space. "I know you don't understand. But we need you to find Lia and Tee. So let me guard your babies, while you *such*—go find. Deal?"

Her ears pricked again. She loved to search for the scent, track down the missing. She'd done that before, towing Lia behind with the long-lead. She trusted Tee to track, too. They both liked this man and trusted him. Could Karma trust him, too?

She watched his gloved hands reach to grasp the bear-toy and put it in the box. Then he picked up one of her babies, and a low growl bubbled deep in her chest. He paused, letting her sniff his hand—Lia-smell—and then place the squealing puppy next to the bear.

"Everybody, stand clear!" He called to the people in uniform watching from some distance away.

Karma whined. Maybe he would help Karma take her babies home? She couldn't carry them all at once. Too far to travel on four paws. She watched as he placed each baby in turn inside the box. When Combs crawled out dragging the container with him, she hurried after, sticking her head inside and sniffing to be sure no damage had been done. He once again held out his Lia-scented gloved hand, and she inhaled deeply, pressing her face into it with a sigh.

He stood, cradling the box with mewling puppies against his chest. Karma jumped up, trying to see inside, but his next words stopped her cold. "Combs *guard.* You know what that means, good-girl? *Guard.*" He gestured with the box, and she cocked her head.

"Karma, *such!* Good-dog Karma, *find Lia!*" He offered his scented glove once again.

Training clicked. Karma lowered her head, and began to track, hearing Combs follow close in her wake with her family. She padded up the wooden steps, scent-trail bright as blood, huffing and hurrying. Her babies would be returned once Karma found her girls—Lia and Tee—and they'd all go home together. Karma couldn't wait! Wouldn't that be fine?

The clear trail couldn't fool her nose. Karma followed the overlapping scent of both her girls, fear-stink bright, until it came to the end. She lay down to announce her find, looked up at Combs, and woofed. He placed the box next to her, dropped Lia's gloves inside, and yelled for help.

Three men in uniform added their muscles when Combs rolled the floor-to-ceiling storage shelf aside, revealing the hidden door. When it opened, Karma flinched at the icy breath of cold air, and heard a weak cry.

Lia! Puppies were safe and warm but her girls—Inside, there! In the cold box!

Dodging past the uniform legs, Karma beat the police to reach her girls.

"Baby-dog, oh Karma."

She bathed Lia's icy face with her tongue. "Combs, thank God you found us. Help her, help my sister, she's in bad shape."

Karma turned to her other girl, and little whines of concern whiffled out. She licked Tee's face, her hands, nudged her hard. But Tee didn't respond. She mewed and cried, blind and deaf to this world. Like her puppies. Karma knew Tee needed her help more than ever.

Chapter 84

Lia patted her hair into place and smoothed the new outfit. Her grandparents didn't approve of her meeting with Combs, never mind she'd explained this wasn't a date but work. She'd stopped measuring success by what they thought. They hadn't reconciled, but her sister was right: there were far worse things than adoption. She added a touch of lip-gloss, took a deep breath, and left the restaurant powder room.

Combs had made an effort, too. His pressed, starched jeans and a pewter wolf's head bolo tie looked sharp against his yellow shirt. She caught him twirling the end of his tie. He looked nervous as she felt, and Lia wondered why.

Smiling, she took her seat. "That's got to be one of the best steaks I've had in a long time." He'd chosen a hole-in-the-wall cowboy joint that only locals knew about. They'd had to wait an hour to get a table, and settled on eating at the copper-topped bar, sharing the space with a couple of wranglers with dirt still on their spurs. Lia didn't mind. This was home.

He smiled, raised his longneck, and she clinked her bottle to his. "Here's to new beginnings."

"So, how's she doing?" Lia didn't have to say the name. Officer Pilikia Teves had been a topic of conversation most of the evening.

"I talked to her partner yesterday. He says she's struggling, but if I told her he said anything, he'd come over here and give me what-for." He grinned. "Paraphrasing, of course."

Lia sipped her drink and toyed with the dessert she no longer had any urge to finish. Tee remained as much of an enigma as the first day they'd met. After a short stay in the hospital, she'd gone home to Chicago without a goodbye. Lia wasn't hurt and didn't blame her. After what they'd gone through, she'd want to see the back end of Texas, too. They weren't best buddies, just because they shared a father. You didn't get to choose your relatives.

"They caught Tony Kanoa, did I tell you? Arrested in California."

"Who? Oh, you mean the import-export guy." She shuddered. "What about the little girl he took?"

"That I don't know. We think he set the fire back in August, and dumped Vicki's body but don't think they can get him on murder charges. But pedophile charges should put him away for a long time." Combs smiled with grim satisfaction. "We're still looking for the Boss, also known as Robin Gillette. Did you know she worked for Doc Eugene for a while? Disappeared after that rash of tornadoes last February, and now she's back in the wind again. Literally." He laughed. "Of course Kaliko Wong back in Hawaii has nothing to say and denies any connection. Says the phone call you overheard never happened."

Lia pushed the dessert away. "I still can't believe Grandfather called you. After all the things we both said." He'd been the one to reach out after she got out of the hospital. Maybe someday she'd bring herself to speak to him. Maybe.

Wyatt urged her to forgive and said holding a grudge only hurt herself. He should know, and said he'd foresworn revenge even on Tony Kanoa and his ilk. She could still hear Wyatt's words, sounding like a prophet from centuries past: *Do not take revenge. I will repay, says the lord.*

She wasn't ready to be that generous. Lia had started taking lessons how to use a gun, and wanted to qualify for open-carry privileges. Hating what guns could do didn't mean you shouldn't respect them and know how to use one, especially if she managed to land the job she wanted with the local PD. Today's lunch was all about convincing Combs to back her plan.

Combs forked a piece of pie, chewed, and swallowed. "Dub Corazon may be a stubborn son-of-a-bitch, but he's as protective of his family as that dog of yours." He took another drink. "Speaking of Karma, how's the little momma doing? Gonzales says his kids are over the moon they get to pick one, but his wife's not thrilled." He laughed. "Can't get over that she's raising a kitten! Took me aback when I saw that orange bit of fluff with the black puppies."

Lia chuckled. She hadn't been hallucinating after all, and she found it bizarre that the tiny thing saved her from being burned into crispy bits. Lots of folks wanted one of Karma's babies. She'd already decided to keep one pup, along with the kitten she'd named Gizmo.

"Interspecies adoption isn't all that rare. When the mommy-hormones kick in, just about any baby will do." Her smile faltered. "You saw how she reacted to Tee. I thought she'd go crazy when the ambulance took Tee away." That moment had changed everything.

Don't think about it! Maybe she'd get used to the notion by the time shipping day came, but now, Lia focused on happier thoughts.

Yes, she'd keep one of the puppies, the one that looked so much like Shadow. Lia remained convinced September's dog fathered the litter, even if others were doubtful.

Lia didn't care. She listened with her heart, and believed what she believed. The pups were five weeks old now, but she'd already begun training her pick of the litter. His shiny coat looked like black glass, with bright ochre paws and kiss-marks on his cheeks. Lia knew he'd be a warrior dog, a Koa like his shadowy father and beautiful mother. She knew because that whisper-tickle connection returned, not with Karma, but with the Magic-pup. Lia smiled, hugging the secret to herself, determined not to share with anyone who would tarnish the gift with skepticism.

"Hey, earth to Lia. Where'd you go?"

"Sorry." She fingered the baby bracelet that spelled out her name. Apikalia. She had another virtual Skype reunion with Wyatt tonight, to finalize the plans, but everything was decided and administered with help from Auntie Isabella. The only stipulation, though, was that it must remain their secret. Tee must never know Wyatt was involved.

"It's great you moved back into your place." Combs took another bite of his pie, swallowed, and wiped his mouth. "Did your Grandfather call off the bank vampires?" He spooned up some ice cream with the next mouthful, and slowly chewed.

She grimaced. No way in hell would she ask for Grandfather's help ever again. But what other explanation could she offer? Lia shrugged. "Family loan."

Wyatt wanted to make up for the lost years. With Auntie Isabella's help, he'd paid off the loan so Corazon Kennels was free and clear in her name. The only pay back he expected was a special favor for Tee, since she refused his overtures.

Officer Teves couldn't afford to buy a $20,000 trained police dog. Lia had a trained dog ready to go, but wasn't a cop. Lia also had family like her newfound cousin September, and friends like Combs, while Tee continued to struggle to connect with anyone. You'd have to be blind not to see the logic Wyatt put forth. But no one could know.

Lia was sure that Karma would love Chicago, too, as long as she was with Tee. And Karma was the only medicine able to heal her sister's pain.

But oh God, it would tear a hole in Lia's heart. She prayed the Magic-pup would heal her own heart. He'd be a part of her future with the police force, if she had anything to say about it.

September already said she'd help with Magic's training, in exchange for temporary lodging. Lia also figured having her as a roommate at Corazon Kennels would be a piece of cake after living with Tee.

She took a deep breath, pushed her desert way, and began her pitch to Combs.

Chapter 85

Karma whined, unable to move much beyond standing and turning in a tight circle. The hard pet carrier bumped every once in a while, and the sound of heavy engines and rushing wind hurt a good-dog's ears. She tried not to be frightened. After all, Karma was a brave dog trained to track down bad people and protect her family.

But her family wasn't here.

Lia brought her to the strange place and hugged and talked with lots of words Karma didn't understand. But Lia tasted of salt and loss when Karma washed her face. So Karma wriggled and jumped and rolled on her back with a Rottie smile to make Lia happy, and they hugged some more.

But then, Karma got shut into a dog crate, and Lia was gone. Strange people picked up the crate and placed it with other boxes and luggage in a big room. That was a very long time ago, though, and Karma needed to pee. She needed a drink, but the bowl of ice had all melted. She sighed and tried to sleep some more. Karma wished Lia would come get her out of the crate, so they could go home.

Karma loved raising her puppies at the boarding kennel. They romped in the grass and chased bunnies and birds. She helped Lia teach them all the special words like "*come*" and "*find*" and "*trip*" games that make a good-dog's life so special. She'd been sorry when Gonzales came with his kids and took away one of the puppies, and Lia's Grandfather claimed another one. But Karma still got to play with Shadow when he and September came to live with them. Her puppy Magic and strange tree-climbing daughter Gizmo kept her tail wagging. At night she slept against Lia's back with Magic and Gizmo snuggled together.

Now, Karma was alone and far from home. Home was safe, home was fun, home was love and familiar smells and snuggles and games that made a good-dog's heart beat fast and tail write joy into the air.

Karma wanted to go home!

When the big room gave a sudden bump, Karma yelped with surprise. The big car moved and bumped along until the loud engine noise stopped.

Maybe Lia would let her out and she could go home again? Karma barked, and then barked again. She needed to pee. And for the first time, her tummy flip-flopped, even though she was very brave.

Men moved her crate out of the big storage place and took her to another area that smelled of dogs and cats and pee and fear. She looked and looked but didn't see Lia anywhere. The cold air smelled different, too, like a city but with snow in the wind. How strange!

Suddenly, Karma heard voices that made her short black fur stand up with excitement. One voice, especially, someone she'd missed and wondered and pined for the weeks and weeks they'd been apart. It hurt her heart when family she loved went away. But maybe...maybe the long day meant an extra special treat? Not a bacon-kind-of-treat but something (she could hardly imagine!) that was so much better? Karma stood up in the cramped crate and couldn't contain herself.

Whines and yelps spilled from her throat. She recognized the distant silhouette of a small figure, who stood silent and frozen for a long moment. And then Tee ran, ran, ran to the crate, fingers reaching through the front grillwork to touch Karma's cold nose, and hot slurping tongue.

"Baby-dog!? Oh my God, it's Karma, you're here!"

Karma shivered with joy, wagging so hard her hips banged and shook the carrier. She'd found her purpose—to love and to serve and protect this woman, this piece of her heart, no matter what.

Home wasn't a place. Home was Tee.

FACT, FICTION & ACKNOWLEDGEMENTS

Thank you for reading FIGHT OR FLIGHT, and I hope you enjoyed this fourth book in the September Day series that includes LOST AND FOUND, HIDE AND SEEK and SHOW AND TELL. I feel like I've won the lottery, to write about my passion and share these stories with the world. There never would have been a series of these Thrillers With Bite without YOU adopting these books. (Can you see my virtual tail wag?)

My publishing pedigree tips heavily toward the nonfiction side of things, and the pet journalist that fuels my curiosity constantly inspires stories ripped from the headlines. Fiction by definition is, as September would say, made up crappiocca. But in order for readers to suspend their disbelief, there needs to be a scaffold of truth holding it together. Below, you'll find the Cliff's Notes version of what's real and what's fantasy.

As with the other books in the series, much of FIGHT OR FLIGHT is based on science, especially dog and cat behavior and learning theory, the benefits of service dogs, and the horror and reality of dogfights and human trafficking. Suspense and thriller novels by definition include mayhem, but as an animal advocate, I make a conscious choice to NOT show a pet's death in my books. All bets are off with the human characters, though.

I rely on a vast number of veterinarians, behaviorists, consultants, trainers, and pet-centric writers and rescue organizations that share their incredible resources and support to make my stories as believable as possible. Find out more information at IAABC.org, APDT.com, DWAA.org and CatWriters.com.

FACT: Selective disobedience is vital in training service dogs. Whether trained as police K9 officers or for other kinds of service, the savvy dogs must learn to think for themselves. For instance, the guide dog must know to disobey his human partner's command to "forward" into car traffic, and canine heroes figure out when to follow the most important trail, or take a bullet to save their human handler.

FACT: Hawaiian cowboys are real, and have a rich heritage. In 1832, three Mexican-Spanish vaquero (cowboys) were hired to train horses to use as working animals in the emerging cattle industry. They became known as paniolo, a variant of the espanol language the vaquero spoke. Today, the term still refers to the Hawaiian cowboys and the unique culture that lives on today. For instance, the *kaula ili* (skin rope) typical of the paniolo was passed down within family lines. Find out more about the fascinating culture of the paniolo at these links:

https://en.wikipedia.org/wiki/Cowboy#Hawaiian_Paniolo

https://hanahou.com/7.3/a-tale-of-two-ranches

http://www.alohacottages.net/ikua_purdy.html

FICTION: Shadow and Karma's viewpoint chapters are pure speculation, although I would love to able to read doggy minds. However, every attempt has been made to base all animal characters' motivations and actions on what is known about canine and feline body language, scent discrimination, and the science behind the human-animal bond.

FACT: Real-life pets inspire some of the pet characters in FIGHT OR FLIGHT. I've held a "Name That Dog/Name That Cat" contest for each of the four novels thus far in the series. Since this thriller continues where SHOW AND TELL left off, some of those same pet names live on in future stories.

Some of you know that my heart-dog Magic inspired Shadow's character. We lost Magic last year, and I've struggled with continuing the series. His best friend Karma-Kat mourned his GSD buddy and slept with Magic's collar for two weeks after he died. To honor their relationship, I included those names in the contest poll for FIGHT OR FLIGHT, and you—the readers—voted overwhelmingly to bless this and future stories with their names. For that reason, **Karma** the Rottweiler police dog (named after dog-loving-Karma-Kat) stars in this thriller. And the puppy-son of Shadow and Karma is named **Magic**, destined to share many future hero dog adventures. (Oh crap, now I'm crying…)

Vickie nominated the name **Thor** in honor of her Bouvier, who she described as very strong and sweet, and I made him the tracking dog hero early in the book. **Una Bell Townsend** suggested her red heeler/blue heeler/Pit Bull mix, a rescue dog she named after **Buster Keaton** due to his bugged out eyes. She says Buster the Pittie is the best watchdog they've ever had, and in the story, Buster helps save Shadow from the flood. **Debbie Glovatsky's** yellow tabby boy **Waffles** won the honor of saving the life of Lenny—Waffles is a blogging star known to have an extra-long tail and an adventurous mancat nature.

Congratulations and THANK YOU to all the winners. I think they all deserve treats. Maybe even bacon!

FACT: Therapy dogs can work wonders when partnered with autistic individuals. Emotional Support Animals (ESA) also partner with a variety of people, from children to adults, including those suffering from post-traumatic stress disorder (PTSD). Only dogs and guide horses for the blind can be *service animals* trained to perform a specific function for their human partner, from becoming the ears for the deaf, eyes for the blind, support for other-abled and alert animals for health and physically challenged individuals. Of course, there are amazing people-pet partnerships that develop without any formal training, and many animals like Shadow and Karma intuitively provide the support their humans need.

Learn about the differences and the benefits of pet-people partnerships at http://petpartners.org. You can also find out about "fake" credentialing services that hurt legitimate partnerships in this blog post: http://amyshojai.com/fake-service-dog-credentials/

FICTION—maybe?: I asked my readers what kind of "new" character they'd like in future stories, and many folks asked for an "animal communicator." Hmnnn.

As a student of animal communication, I respect the ability of dogs, cats (and other creatures) to express themselves in species-specific ways. Our animal companions "talk" with whisker twitches and eye-blinks, body position and fur elevation, woofs and purrs, growls and hisses, and even smelly Post-It notes and silent meows humans can't detect. Cats and dogs understand so much about us by paying exquisite attention to our actions, expressions, and (dare I say) smell-signals but we'd love to attribute their ability to telepathy.

I have colleagues who tout their ability to communicate telepathically with animals. But as a "just the facts" journalist with a science bent, I want to see studies quantifying this mystery. I'm intrigued by the brilliant scientist author Temple Grandin (Thinking In Pictures and Animals In Translation) who describes her perceptions as an autistic person and offers ways to better understand non-human creatures.

The novelist in me loves a good fantasy. In fact, I write "dog viewpoint" because I love the idea so much and wish it was fact. If telepathy between humans and other species is possible, a common language would be necessary. So I'll explore the notion further in future stories, with September-the-skeptic and her cousin Lia.

FACT: Dogfights are a sad reality in much of the world. Animal fighting is a federal crime and dog fighting is a felony in all 50 states. That's due in part to the relationship between the fighting events and illegal gambling, guns and drugs. In Texas and Oklahoma both dog fighting and cock fighting remain a problem, where sometimes whole families attend including little kids. Children brought up in the culture of dogfights consider them normal, and perpetuate the horror. To combat the crime of dogfights, the Missouri Humane Society, the ASPCA, the Louisiana SPCA, and the UC Davis Veterinary Genetics Laboratory collaborated to establish the first ever database. Find out more about Canine CODIS here:

http://www.vgl.ucdavis.edu/forensics/CANINECODIS.php

FACT: Pit Bulls are not inherently "evil" or "aggressive." Because of their heritage, these dogs have an increased propensity for dog-on-dog aggression, as do many other terrier breeds (remember the mention about Thor the Bouvier?). Pit Bulls do not bite people more readily than other breeds. Sadly, that statistical distinction goes to German Shepherds. (Don't tell Shadow!) All dogs bite, and every breed has challenges, so be educated and prepared for whatever animal friend steals your heart.

FACT: According to the CDC and others, Autism Spectrum Disorder (ASD) affects about one percent of the world population, and about one in 68 children. The challenges facing these children and their families vary from mild to severe, and can prove devastating to those who love them. Some of these gifted individuals rise far above their challenges (think of Temple Grandin and Albert Einstein for example). These types of characters make great fodder for fiction authors. After putting Steven and others through hell in the first book LOST AND FOUND, it seemed only fair to give them a turn at playing hero in future stories. Refer to these resources for

more information on ASD:
http://www.cdc.gov/ncbddd/autism/data.html
http://psychcentral.com/lib/autistic-and-gifted-supporting-the-twice-exceptional-child/

FACT: Both dumpsters and straw bales float. I checked.

FACT: Eighty-six percent of missing children suspected of being forced into sex work came from the child welfare system, national data shows, and a state-funded study estimated that the vast majority of young victims in Texas had some contact with Child Protective Services (CPS). Anti-trafficking efforts in Texas have focused more on putting pimps in prison than rehabilitating their prey. More information on this heinous situation can be found at these links:

http://www.heralddemocrat.com/news/20170303/texas-couldn8217t-help-this-sex-trafficked-teen-so-authorities-sent-her-to-jail

http://www.heralddemocrat.com/news/20170224/when-foster-care-couldn8217t-help-this-16-year-old-she-ran-to-pimp

https://www.texastribune.org/2017/02/13/how-texas-crusade-against-sex-trafficking-has-left-victims-behind/

https://www.texasattorneygeneral.gov/cj/human-trafficking

FACT: This book would not have happened without an incredible support team of friends, family and accomplished colleagues. Cool Gus Publishing, Jennifer Talty and Bob Mayer made these thrillers with "dog viewpoint" a reality when many in the publishing industry howled at the notion. Special thanks to my first readers for your eagle eyes, spot-on comments and unflagging encouragement and support. Wags and purrs to my Triple-A Team (Amy's Audacious Allies) for all your help sharing the word about all my books. Youse guyz rock!

I continued to be indebted to the International Thriller Writers organization, which launched my fiction career by welcoming me into the Debut Authors Program. Wow, just look, now I have four books in a series! The authors, readers and industry mavens who make up this organization are some of the most generous and supportive people I have ever met. Long live the bunny slippers with teeth (and the rhinestone #1-Bitch Pin).

Finally, I am grateful to all the cats and dogs I've met over the years who have shared my heart and oftentimes my pillow. Magical-Dawg (the inspiration for Shadow) and Seren-Kitty continue to live on in my heart. Newcomer Bravo-Boy the Bullmastiff pup and Karma-Kat inspire me daily.

I never would have been a reader and now a writer if not for my fantastic parents who instilled in me a love of the written word, and never looked askance when my stuffed animals and invisible talking wolf and flying cat friends told fantastical stories. And of course, my deepest thanks to my husband Mahmoud, who continues to support my writing passion, even when he doesn't always understand it.

I love hearing from you! Please drop me a line at my blog https://AmyShojai.com or my website https://shojai.com where you can subscribe to my PET PEEVES newsletter (and maybe win some pet books!). Follow me on twitter @amyshojai and like me on Facebook: http://www.facebook.com/amyshojai.cabc

ABOUT THE AUTHOR

Amy Shojai is a certified animal behavior consultant, and the award-winning author of more than 30 bestselling pet books that cover furry babies to old fogies, first aid to natural healing, and behavior/training to Chicken Soupicity. She has been featured as an expert in hundreds of print venues including The Wall Street Journal, New York Times, Reader's Digest, and Family Circle, as well as television networks such as CNN, and Animal Planet's DOGS 101 and CATS 101. Amy brings her unique pet-centric viewpoint to public appearances. She is also a playwright and co-author of STRAYS, THE MUSICAL and the author of the critically acclaimed THRILLERS WITH BITE pet-centric thriller series. Stay up to date with new books and appearances by subscribing to Amy's Pets Peeves newsletter at https://www.SHOJAI.com.

CPSIA information can be obtained
at www.ICGtesting.com
Printed in the USA
FSHW020647090119
54919FS

9 781948 366021